Praise for
BURN FOR ME

"With heart-pounding romance
and non-stop action,
this is Ilona Andrews at her best!"
—Jeaniene Frost, *New York Times* bestselling author

"Addictive, imaginative, and incredibly sexy."
—Eloisa James, *New York Times* bestselling author

"Staking out her ground in
paranormal romance, uber-talented
Andrews proves that, no matter the genre,
she is a storyteller extraordinaire."
—*Romantic Times* BOOK*reviews* (Top Pick)

D0089179

White Hot

A tall man was striding from the far end of the hallway. He wore the black robe and it flared around him, the wings of a raven about to take flight. He walked like he owned the building and he'd spotted an intruder in his domain. Magic boiled around him, vicious and lethal, so potent I could feel it from thirty yards away. He wasn't a man, he was an elemental force, a thunderstorm clad in black about to unleash its fury. People flattened themselves against the walls, trying to get out of his way. I saw his face and recoiled. Chiseled chin, strong nose, and blue eyes blazing with power under dark slashes of eyebrows.

Mad Rogan.

By Ilona Andrews

ATTENTION: ORGANIZATIONS AND CORPORATIONS
HarperCollins books may be purchased for educational, business, or sales promotional use. For information, please e-mail the Special Markets Department at SPsales@harpercollins.com.

ILONA
ANDREWS

WHITE
HOT

A HIDDEN LEGACY NOVEL

Security Public Library

715 Aspen Drive

Colorado Springs, CO 80911

AVONBOOKS

An Imprint of HarperCollinsPublishers

HarperCollins
PUBLISHERS
Since 1817

This is a work of fiction. Names, characters, places, and incidents are products of the author's imagination or are used fictitiously and are not to be construed as real. Any resemblance to actual events, locales, organizations, or persons, living or dead, is entirely coincidental.

Excerpt from *Wildfire* copyright © 2017 by Ilona Gordon and Andrew Gordon.

WHITE HOT. Copyright © 2017 by Ilona Gordon and Andrew Gordon. All rights reserved. Printed in the United States of America. No part of this book may be used or reproduced in any manner whatsoever without written permission except in the case of brief quotations embodied in critical articles and reviews. For information, address HarperCollins Publishers, 195 Broadway, New York, NY 10007.

First Avon Books mass market printing: June 2017
First Avon Books hardcover printing: May 2017

ISBN 978-0-06-228925-4

Avon, Avon & logo, and Avon Books & logo are registered trademarks of HarperCollins Publishers in the United States of America and other countries.

HarperCollins is a registered trademark of HarperCollins Publishers in the United States of America and other countries.

17 18 19 20 21   QGM   10 9 8 7 6 5 4 3 2 1

If you purchased this book without a cover, you should be aware that this book is stolen property. It was reported as "unsold and destroyed" to the publisher, and neither the author nor the publisher has received any payment for this "stripped book."

Acknowledgments

We'd like to thank our editor, Erika Tsang, for her guidance, understanding, and continued belief in the story.

We are very grateful to our long-suffering agent, Nancy Yost, who puts up with us despite our shenanigans and the wonderful team of NYLA, especially Sarah Younger and Amy Rosenbaum.

Special thanks to Andrew Suh and Chris Burdick for their advice regarding firearms. All errors of fact are our own and were made despite their help.

We would also like to thank the following readers who generously donated their time to read the early draft and offer feedback: Nicole Clement, Robin Snyder, Jessica Haluskah, Shannon Daigle, Kristi de Courcy, Sandra Bullock, Joe Healy, Omar Jimenez, Kathryn Holland, Laura Hobbs, Jan and Susan, and others.

Finally, we would like to thank our readers. Sorry you had to wait for so long.

Prologue

A wise man once said, "A human mind is the place where emotion and reason are locked in perpetual combat. Sadly for our species, emotion always wins." I really liked that quote. It explained why, even though I was reasonably intelligent, I kept finding myself doing something really stupid. And it sounded much better than "Nevada Baylor, Total Idiot."

"Don't do this," Augustine said behind me.

I looked at the monitor showing Jeff Caldwell. He sat shackled to a chair that was bolted to the floor. He wore prison orange. He didn't seem like much: an unremarkable man in his fifties, balding, average height, average build, average face. I read a news article about him this morning. He had a job with the city; a wife, who was a schoolteacher; and two children, both in college. He had no magic and wasn't affiliated with any of the Houses, powerful magic families that ran Houston. His friends described him as a kind, considerate man.

In his spare time, Jeff Caldwell kidnapped little girls. He kept them alive for up to a week at a time, then he strangled them to death and left their remains in parks surrounded by flowers. His victims were between the ages of five and seven, and the stories their bodies told made you wish that hell existed just so Jeff Caldwell could be sent there after he died. The night before last he had been caught in the act of depositing the tiny corpse of his latest victim in her flower grave and was apprehended. The reign of terror that had gripped Houston for the past year was finally over.

There was just one problem. Seven-year-old Amy Madrid was still missing. She had been kidnapped two days ago from her school bus stop, less than twenty-five yards from her house. The MO was too similar to Jeff Caldwell's previous abductions to be a coincidence. He had to have taken her and, if so, it meant she was still alive somewhere. I had followed the story for the past two days waiting for the announcement that Amy was found. The announcement never came.

Houston PD had had Jeff Caldwell for thirty-six hours. By now the cops had scoured his house, questioned his family, his friends, and his coworkers, and pored over his cell phone records. They interrogated him for hours. Caldwell refused to talk.

He would talk today.

"If you do this once, people will expect you to do it again," Augustine said. "And when you won't, they'll be unhappy. This is why Primes don't engage. We're only people. We can't be everywhere at once. If an aquakinetic puts out one fire, the next time something goes ablaze and he fails to be there, the public will turn on him."

"I understand," I said.

"I don't think you do. You're hiding your talent precisely to avoid this kind of scrutiny."

I hid my talent because truthseekers like me were extremely rare. If I walked into the police station and wrenched the truth from Jeff Caldwell, a couple of hours later I would get visitors from the military, Homeland Security, FBI, CIA, private Houses, and anyone else who had the need of a one hundred percent accurate interrogator. They would destroy my life. I loved my life. I ran Baylor Investigative Agency, a small, family-owned firm; I took care of my two sisters and two cousins; and I had no plans to change any of it. What I did wasn't admissible in court. If I took any of those people up on their offer, I wouldn't be in the courtroom testifying in a nice suit. I'd be at some black site facing a guy tied to a chair and beaten to within an inch of his life, with a bag over his head. People would live or die on my word. It would be dark and dirty, and I would do almost anything to avoid that. Almost.

"I've taken every precaution," Augustine said, "but despite my best efforts and your . . . outfit, the chance you will be discovered exists."

I could see my own reflection in the glass. I wore a green hooded cape that hid me from top to bottom, black gloves, and a ski mask under the hood. The cape and the gloves came courtesy of an Alley Theatre production and belonged to Lady in Green, Scottish Highwaywoman and Heroine of the Highlands. According to Augustine, the outfit was so unusual that people would concentrate on it and nobody would remember my voice, my height, or any other details.

"I know we've had our differences," Augustine started. "But I wouldn't advise you to act against your self-interest."

I waited for the familiar mosquito buzz of magic telling me he lied. None came. For whatever reason, Augustine was doing his best to talk me out of an arrangement that directly benefited him, and he was sincere about it.

"Augustine, if one of my sisters was kidnapped, I would do anything to get her back. Right now a little girl is dying of hunger and thirst somewhere. I can't stand by and let it happen. I just can't. We have a deal."

Augustine Montgomery, head of House Montgomery and owner of Montgomery International Investigations, held the mortgage on our family business. He couldn't force me to take clients, but he'd called my cell earlier this morning, just as I was walking to the police station, about to destroy my life. He had a client who'd specifically requested my services. I promised to hear the client out if he arranged for me to have an anonymous shot at Jeff Caldwell. Except now he seemed to be having second thoughts.

I turned and looked at Augustine. An illusion Prime, he could alter his appearance with a thought. Today his face wasn't just handsome; it was perfect in the way the greatest works of Renaissance art were perfect. His skin was flawless, his pale blond hair brushed with surgical precision, and his features had the kind of regal elegance and a cold air of detachment that begged to be immortalized on canvas or, better yet, in marble.

"We have a deal," I repeated.

Augustine sighed. "Very well. Come with me."

I followed him to a wooden door. He opened it. I walked through into a small room with a two-way mirror in the far wall.

Jeff Caldwell raised his head and looked at me. I searched his eyes and saw nothing. They were flat and devoid of all emotion. Behind him a two-way mirror hid observers. Augustine assured me that only the police would be present.

The door closed behind me.

"What is this?" Caldwell asked.

My magic touched his mind. Ugh. Like sticking your hand into a bucket of slime.

"I did nothing wrong," he said.

True. He actually believed that. His eyes were still flat like those of a toad.

"Are you just going to stand there? This is ridiculous."

"Did you kidnap Amy Madrid?" I asked.

"No."

My magic *buzzed* in my brain. *Lie. You scumbag.*

"Are you holding her somewhere?"

"No."

Lie.

My magic snapped out and clamped him in its vise. Jeff Caldwell went rigid. His nostrils fluttered as his breathing sped up, racing in tune to his rising pulse. Finally, emotion flooded his eyes, and that emotion was raw, sharp terror.

I opened my mouth, letting the full power of my magic saturate my voice. It came out low and inhuman. *"Tell me where she is."*

Chapter 1

Figuring out when people lied came naturally to me and required no effort. Compelling someone to answer my questions was a whole different ball game. Until a couple of months ago I didn't even realize I had the power to do it. Picking through Jeff Caldwell's mind was like swimming through a sewer. He fought me every step of the way, his will bucking in panic, threatening to shatter his own mind in self-defense. The trick wasn't getting the information; it was keeping his mind intact enough to stand trial. I'd gotten what I wanted anyway, and when I exited MII's building, a caravan of cop cars had taken off down Capitol Street, an urgent cacophony of sirens demanding right of way.

Jeff Caldwell had drained me down to nothing. Driving was an effort. Somehow I made it through Houston's notorious traffic, turned onto the road leading to our house, and almost blew through a stop sign. It was a bad place, too; delivery trucks had a nasty habit of rolling out this way as if other cars didn't exist.

Nothing rolled out today. I glanced down the access road anyway. A two-foot-high steel barrier bristling with thick six-inch-long spikes blocked the street. Judging by the indentations in the pavement it could be lowered into the ground. If you added some blood and tattered cloth on the spikes, it would fit into any postapocalyptic movie. The barrier hadn't been here a couple of days ago. The last time two trucks collided here must've resulted in some serious lawsuit.

I yawned and kept going. Almost home. Almost. I pulled into the lot in front of our warehouse and parked my Mazda minivan between my mother's blue Honda Element and Bern's 2005 Ford Mustang. My cousin's ancient Civic had died a sad death a month ago, when the descendants of two magical families decided to have words in the college parking lot. Their words involved trying to crush each other with five-hundred-pound decorative rocks from the landscaping display. Unfortunately, their aim turned out to be crap and they survived. Their families reimbursed us—and five other car owners—for the damages. Now a gunmetal-grey Mustang occupied the Civic's former spot.

No charges had been filed. In our world, magic was the ultimate power. If you had it, you suddenly found that many rules bent around you.

I dragged myself out of the car and punched the code into the security system. The heavy-duty door clicked; I swung it open, stepped inside, and shut it behind me. The familiar office walls, plain beige carpet, and glass panels greeted me.

Home.

Today was over. Finally. I exhaled and took off my shoes. I had stopped by a client's office before dressing up as a Scottish highwaywoman, so I was still wearing one of my "we're not poor" outfits. I owned two expensive suits and two matching pairs of heels, and I wore the first when I went to see a client who might be impressed by appearances and the second when I came to collect the payment. The heels I had to put on today should've been banned as evil torture devices.

Someone knocked.

Maybe I'd imagined it.

Another knock.

I turned and checked the monitor. A blond man stood in front of my door. Short and compact, with a serious face and thoughtful blue eyes, he was in his late twenties. A zipped-up brown leather folder rested in his hands. Cornelius Harrison of House Harrison. A few months ago Augustine had strong-armed me into looking for Adam Pierce, a lunatic pyrokinetic with the highest magical pedigree. Cornelius had been forced by his family to play the role of Adam's "boyhood companion," a role he had detested. Cornelius had helped me in my investigation. His older sister currently ran House Harrison.

The Cornelius I remembered was clean-shaven and meticulously dressed. This Cornelius was still well-dressed, but his cheeks were rough with stubble and an unsettling shadow darkened his eyes, as if he had seen something that disturbed him to the very core and was still reeling from the impact.

A little girl stood next to him, carrying a small Sailor Moon backpack. She had to be about three or four years old. Her hair was dark and straight and her eyes pointed at an Asian heritage, but her features reminded me of Cornelius. Their expressions, solemn and serious, were completely identical. I knew he had a daughter but I'd never met her. A large Doberman Pinscher sat next to the child, as tall as she was.

What would a member of Houston's magical elite want from me? Whatever it was, it wouldn't be good. Baylor Investigative Agency specialized in small-time investigations. Contrary to the PI novels, gorgeous widows in search of their husband's killer or billionaire bachelors with missing sisters rarely darkened my doorstep. Insurance fraud, cheating spouses, and background checks were our bread and butter. *Please don't let this be a cheating spouse.* Those were always so difficult when children were involved.

I unlocked the door. "Mr. Harrison. How can I help you?"

"Good evening," Cornelius said, his voice quiet. His gaze snagged on the shoes in my hand and moved on to my face. "I need your help. Augustine said I could come by."

Augustine . . . Oh. So Cornelius was the client Montgomery wanted me to see.

"Come in, please."

I let them in and shut the door.

"You must be Matilda." I smiled at the little girl.

She nodded.

"Is that your dog?"

She nodded again.

"What's his name?"

"Bunny," she said in a small voice.

Bunny looked at me with the kind of suspicion usually reserved for rattlesnakes. Cornelius was an animal mage, a rare brand of magic, which meant Bunny wasn't a dog. He was the equivalent of a loaded assault rifle pointed in my direction.

"He can smile," Matilda offered. "Smile, Bunny."

Bunny showed me a forest of gleaming white fangs. I fought an urge to step back.

"Is there a place Matilda can wait while we talk?" Cornelius asked.

"Of course. This way, please."

I opened the door to a conference room and flicked on the light. Matilda took off her backpack, put it on the table, then climbed into the nearest chair. She opened her bag and took out a tablet, a coloring book, and some markers.

Bunny took a spot by Matilda's feet and gave me the evil eye.

"Would you like some juice?" I opened the small refrigerator. "I have apple and kiwi-strawberry."

"Apple, please."

I handed her a juice box.

"Thank you."

There was something oddly adult about the way she held herself. If this was what Cornelius was like when he was a child, Adam Pierce and his chaos must've driven him insane. It was no wonder that he'd distanced himself from both Houses.

"Do you have many clients with children?" Cornelius asked.

"A few, but the juice boxes are mine. I'm hiding them from my sisters. This is the only place they won't raid. Let's talk in my office."

I led Cornelius across the hallway to my office and my head almost exploded. A page from *Bridal* magazine was taped to my office glass door. It showed a woman in a spectacular gown made with long white feathers. Someone—probably Arabella—had cut out my head from some selfie and pasted it over the bride's. A big heart, drawn in a pink marker and sprinkled with glitter, decorated the bride's dress. Inside the heart someone had written *N+R = LURVE*. Little pink hearts floated around my face.

Killer way to make the first impression. I wished I could fall through the floor.

Through the glass I could see another bridal photograph, this one embellished with glittering dollar signs, waiting on my desk. On the bride's dress, big block letters written with Catalina's painstaking precision, said *Marry him. We need college money.*

I had to murder my sisters. There just wasn't any way

around it. No jury on this earth would convict me. I could represent myself and I would still win.

I pulled the photograph off the glass and swung my office door open. "Please."

Cornelius settled into one of my two client's chairs. I grabbed the second photograph off the desk, crumpled both, and threw them in the trash.

"Are you getting married?" Cornelius asked.

"No."

R stood for *Rogan*. Connor Rogan, except nobody called him that. They called him Mad Rogan, the Scourge of Mexico, the Butcher of Merida, the man who'd nearly leveled downtown Houston trying to save the rest of the city. Mad Rogan and the rest of humanity were never on a first-name basis. He cut buildings in half, threw buses like they were baseballs, and when he and I were done with Adam Pierce, he'd invited me to become his . . . *mistress* would be the polite term. It took all of my will to turn him down. Even now, when I thought about him, my pulse shot up. Unfortunately, my grandma witnessed our parting fight and decided that sooner or later we would get hitched, a fact she shared with my two sisters and two cousins, and since three of them were under the age of eighteen, the teasing was relentless.

"Coffee? Tea?" I asked.

"No, thank you."

If I closed my eyes, I could imagine Mad Rogan in my office. I remembered the feel of his hands on my skin. I remembered his taste. I slammed a mental door on that thought so hard my whole skull rattled. Rogan and I were over before we even had a chance to start.

I took my seat, trying to remember everything I could about Cornelius. He had distanced himself from his House and moved out of their territory to a very comfortable, but modest by the House's standards, residence. He was a stay-at-home dad, while his wife worked somewhere—I had no idea where. He detested the entire Pierce family. That was pretty much it.

"Why don't you tell me about your problem and I can tell you whether or not we're equipped to handle your issue."

"My wife was murdered on Tuesday night."

Oh my God. "I'm so sorry."

Cornelius sank deeper into his chair. His eyes turned dull as if dusted with ash. His words sat there between us, lead bricks on the table.

"How did it happen?"

"My wife is . . . was employed by House Forsberg."

"Forsberg Investigative Services?"

"Yes. She was one of the attorneys in their legal department."

Private investigation was a small field and you got to know your competitors pretty quickly. Full-service juggernauts similar to Augustine's MII were rare. Most of us tended to specialize, and Matthias Forsberg's firm concentrated on the prevention of corporate espionage, which meant they did bug sweeps, information security audits, and risk assessments. The word on the street was that occasionally, if the check was big enough, they would change hats and engage in the very things they offered to protect you from. Once in a while you'd hear rumors about possible legal action, but no cases had ever reached the public eye, which meant House Forsberg had a robust legal department.

"On Tuesday night my wife called at nine thirty to tell me she would be working late." Cornelius' voice lost all emotion. "At eleven, she and three other lawyers from her department walked into Hotel Sha Sha. They came out in body bags. There is an established way to handle matters when someone dies in the service of your House. When I approached House Forsberg this morning, I was told that my wife's death is a private matter, unconnected to her job."

"What makes you think it was connected?" Hotel Sha Sha was an expensive boutique hotel, located on Main Street. It was small and private and just upscale enough to add glamor to a clandestine meeting without breaking the bank. I'd tailed more than one cheating spouse there.

"I may not be a Prime, but I'm still a Significant and a member of a House. When I ask for information, I get it." Cornelius reached into the folder and handed me a piece of paper. "Nari was shot twenty-two times. Her body"—his voice caught—"her body was riddled with bullets."

I scanned the ME report. Nari Harrison's body showed bullet wounds from left and right sides. They had to have occurred simultaneously, because the trajectory of the projectiles would've changed once she fell. Two of the gunshot wounds were in her forehead. The ME noted that her face showed signs of gunfire stippling. In the margins of the report someone had scrawled notes in shorthand, as if writing something in hurry. *HK 4.6 x 30 mm. Traces of HTSP. Stippling, twelve to eighteen inches.*

I had this terrible feeling in my chest, as if a heavy cold ball somehow formed just under my heart and was growing larger and heavier by the second. "Who made these notes?"

"The leading detective. This is all he could give me and it took a lot to get that much."

"Did he explain this to you?"

Cornelius shook his head.

The woman he loved was dead. Now I would have to explain how she died. He was sitting right in front of me, a living, breathing human being. His daughter was in the next room.

I took a deep breath to steady my voice. He'd come to me for professional advice. I had to give him my best opinion.

"Your wife was hit by armor-piercing rounds from a Heckler & Koch MP7. It's a vicious weapon developed for the German army and the counterterrorism division of the German police and designed specifically to penetrate body armor. It's meant for military use. The pattern of the gunshot wounds indicates that your wife was in the center of two intersecting fields of fire."

I took a mug with a little kitten on it and set it in the center of the desk, grabbed two pens, and lined them up diagonally in front of the mug, one pointing to the left, the other to the right.

"HTSP stands for High Tensile Strength Polyethylene. She was wearing a ballistic vest."

"That makes no sense." Cornelius stared at me. "She had a bulletproof vest, but she died anyway."

"Yes. In fiction, vests stop everything. In reality, ballistic vests are only bullet resistant. They come in different levels of protection. Your wife was likely wearing a vest rated up to Level III, which means it would probably stop several 7.62mm rifle rounds. Even then, being shot in a bulletproof vest feels like taking a hammer to the body. In this case, your wife was shot multiple times by personal-defense-class military-grade firearms designed to pierce body armor. Death was instant." At least I could offer him that.

He didn't seem to draw any comfort from it.

I had to keep going. I'd started this; I had to finish. "The gunpowder stippling occurs when someone is shot at a close range and gunshot residue is deposited on the victim's skin. This includes gunpowder burns, soot, and pitting and tearing of the top layers of the skin, if the gun discharged close enough."

He clenched his right fist. The knuckles of his hand went completely white. He was probably picturing Nari's face in his head.

"According to this report, after your wife was already

dead and prone on the ground, someone pumped two bullets into her forehead. The lead detective estimated the range to be between a foot and a foot and a half." Just about right for someone holding a Heckler & Koch straight down.

"Why? She was already dead."

"Because the people who did this were well trained and thorough. If we get reports on the other three lawyers, it's highly probable they were also shot in the head. A group of people ambushed your wife and her colleagues, killed them with military precision, and then lingered long enough to walk through the scene and put two bullets in the heads of those present to ensure there were no survivors. They did this in the middle of Houston, they made no effort to be subtle about it, and they got away clean. This wasn't just a professional hit. This was a message."

"We're stronger than you are. We can do this anytime, anywhere, to any of your people," Cornelius said quietly.

"Exactly."

He understood the House politics better than I. He'd had a front-row seat to them most of his life.

"Mr. Harrison, you came to me for my opinion. Based on what you told me, I believe House Forsberg is involved. We don't know if your wife . . ."

"Nari," he said. "Her name is Nari."

"We don't know if Nari acted in the interests of the House or against them. We do know that House Forsberg is pretending that nothing happened, which either means that House Forsberg killed your wife and others as a warning to their people or that they got the message the killers sent and it scared them. My recommendation to you is to walk away."

All of the muscles in Cornelius' face were clenched so hard that his skin looked too tight. "That's not an option for me."

He wouldn't survive this. I had to talk him out of it. I leaned forward. "This is a war between Houses. Last time we spoke, you told me you deliberately distanced yourself from yours. You said that you loved your family, but they used you and you didn't enjoy being used."

"You have a good memory," he said.

"Has that situation changed? Will your House help you?"

"No. Even if they were inclined to do so, their resources are limited. House Harrison isn't without means, but my family is reluctant to engage in combat, especially on my behalf. I'm the youngest child and not a Prime. I'm not necessary for the future of the House. If it was my brother or sister, things might be different."

He said it so matter-of-factly. My family would do anything for me. If I was trapped in a burning house, every single one of them, my knucklehead sisters and cousins included, would run in there trying to save me. Cornelius' wife was dead and his family would do nothing. It was so unfair.

"It's up to me," he said.

I lowered my voice. "You don't have the resources to fight this war. Your daughter is sitting in the next room. She already lost her mother. Do you really want her to lose her father too? You are the only parent she has left. What will happen to her if you die? Who will take care of her?"

"I could have an aneurysm in the next ten seconds. If that happens, Nari's parents will raise Matilda. My sister hasn't seen my daughter since she was a year old. My brother never met his niece. Neither of them is married. They wouldn't be good caretakers."

"Cornelius . . ."

"If you are planning on telling me that revenge doesn't make one feel better . . ."

"It depends on the revenge," I said. "Punching Adam

Pierce was one of the best moments of my life. Every time I think about it, it makes me smile. But revenge has a price. My grandmother almost burned to death. My oldest cousin nearly died in the collapse of downtown. I nearly died half a dozen times. The price for this will be too high."

"That's for me to decide."

His eyes had that steely cold look to them. He wasn't going to back down.

I leaned back. "Very well. But you'll have to find someone else to help you with your suicide mission."

"I would like your help," he said.

"No. I understand that you are determined to hang yourself, but I won't be holding the rope for you. Not only that, but Baylor Investigative Agency is a very small firm. We specialize in low-risk investigations. I'm not qualified."

He pointed at the ME's report. "You seem very qualified."

"I know about guns, Mr. Harrison, because there is a long tradition of military service on my mother's side of the family. My mother and my grandmother are both veterans. It doesn't mean I'm capable of taking on this investigation. Hire someone else."

"Who?"

"Augustine."

"I've already spoken with Augustine. He did me the courtesy of being candid. With the amount of money at my disposal, I can't afford a full investigation. My money will buy me some surveillance and the due diligence of his people, but it's not really lucrative enough for him to throw the full power of his team behind it. Even if he does so, House Forsberg is very well prepared for any traditional level of scrutiny. This means a drawn-out, expensive investigation, and I would run out of money before we obtained any results. According to Augustine, you're capable of nontraditional scrutiny. He said that you were able, professional, and honest, and that you had good instincts when it came to people."

Thanks, Augustine. "No."

"My finances aren't enough for MII but they allow me to make a very attractive proposal to a smaller firm."

"The answer is no."

"I mortgaged our house."

I put my hand over my eyes.

"I can pay you a million today. Another million when you explain to me why my wife was murdered and who was responsible."

Absolutely not. "Good-bye, Mr. Harrison."

"My wife is dead." His voice shook with barely controlled emotion. His eyes glistened. "She's my light. She found me in the darkest time of my life and she saw something in me . . . She believed I could be a better man. I didn't deserve her or the happiness we had. She loved me, Nevada. She loved me so much, in spite of my faults, and I was the luckiest man alive because when I opened my eyes in the morning, I saw her next to me. She had integrity. She was kind and intelligent, and she tried her hardest to do the right thing so this world would be a better place for our child to grow up in. She didn't deserve this. She deserved to be happy. She deserved a full and long life. Nobody had the right to rob her of it."

His face contorted with raw pain and grief. I was trying so hard not to cry.

"I love her determination. I love her spirit. I'm proud to have been her husband. And now she's dead. Someone took this wonderful—this truly beautiful—human being and turned her into a corpse. I saw her on the morgue table. She's just . . . cold and lifeless as if she never was. Everything is gone except for our daughter and my memories. I have to strive to be the man she thought I was. When my daughter grows up, she'll ask me why her mother was murdered and I'll have to answer her. I have to account for my actions. I want to tell her that I found those responsible and I made sure they wouldn't hurt anyone else."

He brushed moisture from his eyes with a furious swipe of his hand. "Nobody else will do this. Her family doesn't have the means, my family doesn't care, and her employer might have murdered her. There is only me. Will you help me? Please."

He fell silent. He was sitting here asking for my help and I couldn't throw him out of my office. I just couldn't. I remembered when Mom sold our house to pay for Dad's bills. I remembered when we mortgaged the business and kept it from him, because it would've killed him faster than any disease. If someone I loved was murdered, I would do the same thing Cornelius did. He had nowhere to turn. If I slammed the door in his face now, I wouldn't be able to look my reflection in the eye.

I reached into the top drawer of my desk and took out the blue new-client folder. I opened it so it faced him, placed it on the table, and wrote $50,000 in the margins on the front. "This is my retainer. This stays with the agency no matter what happens. It's nonnegotiable." I used my pen to circle the bottom number on the right side. "These are our rates. This job is likely to be high-risk, so the top rate right here will apply. As you can see, it's a daily and not hourly rate. Depending on the situation, I may have to charge you hazard pay or additional expenses. The retainer acts like a deductible. Once the amount billed to you exceeds it, you will make additional payments in installments of $10,000. After we're done here, you may want to go to the bank and withdraw at least $20,000 in cash. We may have to bribe people . . ."

"Thank you."

"This is a bad idea. Please reconsider."

He shook his head. "No."

I walked him through the privacy policy and had him sign all of the waivers. "What happens once we find whoever is responsible?"

"I'll take care of things from there."

"Meaning you'll kill your wife's murderer."

"It's the way Houses handle things," Cornelius said.

"Well, I'm not a House. I'm a person with a family, and I respect and try to obey the laws of this country. I won't hesitate to defend you or myself, but I won't condone murder."

"Understood," Cornelius said. "How do we start?"

"I need to be able to speak to Matthias Forsberg. I need face-to-face time so I can ask him some questions. I can make the necessary calls tomorrow, but he'll refuse to see me."

"You don't have the social status and you work for his competitor." Cornelius nodded. "Matthias is an active participant in the Assembly. He never misses a session. Tomorrow happens to be December 15th. The session starts at 9:00 a.m."

"I don't have admission to the Assembly." The Assembly was an unofficial executive body that governed the magic users at state and national levels. The Texas State Assembly met in Houston. A family had to have at least two Prime-caliber magic users in three generations to be considered a House and each House had a single seat. Technically the Assembly had no power within the U.S. government, but, practically, when the Houses spoke in one collective voice, both Congress and the White House listened.

"A family name has to be good for something, right?" Cornelius smiled. It never reached his eyes. They stayed bitter and haunted. "As a Significant and a scion of a House, I'm free to attend the Assembly and bring a companion of my choice. I intend to be an active participant in this investigation, Ms. Baylor."

"Call me Nevada," I told him. "Good. Then we'll meet here tomorrow at seven."

Cornelius and Matilda left, the hellhound Bunny in tow. I sat at my desk for a few moments, long enough to shoot a quick email to Bern with everyone's names and a brief description of what happened, then took a deep breath and let the air out slowly. Breaking this to my family would be hard. My mother might disown me.

I fished the dollar-sign bride out of the trash, smoothed her out the best I could, and stuck her and the ME report into a manila folder. This job would affect the entire family. They had the right to know the risk. Besides, experience proved that keeping secrets when you were a Baylor didn't work. Sooner or later all your hidden schemes exploded into the light, and then there was hell to pay and hurt feelings.

I tucked the folder under my arm and grabbed my book, *Hexology* by Stahl. A few weeks ago a package of books had arrived at our doorstep in a padded yellow envelope, six books in all, dealing with spells, arcane circles, and magic theory. A plain rectangular label had just one word printed on it—*Nevada*. Interrogation of my family provided no leads. They didn't know where the books came from, they didn't order them, and they had no idea who did, although they offered many wild theories.

I'd dusted the envelope for prints but I didn't find any. The label proved to be a generic four-by-four inches, and a half-dozen office stores in the ten-mile radius carried identical labels. And of course, they also carried the same yellow envelopes. My name was printed in Times New Roman font, 22 pt size. I briefly considered swabbing the

34366000051003

envelope for DNA and paying a private lab to analyze it to eliminate my family and run it through their database for possible matches, but the lab quoted $600 to run the swab and I couldn't justify the expense to myself. It was still driving me nuts.

The books had proven incredibly useful and I'd been reading them nonstop trying to catch up on years of neglected education in magic theory. This particular book was on hexes—magic constructs that locked information within a human mind. I had encountered a very powerful hex several weeks ago and had to peer under it to save the city. The book confirmed that I had come perilously close to killing a man through sheer ignorance.

I made my way through the office back door into a wide hallway. The delicious smell of seared carne asada swirled around me. I turned right and headed toward the kitchen.

When Dad was fighting his losing battle with cancer, we sold our house. We sold everything we could, but we still had to survive and make a living, so a strategic decision was made: we used our business to purchase a large warehouse. On the east side, the warehouse was the front for Baylor Investigative Agency. We installed interior walls and a drop ceiling, making a small but comfortable office space: three offices on one side and a break room and conference room on the other. On the west side, the warehouse turned into a motor pool, where Grandma Frida worked on tanks and armored vehicles for the Houston elite. Between the office and the motor pool, separated from the latter by a large wall, lay three thousand square feet of living space.

My parents had this vision of making our living space look like the inside of an ordinary house. Instead we succeeded in throwing walls where they were needed and sometimes not at all, so in certain areas our place bore a startling resemblance to a home-improvement showroom.

The kitchen was one of those spots. Square, roomy, with a generous island and a big kitchen table made from an old slab of reclaimed wood, it would give most cooking shows a run for their money. Right now it sat half empty: my mother, Grandma Frida, and my oldest cousin, Bern, were the only ones left. My two sisters and Bern's younger brother, Leon, must've run off already. Just as well.

Small bowls filled the center of the table, holding everything from grated cheese and pico de gallo to guacamole. Soft-taco night. I refrained from cheering, grabbed an apron out of the kitchen drawer, put it on, and landed in a chair next to Grandma. There was no way I could get stains on my hideously expensive suit, and taking it off and changing into casual clothes would've taken too long. I was too hungry.

"And the hunter home from the hill," Bern announced.

I squinted at him. "Decided to take British Literature after all?"

"It was the lesser of two evils. The next semester will try my patience." Bern wolfed down his food and reached for another taco. Over six feet tall and two hundred pounds, most of it bone and muscle, Bern went to judo twice a week and ate with all the appetite of a bear preparing to hibernate for winter.

I pulled a warm soft-taco shell out and began filling it with delicious things. I'd had to bust my butt to get through college as fast as I could, because I was the primary breadwinner. But now the business was making money. We weren't rich—we probably barely scraped the bottom of the middle class—but we could afford for Bernard to take his time with his education. I wanted him to have the whole college experience. Instead he took every opportunity to pile more course work on himself.

I eyed my mom's plate. One lone taco. Where Grandma Frida was naturally thin, with a cloud of platinum-white curls and big blue eyes, my mother used to be muscular and athletic, built with strength and endurance in mind. That was before the war left her with a permanent limp. She was softer now, rounder around the edges. It bothered her. She'd been eating less and less and a couple of weeks ago we realized she'd begun skipping dinner altogether.

"This is my third one," Mom said. "Stop staring."

"It is," Grandma Frida confirmed, poking at her taco salad. "I watched her eat two."

"I'm just making sure all of our business assets are in fighting condition." I stuck my tongue out at her. "Can't have you passing out from hunger on the job. Any news on Senator Garza's thing?"

"Nope," Grandma Frida said.

"It's all harebrained conjecture at this point," Mom said. "The talking heads are trying to drum up hysteria, saying it was a Prime who had to have done it."

Senator Timothy Garza died on Saturday in front of his cousin's house. His security detail died with him. The story was so sensational it even pushed Jeff Caldwell's arrest onto the back burner. The police weren't releasing any information connected to the senator's murder, which caused the news media to froth at the mouth in outrage. Without any data, they were forced to marinate in their own speculation, and the theories were getting wilder by the minute. If a Prime had been involved, I wouldn't be surprised. Garza had run on a platform of limiting the influence of the Houses, which didn't exactly make him the darling of Texas magic elite. The debates during his election campaign had turned ugly fast.

"What have you been up to?" Mom asked.

I stuffed a chunk of soft taco into my mouth and chewed to buy some time. I would have to come clean. I swallowed. "I took a high-risk job."

"How high-risk?" Mom asked.

I opened the folder and slid the ME's report toward her. She read it. Her eyebrows furrowed. "We're solving murders now?"

"Who got murdered?" Grandma Frida asked.

"Do you remember the animal mage I told you about? The one with a raccoon who was bringing juice to his daughter in a sippy cup?"

"Cornelius Harrison," Bern said.

"Yes. His wife."

My mother's expression was growing grimmer by the second. She passed the ME report to Grandma.

Grandma glanced at the report and whistled.

"This is above our pay grade," my mother said.

"I know," I told her.

"Why would you take this?"

Because he'd sat in my office and cried, and I'd felt awful for him. "Because she's dead and nobody cares. And he's paying us very well."

"We don't need the money that badly," my mother said.

"According to my sisters, we do." I slid the photograph with dollar signs toward her.

Mom swung toward Grandma Frida. "Mom!"

Grandma Frida's eyes got really big. "What? Don't look at me!"

"You started this."

Ha! Attack deflected and redirected.

"I did no such thing. I'm innocent. You always blame me for everything."

"You started it and you encouraged it. Now look, she's taking on murders because you're guilt-tripping her to put food on the table. And what kind of message does this send?"

"A true-love kind of message." Grandma Frida grinned.

Bern got up and leaned to me. "You want me to run the background on everyone?"

"Yes, please. I sent you an email. I'm going to the Assembly tomorrow, so something on Matthias Forsberg would be great."

"Will do." He took his plate to the sink.

"Your granddaughters don't need a rich Prime to pay for their college!" my mom said. "That's why their sister, their mother, and their grandmother work long hours. We pay our own way in this family."

"Oh, come on, Penelope, you know I didn't mean it that way."

"Well, how did you mean it exactly, Mother?"

Grandma Frida waved her hands. "I meant it to be funny! Nevada's been moping for two months now. She's turned into that sad donkey from the cartoons, the one that always gets rained on."

"I haven't been moping. I told Rogan no and if I never see him again, it will be too soon."

"Oh, please." Grandma rolled her eyes.

"I mean it, Grandma. Let it go. It's not like he's beating down our door and proclaiming his undying love to me."

And in my secret shameful moments I daydreamed that he would do just that. I had woken up in the middle of the night once, convinced that Rogan was outside. I almost ran out there in my nightshirt. Thankfully, nobody saw me before I came to my senses.

He'd never shown up. He'd never called. He'd never emailed. He hadn't fought for me, not even a little bit. It hammered home the fact that I was right to turn him down when he stood in my garage, told me to pick a spot on the planet, and promised me he would take me there. Mad Rogan wanted a plaything. I said no and he moved on.

"He sent you those books!"

"You don't know that."

"Well, who else would?" Grandma Frida spread her arms.

"Maybe it was Augustine." Yeah, hell would freeze over first. Augustine wouldn't move a finger unless it helped his bottom line.

"You and Rogan aren't done." Grandma pointed her fork at me. "Just watch. Fate will throw you two together. One day you'll just run right into him and boom! True love."

"Well, if Fate ever does throw us together, I'll be sure to punch her in the face." I turned to my mother. "Are you with me on this case or not? Because if you want to fight with me some more, now is the time to do it."

She looked at me for a long moment.

Oh. I'd just raised my voice at my mother for no reason. "I'm sorry."

"You told me yourself, it's your business."

"Mom . . ."

"Of course we're with you," she said. "But I don't have to tell you this is a professional hit. You need to be careful."

"I will be."

"We don't know what kind of pot you'll be stirring. They'll come after both you and him. They might come after us as well. Does your client have any House support?"

"No. He chose to live with his wife and daughter in Royal Oaks. He was very proud of his independence."

"Any security on his residence?"

"Not really." Technically, Bunny counted as security, but there was only so much one dog could do against killers with guns.

"Wife's parents?"

"They're not affiliated with any prominent families, as far as I know."

"What's your take on him?"

I grimaced. "He worshiped his wife. He'll do anything for revenge."

My mother nodded. "You may want to talk to him. His little girl will be safer here with us than with his grand-parents."

"Thank you," I said.

She sighed. "It's my job as a mother. I can't make you stop doing something stupid but I can help you do it in the least dangerous way possible."

I turned and headed toward the ladder leading to my room.

"Did you see how she got all hot under the collar?" Grandma Frida said in a theatrical whisper behind me. "She's not over him."

"I can hear you!" I climbed the ladder and pulled it back up after me. My little loft apartment greeted me—a large bedroom and a bathroom. When we'd originally moved into the warehouse, I really wanted my privacy, and the older I grew, the more I treasured it. I took off my suit, carefully put it in the garment bag, and hung it up in the back of my closet.

I wasn't over Rogan.

When I kissed him inside the null space, I'd almost seen into him. For a few brief moments he wasn't Mad Rogan. He wasn't even a Prime. He was just . . . Connor. A man. And I wanted to know that man so badly. But he'd slammed that door shut as soon as he noticed it was cracked open.

I turned on the shower to let the water warm up, and stripped. Obsessing over something that would never be did me no good. Shower, clean clothes, sleep. I had a big day tomorrow and I'd need to do some research for it before bed.

Chapter 2

The morning brought rain and Cornelius, who arrived at exactly 6:55 a.m. in a silver BMW i8. The hybrid vehicle, sleek and ultramodern, looked slightly odd, its lines varying just enough from the established norms of the gasoline cars to draw attention.

Of course he would drive a hybrid car. He likely never bought bottled water either. Bern had run all of the usual checks on him yesterday. Aside from that new mortgage, Cornelius was debt-free. He had excellent credit history and no criminal record, and he generously donated to an animal charity. He also had been right about House Forsberg's involvement in his wife's death. The story was getting no press. Even with Garza's murder flooding all available news channels, a brutal slaying of four people in a hotel downtown was at least worth a quick mention. It hadn't received one, which meant someone somewhere was actively suppressing it. If House Forsberg truly had nothing to do with it, they'd have no reason to keep it quiet.

Cornelius stepped out of the car. He wore a white dress shirt open at the collar, with sleeves rolled up, dark brown pants, and scuffed-up brown shoes that looked ancient.

Comfort clothes, I realized. He must've chosen the outfit on autopilot and his subconscious made him reach for something old and familiar.

A large reddish bird swooped down from the overcast sky and landed on the branch of a big oak tree across the parking lot.

"This is Talon," Cornelius said. "He's a red-tailed hawk, commonly known as a chicken hawk, although really it's a misnomer. They hardly ever target adult chickens. The Assembly won't permit me to bring in a dog. It won't permit you to bring in a gun either. However, on the fourth floor there is a bathroom where the window has been altered so it doesn't trip the security system. It's frequently left open."

"Is it the secret smoking bathroom?" I guessed.

Cornelius nodded. "It's just far enough from the smoke detector that an open window lets them get away with it. Are you armed?"

"Yes." Before Adam Pierce, I got away with carrying a Taser 90 percent of the time. Now I didn't leave the house without a firearm and I practiced with my guns every week. My overtime at the gun range was making my mother very happy.

"Can I see it?"

I pulled my Glock 26 out of the holster under my jacket. It was accurate, relatively light weight, and made for concealed carry. I'd opted for one of my cheap pantsuits primarily because I could get away with the kind of shoes that let me run and because the jacket was loose enough to obscure my firearm. Besides, I seriously doubted they would let me into the Assembly building in my typical attire of old jeans, running shoes, and whatever top wasn't too wrinkled after one of my sisters dumped my laundry on my bed to make space for her own load in the dryer. I'd have to clear an X-ray and a metal detector as well.

Cornelius examined the gun. "Why does it have this bright blue paint on this part?"

"It's matte fingernail polish. The black on black sight makes it harder to hit dark targets and the fingernail polish fixes that problem and cuts down on the glare."

"How much does it weigh?"

"About twenty-six ounces." I'd stuck with the standard 10 round magazine, hollow point. And I carried a lot of extra ammo. My adventures with Rogan made me paranoid.

"Talon can carry it through the bathroom window for you."

Okay, I had to nip this in the bud. It's not that the idea of walking into a building filled with the top crust of Houston's magic users unarmed wasn't giving me anxiety. It was. My favorite strategy when confronted with danger was to run away. People who ran away survived and avoided costly medical bills, loss of work hours, and increases in insurance premiums. They also escaped being lectured by their entire family about taking unnecessary risks. I used a gun only when I had no choice. Confronting a Prime inside a building filled with other Primes would make running away very difficult, so going in armed was tempting. But bringing a firearm into the Texas Assembly was suicide. Might as well pin a target to my chest with the words *Terrorist. Shoot Me.*

"Why would I need to bring a gun into that building?"

"It might be useful," Cornelius said quietly.

Right. "Cornelius, if we're going to work together, we have to agree on full disclosure. You want me to bring the gun into the Assembly because you're convinced that Forsberg killed your wife and you want me to shoot him."

"When I talked to them yesterday before coming to see you, one of his security people suggested that Nari may have been having an affair with one or both of the other two lawyers. When I told him it was unlikely, his exact words were, 'We don't always know the people we marry. Who knows what the investigation will uncover? I've seen it all, embezzlement, sex addicts, drugs. Terrible what sometimes comes to light.' They're not simply content to ignore her death. They're now actively distancing themselves from her and, if I keep making noise, they're threatening to smear her name."

"That's awful of them. But it doesn't tell us that Matthias Forsberg is guilty. It only indicates that Forsberg Investigative Services employs scumbags and they're trying to cover their asses."

Cornelius looked away.

"You came to me for the truth. I'll get the truth for you. When I point out the guilty person to you, it won't be because of a hunch or a feeling. It will be because I'll present you with the evidence of their guilt, because accusing someone of murder should never be done lightly. You want to be sure, right?"

"Right."

"Good. We need evidence. We'll search for this evidence together and we'll do it as safely and carefully as possible, so you can come home to Matilda. According to my research, the security at the Assembly is very tight. You can't even get into the Allen Parkway parking lot without showing ID and having a reason to be there. If we were to follow your plan, and someone discovered that I carried a firearm into that building, the security wouldn't detain me. They would shoot me and whoever I was with."

His face told me he didn't like it.

"What happens if Forsberg attacks?" he asked.

"On a crowded Assembly floor? In plain view of his peers, while we're unarmed?"

Cornelius grimaced.

I smiled at him. "I think we should table the gun idea for now. If he attacks, I'll do my best to handle it."

I wasn't exactly defenseless. As long as I could get my hands on my attacker before he or she killed me, they would be in for one unpleasant surprise. The military had been employing more and more mages. Military service wasn't exactly a stress-free environment, and the people in charge had quickly figured out that they needed a method for neutralizing magic users. That's how the shockers came on the scene. Getting them installed involved a specialist who reached into the arcane realm, the place beyond our fabric of existence, pulled out a creature nobody fully understood, and implanted it into your arms. I'd had mine implanted when I was hunting Adam Pierce. You primed them with your magic, suffering through some pain, and if you grabbed your victim, that pain would hit them and blossom into a convulsion-inducing agony. The shockers were supposedly nonlethal, but I had too much magic. I could kill an Average magic user, and although I had used them on a Prime only once, barely, he'd definitely felt it.

"I'll defer to your judgment." Cornelius opened the door of his vehicle. "Please."

"Let's take my car," I said, nodding at my minivan.

He glanced at the Mazda. His face turned carefully neutral. My aging champagne mom-minivan clearly failed to make the right impression.

I walked to the minivan and opened the passenger door. "Please."

Cornelius opened the trunk of his car and lifted out a large plastic sack similar to one of those fifty-pound bags of cheap dog food, except this one was plain white and unmarked. He heaved it onto his shoulder and carried it over to the Mazda. I opened the trunk and let him slide it in there.

We got into my car and buckled up. I drove out of the

parking lot and turned right, heading to Blalock Road. Anything to avoid the hell that was the 290. Cornelius' face was a grim mask. He didn't trust me yet. Trust took time.

"May I ask, why your car?"

"Because I'm familiar with the way it handles and we may have to drive very fast. In addition, this type of car blends into traffic, while your vehicle stands out." Also because my grandmother made some modifications to the engine and installed bulletproof windows after my Adam Pierce adventure, but he didn't need to know that. "What's in that bag?"

"It's a private matter, unrelated to our visit to the Assembly."

Okay. Fair enough. But now, of course, I was dying to figure out what was in there.

"Do you smoke?" I asked.

"No."

"How do you know about the smoking bathroom?" Here's hoping he hadn't shared with anyone that we were planning to visit.

"My brother is deeply offended by its existence. He's asthmatic."

True. So far he hadn't lied to me.

"My turn," Cornelius said. "What do you hope to gain by speaking with Forsberg? He won't admit any guilt."

"I have a lot of experience with watching people, and I can usually tell when they're lying."

And we ran into roadwork. Of course. Now I would have to merge onto Katy Freeway.

"Curiously, that's almost exactly what Augustine told me about you," Cornelius said.

Augustine had kept my secret. Primes didn't do anything without some ulterior motive. I wasn't looking forward to finding out what he was planning.

"Are you having second thoughts? It's not too late. We can turn around and I'll refund your retainer."

"No." Cornelius looked out the window. "When I woke up this morning, I thought of kidnapping Forsberg and torturing him until he told me everything he knew."

Homicidal fantasies were never a good sign. "That would be a terrible idea. First, it's illegal. Second, we don't know if Forsberg is involved. If he isn't, you would've tortured an innocent man. Third, my cousin ran the background on House Forsberg. While they are not the wealthiest House in Houston, their net worth is substantial and so is their private security force. If you were to kidnap Forsberg and not die in the attempt, you would be hunted down and eventually killed."

Cornelius didn't answer.

Bern and I had stayed up way too late with House Forsberg's file. Matthias Milton Forsberg, fifty-two years old, was a fourth-generation Texan and very proud of it—so proud that he'd gone to the University of Texas instead of the usual Ivy League schools. He'd become the head of his House twelve years ago, when his father retired. He was married, with two adult children, Sam Houston Forsberg and Stephen Austin Forsberg, which made me laugh a little last night while drinking coffee. It was good that he'd stopped at two, because nobody was quite sure which man Dallas was named after. Matthias had never been arrested, never served in the military, and never declared bankruptcy. He did own a lot of houses.

Magically he was a hopper. Hoppers compressed the space around them, propelling themselves or others through it. Usually their hops were short-range, topping out at thirty yards. Still, they could cover short distances very quickly and were hard to target while hopping, which made them highly sought after by the military. I'd never encountered one before, so I had watched some

YouTube videos. Most of them consisted of guys between the ages of fifteen and twenty-five launching things at walls with their magic, such as watermelons, pumpkins, cans of paint, and in one particular extra-stupid video, a gallon of gasoline with a lighted fuse made out of a long sock. That went about as well as you would expect. Most of them tried to throw each other or themselves as well, but none had enough power. The best they could do was stagger their friends a few feet. According to Bern, the mass and size of the object were a factor.

The internet claimed that Prime-rank hoppers could pass through solid walls if they timed their jumps right. If that was true, Forsberg's reputation for flirting with corporate espionage made perfect sense.

Public records and YouTube videos weren't much to go on, but unlike me, Cornelius had access to the House database and he'd probably met Forsberg.

"What can you tell me about Matthias Forsberg?" I asked.

"He's a typical Houston Prime; he safeguards the family wealth, he has firm ideas of what is and isn't proper for a person of his social standing, and he avoids public scrutiny. He considers very few people his equals and treats the rest with contempt."

"Can he hop through walls?"

"Yes. Could you take the next exit, please?"

I pulled off the freeway.

"Make a right and park, please."

We made a right and stopped before a construction site. The steel bones of the building were beginning to take shape, wrapped in scaffolding. Cornelius got out, took the sack out of the trunk, and walked down the road between the buildings, disappearing from view. Talon swooped down, following him.

What could be in the sack? It was plastic, reinforced

with mesh. He could have body parts in there and I would never know.

I drummed my fingers on the dashboard and turned on the radio. "*. . . no updates on Senator Garza's murder investigation. The police department remains . . .*"

I turned it off.

It couldn't be body parts. They would've made bulges. The sack seemed uniform, so unless he'd minced the body parts into mush . . . Okay, this was just morbid. Four months ago it wouldn't even occur to me that there might be body parts in the sack.

Cornelius reappeared, carrying an empty sack. If it had been filled with something nasty, I would smell it when he put it back in the car.

He folded the sack carefully and put it in the trunk. Nope, no weird smells. No suspicious dripping.

"Thank you," he said. "We can be on our way now."

The Assembly occupied the America Tower, a graceful skyscraper on the corner of Waugh Drive and Allen Parkway. The forty-two stories of pale concrete and dark windows rose in elegant curves to almost six hundred feet above Houston's midtown. This December had brought endless rain, complete with floods, and a perpetually gloomy overcast sky. The America Tower stood out against this dark backdrop as if some wizard's mystical spire had escaped its legend and appeared in the middle of Houston. It was filled with mages, except this kind of mage wouldn't sing songs in a bumbling, adorable way or send you on a heroic quest. They would murder you in an instant and then their lawyers would make any hints of a criminal investigation disappear.

We cleared a security booth, where Cornelius had to show his ID, then parked and stepped out of the car. Talon dived over us and took off, flying past a large dandelion-shaped fountain wrapped in a white fuzz of mist to the trees on the side.

We walked past the perfectly manicured emerald-green lawn toward the glass entrance. I missed the weight of my gun, but the Glock had to stay in the car.

"How does your magic work?" I asked softly. "Are you telepathically controlling Talon? Could you see through his eyes?"

"No." Cornelius shook his head. "He's his own bird. I give him food, shelter, and affection, and in return, when I ask for a favor, he answers."

Talon wasn't just a bird, he was a pet. That probably meant that Bunny was also a pet. If any of his animals got hurt, Cornelius would react very strongly. I would have to keep it in mind.

We were almost to the doors.

"Forsberg probably won't dignify any of my questions with an answer," I said.

"I agree."

"You may have to do the asking. I want you to be blunt. Yes-or-no questions are best."

"So you need me to walk up to him and ask him if he's responsible for Nari's death?"

"No, that's too broad a term. He may have had nothing to do with it, but he may feel guilty or upset because of what happened to her. We know that he himself didn't do it, because at the time of the murder, he was photographed by about fifty people at the Firemen's Annual Fundraiser Dinner. Ask him if he ordered her killed. No matter what he answers, your second question should be 'Do you know who did?' We need to see his reaction. Keep your questions short and to the point and don't elaborate so he doesn't have a way to weasel out of it. Silence puts people under a lot of pressure and they'll try to respond. If I think he's lying, I'll nod."

Cornelius held the door open for me and we walked into the lobby. The blast of air-conditioning after the rain made me shiver. The temperature outside hovered around the low seventies, but inside it must've been barely above sixty degrees. The floor, high-gloss sandy-brown marble, gleamed like a mirror. Logic said they had to have installed it in tiles, but I couldn't even see the grout lines. The same marble sheathed the walls. In the center of the floor, three banks of elevators offered access to upstairs. Four guards, dressed in crisp white shirts and black pants and armed with Remington tactical shotguns, stood at the strategic points near the walls. Three more manned the desk in front of the metal detector. The Assembly's guards weren't playing. Prime or not, a tactical shotgun would make me reconsider any mischief really fast.

If I pointed a gun in their direction, they would fire without a second thought and whoever was in the immediate vicinity would be caught in that blast.

"You were right," Cornelius said quietly.

"Thank you."

We reached the desk, where Cornelius got a "Welcome, Mr. Harrison. We're glad to see you again." I got to pull out two forms of ID and fill out a three-page questionnaire that included my blood type and medical-insurance provider before they eventually issued me a one-day pass.

Finally, we made our way to the elevators. According to Cornelius, Forsberg would be on the twenty-fifth floor. I pushed the appropriate button and the elevator rose. The doors opened on the fourth floor and a man in a hooded robe strode in. The robe was jet black, split on the sides like the tabard of some medieval knight, and equipped with a deep hood that hid its owner's face. Only his chin with a carefully trimmed red beard was visible. A dark green stole draped his shoulders, shining with silver embroidery. Underneath the robe the man wore black pants tucked into soft black boots that came halfway up his ankle, and a black shirt. He looked frightening, almost menacing, like a mage ready for war.

I took a step to the side, giving him room.

The man pushed the button for the tenth floor. A moment later the doors opened and he stepped out.

Another robed person, a woman this time judging by the braid of dark hair spilling from the hood, walked up to him before the doors closed, hiding them from view.

"Why are they dressed that way?" I murmured.

"It's tradition. The Assembly has a Lower Chamber, where every Prime and Significant of a qualified House can vote, and the Upper Chamber, where only Prime heads of Houses can vote. The robes mean they belong to the Upper Chamber."

The elevator stopped three floors later and another robed man got in, his stole gold embroidered with black.

"Cornelius!"

The mage pulled back his hood, revealing the handsome face of a man in his early sixties, with bold features, a broad forehead, and smart hazel eyes caught in the network of wrinkles. A short beard, black and sprinkled with silver, hugged his jaw. His hair, once probably dark with some white, but now mostly white with some dark, was brushed away from his face. He looked like your favorite uncle who lived somewhere in Italy, owned a vineyard, laughed easily, and hugged you when you came to visit. Right now his face showed concern, and his eyes were saddened.

"My boy, I just heard." The man hugged Cornelius. "I'm so sorry."

His regret was genuine. How about that?

"Thank you."

"Words can't express . . ." The man fell silent. "You, the young, you're not supposed to die. Old men like me, we come to terms with our own death. We've lived full lives. But this . . . this is an outrage. What is Forsberg doing about it?"

"Nothing," Cornelius said.

The man drew back. His deep, resonant voice rose. "Nari was an employee of his House. What do you mean he's doing nothing? It's his duty. The honor of his House is at stake."

"I don't believe he cares," Cornelius said.

"This would've never happened under his father. There are certain things that the head of a House simply does. Let me see what I can do. My voice may not be as loud as it once was, but people still listen to it. If you need anything, anything at all, you know where to find me."

True. A sincere Prime who actually showed compassion.

"Thank you."

The man got off on the twentieth floor.

"Who was that?" I asked.

"Linus Duncan," Cornelius said. "Very old, very powerful House. He used to be the Speaker of the Upper Chamber. The most powerful man in Houston. Until they drove him out."

"Why?"

"Because he was honest and he tried to change the Assembly for the better," Cornelius said.

It didn't surprise me. Houses feared change like it was a rabid tiger.

The elevator chimed, announcing our floor. We stepped off and turned right. Near the middle of the long hallway, by an open door, three men stood together discussing something, all dark-haired, middle-aged, and wearing black robes with their hoods down. One of them was Matthias Forsberg. Of average height but with the broad, sturdy frame of an aging football player, Forsberg stood out. His shoulders were wide and heavy, his stance direct. He planted his feet as if he expected to be run over. His face, with dark eyes, wide eyebrows that angled down without any hint of an arch, and a hint of softness around the chin, didn't match his body.

Cornelius sped up, heading toward the men. I chased after him. Forsberg raised his head, glancing in our direction. His expression changed from tense to alarmed. The two other men looked in our direction and moved to the other end of the hallway, leaving Forsberg alone.

"Harrison," Forsberg said, looking like he just found some rotten potatoes in his pantry. "My condolences."

"Did you order the death of my wife?" Cornelius asked. His voice rang out. People looked in our direction. Smart. Forsberg would have to respond now and it was clear he wasn't used to backing down.

"Are you out of your mind?" Forsberg growled.

"Yes or no, Matthias."

"No!"

Truth.

"Do you know who did?"

"Of course not."

My magic buzzed, an angry invisible mosquito. Lie. I nodded.

"If I did, I'd take action."

Lie.

"Was her death connected to the business of your house?"

"No."

Lie.

Cornelius looked at me. I nodded again.

"Tell me who killed my wife," Cornelius ground out through his teeth.

Argh. Wrong question.

"You're delusional and grieving," Forsberg said. His expression hardened. "This is the only reason you're still breathing. I'm going to give you one chance to get out of this building . . ."

His gaze snagged on something behind me. His eyes opened wide and I saw fear ignite in their depths. It was so at odds with the bullheaded arrogance he projected, I almost did a double take.

I looked over my shoulder.

A tall man was striding from the far end of the hallway. He wore the black robe and it flared around him, the wings of a raven about to take flight. He walked like he owned the building and he'd spotted an intruder in his domain. Magic boiled around him, vicious and lethal, so potent I could feel it from thirty yards away. He wasn't a man, he was an elemental force, a thunderstorm clad in black about to unleash its fury. People flattened themselves against the walls, trying to get out of his way. I saw his face and recoiled. Chiseled chin, strong nose, and blue eyes blazing with power under dark slashes of eyebrows.

Mad Rogan.

My heart hammered so fast; my chest was about to explode.

He was coming toward me.

Our stares connected. I clamped all my thoughts into a steel fist, trying to keep my reaction under control.

His expression softened and for a fraction of a second I saw him looking at me with a mix of surprise and relief. Then the gaze of those furious eyes fixed on Forsberg with predatory focus. I knew that expression. It said, "Murder."

I whipped around. Panic drowned Forsberg's face.

Magic contracted around him, compressing in on itself like a spring coiling under pressure. The hallway around me stretched back as if marble and metal suddenly became elastic.

I shoved Cornelius out of the way.

The hallway compacted like an aluminum can flattened by pressure and suddenly I was airborne. I hurtled through the air, straight at Mad Rogan.

Fate threw us at each other. I could never tell Grandma.

I crashed into Rogan. Strong arms caught me. The impact spun us around, and I landed upright on the floor to the right of him. Before my feet touched the marble, Rogan hurled a handful of quarters in the air. The coins streaked at Forsberg, flattened bullets driven by Rogan's power, dodging random people in the hallway as they shot toward their target.

The air around Forsberg shimmered. The coins collided with the shimmer and fell to the ground, bouncing from an invincible barrier. Forsberg blurred, landing twenty yards back from where he'd been.

"Shoot him," Rogan said, his voice clipped.

"No gun."

Forsberg looked scared to death. People who panicked didn't think; they ran. I dashed toward the elevator. We had to beat him to the lobby.

Forsberg jumped straight up, blurred, and then fell through the floor. I caught myself on the corner of the short hallway leading to the elevator, slid on the marble floor, and mashed the button going down. Rogan was only a step behind me.

The elevator doors slid open and we rushed inside. I hit the button for the lobby. The door began to slide closed and Cornelius squeezed through the gap at the last moment, causing them to reopen. Rogan jerked the animal mage off his feet, slamming him against the elevator wall, his forearm pressed against the blond man's throat. Cornelius groaned, his feet above the ground, all of his weight pushing his neck against Rogan's forearm.

"Drop my client!" I barked.

Rogan pressed harder. Cornelius' face turned red. I'd seen what Rogan could do with his bare hands to a person. If I didn't pry Cornelius away from him, Rogan would crush his windpipe.

"Rogan! He's a . . . he's a civilian!"

Rogan stepped back as if I'd thrown a switch. Cornelius dropped to the floor, gulping air. Apparently I'd said the magic word.

"Try that again and I'll shock you into oblivion," I ground out.

The elevator doors opened. Twelfth floor. Rogan pushed the button, forcing the doors to close, and peered at Cornelius. "Is this my replacement?"

What? "I didn't replace you!"

"Of course not. I'm irreplaceable."

Cornelius finally managed to squeeze out a word. "Rogan? The Butcher of Merida? *Mad* Rogan?"

"Yes," Rogan and I said in unison.

"Is this the *R* on the dress?" Cornelius' eyes were wide.

Think of clouds, think of bunnies, don't think about the wedding-gown pictures. Rogan claimed he wasn't telepathic, but he could project images, which meant he could probably pick up impressions if I concentrated on things too much.

"Dress? What dress?" Rogan asked, honing in on the word like a shark sensing blood in the water.

"Never mind," I told him. "Cornelius, not another word or I walk."

Rogan's eyes narrowed. He'd recognized the name. He was involved in this thing with Forsberg up to his elbows. Just my luck.

Number two above us blinked. Almost there.

Rogan tossed the coins in the air and the quarters hung around him motionless. His magic brushed past me, a raging, terrible beast. Shivers ran down my spine. Suddenly the past two months of normal life tore apart, like fragile paper, and I was right back next to Rogan, about to charge into a fight. And it felt right. It felt like I'd been sleepwalking and had suddenly woken up.

I had to get away from him as soon as I could. He was bad for me on every level.

"Alive!" I told him. "I need Forsberg alive."

The doors chimed and opened. We burst into the lobby to a wall of shotguns pointed in our direction. Behind the security, Forsberg lay on the floor on his back. A puddle of red slowly spread from his head. His eyes were gone. In their place two blood-filled holes gaped at the ceiling.

Rogan swore.

ℕormally it would've taken me days to extricate myself from the clutches of the Assembly's security. With Rogan emanating menace and Cornelius explaining things in a calm, patient tone one normally used with small children, we walked out of the building in twenty minutes. They stuck to the truth: Forsberg attacked Rogan without provocation. Cornelius and I just happened to be in the way, and there were a dozen witnesses who would confirm it. When one of the security people asked if Rogan had threatened Forsberg, the Scourge of Mexico looked at him for a moment and condescended to explain that he hadn't threatened anyone. He had been moving though the hallway with a purpose because he had someplace to be and if they had a problem identifying the difference between that and him actually threatening someone, he would be happy to demonstrate. They decided not to question him further after that.

Outside, Rogan raised his head and squinted at the sun that broke through the overcast sky. The robes were really too much. He needed some crimson banners and a glowing staff and he'd be all set.

His face was tight. He was pissed off. I was pissed off too. We'd lost Forsberg and we had no idea how he'd died, let alone any clues as to who might have helped him on his way. House Forsberg would circle the wagons and hunker down now. Everything about this investigation had just become a lot harder.

"Since when did you stop carrying your gun?" Rogan asked.

"Mr. Rogan . . ."

"Oh no." Rogan glanced at Cornelius. "We're back to formal ground. I'm clearly out of favor."

"Mr. Rogan . . ."

"Why are you mad at me?"

I made a heroic effort to keep my voice calm and measured. "You panicked the witness I was interrogating, causing him to throw me around like a rag doll, hop his way through the floors, and get himself killed, which really complicates my life and robs my client of an opportunity to discover why his wife was murdered, and then you almost strangled said client in an elevator."

"It does sound bad when you put it that way, Ms. Baylor."

His words were meant to sound light, but his eyes remained dark and grim. Something bad had happened to Rogan. I almost reached out, then caught myself. No.

No.

The man was a disease and I couldn't get rid of the infection as it was. I so didn't need another outbreak of Rogan fever.

Two Range Rovers pulled up, one gunmetal grey, the other white, both with familiar thick and tinted windows. Rogan owned a fleet of VR9 armored cars. They were state-of-the-art custom vehicles, built to be armored from the ground up while looking perfectly normal and blending into traffic, and they handled like a dream. I'd ridden in one just before Adam Pierce blew it up.

An athletic man in his twenties, with short blond hair and military bearing, jumped out of the grey Range Rover and brought the keys to Rogan. "Sir. Ms. Baylor."

"Hello, Troy." I was there when Troy had his job interview and was hired. He was ex-military and Rogan had saved him from a foreclosure. Today Troy wore a hip holster, full and in plain view.

"How is being an evil henchman treating you?"

"Can't complain, ma'am. It's a good gig if you can get it."

Of course. Complaining wouldn't be evil-henchman-like. Rogan's people worshiped the ground he walked on. If Troy was any indication, he found them at the lowest point of their lives and offered them a chance to be somebody. To matter, to have a well-paying job they would be really good at, and to provide for their families. A pack of hounds raised from puppies couldn't be more devoted. I just wasn't sure he ever saw them as anything more than assets at his disposal.

Rogan turned to me. "Come with me to my house. I have some information you'll want."

Enter my lair, said the dragon. I have shiny treasure for you to play with, I'll keep you warm and safe, and if it suits my purpose, I'll chain you to the floor and kill your client by throwing quarters at him with my magic. Been there, done that.

"I don't think so. But I'll be happy to discuss things with you in daylight in a very public place. Would you like my card?"

When I was in college, one of my professors liked creative descriptions, and whenever he had to indicate that some historical figure was in a moment of monumental rage, he'd say he had thunder on his brow and lightning in his eye. I never understood what that phrase meant until Rogan's face demonstrated it for me.

Cornelius took a careful step back. Troy backed up too. Yes, I did just tell Mad Rogan no, and look, the planet was still turning.

"Your card?" Rogan said, his voice very calm and quiet.

"It's a little piece of paper that has my phone number, email address, and other contact information on it." I waited to see if his head would explode. I shouldn't have taunted him, but I was really pissed off. We'd had Forsberg until he butted in.

Rogan pivoted to Cornelius. "My condolences on your loss. It would be my honor to have you as my guest tonight. Permit me a chance to make up for our earlier misunderstanding."

How nicely put. "You mean the part where you almost choked the life out of him?"

"Yes."

"Please don't get into his car," I told Cornelius. "He's dangerous and unpredictable."

"Thank you," Rogan said.

"Your life means absolutely nothing to him," I continued. "When he doesn't like somebody, he hits them with a bus."

"I have no desire to start a feud with House Harrison," Rogan said.

Truth.

"I guarantee your safety."

Also truth.

"And I have a recording of your wife's final moments," Rogan said.

Bastard.

Cornelius glanced at me.

"He isn't lying," I told him. "But if you get into that car, I don't know if he'll let you leave. Please don't do this."

Cornelius squared his shoulders. "I'd be delighted to accept your invitation."

Damn it. Why don't people ever listen to me?

Rogan opened the back passenger door of the Range Rover. Cornelius got in. Rogan leaned over the open door to look at Cornelius.

"Would you mind if your employee joined us?"

"Of course not," Cornelius said.

Rogan turned to me. "See? Your employer doesn't mind. If I'm such a villain, why don't you tag along to ensure his safety?"

He was insufferable. That was the long and short of it. And getting into the same car with him was out of the question. The more distance between us, the better. Except now he had my client in his claws.

"I'll follow you in my car. Cornelius, he also projects, so try not to think about anything you don't want him to pick up."

Rogan stepped close to me. Too close. I wished my body would stop betraying me every time he shortened the distance.

His voice was intimate. "I'm not one to judge, but it seems to me that you're not taking me seriously as a threat. I could kill him en route."

I crossed my arms on my chest. "Really? You're actually going to stoop to direct threats now?"

"You think the worst of me, and you know how I hate to disappoint. Troy will be happy to drive your vehicle."

Okay, something was definitely off with him. The Rogan I remembered was direct, but he could also be subtle. This wasn't even remotely subtle. He had another car following him and usually he preferred to travel alone. He was twisting my arm trying to get me into his armored vehicle. The cars had parked so their bulk blocked us from anyone entering the parking lot. Troy wore his sidearm in plain view. This wasn't about abducting Cornelius or forcing me to do something I didn't want to do. This was about safety. Both Cornelius and I would be much safer in a state-of-the-art armored vehicle than in my minivan.

As much as I wanted to be away from Rogan, if he was concerned about safety, I'd be an idiot not to take it seriously.

I handed the keys to Troy. "Mazda van over there. She handles light."

Troy nodded and jogged around the cars.

I walked up to Rogan's Range Rover, sat in the front passenger seat, and buckled my seat belt. I'd just have to endure and not think of him sitting next to me.

You'd think two months of not seeing him would've made a difference, and it had. It made whatever was pulling me to him worse. *Yeah, do you remember how you woke and ran downstairs, because you thought you saw him, and when you opened the door, nobody was there?*

He shut my door and got into the driver's seat, scanning the parking lot in front of us with a thousand-yard stare. "There is a Sig in the glove compartment."

I opened the glove compartment, took out the Sig, checked it, and put it on my lap.

"What happened?" I asked quietly.

"I lost some people," he said. There was an awful finality in his voice.

I hadn't thought he cared. I'd thought he viewed his people as tools and took care of them because tools had to be kept in good repair, but this sounded like genuine grief—that complicated cocktail of guilt, regret, and overwhelming sadness you felt when someone close to you died. It broke you and made you feel helpless. Helpless wasn't even in Rogan's vocabulary. Maybe I'd been wrong then or maybe I was wrong now. Time would tell one way or the other.

I closed my mouth and watched Houston slide by outside the window, searching the warm winter day for something I might have to shoot.

Chapter 3

(M)ost of the Houston Houses had mansions inside the Loop, a long road that encircled the downtown and the pricey neighborhoods such as River Oaks. Having an address inside the Loop was as much of a status symbol as driving luxury cars and owning personal yachts.

However, Rogan was a fourth-generation Prime. He had no interest in impressing anyone. We climbed northwest instead, leaving the city, and then the main road, behind. Old Texas oaks spread their branches over green grass, stoically enduring the rain of Houston's December.

My phone rang. Bern.

"Yes?"

"Hey, the Internet is buzzing with some sort of disturbance at the Assembly."

Well, that didn't take long.

"Do you know what's going on?"

"Forsberg is dead. I didn't kill him."

"Are you okay?"

"Yes."

"I'm showing you moving northwest."

He'd tracked my phone. "That's right."

"Where are you?"

"I'm going to Mad Rogan's house."

Silence.

"Don't tell Mom," I said.

Rogan grinned next to me, a quick parting of lips.

"I won't," Bern promised.

I hung up.

"Were you trying to murder Forsberg?" I asked.

"If I was trying, he wouldn't have left the floor."

"You looked like you were about to kill him."

"I wanted answers and he was going to give them to me. If he didn't, I probably would've."

I didn't even need my magic to tell me he meant it. "Will you be able to get your hands on his autopsy report?"

Rogan spared me a glance. Yes, of course. What was I thinking doubting the great Mad Rogan?

"How was he able to hop while dead?" I asked.

"Hopping is a two-step process," Rogan said.

"It's similar to breathing," Cornelius explained from the back seat. "Forsberg pulled the magic in, inhaling, then let it out, exhaling, and it carried him forward. If someone killed him just as he exhaled, the jump would still occur."

I really needed access to the House network and its explanations of higher magic talents. Unfortunately, I wasn't a member, nor would I ever get to be one.

We came to a wrought-iron gate that swung open at our approach and Rogan drove up the long curving driveway, past the picturesque plants. The path turned and a massive Spanish Colonial house sitting atop a low hill came into view. Two stories tall, with thick stucco walls and red tile roof, it looked at the world with arched windows. A large round tower graced the right side, and a covered balcony offered the view from the second story on the left. Red-and-purple flowers dripped from flower baskets, stretching over the balcony's dark wood rail. In the middle, a heavy rounded door, old wood with wrought ironwork, offered access to the inside of the home. It was impossibly romantic. If they ever made another Zorro movie, I knew just the place where they could film it. You half expected a man in a black mask and a cape to sword-fight his way across the balcony, leap onto a jet-black Andalusian horse, and gallop past us down the driveway.

I realized that Rogan leaned next to me.

"Do you like it?" he asked quietly.

People lied to me every day, several times a day, with the best and the worst intentions. I made it a point to lie as little as possible. "Yes."

A self-satisfied smile lit up his face. Oh, for crying out loud, it wasn't as if he had built it with his bare hands . . . Why was it even important if I liked it?

We followed him through the door into the formal entrance, with a cool limestone floor and massive columns. On the right, a curved staircase with a wrought-iron railing led to an upstairs hallway. On the left, a vast living room waited under the high ceiling crossed with rough wooden beams and lit by three rustic chandeliers, rings of metal studded with candle-shaped bulbs, that could've come from a medieval castle. Wide window-filled arches supported by stone columns interrupted the wall to the left, letting the light of the late morning stream into the space. Red-and-white Oriental rugs lay across the floor. The furniture was old and heavy, the cushions of the couches oversized and plush. A massive fireplace took up the far wall. It could've easily turned into a stuffy dark space, but instead it was light and airy, welcoming and clean. Plants stood here and there in large pots, adding bright spots of green to the stone walls.

Mad Rogan owned my dream house. Life just wasn't fair. That was okay. I would work really hard and one day I would buy my own house—maybe not quite as big, or as tastefully furnished, but it would be mine.

Rogan went up the staircase and we followed him across an indoor balcony that spanned the living room to a hallway. Rogan turned right, and we walked up another short staircase to a metal door. He held it open for me.

I walked into a square room. The wall on my left and the one directly in front of me were thick tinted glass that showed a wide covered balcony and more walls—these windows opened into the inner courtyard. The other two walls were taken up by screens and computers, manned by two people with headsets.

"Leave us," Rogan said.

They got up and left without a word. Rogan invited us to a U-shaped blue couch arranged around a coffee table. We sat.

"Bug!" Rogan called.

"Coming, Major," a voice responded from some speaker.

Rogan looked at Cornelius. "Did you bond with your wife, Mr. Harrison?"

Cornelius hesitated. "Yes."

What kind of a question was that?

"Was it a true bond?'

"Yes."

Rogan looked at me. "Is he telling the truth?"

"You do realize that I work for him and not you?"

"If he's lying to me, and I show him this, I may have to kill him."

I looked at Cornelius. "Do I have your permission to tell him?"

"Yes," he said.

"He's telling the truth."

Rogan walked over to the wall, slid the panel open, and came back with a glass and a bottle of Jack Daniels. He set the glass and the bottle in front of Cornelius.

"I don't drink," Cornelius said. "I'll be sober for this."

"What will happen after you find your wife's killer?" Rogan sat down to my left.

"I'll fire Ms. Baylor," Cornelius said.

"Because of Ms. Baylor's stubborn inability to compromise when it comes to legal matters?" Rogan asked.

"She made it clear she doesn't want to be involved in what would follow."

I waved at both of them in case they forgot that I was sitting right there.

"How committed are you to this course of action?" Rogan asked.

"I've taken measures already," Cornelius said.

Rogan sat back, his eyes calculating. "I'm going to share some confidential information with you. It has wide-reaching implications. If you would rather not be involved, tell me now. The lives of my people depend on your discretion and if you betray my confidence, I'll have to eliminate you."

"Understandable," Cornelius said. "Likewise, if I discover that you in any way caused Nari's death, I'll take the appropriate actions."

This wasn't the world of normal people. Yet somehow I kept getting stuck in it.

"For the record, I don't consent to being killed," I said.

They both looked at me.

"Just getting it out there in case there are any questions later."

A careful knock sounded and Bug bounced into the room. One of my mother's friends had a cairn terrier called Magnus. Cairn terriers were bred to catch vermin among the cairns of the Scottish Highlands, and Magnus was physically unable to sit still. He dashed about the back yard, he ran on walks, he chased toys, and if you blew bubbles, he turned into a bolt of black furry lightning until he murdered every single one. Moving was his job and he devoted himself to it.

Bug was Magnus in human form. He was always moving, typing, talking, tracking . . . Even though he often sat for most of the day, he wasn't sedentary. He was never without a purpose or a task, and I had a feeling that if only he could stop doing all of his things and eat a sandwich once in a while, he would put on the twenty-five pounds his skinny frame was missing.

Bug was a swarmer. The U.S. Air Force had bound him to something they'd pulled out of the arcane realm. They called it a swarm because they had no better name for it. The swarm had no physical form. It lived within Bug somehow, which let him split his attention, process information faster, and made him into a superior surveillance expert. Most swarmers died within two years of being bound, but Bug had somehow survived and, until recently, lived in hiding, detesting all authority, especially the military variety. I'd occasionally bought his services with Equzol, a military-grade drug designed to even him out. Then Rogan had lured him from his hiding place with promises of Equzol, advanced computer equipment, and whatever else was part of the devil deal they struck.

Being lured into Rogan's clutches agreed with Bug. His skin had lost its sallow tint, and while his eyes still brimmed with nervous energy, he wasn't twitching or freaking out.

Bug dropped onto the couch and placed a laptop in front of him on the table. "Hey, Nevada."

"Hey."

A plump dog that was mostly French bulldog and part something unidentifiable sauntered into the room and rubbed its face on my pants leg.

"Hi, Napoleon." I reached down and patted his head. Bug's dog rambled over to Rogan and unceremoniously flopped on his feet. Rogan reached down without really looking, on autopilot, picked Napoleon up and put him on the couch next to him. The French bulldog sighed contently, wedged his butt deeper into the couch, and closed his eyes.

Rogan leaned back. "In the fall, Ms. Baylor and I were involved in apprehending Adam Pierce."

"I know," Cornelius said. "That's how we met."

Bug pulled a tablet out of his sweatshirt and began messing with it. A screen slid from the wall on the side.

"Adam Pierce didn't act alone," Rogan said. "Someone loaded him like a gun, aimed, and pulled the trigger."

"Who?" Cornelius asked.

"We don't know," Bug said.

"We became aware of the conspiracy surrounding Pierce when we learned he was moving about the city undetected," I said. "He didn't just have a single mage cloaking him. There was an entire team shielding him. We know that an animator Prime was involved."

In my head I flashed back to running across a parking lot as Rogan fought a whirlwind of metal and pipes that tried to crush him. We never did find out who the animator was.

"Pierce used a teenager to do some of his dirty work," Rogan explained. "His name is Gavin Waller. Gavin's mother is my cousin. I found out that she was part of whatever cabal was pulling Adam's strings."

That was news to me. So Rogan's own cousin had betrayed him. Would he care? Would it even matter to him? He hadn't seemed to have taken any interest in Kelly Waller or her son, until Adam Pierce made Gavin a part of his murder-and-arson spree.

"Whoever was behind Adam is well funded and powerful," Rogan continued. "Fortunately for me, they overlooked a weak spot in their armor."

Bug tapped the keys on the laptop. The screen ignited, showing a woman in a skin-tight black dress kneeling on a tall chair, her arms bent at the elbow, her forearms resting on the chair's back so she could stick her butt out. A high-heeled shoe hung from the index finger of her left hand. She was looking straight at the camera with light grey eyes, her makeup fresh and flawless. Her strawberry-blond hair framed her face in a perfectly straight shimmering curtain. Her expression was vapid. She was biting her lower lip.

Ugh.

"Harper Larvo," I murmured.

"Who is she?" Cornelius asked.

"A socialite," I said. "She was involved with the people behind Adam Pierce."

"I put her under surveillance," Rogan said.

"We bugged her apartment, her phone, her cell, and her car," Bug said. "We bugged all the shit."

"A month ago Harper began an affair with Jaroslav Fenley," Rogan said.

Cornelius leaned forward. Jaroslav had worked with Nari. He was one of the three other lawyers murdered with her.

"Then, last Friday we got this." Rogan nodded at Bug, who reached over the top of the laptop and pressed a key.

"It's happening," Harper's voice said. *"They're going to hand it over. They don't want it leading back to them, so they're looking for security for the meeting now."*

"We need the time and place," an older female voice said.

A muscle jerked in Rogan's face.

"I'm tired. Can I just be done? He's boring and he smells. The BO is through the roof."

"Do you need me to remind you who's holding your leash?"

"Fine. I'll call you when I get it."

"The other woman on the tape is Kelly Waller," Rogan said. His blue eyes were glacier-cold. He cared about Kelly Waller's betrayal. He cared very much. If I were Kelly Waller, I'd make arrangements to run away to another continent.

Bug grimaced. "She used a burner phone. If she wasn't clutching Sassy at the time, we wouldn't have caught it."

"Sassy?" I asked.

"Her foo-foo poodle," Bug said.

"You bugged her dog?"

Bug drew back, outraged. "I bugged her collar! What, you think I'm a complete fart muffin? She shouldn't have that dog anyway. She treats her like shit. She doesn't deserve Sassy." Bug tapped the keys. "We combed the net and the usual places a dimwit—"

Mad Rogan glanced at him.

"—a man who doesn't know what the hell he's doing might look for private security. We found Fenley's job and we took the contract."

"We?" I asked.

"I own a private security company," Rogan said.

Of course.

"Fenley indicated that they were meeting with another party to exchange some data," Rogan said.

"At Hotel Sha Sha," Cornelius guessed.

Rogan nodded. "The timing and location weren't ideal, but I took the risk. If my cousin wants this data, I want it more."

He took the risk and his people had died. He blamed himself. It didn't reflect in his face, but I saw it in his eyes for a brief moment, before they went back to their icy blue. The last time we talked, I was almost completely convinced that he was a sociopath. He seemed invulnerable, as if nothing could bother him. This did.

Bug pushed a key on the keyboard. I braced myself.

A woman in her mid-thirties wearing grey pants, a black shirt, and an odd-looking bulletproof vest appeared on the large screen. A thin strip of metal and plastic adhered to the left side of her forehead, disappearing under her dark hair, pulled back from her face. She touched it and the view shifted slightly. She was looking into a mirror.

"Stop screwing with it," Bug's voice said.

"It's distracting." Her voice carried traces of Louisiana. *"I don't like distracting."*

"It the best tech on the market," Bug said. *"And you broke the last two, Luanne."*

"They were also distracting."

"Do you see the care in my eye?"

Luanne looked athletic and strong, and the way she held herself projected a dispassionate calm. Not serenity, just a quiet, competent alertness devoid of any emotional connection. I'd met her type before. She was a professional private soldier. You would look into her eyes and see nothing, and then she'd shoot you in the face, and as the bullets were flying, you'd still see nothing. It didn't reach her, maybe because of her experience or perhaps it just never did. In everyday life, she'd look completely normal. You'd see her at the supermarket and never imagine that she could kill people for a living.

Behind her men and women in identical garb were checking their weapons.

"What kind of a vest is that?" I asked. It looked segmented under the grey fabric, as if made of small hexagonal sections. Flexible too. The hexagons shifted slightly as Luanne moved.

"That's a Scorpion V," Bug said. "Latest, greatest, classified, and civilians aren't supposed to have them, so don't see it or we'll have to gouge your eyes out."

"No heroics, Luanne," Rogan said off camera. *"I just want to know what they're trading. Get in, stay alive, get out."*

"With all due respect, Major, this isn't my first dance," Luanne said.

"Major worries," a younger man with a freckled face said as he rested a firearm on his lap. Heckler & Koch MP7.

I glanced at Rogan. His face was blank.

"Major always worries," an older man said.

"It's our job to prove that he's worried for nothing, Watkins." Luanne turned and the view swung to a group of private soldiers. *"Time to earn the big money."*

The screen split into four, each feed attached to a different soldier.

"Fast forward," Rogan said quietly.

The recording sped up. They divided into four huge black Tahoes, picked up the lawyers—putting them only into two Tahoes—and took separate routes to the hotel. The video slowed to normal speed. We watched them get out and escort two men and two women, all in Scorpion bulletproof vests, into the hotel, where another private soldier met them at the door. Rogan's team must've scouted the location beforehand and done a walk-through.

As the lawyers were hustled into the hotel, the recording caught the taller woman's face.

Cornelius took a sharp breath.

She was about twenty-eight or so, Asian, possibly of Korean descent, with a round face and large smart eyes that looked just like her daughter's. Worry twisted her face. She seemed so alive there on the recording.

I was watching a dead person walking.

The lawyers and the private security people moved into the building. Four went ahead. The group directly responsible for the lawyers' lives followed, clearing the hotel's corridors in the "hallway" formation: one guard in front, the other slightly behind to his left, then the lawyers, then the third guard on the right and the final guard almost exactly behind the first. From above it would look like a rectangle set on a corner. Four remaining guards brought up the rear. They moved fast, took the stairs instead of the elevator, and arrived at a suite on the second floor. Another private solider, a woman this time, stood at the doors of the suite.

"Any security on the outside?" I asked.

"There are two people," Rogan said. "One on the building northwest, covering the entrance, and one on the museum's roof to the north, covering the two windows."

Thorough. He'd covered the exit and the windows, so if anyone or anything that presented a threat tried to enter the hotel, his people would know instantly and neutralize it. I never took any private security jobs, but back when my father was alive, he and my mother had insisted I take a course on it at a training facility in Virginia. From what I could remember, Rogan's people had crossed every *t* and dotted every *i*.

The lawyers and their bodyguards filed into a spacious suite. A dark coffee table—some sort of wood, nearly black and sealed to a mirror shine—stood in the middle of the room, flanked by a dark grey sectional sofa and two chairs, one upholstered in royal purple and the other in zebra print. The lawyers sat down. Rogan's people spread through the room, one by the dark red draperies, one by the door to the bathroom, and the rest by the walls, forming a killing field in front of the door. Four people stayed with the lawyers.

The four feeds on the split screen showed every angle of the room. On two of them Luanne's face was clearly visible and she was frowning. She was looking at the window. What did she see . . . ?

Condensation. A thin layer of fog tinted the glass.

"Bug," Luanne said quietly. *"What's the humidity in here?"*

"Ninety-two percent."

"What's the humidity by Cole on the roof?"

"Seventy-eight."

"Abort." Luanne bit off the word. *"Move them out now."*

The room iced over. In a blink a layer of ice sheathed the walls, the weapons, and the furniture.

"I'm reading a temperature drop!" Bug's voice called.

Then everything happened all at once.

A short African American soldier standing by the lawyers clenched her fists and jerked them down, as if ripping something. A low sound rolled through the room and the air around her turned pale blue. An aegis, a human bulletproof shield.

Three other soldiers by the aegis jerked the lawyers to their feet and shoved them into the blue sphere.

At the door another soldier grabbed the handle, yanked his hand free as if burned, and kicked the door. It held. The layer of ice on it kept growing, at least an inch thick.

"Make a hole!" Luanne barked.

The two men by the door snapped into mage poses, arms slightly raised, palms up as if holding an invisible basketball in each hand. Crimson lightning flared around their fingertips. Enerkinetics, commanding the raw magic energy. The wall was about to explode.

Suddenly Luanne's face turned blank. She snapped her MP7 up and shot both enerkinetics in the head.

Across the room a middle-aged African American man spun toward her and fired. The bullets smashed into Luanne, jerking her back with each hit. The view of her camera trembled as each projectile ripped into her body. A small explosion flared before her camera, the bloody mist flying. A bullet hit Luanne in the skull.

She turned, oblivious to the stream of bullets. She should've been dead. She had to be dead, but her body rotated, swung the MP7 around, and unloaded the full blast into the aegis's blue sphere. The bullets slid through, making ripples in the barrier and clattering harmlessly to the floor. The middle-aged man who'd shot her turned as well, the same slack expression on his face, and pumped a stream of bullets into the shield.

What the hell was going on?

I looked into Rogan's eyes. I had expected anger and pain, but what I saw in their depths made me want to cringe. They were full of darkness, as if a layer of ice had formed over bottomless black water. There were terrible things in that water.

"Give me an exit!" the aegis screamed.

The soldiers near her fired back. Luanne careened and crashed down, her head bouncing off the floor, her camera still recording.

The two soldiers, one by the door and the other by the window, spun in unison and sprayed the room, cutting down the lawyers' guards like they were straw, then turned their weapons onto the shield. The aegis screamed as multiple impacts ripped into her sphere. Blood poured from her nose. Her hands shook with effort.

The faces of the lawyers behind the shield were so frightened—contorted with panic and helpless.

The first bullet broke through and hit the young blond lawyer in the throat. Blood landed on Nari Harrison's cheek and I saw the precise moment when she realized she wouldn't be going home.

The blue sphere vanished as the shield failed. The aegis dropped to her knees, blood pouring from her mouth. Bullets ripped into the unarmed attorneys. For a few moments they jerked, suspended by the stream of armor-piercing rounds tearing into their flesh, and then collapsed. Nari landed four feet away from the camera. Her wide-open dead eyes stared at us through the screen.

Cornelius made a strangled sound.

A boot blocked Luanne's camera view. Two shots popped like dry firecrackers. The boot moved as the soldier stepped over to Nari. A gun barrel loomed over her head. Two bullets punched her temple, misting blood onto her face. The soldier walked from lawyer to lawyer, pumping bullets into their heads, then stopped by the blonde female lawyer's body. Blood soaked her blond hair. He crouched, pulled something from her hand, and stepped away. Glass shattered. He returned to sink two bullets into her skull.

The camera in the left top corner swung up and we saw the soldier's young freckled face. His eyes were brimming with pain and fear. Slowly, he raised his middle finger and held it. A little message to Rogan. Fuck you.

The soldier pulled his sidearm out. His hand shook, as if he strained against the movement. His lips quivered. His eyes, wide open, nearly black with desperation and fear, stared straight at us. He pressed the huge black barrel of the Smith and Wesson against his own temple and pulled the trigger.

The camera clattered to the floor.

It hurt to breathe. I wanted to cry, to stomp, to do something to let what I'd seen out of my head, but instead it sat there, hot and painful, while I grew numb. I looked at Rogan and saw everything at once: his impassive face, his hands quietly locked into a single fist, and his eyes, dark with rage and grief.

"May I have some privacy?" Cornelius asked, his voice ragged and broken.

Rogan and I rose at the same time.

Rogan led me across the room and we walked out onto the balcony. Comfortable chairs and a chaise lounge with blue cushions circled a coffee table. I sat down.

Rogan pulled off his tabard. The black pants and the shirt hugged his frame, showing off his flat, hard stomach, his chest, and his wide shoulders. Normally I would've stared. Now I was too numb.

The menacing elemental force that had terrified Forsberg was gone. Instead Rogan was grim and resolute now, his magic coiling around him like an injured wolf with savage fangs ready for revenge.

"Beer?" he asked, his eyes dark.

"I can't."

He walked over to the fridge built into the stone side of the balcony and brought me a bottle of cold water.

"Thank you."

I took the bottle and stared at it, trying to purge the visions of blood, Nari Harrison's dead eyes, and the young soldier's desperation. Right now Cornelius was inside struggling with images of his wife dying. The tinted wall of glass, opaque from the outside, hid him from us. Bug was probably monitoring Cornelius via his tablet. The swarmer had escaped through the back door as Rogan and I stepped out, but I highly doubted Rogan would leave Cornelius completely unsupervised.

"Can Cornelius hear us?" I asked.

"No. He can see us, but I'd guess he's currently preoccupied."

"Why did you ask him if he was bonded to his wife?"

"Pretium talent," Rogan said.

The price of talent? "I don't understand."

"Animal mages bond with animals at a very young age, some in infancy. They're too young to control their magic and they become attuned to dogs, cats, wild birds, squirrels, any living creature their talent can reach. That power comes at the cost of cognitive development and their relationship with humans. Some of them never learn to talk. Most don't develop empathy toward other people, except for a bond with their parents, but, when parents themselves are animal mages, they don't always bond with their offspring. It's not something they advertise for obvious reasons. Meaningful adult relationships are very rare for them."

"But Cornelius loved his wife."

Rogan nodded. Sadness softened his harsh expression for a brief moment. "Yes. Somehow she broke through to him. She gave him something he thought he would never have and now she's dead. He knows he probably will never experience that again."

That explained so much and made everything even more horrible.

We sat in tense, heavy silence. The anger boiled inside of me, a self-defense against shock and brutality. I wanted to punch something. I rested my elbows on my knees and buried my face in my hands, trying to keep calm. *Don't rewind it in your head. Focus on the job. Focus on doing something about it.*

"Do you think an ice mage was responsible?" I asked.

"Yes. To drop the temperature that fast, it would have to be a Significant, but probably a Prime," Rogan said, his voice clinical and calm. "And an egocissor."

"A manipulator?"

He nodded again, wrapped in an icy detachment. "Definitely a Prime."

Manipulators were dangerous as hell. They could impose their will on others and their victim was usually aware of what they were doing. Luanne knew she had fired at her own people. She watched herself do it, but couldn't do a thing about it. The freckled soldier had put bullets into his friends and was powerless to stop it.

And Rogan had watched it all. Knowing him, he had gone over that recording moment by moment, studying it, searching for the instant it had all gone wrong, looking for some slight hint of the enemy betraying themselves. How many times had he watched his people die? I searched his face and saw the answer—too many. They'd had his people murder each other and sent him a special *fuck you* at the end. They'd made it personal. They wanted him to blame himself and feel helpless. In his place I would've raged. I didn't know these people. They weren't my friends or employees, but after watching that, I had trouble keeping it together. He sat across from me, cold and calm.

An officer, I realized. He was acting like a capable military officer whose unit had taken heavy casualties— methodical, almost serene, while his mind feverishly sorted through threats and strategies. Rogan wouldn't fall apart. He would stay just like that until he eradicated every last person responsible for his people's death.

"Bug's equipment says Luanne's heart stopped beating three seconds after Rook fired at her," Rogan said. "She was clinically dead. Only a Prime manipulator could've held on to her for a full ten seconds after death. An ice mage and a manipulator of that caliber working together means two different Houses."

It meant a conspiracy and an alliance, the same type we had seen behind Adam Pierce. Rogan was right. Something big was happening and we had just grazed the edge of the storm.

"How many ice mages with that kind of capability are in Houston?" I asked.

"Sixteen, by conservative estimate. Twenty-two, if we're being generous. Four Houses."

Too many. "Manipulators?"

"Three Houses, but that doesn't help us. I told you that animal mages don't like to advertise the side effects of their powers."

"Manipulators may not admit to being manipulators?"

Rogan nodded. "They rank as other telepathic specialties. Psionic inundation is a heavy favorite."

Psionics had the ability to temporarily overload other minds. A psionic Prime could generate a field of mental effect and everyone caught in it would go blind, or fall to the ground in pain, or flee for their life.

"What about the glass breaking toward the end?"

"He dropped something out of the window. Bug thinks it may have been a USB drive. Whatever it was, a vehicle drove up and one of the passengers grabbed it off the pavement. My sniper had no clear shot because of the traffic."

We sank into silence again. The recording kept playing over and over in my head, so visceral it shot right past all of my normal brakes and reached deep into the vicious part of me that usually woke only when my family was threatened. I wanted to kill the people who did this. I wanted to murder them and watch them die. It would be just. It would be fair.

I met Rogan's gaze. "Do you have any leads?"

"Do you?" Rogan asked. "Did you get anything from Forsberg?"

"Yes."

"Are you going to tell me?"

"No."

He stared at me.

"You're not my client," I told him. "I don't work for you and I'm not going to share confidential information with you unless my client directs me to do it. Even then, I have misgivings. I'm still trying to come to terms with what happened to his wife." Her death kept playing though my head, stuck on a perpetual loop.

He leaned back and studied me. An imperceptible shift took place in the way he sat, in the line of his shoulders, and in his eyes. Apparently we were done talking about work.

"What?"

"I missed you," he said, his lips stretching into a slow, lazy smile. The ice in his eyes began to melt. "Did you miss me, Nevada?"

He said my name. "No."

"Not even a little bit?"

"No. Never thought of you." Just because I usually chose not to lie didn't mean I couldn't.

Rogan grinned and all of my thoughts went to the wrong places. He was almost unbearably handsome when he smiled.

"Stop it," I growled.

"Stop what?"

"Stop smiling at me."

He grinned wider.

"Why did you even get involved in this? Trying to punish your cousin?"

"Yes."

And he'd just lied. I squinted at him. "Lie better."

"Nice, Ms. Baylor. That was a partial truth and you still tagged it. Been practicing?"

"None of your business." I hadn't just been practicing. I'd been actively working on being better. I studied my books, I worked on arcane circles, and I experimented with my magic. I enjoyed it too. Using my magic was like stretching an aching muscle. It felt good.

"Mmm, prickly."

"You're not answering my questions. Why should I answer yours?"

He surveyed me, his eyes half closed, as if wondering if I were a delicious snack. I had an image of a massive dragon circling me slowly, eyes full of magic fixed on me as he moved, considering if he should bite me in half.

"Dragons." Rogan snapped his fingers.

Oh crap.

"I wondered why I kept getting dragons around you." He leaned forward. His eyes lit up, turning back to their clear sky blue. "You think I'm a dragon."

"Don't be ridiculous." My face felt hot. I was probably blushing. Damn it.

His smile went from amused to sexual, so charged with promise that *carnal* was the only way to describe it. I almost bolted out of my chair.

"Big powerful scary dragon."

"You have delusions of grandeur."

"Do I have a lair? Did I kidnap you to it from your castle?"

I stared straight at him, trying to frost my voice. "You have some strange fantasies, Rogan. You may need professional help."

"Would you like to volunteer?"

"No. Besides, dragons kidnap virgins, so I'm out." And why had I just told him I was not a virgin? Why did I even go there?

"It doesn't matter if I'm the first. It only matters that I'll be the last."

"You won't be the first, the last, or anything in between. Not in a million years."

He laughed.

"Rogan," I ground out through my teeth. "I'm on the clock. My client is in the next room mourning his wife. Stop flirting with me."

"Stop? I haven't even started."

I pointed my bottle at him.

"What does that mean?" he asked me.

"It means if you don't stop, I'll dump this bottle over your head and escape this compound with my client."

"I'd like to see you try."

The door opened and Cornelius stepped out. His face was flat, his eyes bloodshot. All my selfish embarrassment evaporated. Rogan's sensual smile vanished and I was once again looking at a Prime—cold, hard, collected, and looking for revenge.

Oh. He'd done it on purpose. He'd riled me up and pulled me out of the terrible place I was in after I saw the video. The awful loop of death no longer played through my brain.

Cornelius sat in a chair and looked at Rogan. "What are you offering?"

"You have an excellent investigator," Rogan said. "Ms. Baylor is competent, thorough, and holds herself to a high professional standard."

I waited for the other shoe to drop.

"But her firm is small. It lacks resources and power. Things I have in abundance."

Was he trying to get Cornelius to fire me?

"I, on the other hand, require Ms. Baylor's services," Rogan said. "She has the ability to greatly speed up the search for the murderer of my people."

"Because she's a truthseeker," Cornelius said.

I sighed.

"I'm not an idiot," Cornelius said quietly.

"We're after the same thing," Rogan said. "I propose we join forces."

"I need a few minutes with Ms. Baylor," Cornelius said.

"Of course." Rogan rose and went inside.

Cornelius waited until the door shut behind Rogan and leaned back against the cushioned seat. "I realize that this is an uncomfortable question, but I have to ask. What's your relationship with Mad Rogan?"

"We cooperated to apprehend Adam Pierce."

"I know that. I meant emotional relationship."

He deserved an honest answer.

"It's the same old story." I made my voice sound as nonchalant as I could. "Billionaire Prime meets a pretty girl with a little magic, billionaire Prime makes the girl an offer, and the girl tells him to hit the road."

And then billionaire Prime makes all sorts of heated promises and dramatic declarations that make the girl think that maybe he might actually view her as more than a pleasant diversion, except he disappears for two months and doesn't follow through.

"Will it be difficult for you to work with him?" Cornelius asked.

His wife was dead, Rogan had offered him the deal of a lifetime, and Cornelius was thinking of my comfort. In his place, I didn't know if I would be capable of that much compassion.

"It's very kind of you to take my feelings into consideration."

"We're a team. I'm asking you to put yourself at risk for my sake. I want to know your opinion."

"I'm a professional and so is he. We're able to put things aside. Whatever discomfort I may or may not feel is irrelevant."

"Do you think I should agree to this?"

"Rogan is a cold-blooded bastard, but he's right. We'll need muscle, money, and firepower. He has them; we don't. And, despite all of his high-handed arrogance, he keeps his word."

"How do you know?"

"He spared Adam Pierce. I needed him alive and Rogan

refrained from killing him even though he would've loved to twist Adam's head off."

A hawk shrieked. Talon swooped past us and a dead mouse fell on the table. The big bird turned and landed on Cornelius' shoulder. The animal mage raised his hand and stroked the bird's feathers gently, his face thoughtful.

The hawk was trying to feed him. Even Talon realized Cornelius was grieving.

"Think of Rogan as a dragon," I told him. "A powerful, ancient, selfish dragon who'll devour you in a blink but who also has an odd sense of honor. If you make a deal with him, make sure to spell out all of the important things now and get him to agree to them."

Cornelius picked up the dead mouse and held it up to Talon. "Thank you. Not hungry. You eat it."

Talon regarded the mouse with his round amber eyes, grabbed it out of Cornelius' hand, and flew off to the tree line. Cornelius walked over to the window and tapped on the glass. Rogan stepped out and joined us at the table.

Cornelius took his seat. "We've considered your proposal and I have some conditions. Only one, actually."

"I'm eager to hear it," Rogan said.

"I understand that there are forces bigger than all of this," Cornelius said. "I'm not interested in that. I want the person who killed my wife. There may come a moment when that person may become extremely valuable to you because of the information he or she carries. You'll want to keep them alive as an information source or a hostage. You must understand that I don't care."

Cornelius' voice dropped into a quiet, fierce growl. The pain was so raw on his face he didn't look quite human.

"No matter how important that person is to you, you'll give them to me. My price is the life of Nari's murderer. I, and I alone, will take it."

A thoughtful expression claimed Rogan's face. His eyes turned calculating.

Cornelius waited.

Rogan offered his hand. "Agreed."

Cornelius took his hand. They shook on it.

"Shall we formalize the arrangement?" Rogan asked.

"Yes," Cornelius said.

Rogan dialed a number on his phone. "Bring me a blank House contract, please."

"You're actually going to write out a contract where you specify that you surrender the right to kill Nari's murderer to Cornelius?"

Both of them looked at me. "Yes," they said at the same time.

I just stared at them.

"He's a member of a House," Rogan said. "Why would I treat him with anything less than courtesy?"

We weren't even from the same planet.

A woman appeared with a blank contract. They worked on it, Cornelius' face haggard and angry at the same time. He and Matilda deserved to know what happened to Nari, and Matilda deserved to have her father return home to her. I had given my word and I was committed already, but if I hadn't been, this would do it. If I walked away, Cornelius would run straight into whatever deep water Rogan was wading through, and keeping up with Mad Rogan was bad for one's life expectancy.

"I need a security team on my house," I said.

Rogan picked up his phone, texted a short word, and looked at me. "Done."

"Were they already waiting somewhere conveniently close?"

"Yes."

I pulled out my own phone and dialed the house.

"Yus!" my youngest sister chirped into the phone. Arabella was fifteen, but going through this weird phase where she acted like she was eight.

"Is Mom home?"

"Yus!"

"Find her and tell her that Rogan's security team is watching our house. Please ask her not to shoot them."

"Okay! Nevada?"

"What?" If she asked me about Rogan, I swear I would . . .

"Will you pick up some sushi for dinner?"

"Yes."

"No nasty mayo sauce?"

"No mayo."

"Will you tell Mad Rogan that he should ma . . . ?"

I hung up and turned to Cornelius. "How would you feel about moving into our house for the duration of the investigation?"

Cornelius blinked.

"This is going to get dangerous and complicated," I said. "The people behind this aren't going to have moral scruples over doing terrible things such as kidnapping and torturing a child. Our warehouse has an excellent security system, and it's protected by Rogan's people. If they somehow get past Rogan's soldiers, they'll have to deal with my mother, who's a former sniper; my grandmother, who builds tanks; and four teenagers who have no fear of death and who all have been taught to shoot properly. You and Matilda will be safe."

"But we have animals," Cornelius said.

"We have a lot of room and an entire guest apartment built into the corner of the warehouse. My sisters would love to watch Matilda."

"She's right," Rogan said. "You're welcome to stay here as well, if you would prefer."

Cornelius blinked. Leaving your daughter in the house of a man who leveled cities when he got upset wasn't the most prudent move.

"Thank you. It would be rude of me to reject Nevada's invitation."

"Of course," Rogan said and winked at me.

And he'd just manipulated Cornelius. This would be one hell of a partnership.

"Do we have a plan?" Cornelius asked.

Both of them looked at me. Right. I was the investigator, so they expected me to investigate.

"Has Bug been able to identify who the lawyers were supposed to meet?"

"No," Rogan said.

I turned to Cornelius. "And you have no idea whom Nari was meeting or why?"

"No," Cornelius said.

"Has anyone talked to the family members of the other lawyers?"

"No," Rogan said.

I got up. "Then I'll start there."

"I'll come with you," Cornelius said.

"Not this time," I said gently.

"Why?"

"Because your wife and their spouses knew each other socially. They may have an emotional reaction to your presence, and we need information. I promise that I'll let you know tonight what I've learned. Also, you have a household to move."

"I'll arrange for escort." Rogan pulled out his phone.

"Thank you but I got it," I said.

"Not yours. His." Rogan texted on his phone. "I'm coming with you. I've agreed to a partnership. I'll participate in this investigation or the deal is off."

I'd just assured Cornelius that Rogan and I could work

together. There was no reasonable pretext to keep him from coming with me. I had to stay professional about this.

"Very well. However, I have some conditions. You have to promise not to kill people I'm about to question or intimidate them unless I ask you to. Specifically, please don't strangle anyone with their clothes again."

Cornelius' eyes widened.

"Fine. Anything else?" Rogan asked, his voice dry.

"Yes. Please change so you look less like a Prime. I don't want anyone to recognize you. It's very hard to get people to open up when they realize the Scourge of Mexico is on their doorstep."

Chapter 4

Half an hour later, the contracts were signed and witnessed by me and the woman who brought them. The woman led me down to the front door, where my minivan waited. The keys were in the ignition. I got into the driver's seat.

I could just drive off and leave Rogan hanging. That would be hilarious. Of course, he would probably chase me down with something ridiculous, like his own private flying fortress or some such nonsense.

The front door swung open, and Bug slipped out and trotted to the car. I rolled down the window.

"Hey." He leaned so his elbows rested in the open window. "Are you going to stick around for a while?"

"Looks as if I don't have a choice."

"Good."

"Why?"

"It's been sixteen-hour workdays around here for the past two months. There was a lot of fallout from the Pierce crap. The major had to testify before the Assembly, and four people tried to bring lawsuits, but the bulk of the work was surveillance. This thing, whatever the hell it is, is bleeding amorphous. You sort of find evidence of it, and then the dick fucker just slips from your fingers. This Forsberg's lawyer meeting was the first solid thing we had, then Tuesday happened . . ."

Getting through the stream of Bug's consciousness was like hacking your way through a jungle.

"We couldn't get to Forsberg until today. Yesterday was rough. He went to notify all the families in person. Luanne was one of the *sixteen*."

Bug looked at me to make sure I understood the gravity of the situation. Except I didn't.

"I don't know what that means."

He made a sour face. "Just . . . stick around. He has a human expression on his face when you're around."

"Thanks, Bug. I'm glad to see you too." Apparently my function was to keep a human expression on Rogan's face. Good to know. And here I thought I was spearheading an investigation. How silly of me.

The door opened, and Rogan came out. Bug took off. Rogan watched him go and strode to the car. He'd abandoned his about-to-go-on-a-sorcerous-rampage outfit for old khaki cargo pants, beat-up boots, and a green Henley. The shirt molded to his shoulders and chest. His biceps stretched the sleeves. He looked strong, and rugged, and rough around the edges. He needed an ax or something, so he could casually swing it while he walked. I tilted my head and just watched.

He opened the door and got in. And suddenly the car was full of Rogan and his magic. I could barely breathe.

How had I ever agreed to this? I needed my head examined.

"What did he say?" he asked.

"Just Bug being Bug."

"You're avoiding the answer."

"You're so perceptive."

Rogan regarded me with his blue eyes, took out a baseball hat, and put it on. Dragon in camouflage, going down to the village to spy on the delicious people living there.

He clicked his teeth, biting through the air.

I had to stop thinking about dragons.

I shifted out of park and concentrated on driving. I liked being in the car with him. God help me, I missed this. I missed him.

"Is that a new perfume?" Rogan asked.

"I'm not wearing any. What does it smell like?"

"Citrus."

"That's probably my shampoo."

Talk about work, look straight ahead, don't think about reaching over and sliding my hand down his chest to feel the solid wall of his abs . . . Don't imagine kissing him . . .

Rogan swore quietly.

"What?"

"Nothing."

I glanced at him. Our stares connected.

Wow. His eyes turned a deep, bottomless blue and they were filled with need. It got away from him and now he was thinking of me naked. A woman would have to be dead not to respond to that, and I wasn't dead. Not even a little bit.

Anticipation zinged through me. I knew exactly how much space separated us. I felt every inch of it, charged with electric energy. If he touched me right now, I'd probably jump a foot in the air. I stared straight ahead. We didn't do well in a small, confined space. This was a terrible idea. Maybe I should roll down the window to let some of the sexual tension out.

We needed a distraction, or I'd end up pulling over and we'd end up in the back seat, doing . . . things.

"It makes no sense to go after Jaroslav Fenley's family," I said. I had spent a fair amount of time with the background on the three other lawyers and I'd refreshed my memory with my notes on my phone while Rogan and Cornelius wrote their contract. "He lived and breathed his career, according to his home computer. Harper was his only significant relationship in the last few months."

"Bernard broke into his computer?" Rogan guessed.

"Yes, in thirty seconds. Jaroslav's router password was 'admin.' Probably explains why he fell for Harper."

"He cut corners," Rogan said.

"Yes. It takes an effort to change your router password. Most people have to look up how to do it. It takes time and effort to maintain a meaningful relationship. Harper didn't require a relationship."

"He could get away with sex and some light pillow talk." Rogan grimaced. "I know the type. The man is a walking security risk. He works only as hard as he has to to get ahead. His goal isn't to do his job, it's to get to the place where he doesn't have to do his job while still getting paid."

"It looks that way. Jaroslav logged a lot of billable hours. It looked good on paper. He slept, worked, and worried about his student loans. Bern's still going through the files, but so far he didn't find anything incriminating. Jaroslav's parents live in Canada and he doesn't keep up with them. His brother just had a baby. It's all over his family's Facebook. Jaroslav hadn't commented on the baby pictures. His family is a dead end, so it's out. I take it you don't want to talk to Harper?"

Rogan shook his head. "She's our only link to this conspiracy. We need to preserve her as long as we can."

"That leaves us with two choices," I said. "Marcos Nather's family or Elena de Trevino's. Nather's is closer."

"Nather it is."

Marcos and Jeremy Nather lived in Westheimer Lakes, in a typical Texas suburban house: two stories, brick, at least three thousand square feet, with four bedrooms, three bathrooms, and a two-car garage. The neighborhood was about seven to eight years old, just enough for the prices to go down slightly. The house wasn't out of their price range, and according to Bern, their credit looked healthy. Marcos Nather had been a successful lawyer and Jeremy Nather worked as a software engineer employed at a start-up that developed fitness apps. His LinkedIn profile showed that Marcos had worked for Forsberg for the last three years. Before that he worked for Zara, Inc., an investment firm. Marcos and Jeremy had been married for six years and neither had any magic talents. I ran through all of that for Rogan while I drove.

"Where do you get your information?" he asked.

"Why? Planning to get into the private investigator business?"

"Call it curiosity."

Aha. "A lot of it comes from online databases. We get public records and we pay for the access to criminal history, credit checks, and so on. Social networks are a gold mine. People post a huge amount of personal information online and all of their social accounts are usually connected."

And that was why, although I had an account at every major social network—including Herald, which was devoted to speculation about Primes, general fangirling, and a lot of fanfic—none of my accounts had any personal information. I didn't vent online, I made no political comments, and I dutifully posted at least one or two cute kitten pictures every week or so, just to reassure the network algorithms that I wasn't a bot.

"What's this?" Rogan pulled a book out of the side pocket on the door. An elaborate arcane circle decorated the front cover. *"Circlework: Practical Applications."*

That was my stakeout replacement for *Hexology*,

which was incredibly useful, but so dry it put me to sleep. I had already read *Circlework* cover to cover, but I hadn't memorized all of the circles I'd marked as important, so I brought it with me and faithfully tried to reproduce the illustrations on my legal pad while I waited for my insurance fraudsters to stumble.

"What about it?"

I could just ask him directly if he sent them. But then I would know. For some reason not knowing seemed like a better option. Some part of me liked to think it was him.

He flipped through the book. "If you're ever in need of instruction, I'll be glad to give you lessons."

I glanced at him. "What will it cost me?"

"I'll think of something." His voice promised all sorts of interesting ideas.

"Bargains with dragons never end well."

A smug smile touched his lips, turning his expression wolfish and hungry. "That depends on what you're bargaining for."

I shouldn't have gotten into the car with him. That was the long and short of it.

The GPS spoke in Darth Vader's voice, informing me that my destination was in five hundred feet on the right. Saved by the Sith.

I parked in the shade under a tree, retrieved my gun, and slid it back into my custom women's on-the-waist holster, where my suit jacket hid it. Men had a much easier time with the concealed carry. I was short-waisted and my hips had a curve to them, so a regular holster just jabbed the gun into my ribs.

Rogan and I made our way to the front door.

I rang the bell. "Best behavior."

"I remember," Rogan growled.

The door swung open revealing a man in his thirties. Of average height, with light brown hair and a short beard, he resembled a typical guy you'd encounter in the suburbs: the kind with a steady job, who went to the gym three times a week, and let himself eat a little more than he had ten years ago. His eyes were hollow.

"Now isn't a good time," he said.

"Mr. Nather, I work for Cornelius Harrison," I said, holding out my card. "My deepest condolences."

He blinked, took my card, and read it. "Private investigator?"

I had to get inside before he shut the door in my face. "House Forsberg is refusing to investigate the murders. Mr. Harrison has asked me to find out what happened to his wife. He wants to be able to tell his daughter that her mother's murderer didn't get away with it. I'm deeply sorry to intrude on you in your time of grief. We just need a few moments of your time."

Jeremy looked at me and sighed. "A few minutes."

"Thank you."

He led us through the foyer to the living room sectioned off from the kitchen by an island. Two young children, a boy and a girl, lay on the rug. The boy, older by a year or two, was playing with an iPad, while the girl was building something with Legos. An older woman, her eyes bloodshot, sat on the couch with a book. She glanced at us, her face haggard.

"Mom, I have to talk to these people," Jeremy said. "I'll just be a minute."

She nodded.

"Hi," the kids chorused.

"Hi." I waved.

Jeremy forced a smile. "Sorry, guys, I'll be right back."

He walked us to the office off the living room and closed the French doors behind us.

"I haven't told them yet," he said. His voice caught. "I don't know how."

"Have you spoken with anybody? A grief counselor?"

He shook his head. An overwhelming pain reflected in his face, the kind of pain that smashed into you like a car moving at full speed and left you broken and dazed. I wished there was something I could do for him.

I pulled out another one of my cards, checked the contacts on my phone, and wrote my therapist's name and phone number on it.

"When my father died, I didn't know how to deal with it. I blamed myself and I dragged my guilt and grief with me like a rock for weeks until I went to see Dr. Martinez. She's very good at what she does. It will still be terrible, but she'll help you take the edge off the worst of it. And if she has no openings in her schedule, she'll be able to refer you to someone who does."

Jeremy stared at me. "Does it get better?"

"There is no such thing as closure," I told him. "It never goes away. But it gets duller with treatment and time. Talking about it helps."

Jeremy took the card and slid it into his wallet.

I took out my digital recorder, pushed the on switch, and said, "Thursday, December 15th. Interview with Jeremy Nather."

Jeremy leaned against the wall, his arms crossed.

"Mr. Nather, do you know why Marcos was in that hotel room?"

"According to House Forsberg, he was there to have an affair with Nari Harrison. Or Elena de Trevino. Or Fenley. Maybe all of them were going to have an orgy." His voice was bitter.

"That's what they told Cornelius as well. With promises of evidence of embezzlement and drug use if the questions continued."

"It's absurd." Jeremy leaned over the table, planting

both palms on it. "Marcos was loyal. It was the core of his character. He was loyal and honest."

"House Forsberg doesn't have the best reputation," Rogan said. "Did he have conflicts at work?"

Thanks. Please do destroy the rapport I'm trying to build.

"He was planning to leave the firm," Jeremy said.

True. "Who else knew about it?"

"Just me and him. Marcos is . . . was a very private man. We were both working too much and missing time with the kids. He wanted to quit and take a year or two at home, but he wanted to pay off the house first. We moved here for the school district, and he wanted to make sure we'd be okay on one income. We're twenty-eight thousand away from owning this house." Jeremy rocked back. "I knew it was making him miserable. Three weeks ago I tried to get him to quit. He promised to put in his notice just before the Christmas break. I should've pushed harder."

"Do you think he was in the hotel room because of his work?"

"Yes."

True. "Do you have any idea what he was working on?"

"No. He didn't bring that home. I'm the one who usually ranted about work. Marcos compartmentalized. He left work at work. When he came home, he was just Marcos."

He dropped into a chair, slumped, and put his hand over his eyes. I wouldn't get anything else out of him.

"Did he have any enemies?" I asked. "Anyone who might . . ."

"Who might murder him in a hail of gunfire?" Jeremy said, his voice dull and flat. "No."

"We're so sorry for your loss," I said. "If you think of something, please call me. We'll show ourselves out."

It had started raining. I stood by my car for a moment and let the drizzle wet my hair. The grief was thick in that house, and I wanted to wash it off.

"Did he lie?" Rogan asked.

"No. He truly doesn't know anything. Neither Nari nor Marcos shared anything with their families, which probably means it was something dangerous."

We had to try Elena's family. She was our last obvious lead.

The De Trevinos lived on a lake next to the Southwyck Golf Club, a good fifty minutes away from Westheimer Lakes. I steered the car down TX-99 South, watching the fields bordered by strips of trees roll by. It looked like we were in the middle of nowhere, someplace in the Texas country. You would never know that just beyond the trees brand-new subdivisions carved the land into orderly rows of nearly identical houses.

I took Alt-90 and we cut our way through Sugar Land and Missouri City, tiny municipalities within the greater Houston sprawl. The traffic was light, the road open.

For a few minutes Rogan had flipped through my book and written a couple of notes in it. It still lay open in his hand, but he wasn't paying attention to it. His jaw was set. He stared straight ahead, his eyes again iced over. This new crystalized rage chilled me to the bone. Whatever was going on in his head was dark—so, so dark. It grabbed hold of him and pulled him under into the black water. I wanted to reach in there and drag him out into the light, so he'd thaw.

"Connor?"

He turned and looked at me, as if waking up.

"What happened to Gavin?"

Gavin was Rogan's nephew. Adam Pierce, with his

motorcycle jacket, tattoos, and deep hatred of any authority, had embodied the image of a cool rebel. Like many teenagers, Gavin had worshipped him, and Adam had preyed on that devotion.

"Gavin made a deal."

I took an exit onto the Sam Houston Tollway. The road repair crews were working on the shoulder again and I had to drive next to the temporary concrete barriers. Never my favorite. At least I could see. Somehow I always ended up on these roads at night, when it was raining and another concrete barrier boxed me in on the other side.

"What kind of deal?"

"A year in a juvenile boot-camp facility, until he turns eighteen, followed by a ten-year commitment to the military in exchange for his testimony against Adam Pierce. If he fails, he'll serve ten years in prison."

"That's a good deal."

"Under the circumstances. He happened to have talent, so we used it as a bargaining chip."

"And you're sure he isn't involved in what his mother was doing?"

"He isn't," Rogan said.

"I didn't know you cared about your nephew. You made it seem like you were estranged."

"Not by my choice."

He looked out the window, slipping away again. I wasn't even sure why it was so important to keep him here with me, but it was.

"Have you been practicing with a gun since our last encounter?" I kept my voice light.

He just looked at me.

"No? Rogan, you said yourself, you're a terrible shot."

Okay, so this wasn't the best way to bring him out, but that's all I could think about.

"You're riding shotgun," I continued. "If bandits attack

this pony express, how are you going to hold them off without a gun? Are you planning on rolling down the window, announcing yourself, and glaring at them until they faint from fear?"

He didn't say anything. He just kept watching me.

I opened my mouth to needle him some more.

The barrier on the right of us cracked as if struck by a giant hammer. The cracks chased us, shooting through the concrete dividers with tiny puffs of rock dust. His magic ripped into cement with brutal efficiency. It brushed by me and I almost swung the door open and jumped out.

The cars behind us swerved, trying to shift lanes away from the fractured barriers.

"Stop," I asked.

The cracks ceased.

"Do you need me to drop you off?" I asked.

"Why would I want that?"

"So you can brood in solitude."

"I don't brood."

"Plot horrible revenge, then. Because you're freaking me out."

"It's my job to freak you out."

"Really?"

"That's the nature of our relationship." A spark lit his eyes. "We both do what's necessary, and after it's over, I watch you freak out about it."

"I don't."

"Oh, I don't want you to stop. I find it highly amusing."

That's the last time I try to cheer you up. Go back into your dragon cave for all I care.

"Would you like me to break one more concrete slab, so you can take a picture for your grandmother?" he offered.

"I changed my mind," I told him. "I don't want to talk to you."

He chuckled.

I should just stop trying.

Grandma Frida would think it was really neat.

I took my phone off the console and held it to him. "Okay, but only one or two more. Just enough for the Vine."

"Your grandmother has a Vine account?" The barriers fractured.

"Yes. She'll probably post it on her Instagram too. Okay, that's enough, thank you, or the driver of the Volvo behind us might have a heart attack."

Elena de Trevino's family lived in a huge house. The Nathers' home was large by most people's standards, and you could fit two of those into the de Trevino homestead. The building sat on half an acre, a huge dark red brick beast that mashed Colonial Revival with chunks of Tudor around the windows. A thick brick wall guarded the yard, with an arch allowing entrance to the inner driveway and the garages, and the chimney of the obligatory fireplace Texans used once in a blue moon mimicked the steeple of a church.

The difference magic made. Both Elena de Trevino and her husband, Antonio, were rated Average. I had found their LinkedIn profiles and they both listed AV in the powers section.

I parked on the street, and Rogan and I walked to the door.

A young Hispanic woman answered the door. "May I help you?"

Her gaze snagged on Rogan. I might as well have been invisible. Women looked at him wherever he went. In the age of magic, many men were handsome. Rogan wasn't just attractive; he projected masculinity. It was in his posture, in the male roughness of his face, and in his eyes. When you saw him, you knew no matter what happened, he would handle it. Little did they know that he solved most of his problems by throwing money at them or trying to kill them. Sometimes at the same time.

I offered her my card. "I've been hired by House Harrison. I would like to speak with Mr. de Trevino."

The woman dragged her gaze away from Rogan to the card. "Wait, please."

She closed the door.

"House Harrison?" Rogan asked.

"Cornelius hasn't been excised."

Excision was the worst punishment a magical family could level on its member. They withdrew all emotional, financial, and social support, effectively kicking the offender out of the family. An excised member of the House became damaged goods: his former allies abandoned him for fear of angering his family, and his family's enemies refused to help him because no excise could be trusted. Cornelius distanced himself from his House by his own choice, but he hadn't left it.

"Look at this house." I nodded at the door. "We wouldn't even get a foot in the door unless we dropped some House's name."

Rogan smiled, a wicked sharp grin. "You should let me knock."

Last time he "knocked" on my door, the entire warehouse vibrated. "Please don't."

The door opened, revealing an athletic man about forty years old. He wore grey dress pants and a light grey sweatshirt, the sleeves pulled halfway up his forearms. His face was pleasant: dark eyes under sloping dark eyebrows and a generous mouth. A dark, carefully trimmed beard hugged his jaw. His hair was also dark and cut very short. Antonio de Trevino. His resume said he worked as an investment analyst.

"Good afternoon." He smiled, showing perfectly even white teeth. "Please, come in."

We stepped inside.

"I'm Antonio. This way. Sorry for the disarray. We're kind of in the middle of things."

He didn't seem broken up about his wife's death. Compared to Jeremy, he seemed downright cheerful.

Antonio led us into a vast living room, to plush beige chairs arranged on a red rug. The furnishings looked expensive, but it was the middle-class kind of expensive: new, probably in the latest style, and nice. The furniture in Rogan's house had weight; it looked timeless. You couldn't tell if it had been purchased by him, his parents, or his grandparents. Compared to that quality, these furnishings seemed superficial, almost cheap. Perspective was a funny thing.

The Hispanic woman hovered in the doorway.

"Coffee? Tea?" Antonio asked.

"No, thank you." I took my seat.

Rogan shook his head and sat in the chair on my right.

Antonio took the small sofa and nodded at the woman. "Thank you, Estelle. That will be all."

She vanished into the kitchen.

"So House Harrison is looking into Mrs. Harrison's death. Understandable, considering how little Forsberg is doing. How may I help you?"

"Would you mind answering a few questions?" I asked.

"Not at all."

I took out my digital recorder, tagged the conversation, and set the recorder on the glass coffee table.

"Do you know why your wife was in that hotel room?"

"No. I would imagine for professional reasons. I can

tell you that the situation at work had been stressful in the day prior to her death. She seemed distracted at dinner."

"Did she mention anything specific?"

"She said, 'I can't pick up John tomorrow. I'm sorry. There's an issue at work. The entire office is in a state of emergency and I'm not sure when I'll be able to get home. Would you mind terribly taking him to his play? It's at seven.'"

He'd said it in his normal voice, but the intonation was unmistakable female.

"You're a mnemonic," Rogan said.

"Yes. We both are, actually. Elena was a predominantly visual mnemonic and I'm auditory. We both have near perfect short-term recall." Antonio leaned back. "I don't want to give you the wrong impression. I'm deeply saddened by Elena's death. I lost a capable, caring partner, and our children lost their mother. She was a wonderful parent. The blow to their childhood is devastating."

True.

"Our marriage was arranged. Our families had agreed that we had a high chance of producing a Significant, so we married and dutifully tried three times. We may have succeeded with Ava, our youngest. Only time will tell. We weren't in love." He said it so matter-of-factly.

"And you consented to this?"

Antonio smiled again. "I'm guessing you're not magically capable. Producing a Significant would be an immense achievement. It would open doors and change our entire social standing. The price is worth it. We're both reasonable people. We hardly suffer."

He raised his arms, indicating his living room.

"We allowed ourselves to seek happiness elsewhere, provided we were discreet for the sake of the children. So, if you want the proverbial pillow talk, you'll have to ask Gabriel Baranovsky. He and Elena had a relationship for the past three years. She went to see him the evening before she died. Perhaps he'll talk to you. Personally, I doubt it. There are Houses and then there are *Houses*."

He'd sunk extra gravitas into the last word just in case I failed to understand its full significance.

"Baranovsky belongs to one of the latter. Elena was very fortunate to have caught his eye, and we've benefited from that connection, which is now severed."

How exactly did he benefit? Did he casually slip it into conversations during business deals? *"By the way, my wife is banging Baranovsky. Your money is safe with me."* Ugh.

"It would take someone of equal social standing to get Baranovsky's attention. House Harrison isn't one of those families. I do apologize; I don't mean to be rude. I simply want to make the matter as clear as possible. Primes aren't like us."

I glanced at Rogan. His face was stoic.

"They breathe the same air and drink the same water, but their power sets them firmly apart and that's the way they like it. The gulf between them and a normal person is enormous. You're an attractive woman, so perhaps with the right attire and a trip to the salon, you might get to his personal secretary. Personally I would go through Diana Harrison. Cornelius' sister is a Prime, which does mean something even to the likes of Baranovsky, so he may condescend to a meeting. In any case, please let Cornelius and Diana know that I'll be happy to assist House Harrison in any way possible."

Five minutes later we made it outside. His wife was dead and all Antonio could think about was how it would affect his social standing. What a colossal asshole.

"The right attire *and* a trip to the salon?" I rolled my eyes, heading for the car. "I may have to break my piggy bank."

"That right there is why I don't socialize," Rogan said.

"It's good that we had him explain all this to us. I feel so unprepared. I had no idea I had to have the right outfit before I talked to a Prime. You should've given me a list of what was appropriate to wear. I hope you're not offended."

I turned and suddenly Rogan was there. I stepped back on pure instinct and my back bumped against the car. All of the ice in his eyes had melted. They were hot, inviting, seducing. He was thinking of sex and that sex prominently featured me.

"I'm not offended."

His big muscular body caged me in. He focused on me as if the rest of the world didn't even exist. When he looked at you like that, he made you feel like you were the most important person in the universe. Every word you said mattered to him. Every gesture you made was vital. It was devastating. I wanted to keep talking and doing things to keep him focused on me just like that.

"I don't care how you come to see me." His voice was casual, almost lazy. "You can come in a suit. You can come in jeans."

He was just screwing around with me now. Well, maybe it was time to take some of that power back from him.

"You can come wrapped in a towel. You can come naked. Really, it's up to you. As long as you come, I don't care."

Aren't you smug? I took a tiny step forward, raising my face as if to kiss him. "What if I don't come at all?"

His voice dropped. "That would be a tragedy. I would use all of my power to prevent it."

His eyes were so blue and they were making promises. All kinds of promises about being an outlaw in bed and doing things I would never forget. I looked right into them and tried my best to make some promises of my own.

"All of your powers?" If I leaned forward an inch, we would be touching. The space between us was so charged with tension, if we brushed against each other, we might spark. I was playing with fire.

"Yes." His magic hovered around him, anticipating and eager, almost daring me to reach out.

"Are we still talking about clothes?" I asked.

"If you say so."

He leaned forward and I put my finger on his lips and pushed him back. "No."

His eyes narrowed. "No?"

I dropped my hand.

"Let's see, you ask me to be your toy, I say no, you move on. You don't call, you don't write, you don't come by. You make no effort to prove to me that you wanted anything more than some casual sex."

His eyes darkened. "There would be nothing casual about it."

I believed him, but it didn't change my point. "You treated me like some cheap amusement."

He leaned an inch closer. "I didn't."

I should've been alarmed, but I had too much emotion pent up to stop now.

"Rogan, do you know how little I mattered to you? You didn't even want to go through the motions of dating me. You just wanted to skip all of it and get straight to sex. You made me feel this small." I held my index finger and thumb apart about an eighth of an inch. "Have sex with me, Nevada. I'm not even going to pretend to want to know you better."

His jaw tightened. "That's not what I meant and you know it."

"I offered you a chance to fight for a relationship and you didn't take it. You clearly moved on. I did too."

A muscle in his face jerked.

"And now that I'm conveniently here, you decide to give it another shot. Is there a shortage of attractive women in your life, Connor?"

"There is a shortage of you in my life," he said.

"Really?"

"A critical shortage. One that must be immediately corrected."

He was being deliberately vague. He couldn't lie to me, so he resorted to making the kind of statements I'd have a hard time qualifying. You had to admire the man's brain.

"Not interest—"

Rogan yanked me to him and jerked his hand up. My Mazda left the ground. A six-foot wide disk of crimson fire slashed into my car and exploded. Chunks of razor-sharp metal blades rained on both sides of us, trailing crimson and hissing. I sprinted for the massive oak behind us. Behind me the Mazda crashed onto the pavement with a metal clang.

I pressed my right shoulder against the bark and pulled the Glock out. Rogan landed next to me. Blood soaked his right thigh.

"You're bleeding!"

"A scratch," he growled. "Are you hurt?"

"No."

My heart pounded too loud and too fast. The bitter taste of adrenaline coated my tongue.

Something thudded into the tree on the right. I almost jumped.

Another thud.

I leaned forward carefully.

A smaller disk of crimson spun right at my face. I jerked back, colliding with Rogan. The wheel of magic whistled past me and sank into the ground, smoking. A metal star, a foot wide, with four double-edged razor-sharp points. Deep red magic boiled off its blades.

"A barrage mage." Rogan leaned on his side and ducked back as another star thudded into the oak. "Two."

"How do you know?"

"Two different shades of red."

On my side a disk shaved off a slice of the tree.

"Can you stop one in flight?" I asked.

Another disk sliced a three-inch-thick slab from Rogan's side of the tree.

"No. They're coated in magic."

That's right. According to my books, an object wrapped in magic lost its physical properties until the point of impact. If he jumped out there, the disks these guys threw would slice right through him.

Another chunk slid from the oak. They were chopping it down from two sides. Running to the house was out of the question. The closest place to hide would be the arched entrance to the De Trevinos' house, which required a fifty-foot sprint. They would hit us. Making an arcane circle was right out too. We were on the grass.

Rogan leaned out. Another thud. He swore, pulling back. All of his magic meant nothing unless he found a target. He could level the entire row of houses across the street, but there were families in those houses.

I dropped down to my knees and peeked from behind the oak.

A shadow moved on the roof of the mansion across from us. A crimson disk hurtled toward me. I threw myself behind the tree. It whistled past me, its magic singeing my shoulder.

"One is on the roof directly across from us."

Rogan's face was grim. "The other is at the next house on our left."

"They're quick."

"I noticed that."

"You can't collapse those roofs."

"Not planning on it."

"This is a family neighborhood. There could be children inside those homes."

He grabbed my hand and looked at me, his blue eyes calm and reassuring. "I know."

He wouldn't hurt them. At least no other people would die because of us.

Disks thudded into the wood, gouging the oak. The tree shuddered from the impact. The barrage mages were ducking and throwing, too fast for Rogan to lock on to.

We had to move. We were running out of the tree.

I leaned back, facing the tree, and turned my head. Nothing to my right. Only houses. Nothing to my left, except more house and a carpet of brown mulch that crawled toward us . . .

Wait a minute.

Not mulch. Ants.

"Rogan, we're about to have company."

He glanced to the left and swore.

The carpet of the ants advanced in thin rivulets, the currents of insects pooling and changing directions as if momentarily confused, then realigning themselves. Whoever was controlling them didn't have a good hold on the ant horde. He didn't need to. We were in Texas, facing an insect mage, and that meant fire ants. They would flush us from behind the tree and the barrage mages would finish us.

The tree shook continuously now. It wouldn't last much longer.

The ants marched on. On my right another street crossed ours and the ants poured around the corner. The insect mage had to be hiding there, out of our line of sight.

The crimson disk sliced a hair from my thigh. I turned sideways, almost hugging Rogan.

This is it flashed in my head. I could die right here on this lawn. One good shot from the barrage mages and I would never see my family again.

"How's your aim?" Rogan asked.

I stomped the fear down. "It will have to be good enough."

He bared his teeth at me. "On three."

I took a deep breath and exhaled slowly.

He held up one finger. Two.

We lunged from behind the tree at the same time. My Mazda snapped in half with a tortured scream of torn metal. The pieces shot up into the air just as the two figures on the roofs ducked from their cover, launching their spinning circles of magic at us. I sighted the one directly across from us. It felt so impossibly slow.

Kill or be killed. I squeezed the trigger. The gun spat thunder. The mage's head jerked back. I turned, sighting the second barrage mage, and fired. The bullet punched into her chest. She slid down the roof and fell into the sea of ants.

The remnants of my Mazda streaked through the air, blocking the course of the two disks. The magic missiles thudded into metal and fiberglass and exploded, hissing.

Rogan grabbed my hand and pulled me into a run. We dashed across the street, through the arched entrance into someone's yard and past their house. The brick fence exploded in front of us. Rogan turned left. He was going for the insect mage.

Behind us a woman howled, "Brown! Get them off of me! Fuck!"

"I'm trying!" a male growled from somewhere down the street.

"There are ants in my fucking bullet wound! Get them off of me!"

We sprinted to the corner of the street and stopped. I raised my gun and sliced the corner, clearing it. A large white van was parked by the curb. Four large metal drums sat on the ground next to it. A dark-haired man leaned around the next corner, his back to us.

The woman screamed and choked, her cry suddenly cut off.

"Serves you right, you stupid bitch," the man muttered.

Rogan marched past me, murder on his face. The insect mage turned. Rogan grabbed his shoulder and sank a vicious punch into the man's stomach. The insect mage doubled over, sinking. Rogan drove his knee into the man's face. Something crunched. The mage crumpled to the ground.

"Stop," I called out.

Rogan moved toward the fallen man.

"Stop, stop, stop."

He glanced at me.

"Everyone else is dead, Rogan. We can't question him if you kill him."

He bent down, grabbed the mage by his throat, hauled him upright, and smashed him against the stone fence. The mage gurgled, struggling to breathe. Blood dripped from his broken nose. His eyes watered. I stepped close and searched him. No gun. I pulled out his wallet. Driver's license for Ray Cannon. I took out my cell and took a picture of it.

"Is there anyone else?" Rogan asked, his voice cold and precise.

"No," the man gasped.

Rogan squeezed, crushing his throat.

"True," I confirmed.

Rogan loosened his hold. The man drew a hoarse breath and looked at me, his eyes pleading. "Help . . ."

Rogan shook him and slammed him back against the fence. "Don't look at her. Look at me. Who pays your bills?"

"Forsberg."

Damn it. I was hoping we'd get a lead on whoever was behind the attack. Instead we'd circled right back to Forsberg.

"Talk," Rogan ordered.

"They told us you killed his old man, Matthias. There are two teams hunting you. We were closer. It was me, Kowaski, and his sister. We came in two cars—the Ford parked down the street and my van. We set up and waited for you to come out."

"How did you know where we would be?" I asked.

"De Trevino called it in."

That cockroach.

The look on Rogan's face sent icy shivers down my spine.

"Rogan, can I please have him?"

All color went out of the mage's face. He realized whom he'd cornered.

Rogan squeezed his neck again.

I reached out and touched his arm. "Please?"

"Fine." He let go. The mage slid to the ground.

"You're going to put the ants back into the drums," I said. "If I see a single fire ant on this street after we're done with De Trevino, I'll ask him to find you." I pointed at Rogan. "You do know who he is, right?"

The mage nodded quickly.

"Gather your ants and go. The next time I see you, I'll put a bullet in your head." There. That sounded dramatic enough.

Rogan ignored the mage and marched on to De Trevino's house. I followed.

He hit the door with the palm of his hand. His magic

smashed into the wood. Every window in the house exploded outward. He strode into the house, his face dark.

Antonio stood in the living room, his face white as a sheet.

"I'm a little irritated." The furniture slid out of Rogan's way. "So I'll ask only once: why did you call Forsberg?"

"I was worried you might impede their investigation . . ." Antonio squeezed out.

"Lie," I said.

"I just wanted to get information . . ."

"Another lie."

The house shook.

This was taking too long and if I didn't do something, Rogan would bring the entire building down. "Look at me," I said, gathering my magic. "Look into my eyes."

Antonio glanced at me. My magic shot out and clamped him. He shook, straining under the pressure. My powers were will-based, and with everything that had happened today, my will had a lot of fuel behind it.

My voice dropped into a low, inhuman register. *"Why did you call Forsberg?"*

The look on Rogan's face was priceless. *That's right. No circle to help me this time. Somebody leveled up while you were away.*

"Money!" Antonio cried out. "If Forsberg confirms Elena's death happened on the job, her life insurance pays double. House Forsberg promised to not impede my insurance claim if I came forward with any information related to anyone looking into her death."

I released him. "That's true," I told Rogan.

Antonio drew a long, shuddering breath.

Rogan kicked the glass table. It shattered. The shards rose into the air.

Antonio froze, petrified.

A boy burst into the room from the right doorway. He ran across and thrust himself in front of Antonio.

"Don't kill my dad!'

He couldn't be older than ten.

"John," Antonio said, his voice breaking. "Go see to your sister."

"Don't kill my dad!" The boy stared at Rogan, his face defiant.

Rogan stared back.

The shards flew through the air and shattered harmlessly against a wall.

"We all choose a side," Rogan told Antonio. "You chose badly."

He turned and walked out.

The street outside of Antonio's house was empty, the river of ants speeding around the corner, probably back into the insect mage's drums. Sirens howled in the distance. Someone had called the cops.

Rogan's magic roiled around him, an enraged tornado.

"Thank you for not killing him in front of his son," I said.

"Adults can make a choice to become my enemy or my ally, or to remain as noncombatants. Children are just children, Nevada. That child lost his mother. I wouldn't take his father from him." He checked his phone. "This way."

We began walking to the right, away from the retreating ant army.

"Enemies, allies, or civilians, huh?" I asked.

"That's right."

"And if someone helps the enemy, like Antonio?"

"Then he becomes an enemy himself."

"And enemies have to be eliminated?" I asked.

"If they present a danger, yes." Rogan's face was merciless.

The light dawned in my head. I knew what this was. I had gone through it before. "That's true in a war. We're not in a war, Rogan."

"Of course we're at war."

"No. We're in a civilian world. Things are not black and white. They have shades of grey. There are degrees of punishment, depending on the severity of the crime."

He faced me, his blue eyes hard and clear, without a shadow of doubt. "This isn't about punishment. This is survival."

What the hell happened to you in the war, Rogan? What did they do to you to cause this much damage?

"So if someone, let's say a young woman, is helping one of your enemies, she's also an enemy. It's okay to kidnap her off the street, chain her in your basement, and interrogate her by any means necessary."

His face told me he really didn't like where I was going.

"Tell me, how close did I come to being murdered?"

"You were never close to being murdered. At the time, I didn't feel you presented a threat. I just wanted information and if I had obtained it, I would've let you go just as I did. I probably wouldn't have driven you home myself, but asked one of my people to do it."

I tried again. "You can't live like this, Rogan. The war is over."

He stopped and pivoted back, where two bodies lay prone on the ground. "What does that look like to you? Because it looks like combat to me."

We resumed walking.

And he liked combat. Combat was simple. It was familiar. He knew who his enemies were because they were trying to kill him, and he knew what his mission was: to survive by eliminating every threat he saw. You didn't fire warning shots in war. You aimed to kill.

But the civilian life was frustrating and complicated. If Rogan went into a bar and a drunk tried to pick a fight with him, they would expect completely different outcomes. The drunk would expect some insults, then some pushing, then possibly a punch or two, followed by grabbing each other's clothes and tussling on a street until the alcoholic temper tantrum wore off. The drunk would expect to go home afterward. Because that was his normal, the civilian world's normal. He had no idea that the moment he designated himself as a threat, a mental switch flipped in Rogan's brain. If the drunk were lucky, Rogan would incapacitate him by choking him out. If he were unlucky or he tried to pull a knife, Rogan would cripple him or even kill him.

He'd been out of the military for years. He'd probably never sought treatment. He probably didn't know anything was wrong with him.

"How are you sleeping?" I asked him.

"Like a baby," he said.

"Nightmares?"

"I came to your house to ask you to be with me. You turned me down . . ."

Way to change the subject. "Right now isn't the best time for this conversation."

"It's the perfect time. I asked you on a date. You said no. I waited. There was no counterproposal."

"A date?" That wasn't how I remembered it. I waited for the buzz telling me he'd lied, but none came. "Oh please. That's not what you were offering and you know it!"

"That's exactly what I was offering."

True. How was he dodging me on this . . . "Are you telling me that you weren't offering a sexual relationship?"

He took a second. "No."

Ha! Got him. To him a date—whatever he meant by it—was a prelude to sex. In his head he did offer me "a date," so technically he wasn't lying. I'd have to be cleverer with my questions.

"I'm not a stalker, Nevada," he said. "I understood no."

"I didn't want you to stalk me, Rogan."

"What did you want?"

"I wanted you to give me a chance to decide if I wanted a relationship with you. You wanted sex. If you're really hard up for some uncomplicated sex, I hear Harper is single."

He made a grunt that might have been no, but it was hard to tell with that much disgust saturating it.

My legs shook. I kept moving. If I told him that the stress was getting to me, he'd probably try to do something ridiculous like carry me. I wouldn't be carried by Mad Rogan, especially not in public.

"I didn't say I just wanted sex."

"Let me quote: 'Do you want seduction, dinners, and gifts? Seduction is a game, and if you pay enough in flattery, money, or attention, you get what you want. I thought you were above the game.' Did you not say that to me a week before you strolled into my garage to invite me on 'a date'?"

"Yes. I wanted to skip the bullshit."

"So what happened? You changed your mind and now you want the bullshit?"

Rogan's phone chimed. "Yes, I want your bullshit."

"Well, you don't get to have any of my bullshit. I'm keeping it." Okay, and that didn't sound childish. Not at all.

"Why not?"

"Because you call it bullshit."

A silver Range Rover slid around the curve of the road and came to a stop in front of us, Troy behind the wheel.

I got into the back before Rogan or I said anything else. I really didn't want to continue this conversation in front of Troy.

Rogan took the front passenger seat. "Home."

Troy drove out.

"I'm not sure I fully understand the concept of bullshit," Rogan said, his voice quiet. "Would you care to discuss it, over dinner perhaps? I'd be happy to listen to an explanation of how I erred. A place of your choice."

No. If I went to dinner with him, I wouldn't be able to resist reaching out. I would kiss him. I would probably do other things . . . More intimate things . . . I wouldn't be able to help myself, and I didn't want to open that door now.

"I would like to go home."

"Would spending an evening with me be such a terrible thing?" he asked.

The sincerity in his voice stopped me in my tracks. The witty replies died.

"No."

"Are you afraid of me?" he asked.

No, I realized. He would never hurt me. I didn't even know where that belief came from, yet I was absolutely sure that he wouldn't. His power terrified me, but it was a deep-seated, instinctual kind of fear. I wasn't afraid of Mad Rogan. I was probably the only person in Houston who wasn't.

"It's not that."

"I realize that the way I act is disturbing to you," he said. "I'll do almost anything to make you feel at ease, but if you want me to be conflicted about eliminating someone who is a threat, I don't think I can. I don't believe I'm capable of it anymore."

This conversation had gone deep really fast. His facade had cracked and the man behind it was looking at me.

"I just killed two people," I said. My voice came out small. "I'm trying to not deal with it, because if I do, I might lose it. Today was a long day. I need to go home and hug my family, so I know they are still okay."

"Of course," he said, his voice carefully controlled.

I saw him close himself off. One moment Connor was there, and the next Mad Rogan reasserted himself.

We'd witnessed so much grief today. So much pain. Cornelius, Jeremy, the faces of Rogan's soldiers . . . Forsberg. Two bodies on the street behind us. Dreams, futures, *lives* severed abruptly. I didn't even know how to process it all. It had to have an effect on him—he wouldn't be human otherwise—and I saw an imprint of today on his face: fatigue, grief, and grim determination in his eyes. He looked older; not worn, but rough, like he hadn't slept for ages. He was still sharp, still deadly, but it was the dangerous edge of a predator backed into a corner after a long chase.

I would go to our warehouse and be surrounded by a warm human chaos. Someone would be cooking; someone would be watching TV or playing video games. My sisters would be sniping at each other; Leon would complain about his never-ending battle with the French language; then Grandma Frida would come in, smelling of engine grease and metal, and poke fun at my mother . . . I would wrap myself in these warm human connections and let them melt away the dark coldness of today.

Mad Rogan didn't have anyone to go home to. He would return to his Zorro house, eat whatever someone brought him, and probably watch that recording again to see if there was anything he'd missed. He had all the power but it brought him no warmth. No human safety net that would catch him when he was sinking and help him keep his head above water.

I couldn't let him do it.

"Have dinner with me," I asked. "At my house. You

can help me explain to my mother and grandmother what happened to my work vehicle."

A hint of a grin touched his lips. His eyes lit up. "Do you think your mother might try to shoot me?"

"Possibly."

"Then absolutely. I wouldn't miss it."

And he would be the politest dragon ever. Tail tucked in, fangs hidden, and talons carefully folded on his lap. I had just invited Mad Rogan to have dinner. Again. My poor mom.

Rogan's phone chimed. He glanced at it and swore.

"What is it?" I asked.

"Luanne's sister just arrived in Houston. I have to meet her."

I tried to sort out the tangled mess of emotions. Was I relieved or disappointed? I wasn't sure. "Rain check?"

"What time is dinner?"

"Usually around five thirty, six."

"I can make it."

I glanced at my phone. It was three fifteen. He could reasonably make it.

"Pull over," Rogan said.

Troy took an exit and pulled into a gas station.

"I'll be there," Rogan promised.

"I'd like that." I meant it.

He opened the door, stepped out, and bent down. "Take Ms. Baylor wherever she wants to go."

"Yes, sir."

Rogan grinned at me and shut the door.

Troy pulled away. "Where to, Ms. Baylor?"

"Nevada. Would you mind making a small detour for me to pick up some takeout?"

"Your wish is my command," Troy said.

Right. I dialed Takara's number. My sisters would get their sushi after all.

Chapter 5

The Katy Freeway slid by outside the passenger window, the traffic unusually light, the five lanes of smooth pavement channeling a handful of cars forward. In an hour, when the workday rolled to a close, traffic would be murder. The sky, torn between rain and overcast drudgery all day, had finally decided on rain. Water poured from above as if some giant had decided to hold a showerhead above the city.

I petted the plastic bag on the back seat next to me. I had spent way too much money on sushi and I didn't care. After all of the nightmarish things I had seen today, I wanted to buy my sisters all the sushi in the world. I was so grateful they were alive I might even hug them when I got home. Of course, they'd freak out and claim I needed to have my head examined.

Troy's reflection in the rearview mirror frowned. "Are you buckled?"

"Yes. Why?"

"A Toyota 4Runner is hanging out behind us. He was speeding and weaving through the lanes until he settled on our ass. I'm going five miles under the speed limit, the left lane is wide open, and he isn't passing."

I pulled my Glock out and glanced behind us through the tinted back window. The black 4Runner stayed about three car lengths back. A driver and a passenger, both dim, dark silhouettes in the rain. I snapped a picture of the license with my phone. Not great, but once we uploaded it and ran it through some filters, we should be able to read it.

"I've got the rear and front cameras recording," Troy said.

Nice. That's the thing I always liked about Rogan and didn't mind admitting: he was thorough and he thought ahead. "The exit to Sam Houston Parkway is coming up."

"Yep." Troy checked his rearview mirror again. "Let's see if he follows."

The sign announcing the exit flashed by. An exit-only lane peeled off from our lane, running parallel to the main road. A concrete barrier loomed ahead, where our lane split: the left side kept going with Katy, the right joined the exit lane and veered toward a high overpass.

The barrier sped straight at us.

Troy took a sharp right onto the exit and stepped on the gas. The Range Rover flew down the lane. The 4Runner behind us picked up speed. We hurtled up the curving overpass, the ground far below.

A black Suburban drew even with us in the left lane. A man in the front passenger window looked at me, his face smudged behind the rain-splattered window. Maybe midthirties, blond hair brushed back. The man leaned closer to the glass and smiled. The Suburban shot past us. The wet pavement behind the large vehicle turned white with frost. Ice sheathed the road.

The Range Rover slid. My stomach jerked left, then right, trying to escape my body. I grabbed the seat in front of me. We fishtailed down the overpass, Troy's face a white mask in the rearview mirror. My heart hammered in panic. The Range Rover veered into the concrete outer rail. A hideous metal screech ripped through the cabin. A hundred feet below us a parking lot yawned.

We were going to die.

Troy wrestled the wheel back. The Range Rover skimmed the icy road like a pinball shot out of the machine, cleared the apex of the curve, and sped down the overpass. Ahead, the Sam Houston Parkway stretched, the entire right lane glistening with ice. We were going too fast, but if Troy slammed on the brakes, we'd skid and die. The Range Rover slid to the left, then to the right. Troy was pumping the brakes gently, trying to shed all of that speed.

A semi roared next to us in the left lane, blocking us in. We fishtailed down the lane, caught between the semi and the concrete rail.

The familiar 4Runner slid behind the semi. The passenger window rolled down.

Here's hoping Rogan's money bought us enough armor.

"Gun!" I warned.

Bullets sprayed the road behind the car. Something hissed—they'd hit our tires. The rubber inserts meant we'd keep going, but steering had just gotten extra complicated.

The Range Rover slid again, skidding on the ice. Troy caught the skid, steering into it.

They hadn't attacked us while Rogan was in the car. They weren't ready for that confrontation, which meant even now they would want to keep their identity a secret. If I didn't want an attack to lead back to me, I'd use stolen cars, and if the 4Runner chasing us was stolen, it had no armor.

I tried the window. Locked.

"Lower the window."

"Can't do that. Stay buckled."

"Troy!"

"I lower that window and crash, you'll fly through the windshield," he growled.

Getting off the highway was our only chance. "If you don't roll down the window, they'll keep shooting us. Even if the car shields us, the bullets will ricochet. There are innocent people on this road. Open the window!"

The window slid down. I unbuckled, took aim at the 4Runner, and fired five shots in a tight pattern. The windshield fractured. The 4Runner dropped back. The semi slid between the 4Runner and us, blocking the shot.

Three rounds left.

Ahead the exit lane for Hammerly Boulevard peeled off the highway.

The semi roared, speeding up. Troy stood on the gas, but it was too late. I locked my seat belt and thrust the gun down to the right, so I wouldn't shoot myself or Troy.

The semi rammed us. The Range Rover jumped forward, slid, hurtling out of control, the truck thundering past us as it veered back into the left lane. We smashed into something solid. The impact punched me. The gun slipped through my fingers. The seat belt burned my shoulder and chest, knocking the wind out of me.

I opened my eyes. The deflated sacks of the front airbags hung from the dash. Troy lay limp in his seat. The impact had bent Troy's door in, forcing his seat all the way back and pinning my knees in place. My Glock was somewhere in the car, probably on the floor by the passenger seat on my right, and I had no way to reach it. Great.

"Troy?"

He didn't respond.

I put my hand on his neck and felt the fluttering of a pulse. Even; didn't seem weak, although I wasn't a doctor. I held my hand close to his nose. Breathing. Okay. Where the hell was that semi?

I tried to turn to look behind me and managed a half glance over my shoulder. The semi was gone.

The 4Runner had stopped ahead of us on the tollway in the right lane, its front toward us, oblivious to traffic that had to flow around it. The driver door swung open. A leg emerged below the door. It ended in a hoof.

A wave of dread rolled over me, a sickly overwhelming fear. My heart raced. Cold sweat broke out all over my body. The hair on my arms stood up. I had to get out. I had to get out now.

A second foot joined the first. Something wide and dark rose above the door. The dark thing unrolled and snapped into a leathery bat wing.

My chest hurt. My throat constricted, choking me. I unbuckled the seat belt with shaking hands and jerked, trying to get my legs free. Stuck.

It couldn't be real. People summoned monsters from the arcane realm, but I'd never heard of anyone summoning actual demons. Yet it was right there, living, breathing, real, and every instinct I had howled and clawed at my logic.

The creature started toward me. Panic clamped me in an icy vise. The demon stood seven feet tall, its enormous leathery wings mottled with green and brown and streaked with thick cables of veins. Python scales sheathed its muscular arms and torso, the ridges of its bones cutting through the scaled hide to form an exoskeleton on its chest. Sharp bone ridges thrust up from its neck and shoulders. Its powerful dinosaur tail snapped from side to side.

Dizziness swirled through me, tiny black dots drifting before my eyes. I had to run away now or I would pass out.

The demon leaped over the concrete barrier separating the tollway from the exit lane. The hooves clattered as they touched the pavement. A ragged hood sat on its head, and within it, a horrible face looked back at me. Pale, wrinkled, with reptilian slits for a nose, it stared at the world with tilted inhuman eyes. They burned with furious violent red. Below the eyes, a wide slash of a mouth bared a forest of narrow, sharp fangs.

I flailed, yanking my legs, but the seat remained wedged. *Let me out, let me out, let me out, please, dear God, let me out . . .*

The demon jerked the door open.

I didn't want to die. I would never hug my mom again. I wouldn't see my sisters grow up. I wouldn't be there when Bern graduated; I would never find out Leon's magic. I would never find out if Rogan and I had a chance.

My family would be lost without me.

I wouldn't die today. Demon or not, I'll be damned if I lay there, petrified, and let him rip the life out of me. Not today. Not ever.

The demon locked his hand on my throat, pulling me toward him. The monstrous face leaned in, the mouth opening wider, teeth glistening, the red burning eyes excited as he squeezed my throat, cutting off my air.

Lie, my magic whispered.

I clamped both hands on its neck and pushed with all my power. Agony exploded in my shoulders, shot down my arms, and burst into a feathery lightning, biting deep into the demon's flesh. The creature in my arms screamed, but the shocker's lightning held it tight and I strained harder, forcing the full reserve of my magic into his flesh.

The scales turned transparent, betraying a glimpse of human skin underneath. Not a demon. An illusion mage. *You bastard! Fry, you sonovabitch. Fry.*

The illusion broke, a curtain jerked aside, and a man's face screamed at me, big mouth contorted with pain.

A glowing thread swam across my vision. I had to let go or I'd kill myself.

I unclamped my hands from the man's neck. He crashed down on top of me. I hit the seat with my side, the dead weight of his body pinning me, nearly crushing me. My back crunched. His feet in black boots drummed the air as he convulsed on top of me. There was nowhere to go. Thick pink foam slid from his lips. I shoved him back as hard as I could and he sagged on the side of the seat, halfway into the car.

I had no idea if he'd survived that. I had to be sure.

My nose was running. Tears rolled down my face, but the panic vanished. I finally saw my gun on the floor, out of my reach.

I gripped the seat and stood straight up, bending forward. My knees popped. I leaned on the left foot and used my weight to wrench the right leg free.

Faint tremors shook the mage's legs. If he lived . . .

I jerked my left leg free, dove across the seat, grabbed my gun, and fired three bullets into the left side of the mage's chest. Well, if he wasn't dead, he definitely wasn't happy. *Great, I've turned into my mother. That's what she would say.*

The 4Runner hadn't moved. Its driver door was still open. Nobody shot at me. Nobody followed the illusion mage.

I grabbed the corpse by the dark long hair and raised his head to see his face. A man in his thirties, tan, sharp-featured, wearing a black T-shirt, a trench coat, and black tactical-gear pants. Never seen him before.

I was a licensed private investigator involved in an accident. The tollbooth camera had likely recorded the crash. All my training said I had to call it in and hold tight until the cops and first responders got here. If Troy had a neck injury and I moved him, he could end up paralyzed. He could be bleeding to death internally.

But Troy and I were sitting ducks here. If that semi

came back and rammed us again, there would be nothing left but a metal pancake and a bloody spot. Right now whoever had sent the illusion mage thought he was taking care of the job. If I called authorities for help and he somehow listened in, he would know we weren't dead. There was no telling who would show up.

I grabbed the corpse by the T-shirt and yanked it deeper into the car. So heavy. The T-shirt ripped. Damn it. I hooked my hands into his armpits and heaved, lifting with my legs. Finally, the body gave and slid forward. I rolled him on his side, bent his knees, and slammed the passenger door closed. So far so good. I popped the right rear door open, keeping the Range Rover between me and the highway, and got into the front passenger seat.

Troy didn't move. No blood. No obvious injuries. I unlocked his seat belt and checked his pulse again. Still alive.

The impact of the crash had crushed the left side of the Range Rover. Most of the hood was almost intact, but the entire driver door looked out of commission. There was no way to open it. I had to move him from inside the cab.

A truck tore past us and swerved to avoid the 4Runner parked on the shoulder. The vehicle showed no signs of life. I could've sworn I'd seen two people in it.

I found the switch on the side of the front passenger seat and flipped it, pushing on the seat's back to flatten it as much as it would go.

Behind us a blue SUV took an exit lane, then veered sharply back onto the tollway before my heart had a chance to jump out of my chest.

I grabbed Troy and gently, an inch at a time, began to slide him over on to the flattened seat, trying not to jostle him. I pulled and heaved until finally he slid in.

The empty driver's seat gaped at me. I climbed over Troy and landed in it. My feet barely reached the pedals.

The switch moving the seat forward didn't respond. I perched on the edge of the seat, pressed the brake pedal, and pushed the engine-start button.

Start. Please, please, please start.

The engine roared to life. There was no sweeter sound.

I put the car into reverse. The Range Rover's door screeched, parting with the booth, and then suddenly we were free. The engine sputtered. I floored it. The warehouse was fifteen minutes away. I turned on Hammerly, made a left on Triway, and zigzagged through the labyrinth of small streets as the rain poured on, flooding the pavement.

Minutes stretched by, slow and sluggish, the Range Rover coughing and creaking, threatening to die any second. Time turned viscous. I kept checking the rearview mirror. No semis.

Troy stirred in the seat. I glanced at him. He was blinking quickly and tried to sit up.

"Stay down," I told him.

He did.

"Where does it hurt?"

"Back of the head. My vision is blurry. What happened?"

"I'm taking you home," I said.

"Need to notify . . ." He patted down his pocket.

"Don't move," I told him. "We're almost there. Rogan has a team watching our house. One of them has to be an EMT."

"Call it in."

"When we're safe."

Streets flashed by. Gessner. Kempwood. When our street appeared out of the rain, I almost cried. I drove around the warehouse to the back. One of the massive industrial garage doors gaped open, and I steered the Range Rover inside, screeching to a stop a foot from the bumper of an armored Hummer.

"What in blazes . . ." Grandma Frida stepped out from behind the Hummer, a wrench in her hands. She saw the mangled side of the Range Rover and saw my face. I must've looked bloodless, because my seventy-two-year-old grandmother sprinted across the floor to hit the button on the door remote. The reinforced door clanged down, cutting off the world outside.

I ran into the living portion of the warehouse as Grandma Frida grabbed the med kit out of one of the metal cages. Cartoon noises floated from the media room. I stuck my head in. Arabella, blonde and short, sprawled on the couch. Catalina, taller, thinner, and dark-haired, sat on the floor among a scattering of brushes and hair ties. Matilda sat on the floor in front of her, between Bunny and a large seal-point Himalayan cat. One half of her hair was twisted into an elaborate braid.

Everyone looked at me.

I forced a smile on my face. "Matilda, where is your dad?"

"He's taking a nap," she said.

"Sushi!" Arabella jumped up off the couch, becoming completely vertical in 0.3 seconds.

"Can I borrow you two for a moment?"

Catalina grimaced. "I can't let this go—I'll have to redo the whole braid."

"Please don't argue."

They must've heard the no-nonsense note in my voice, because my sisters moved.

"There is a dead body and an injured man in the motor pool," I said quietly. "Grandma is watching them. Catalina, keep Matilda in this room. Do whatever you have to do to protect her. I mean *whatever* you have to do. If you need to use your powers, do it."

Catalina's face paled. "Understood."

"Arabella, is Bern home?"

"He's in the Hut of Evil."

"Tell him to put us on lockdown. Where is Mom?"

"In the tower."

"Leon?"

"Playing *Grim Souls*."

Good; Leon was with his brother in the computer room.

"Are you okay?" Catalina asked.

"Yes."

"Is someone coming for us?" Arabella whispered.

"I don't know. Go."

Arabella took off like a rocket, Catalina ducked back into the media room, and I ran for the intercom in the hallway.

"Mom?"

"Yes?"

"I was attacked. One wounded, one dead body in the motor pool. We need an EMT. Can you get ahold of Rogan's team?"

"Stand by."

I waited.

The intercom came to life. "Open the front door."

I sprinted to the office through the hallway, then to the door and checked the monitor. Two men in tactical gear ran up to the door through the rain, one carrying a medical bag. I opened the door, made sure it was locked behind them, and led them to the motor pool.

The medic went straight for Troy, while the other man went for the corpse and began speaking quickly into his headset.

I dialed Rogan's number. I didn't have to look at contacts. To my shame, I had it memorized. The call went straight to voice mail. There was no message, no introduction, just a beep.

I cleared my throat. "We were attacked on the Sam

Houston Tollway. Troy is injured. Your people are taking care of him. Three vehicles were involved: a semi, a Toyota 4Runner, and a black Suburban. There was an ice mage in the Suburban. He iced the road, then the Toyota shot at us and the semi pushed us off the tollway, and we crashed into a tollbooth. An illusion mage came after us. I killed him, and I have his corpse. Call me back, please."

I hung up and trotted to the medic.

By the time Rogan's medic examined Troy and declared that he had a concussion, all of my adrenaline had worn off. I took several pictures of the dead guy with my phone, and walked away. I should've checked on Cornelius, but right now I wasn't in any shape to give a day's report. I headed to the tower where my mother was instead. *Tower* was really a grandiose name for it. It was a square chute that led up to the crow's nest near the roof, equipped with a sturdy wooden ladder. My mother had climbed it despite her permanent limp, which meant she was really worried about our safety.

I climbed the ladder and emerged through the trapdoor into a small room, built at the very top of the warehouse. The ceiling here was barely five feet high, just enough to comfortably crawl up and sit on the low stool, which was exactly what my mother was doing. Her .300 Winchester Magnum sniper rifle was keeping her company. Dad and she had customized the roof, installing some very narrow windows, but they'd never gotten around to putting in the sniper tower. That had come later, courtesy of Grandma Frida and my mother, after Adam Pierce used some kids to blow up Rogan's car in front of our warehouse.

From this vantage point, my mother had a perfect view of the north, south, and east sides of the warehouse and the adjoining street and parking lots. The warehouse was rectangular, and the west side, where Grandma's Frida's motor pool opened to the street, was too long. The roof blocked the view of that parking lot, so there was no clear shot.

I sat next to my mother.

She reached over and hugged me.

I felt like crying.

"How's the injured?" she asked.

"A concussion. The collision knocked him out."

"Nothing major?"

"Not that the medic found so far." My voice sounded dull. "The Mazda is totaled."

She didn't even blink. "How did that happen?"

"Enerkinetic barrage mages had us pinned down and Rogan broke it in half and used it as a shield."

"Are you injured?"

"Not seriously."

"Is he?"

"Not seriously."

"Are they hurt?"

"I killed them."

"So everything is good then."

"Yes. No."

I opened my mouth and things just came out. I told her about Forsberg throwing me and then dying and about his eyes being two bloody holes I couldn't unsee, watching the recording of lawyers being murdered, about the ice on the overpass and the parking lot below, and the demon, and hoping Troy didn't have a broken neck.

She didn't say a word. She just hugged me again.

"I should tell Cornelius," I said.

"Cornelius won't be up for a while. I gave him two sleeping pills," Mom said.

"Oh."

"He moved everything in, brought in all the animals,

then tried to cook for Matilda, but the girls offered to make her oatmeal with raisins and brown sugar, so she decided to eat that instead. Then he sat in the kitchen staring off into space and his hands were shaking. I made him take a hot shower, watched him take two pills, and the last I saw, he was sleeping like a log. He needs it. He hasn't slept since his wife died."

"I see." One didn't say no to my mother.

Mom reached over and brushed my hair out of my face. "Rough waters."

"Yes. That's okay. I climbed into them of my own free will."

My phone rang. I looked at it. Rogan.

"Yes?"

"I'm on my way," he said and hung up.

I stared at my mom. "The Scourge of Mexico is on his way. We're saved."

Mom snorted. "Lie down." She pointed to a narrow mattress on the floor.

I did. She put a soft blue blanket over me. It was so warm up here, cozy under the blanket. My limbs felt very heavy. I was suddenly so tired, but I was safe. Mom would watch over me.

"Try to rest."

"I feel so weird." Like all those terrible things had happened to someone else.

"You're in shock. Magic-induced panic has strange side effects. Your body needs time to recover. Try to relax and let it go. I'll tell you when your Rogan gets here."

"He isn't mine."

Mom smiled at me. "Sure he isn't."

I yawned. "He's bad for me. Why do I have to like a man who's bad for me? Why couldn't I have found someone who is solid and normal and not whatever the hell he is?"

"I don't know." Mom spread her arms.

I squinted at her. "You're an adult."

"You're an adult too."

"But you're an older adult. You've had more practice." Mom leaned back and laughed.

"Listen to me. I sound like I'm fifteen years old." I tried to scrounge up some embarrassment, but I was too tired.

"When I was five years younger than you are now, your grandpa asked me the same question," Mom said.

"What?" Grandma Frida always told me that she and Grandpa Leon loved my dad. Was it before Dad? It couldn't have been. Mom had me when she was twenty.

"Your dad had a really rough life," she said. "He had problems."

"Like what?" I desperately tried to stay awake.

"He couldn't do crowded places because he was convinced someone was following him and people were looking at him as if there was something wrong with his face."

"Dad?"

"Yes. He couldn't hold down a job. He only had a high school diploma, and the kind of jobs he took often meant he had to keep his mouth shut and do as he was told. But instead he would try to improve things. He'd point out ways to make the job better or to produce more, and he was usually right. He refused to cut corners and didn't get into workplace politics so he would eventually get fired."

That I could believe. Dad had a very strong sense of right and wrong. He was professional in all things and he'd never do anything unethical.

"And then you came along. We had very little money and no medical benefits. Your grandparents pushed your dad to enlist."

That didn't surprise me either. Both Grandpa Leon and Grandma Frida had made their careers in the army. To them enlisting meant a steady paycheck, medical, dental, commissary benefits, and, despite deployments and wars, an odd kind of stability the civilian world couldn't deliver.

"Your dad couldn't enlist. He was hiding and there were too many red flags that would light up."

"Hiding from what?"

Mom sighed. "It's complicated. I promise he had his reasons and they were good ones. My parents didn't understand. They saw a deadbeat loser who'd managed to make a baby and now wouldn't step up to the plate to take care of her. Grandpa Leon called him a coward to his face. Grandma Frida took me to this lunch where she tried to convince me to leave him and come back to their house. Her exact words were 'And if he tries to bother you again, I'll pull his legs out.'"

I remembered to close my mouth.

"She was very convincing. I remember I had a moment where I thought she might be right and it would be easier to just walk away. In the end, it didn't matter. I loved him. I understood why he was the way he was. He loved me so much and he did everything in his power to make things better. So when you were six months old, I enlisted instead and I left you at home with your dad," Mom said. "Hardest thing I've ever done. That's when your grandma began to thaw. She walked into our house a month after I left for boot camp, expecting a trash heap of dirty diapers and your dad at the end of his rope. Instead the place was spotless, you were clean and fed, and he made her lunch. Your dad did a good job taking care of you, and later, of your sisters. He built a business that still puts food on our table. And when Grandpa Leon needed help, your dad always offered it and never once asked for any acknowledgment. He was a good man, your father. I was proud of him and proud to be his wife."

"He wouldn't have left the scene of an accident."

"If your life was on the line, he wouldn't have even thought twice about it. Your dad would do anything to keep us safe. If he had to pick up a gun and shoot someone between the eyes, he wouldn't hesitate. You had an injured teammate in the car. You did what had to be done to keep him safe. Your father would be proud of you. Don't ever doubt that. The agency is his legacy, Nevada. You make sure that it thrives and its name stands for something."

Right now it stood for "we get ourselves into violent messes and then heroically try to get out of them."

"Anyway, the moral of that long story I just told you wasn't to compare you to your dad. It's to remind you that it's your life, Nevada. You own the responsibility for it. I can't be in charge of it and I don't even want to give you advice. There is no point. No matter what I say, you'll do what feel right to you in the end. So." Mom folded her hands on her lap. "What feels right to you, Nevada?"

"I don't know."

"Well, when you figure it out, let me know. If I have to shoot Mad Rogan, I'd like to be properly prepared for it."

"I was wrong about him, you know," I said quietly, half asleep. "I thought he was a sociopath, but he cares about his people being killed."

"You sure he isn't just pissed off because they failed?"

"No. He tries to hide it but you can tell it tore him up inside. He went to notify all the families personally yesterday. When we were tracking Adam, he was really angry about the way the Air Force had treated Bug. I didn't think that much of it at the time, but now it makes sense."

"So he's human after all."

"Sort of. He cares about his people. I just don't know if he cares about anyone else. He still thinks he's at war, Mom. It's kill or be killed. There is no middle ground with him."

"Mhm."

I yawned. "I invited him for dinner. I just wanted to tell you so you don't have a heart attack."

She said something back, but she sounded far away and I couldn't make it out. Thoughts crawled around my head in all directions like big lazy caterpillars. I gave up, closed my eyes, and let myself drift.

Chapter 6

I woke up because I heard voices. I opened my eyes. My mom was gone. The tower was empty and the only light came from the outside filtering through the narrow slits of the windows and from the square opening that led down. I checked my phone. I'd slept for forty minutes, and now I felt kind of woozy. I didn't want to get up. I wanted to lie right here on this cozy air mattress and stay warm and comfy. And maybe sleep some more.

The creaking of a ladder announced someone climbing up into the tower and moving fast.

I flipped onto my stomach, sat up, and leaned toward the opening, my hands on the floor, to see who was coming up the stairs. In that exact moment Rogan raised his head. We were face to face. An overwhelming relief flooded his eyes.

I was so glad to see him.

"Are you hurt?" he asked. Mere inches separated us.

"That's the second time today you asked me that." I leaned closer. I couldn't help myself. "You should really come up with a better pickup line."

He surged up, halfway into the room, his upper body in, his feet still on the stairs. His mouth closed on mine.

His lips burned me. The sleepy wooziness evaporated in a heart-fluttering rush. He smelled of sandalwood, and my head was spinning. I licked his lips. He tasted so good. A hoarse male noise escaped his mouth. *Yes, growl for me.*

His hand stroked the back of my neck, his teeth bit my lower lip, and I gasped as my breath caught in my throat. Heat warmed my skin from within, each sensation magnified. I felt so alive. I wanted his hands on me. I wanted the heat of his rough fingers on my skin. I wanted him inside me. I opened my mouth, shocked at the thought, and he took it, his tongue brushing mine and withdrawing, perfectly in tune with my breath, conquering and seducing, teasing and pulling back, pretending I could get away and then claiming my mouth as his.

A velvet heat dripped down the back of my neck, a phantom molten honey sizzling on my skin, as Rogan's magic bound us. It slid down my spine, inch by inch, setting every nerve on fire in its wake, my body eager for the repeat of ecstasy it remembered. Oh my God, how could this feel so good?

Rogan's hand slid over my chest to cup my breast. *Yes, yes, please.* He took a step up. Another.

If he came up all the way, we'd have sex right here, right now.

On my *mother's* air mattress.

I pushed him. For a fraction of a second he stayed where he was, grasping the air for balance, and then he slid down the stairs with a thud.

I leaned into the opening. He caught himself midway down the ladder, looked up at me, and spread his arms, his face puzzled.

"What's going on?" Mom called from somewhere below.

"Mad Rogan fell down the stairs." I squeezed my eyes shut for a second, cringing inside.

"Does he need a medic?"

Yes, Rogan mouthed and pointed at me.

Aha, no, I'm not giving you any sexy healing. "No, he's fine."

Rogan started back up the stairs, his face determined.

"He's coming down," I announced. "Now."

He gave an exaggerated sigh, went down the stairs and stayed there. Great. Now I would have to climb down the stairs while he entertained himself by looking at my butt. Maybe he would move.

He didn't.

However, by the time I got down the stairs, he'd slid back into his I'm-a-Prime-and-I-can-kill-you-with-my-pinkie expression. Probably because my mother and my grandmother were both in the vicinity, standing in the doorway of the media room and looking at something on the screen. Leon hovered nearby, gazing at Rogan with all of the puppy love his evil teenage heart could muster. For some odd reason, Leon hero-worshiped Rogan with the passion of a thousand burning suns.

I went to the media room. Rogan followed me. One of his people, an African American woman, sat cross-legged on the floor by a laptop connected to our TV with a cord. The other, a trim athletic man in his forties, sat on the couch, leaning forward and keeping most of his weight on his feet, expecting to jump up any moment. An image of an iced-over overpass stretched on the screen and the view was flying down the ice, veering left and right.

Mom and Grandma Frida had identical expressions on their faces: dark and angry.

"Troy should get a raise," I murmured.

"He will," Rogan promised, his voice hard. "Thank you for saving his life."

"I didn't . . ."

"I've already watched this," Rogan said. "You did. Thank you for taking care of him."

On the recording I snapped, "Open the window!"

I hadn't realized I barked like that.

The woman's hands flew on the laptop keyboard. The view switched to the rear camera and the windshield of the 4Runner fractured.

"Clean kill," Mom said.

"What?"

"Zoom in," Mom said.

The recording rewound a few seconds and crept forward at a fraction of the normal speed, zooming in on the windshield. The bullets tore into the glass and punched the dark shape in the passenger seat. It jerked and went limp. That's why nobody came out of the 4Runner after the illusion mage. I'd killed the passenger.

"That's a hell of a shot," Rogan's man said.

Mom turned to Grandma Frida. "Threat-based?"

"Probably." Grandma Frida grimaced. "Well, at least Bernard takes after me."

"I don't get it," I said.

"Pause it," Mom said. The woman paused the recording.

"You and your mom get your shooting from your grandfather," Grandma Frida said. "You more than her. Your Grandpa Leon was crap with a sniper rifle, but if he were under fire, he returned it with deadly accuracy. That's the way his magic worked. Penelope lies there with her rifle and goes to her happy place, but you have to have people shooting at you to hit the target."

"Dual," Rogan said and smiled. He had a really smug expression on his face, like a cat who'd snuck into the pantry and stolen a bag of catnip.

"Keep going," Mom said.

I would have to ask him later what that meant.

The recording restarted. We crashed. A demon got out of the car and walked toward the camera, his trench coat flaring. A smirk curved his lips, baring serrated teeth. Wow. True illusion. There were several kinds of illusion magic. Cloaker mages could make you invisible, but they accomplished it by affecting the minds of others, and a camera would still record you as you were. True illusion mages, like Augustine, not only affected minds, but also altered their physical appearance. Their reflection and pictures showed only what they wanted you to see.

The view switched to the internal camera. I sat petrified on the back seat, breathing fast through my mouth. My pupils were so large that my eyes looked completely black on a bloodless face. I wanted to close my eyes, but instead I watched myself fry him. I'd taken his life. I had to own it.

The doorbell chimed.

"I got it!" Arabella chirped from somewhere inside the house.

"Bug scrambled the footage from the toll road," Rogan said. "The cops got to the 4Runner before my people did, but you have nothing to worry about."

"They will find bullets from my gun in his car," I said.

"Yes. And I've sent an excellent lawyer down there to explain that the car was used to attack one of my vehicles. You may have to give a statement at some point."

"That's it?"

"House wars, House rules," Rogan said. "They aren't interested unless a civilian is involved and often not even then."

"What about the car itself?"

"It was stolen this morning from an office building's parking lot. The Suburban was appropriated from another office building, and neither lot had cameras pointing in that specific direction. And this guy's prints aren't in any databases so far."

"So we have no leads."

"No." Rogan's eyes hardened. He was looking at something on my neck.

I pulled out my phone and checked the camera. Red welts marked my throat, four on one side and one on the other. A souvenir from the illusion mage's fingers.

"Why did you shoot him in the back?" Leon asked from somewhere to the left. "Head would be better."

"Because we need his face for ID." I turned to Rogan. "I saw one of the people in the Suburban."

His eyes lit up.

"The view wasn't great," I said. "It was raining. But I'm sure it was the ice mage. He was in his thirties, I think. Blond, wearing a suit. It's not much, but if Bug puts together possible ice mage candidates, I can look at them. He smiled at me."

"Smiled?" Rogan said, his face dark. "I'll remember that."

My imagination painted him standing over the blond mage, holding the man's guts in his hand. Okay then.

On the screen, I was driving, my eyes empty. I looked like a zombie. We had to be on the right track, at least. Rogan's people were iced before they died. Only an ice Prime could've frozen that overpass so quickly and completely. Something we had done had convinced Nari's murderer that either I or Rogan was a threat.

Troy said something. I replied, my eyes scanning the windshield. I didn't quite have the thousand-yard stare, but it was close. Anxiety splashed me in a cold gush, an echo of driving to the warehouse expecting to be forced off the road any second. I felt the urge to cross my arms to try to put some distance between me now and me on that screen.

A warm hand touched me. Rogan's strong fingers wrapped around mine, forging a link between us. He didn't look at me, his gaze still on the recording. He just held my hand, anchoring me here and now. I'd survived. I'd made it, and now the look in his eyes promised me that he would put himself between me and whatever tried to hurt me next. I could've jerked my hand away, but I didn't. I held on to him.

"You need to switch to Akula tires," Grandma Frida said. "See how the vehicle is lurching? Akula has thicker inserts and an inflated inner chamber."

"I'll take it under advisement," Rogan said.

"This way," my sister said.

I turned and leaned to glance out of the room. Augustine Montgomery was striding down the hallway toward me, with Arabella by his side. My mother had never forgotten that he'd threatened to terminate our mortgage to force me to apprehend Adam Pierce. If she saw him, she'd probably murder him.

"I'll be right back," I announced, slipped my hand out of Rogan's hold, and left the room to intercept the incoming disaster.

Arabella offered me a cherubic smile.

"Why did you let him in?" I hissed in a loud whisper.

"Because he's so very beautiful."

Augustine was remarkably beautiful today. His skin all but glowed, his frost-blond hair barely short of perfect. The quality of his illusion was off the charts.

"He's too old for you. You can't just let someone in the house because you think they're pretty."

Augustine's eyes narrowed. He must've seen Rogan behind me.

"What are you doing here?" Rogan asked, his voice suffused with menace.

"What are *you* doing here?" Augustine snapped, his gaze fixed on Rogan.

"Shhh!" I hissed. "Into the office, before people see us." My mother had stopped coming into the office when I formally took on the leading role in our firm. I didn't care, but she considered it to be my professional domain.

I herded everyone in and shut the door behind me.

"Ms. Baylor . . ." Augustine pushed his glasses up his nose.

Arabella snapped a picture of Augustine.

"Stop that," Augustine and I said at the same time.

"Augustine, don't tell my sister what to do. Arabella, stop it."

"Why do you even associate with him?" Augustine pointed his hand at Rogan. "Was your last adventure not enough?"

Most people, even Primes, gave Rogan a wide berth. Augustine met him head on. He and Rogan had gone to college together and at one point they'd been friends, but now they mostly snarled at each other. The last time they'd met in my office, they nearly destroyed it in their pissing contest. If they tried that again, they would sorely regret it.

Leon slipped into the office, a slender shadow. Great, more witnesses if anything went wrong.

Augustine was waiting for my answer.

"I'm associating with Mr. Rogan because it's in the best interests of my client—the one you sent to me. They have signed a professional agreement, and I have to abide by its terms." That sounded a lot better than "because he makes me feel safe and every time I think about kissing him, I feel a little electric thrill."

"Mr. Montgomery, was there a point to your visit or did you just come here to critique my choice of professional partners?"

"You know perfectly well why I'm here. I warned you it was a terrible idea and I was right."

I took a deep breath. "I have no idea what you're talking about."

Augustine blinked. "Don't any of you watch the news?"

I tapped my keyboard to get my PC to wake up. "What am I looking for?"

"Amy Madrid, press conference."

A dozen links popped up. I clicked the first one. An older woman held seven-year-old Amy in her arms. A man stood next to her, hugging them both. Amy looked like a deer in the headlights.

I smiled.

"Fast forward to the nine-minute and thirty-seven-second mark."

I did.

". . . finally found . . ." some reporter was saying.

"It was the Lady in Green," Amy's mother said, the words bursting out of her. *"They told me. She made him tell her where our daughter was. We love you. Thank you, thank you for saving our daughter. We'll never forget. Eres una santa . . ."*

The mike died. A man in a suit clamped his hand over it and called out, "That is all for today."

"You?" Rogan asked, his expression resigned.

"She would've died," I told him.

Rogan turned to Augustine. "And you helped her do this? How many lunchtime martinis did you have before it seemed like a good idea?"

Augustine recoiled in outrage. "I tried to talk her out of it. She wanted to just walk into the police station. I helped her do it as anonymously and secretly as possible."

Rogan crossed his arms. "Someone told that woman exactly what took place. The video has two million views already. Now she is a damned urban legend. If that's your definition of *secret*, you need to get your head examined."

"Her face and her entire body was obscured. Anyway, I didn't come here to be insulted." He turned to me. "I came here to warn you, just like I did before. This act will have consequences, ones you're likely unable to anticipate. Make your preparations."

Sure, let me get right on that. "If I can't anticipate the consequences, how can I prepare for them?"

"That's for you to figure out." Augustine turned to leave.

"Wait," Rogan said, a speculative look on his face. "I'd like to show you something."

Augustine grimaced. "Is it work related at least?"

"Yes. Nevada, may we enter the motor pool?"

"Follow me. Quietly, please. I don't want to upset my mother." I opened the door and checked the hallway. Clear.

"Why would your mother be upset that I'm here?" Augustine asked.

"Think about it," I said. "It will come to you."

We crossed the hallway and I opened the door to the motor pool.

"Is this about that nonsense of me being a terrible person?" Augustine asked.

Rogan strode through the motor pool, heading for the Range Rover parked in the middle and watched over by a Hispanic woman.

Augustine squinted at the two track vehicles—a tank and a mobile flamethrower. "What exactly does your grandmother do?"

"She tinkers," I told him.

Augustine opened his mouth to say something else, saw the mangled Range Rover, and closed his mouth.

Rogan walked up to the stretcher covered with a dark

brown tarp they must've stolen from Grandma Frida and nodded to the woman. "Thank you, Tiana. Take a break."

"Yes, Major." Tiana trotted outside.

Rogan pulled the tarp, revealing the illusion mage's face. "Do you know this asshole?"

Leon and Arabella climbed up on the nearest track vehicle to get a better view.

Augustine grimaced. "Yes. I do know this asshole. Who did he go after?"

"Me," I said.

"Did he look something like this?" Augustine took off his glasses. His flesh boiled. He expanded, growing to eight feet. Enormous leathery wings thrust out from his shoulders, issuing a challenge. Muscle sheathed his tree-trunk legs, covered in mottled python scales. Hooves formed over his feet. Carved arms stretched forward, armed with razor sharp talons. The horrible face stared at me with ruby red eyes, dripping fire onto the cheeks. A mane of bright roiling flames fell onto his shoulders and back.

"Holy crap!" Leon almost fell off his perch.

Arabella laughed. I threw her a warning glance. *Don't you do it.* The last thing we needed was for her to show off.

The demon flexed his colossal shoulders. I could feel the heat of the fire. I smelled it. How was that even possible? The other guy's illusion had looked real. This *felt* real. I swallowed.

"Yes, he looked like that. Except he was a foot shorter and there were no flames. He had a hood."

"Dilettante," the demon said in Augustine's voice. "Living fire takes concentration."

The demon deflated in a rush, snapping back into Augustine. He slid his glasses back on. "Philip McRaven. Also known as Azazel, mostly because he attempted to get everyone he ever worked with to call him that. He cost me a great deal of money."

"How?" I asked.

"He was a Significant, related to the San Antonio McRavens. They excised him twelve years ago for various offenses and when I met him, he was working as a free agent. He advertised himself as a decent tracker. We were looking to expand our staff and I can always find use for a good illusion mage, especially one with a secondary talent. In addition to being an illusion mage, he was also an upper-range Average psionic."

That explained the panic.

"I put him on a skip trace. One of the Houses had a runaway spouse who married into the House and six months later took off."

"Took the good silver?" I asked.

"Nothing so pedestrian. He made his getaway in a California Spyder."

"Good taste," Rogan said.

I glanced at him.

"It's a 1961 Ferrari. Only fifty-three ever made," Rogan explained.

"The last one to come on the market sold for seven million," Augustine said, his voice dry. "The man was a gambler who used to frequent Vegas. A relatively easy job. McRaven was to find him and call in the local team so we could deliver him and the car back to his heartbroken wife. McRaven found the runaway, put on his demon routine, and then choked the man to death. To add insult to injury, the thief voided his bowels while still in the car."

"How inconsiderate of him." Rogan's expression was perfectly placid.

"Yes, how dare he ruin the upholstery," I murmured.

Our sarcasm flew right over Augustine's head. "It's incredibly difficult to remove the stench of human waste once it soaks into the carpet fibers. I almost killed McRaven. When I asked him why he did it, I got psychosis on parade with all flags flying and a marching band. According to him, he had done it because he liked, and I quote, 'to see light go out of their eyes as they wet themselves in terror.'"

"Charming," I said. Whatever mild tinges of guilt I felt about killing a man who'd tried to murder me evaporated.

"I seriously considered making him disappear," Augustine said.

"Why didn't you?" I asked.

"One, he was my employee. There were plenty of warning signs in his background check, so the fault was mine for hiring this psychopath in the first place. And two, his mother came to see me from San Antonio. The McRavens may not be a full-fledged House, but there are four Significants in that family and now they owe me a favor." Augustine studied Rogan for a long moment. "How do you fit into this? What are you involved in?"

"I'd tell you but I'd have to kill you," Rogan said.

Nobody laughed.

"You should wink next time you make a joke," I told Rogan. "So people know when to laugh."

"I'm not joking," he said.

"He isn't." Augustine pushed his glasses back up his nose. "Except I'm obviously not trembling in terror. Let me break this down for you. I own the largest investigative firm in Houston. Obtaining information is literally what I do for a living. I'm now intrigued enough to divert resources from other, profitable ventures, to look into this. I will put the two of you under enough surveillance that you won't be able to breathe. I'll bug your offices and your vehicles, I'll hack your computers, and I'll have you followed by people who change their faces and bodies with a thought. You can devote an enormous amount of resources to fight me off or you could just tell me, because we all know I'll figure it out in the end. I can be a nuisance or I can be an ally. Your choice. Either way is fun for me."

Rogan considered it.

Augustine waited.

Rogan leaned back. "Do you know how Forsberg's people were killed?"

Augustine peered at him through his glasses. "You realize I referred Harrison to Nevada?"

"I meant, do you know what really happened?"

"No, but I'm all ears."

I sighed and headed to the counter, where Grandma Frida's coffeemaker waited. This would be a long conversation and I needed coffee for it.

By the time Rogan was done talking, we'd moved back into my office, since there was less chance of discovery there. I chased Leon and Arabella off, then checked up on Mom and Grandma and told them I was discussing things with Rogan just in case they decided to look for me. I was on my second cup of coffee, it was barely eight o'clock, and I was still sleepy.

Augustine took his glasses off and rubbed the bridge of his nose. A modern angel, urbane, well-dressed, and carrying a briefcase filled with savage weapons.

"So there is a conspiracy, probably involving several major Houses. To what end?"

"They are trying to destabilize Houston's status quo," Rogan said.

"Yes, but what's the end game?" Augustine frowned. "They're committing a great deal of money and resources. There are only a handful of reasons that motivate people to risk that much of their assets."

"Power, greed, or revenge," I said.

Augustine nodded. "Precisely. Let's say Adam had succeeded and Houston's downtown is in ruins. The stock market crashes. Theoretically, one could make money from that crash, but the local economy would be recovering for years. Long-term outlook for doing business is poor."

"Not only that, but backlash against the Houses would spike," Rogan said. "It would make sense if one of the anti-House radical groups was involved, but this is coming from within House elite. You know what this means. It will eventually explode."

"And when it does, everyone will have to pick a side." Augustine sighed again. "I don't like it. I don't like not knowing what the hell is going on. In fact, I make it my life's mission to know what is going on at all times."

Out of Augustine's view, Rogan rolled his eyes.

Augustine grimaced. "I'm tired of odd things happening. I don't want excitement, I want boredom. Boredom is good for business."

Him and me both.

Augustine glanced at me. "I understand Rogan's involvement. But what about you? You do realize the full danger of this mess?"

"Yes," I said.

"Then why?"

"I'm here because I want to help Cornelius. But mostly because of Nari Harrison."

Augustine's eyebrows rose.

"When we talk about the deceased, we usually mention whom they left behind," I explained. "We say, 'She was a wife and a mother' or 'He leaves behind two children and three grandchildren.' It's almost as if the dead have no value unless we know that someone they are related to is still alive and mourning them. I feel terrible for Cornelius and Matilda. But I feel even worse for Nari. She expected to have a long life ahead of her. She had dreams. She won't see them come true now. She won't see

Matilda grow up. She'll never grow old with Cornelius. She'll never experience anything again, because some scum decided to kill her. Someone should care that this happened. Someone should fight for her and make sure that her murderer never takes another life and that he or she pays for what they did. If I die, I want someone to care. So, I'm that someone for her."

A short figure walked down the hallway toward us. I fell silent.

Matilda stopped in the doorway of my office. She was carrying the huge Himalayan cat and a little plastic bag. The cat hung limp in her arms, perfectly content to be dragged around like a stuffed teddy bear.

Matilda looked at the three of us, walked up to Rogan, and held out the cat to him.

"I need to clean his eyes." Her voice was so cute. "His tears are brown because of his smushed nose and he gets infected. He won't hold still. He can't help it."

Rogan stared at her, stunned. I'd never seen that expression on his face before. It was almost funny.

"Will you hold my cat?"

Rogan blinked, reached out, and carefully took the cat from her arms. The cat purred like a runaway bulldozer.

Matilda opened her little Ziploc bag, took out cotton pads and a small plastic bottle, her tiny eyebrows furrowed in concentration. She wet the cotton and reached out to the cat. He tried to turn away, but Rogan held him tight.

"Hold still. Be a good kitty." Matilda stuck her tongue out of the corner of her mouth, held up her cotton ball, and carefully wiped the cat's left eye with it.

It was such an odd thing. Rogan—big, frightening, all coiled violence and icy logic—gently holding a fluffy cat for a tiny child a fraction of his size. I should take a picture, but I didn't want to ruin it. I wanted to remember it just like this, serious Matilda and shocked Rogan, his eyes soft.

Matilda finished. I held out the trashcan to her. She threw away the cotton pads stained with brown, packed away her bottle, and took the cat from Rogan, settling his front paws over her shoulder. She petted the fur. "There, there. It wasn't bad. You're okay."

The cat purred.

Catalina ran down the hallway, her face flustered. "There you are. I went to the bathroom for a second and you disappeared. Come on, we'll make some cookies."

Matilda held out her hand to her. My sister took it.

"Thank you!" Matilda said to Rogan.

"You're welcome," he said with all of the formality of a man accepting knighthood.

Augustine was smiling.

Rogan looked back at me. "Why me? Why not you?"

"Cornelius is a stay-at-home dad," I said. "She views men as caretakers. Usually he probably holds the cat, but he wasn't available."

Rogan leaned back in his seat.

"It's terrible when he's reminded he is human," Augustine said to me. "He doesn't know how to deal with it. Just think, Connor, one day you might be a father and get one of your own."

Rogan stared at him as if someone had dumped a bucket of cold water on his head.

Payback time. "I doubt it. He'll never marry. He'll stay in his house and brood in solitude being cynical and bitter."

"And entertain himself with his piles of money and high-tech toys," Augustine said. "Like a broody superhero."

Augustine had a sense of humor. Who knew? "Maybe we should invest in one of those searchlights with a Rogan symbol on it . . ."

Rogan reached into his wallet, pulled out two dollar

bills, pushed one toward me and the other toward Augustine. "I hate to see comedians starve. Our only lead is Gabriel Baranovsky, who was Elena's lover, according to her douchebag of a husband. Are you going to help me with Baranovsky, Augustine?"

"I wasn't planning on attending," Augustine said. "But I might now. I want in. Not because I have some altruistic motives, but because when this thing finally bursts out in the open, it will be like an earthquake. It will shake the House politics not only in Houston, but probably in the entire country, and I can't afford not to know where the pieces land."

"Attending what?" I asked.

"How much do you know about Baranovsky?" Augustine said.

"Nothing," I told him. "I haven't had a chance to do any research. I was busy trying not to die."

"Gabriel Baranovsky is an oneiromancer," Rogan said.

Oneiromancers predicted the future by dreaming. Since the beginning of time, people have been trying to catch a glimpse of things to come by any means they could, from casting bones to examining cheese. Dreaming about it proved to be one of the more commonly used methods.

"He's a very accurate short-term precog," Rogan continued. "He dreams specifically about the stock market."

"Dreams during the night, trades during the day," Augustine said. "He made his first billion before he turned thirty."

"His first billion?"

"He's worth more than the two of us combined," Rogan said. "He stopped at three billion because he got bored."

"Wife?" I asked.

"He never married," Rogan said.

"But he's a Prime." That was extremely odd. Finding the right person to marry and producing a gifted child dominated everything Primes did. In our world, magic equaled power, and the Primes feared losing power more than anything. "If there is no wife, then there is no heir and his family will lose the House designation."

A family had to have at least two living Primes in three generations to be considered a House and to qualify for a seat in the Assembly.

"He doesn't care," Rogan said. "He never attends Assembly or socializes."

"Much like someone else we know," Augustine said. "Rumor has it, there is a bastard child. But nobody's ever seen him or her."

"So what does he do with all that money?"

"Whatever the hell he wants." Rogan shrugged.

"Baranovsky is a collector," Augustine said. "Rare cars, rare wine, rare jewels, rare art."

"Rare women," Rogan said. "He was likely Elena's only lover, but for him she was one of many. It's a compulsion. He can't help himself. The more unusual and unique a thing is, the more he wants it. What he wants very, very badly is the 1594 *Fortune Teller* by Caravaggio."

"Caravaggio was a rebel," Augustine explained. "In the 1590s most of the Italian art scene consisted of Mannerist works—posed, stilted arrangements of people with unnaturally long limbs painted in jarring colors. Caravaggio painted from life. His works showed ordinary people and they were hyper-realistic for the time, funny and sly. Later on he would become massively influential."

That made sense. "Baranovsky identifies with Caravaggio," I said. "They both rejected the established artificial status quo and did what they thought was real and important."

"Precisely," Rogan said.

"*Fortune Teller* was Caravaggio's first work in his style," Augustine said. "It was the genesis of everything he created. The painting exists in two versions, and Baranovsky already bought the later version from the French for an outrageous amount of money."

"But he doesn't have the 1594 version," I guessed. "And it's killing him. It's the original. He has to have it."

"You should come work for me," Augustine said.

"I do work for you, by proxy."

"Long story short," Rogan said, "the Museum of Fine Arts here in Houston owns the original *Fortune Teller*. Baranovsky tried everything to buy it, but MFAH refuses to sell. When the painting was donated, the owner stipulated that it could never be sold or leased for monetary compensation. And yet, MFAH wants Baranovsky's money."

"So they are letting him display it," Augustine finished. "In return—because they can't take money—once a year he organizes a huge charity gala. Minimum ticket price is two hundred thousand per family."

I choked on the last of my coffee.

"Baranovsky won't talk to me," Augustine said. "I'm not flashy enough as Primes go. I'm very much in line with the status quo. He might talk to Rogan, since he's the most dangerous man in Houston."

"Is that the official title?" I asked.

"No," Rogan said. "It's a statement of fact."

I couldn't resist. "It's so refreshing to meet a Prime with such humility."

"Anyway," Augustine cut in. "Even if Baranovsky talked to Rogan, it wouldn't do us any good. We all know that Rogan has the interrogative subtlety of a howitzer."

"I can be subtle." He actually managed to look offended.

"Let's ask her." Augustine looked at me. "How do you think Rogan would try to get information from Baranovsky?"

I said the first thing that popped into my head. "He'd hold him by his throat from some really tall balcony."

"I rest my case."

"Holding people by their throat is effective and rapidly produces results," Rogan said, completely matter-of-fact.

Augustine shook his head. "Two of the people in this room are private detectives who routinely extract information from people. You're not one of those two. We need better bait."

They both looked at me.

"What makes you think he would be interested?" I asked.

"Because Rogan will show up," Augustine said. "He never shows up, but this time he will and he'll pay very obvious attention to you. You will also be in my company. You're beautiful and new, and you will seem to command the attention of two Primes. Baranovsky will want to know what's so special about you."

"When is it?"

"Friday."

"I'll need a dress," I said. "And money."

Rogan leaned forward, a warning in his eyes. "Right now the only two Primes that know about you are Augustine and me. If you walk into that benefit dinner, this will change."

Augustine's eyes narrowed. He was watching Rogan very carefully. "You want to get to Baranovsky. This is the best and most efficient way."

Rogan ignored him. "Nevada, I know that you're keeping your talent quiet. There will be no turning back after this."

Either he genuinely worried about me, which was really touching, or he had some clandestine reason to keep the fact of my existence quiet so he could continue utilizing my power. I wish I knew which.

"Don't be dramatic," Augustine said. "As long as she doesn't stand in the middle of the floor and announce that she is a truthseeker, nobody has to know she has any magic at all."

"There will be consequences," Rogan said. "It will be difficult to fade into obscurity after this. At worst, people will realize what you do. At best, you will be dismissed as a woman Augustine or I are using. I know your reputation is important to you. Think about it."

I waited until both of them stopped talking.

"Augustine, are you attending in your professional capacity?"

"Of course. I'll be using MII's corporate account. The charitable contribution is tax deductible."

"Then I'll attend as your employee." I looked at Rogan. "If he introduces me as his employee, it'll explain why I'm there. Your kind of people don't look too closely at hired help. It will look like I'm one of Augustine's investigators and you're trying to get into my pants to aggravate him. If the two of you act the way you've been acting every time I've seen you together, nobody will doubt it."

"What do you mean, the way we've been acting?" Augustine leaned back.

"Have you ever seen a betta fish?" I asked.

"Of course."

"Well, when you and Rogan come into each other's view, you act like two male betta fishes. You puff your fins out and swim around trying to intimidate each other. Just keep doing what you're doing, and everyone will realize that it's really about the two of you and I'm just collateral damage. Everything will be fine."

"I take offense at that," Augustine said.

"You're giving Augustine too much credit," Rogan said. "His fins don't impress me."

He'd delivered that reply on autopilot. His eyes were distant. He was probably still thinking about the gala and he didn't like it.

"I still need a dress."

"I'll handle the dress," Rogan said.

"No," I told him firmly. "You'll give me money and I'll buy my own dress. Also Cornelius will likely want to attend. He'll need financial assistance as well."

"I'll take care of it," Rogan said.

"It's decided then," Augustine said. "Why do I have this nagging feeling this won't end well?"

"Never fear quarrels, but seek hazardous adventures," Rogan said, obviously quoting. He still didn't seem enthusiastic about it.

"Where is that from?" I asked.

"The Three Musketeers." Augustine shook his head. "Rogan, everything about you is hazardous. It's late and I have things to take care of. You can have your broody Athos all to yourself, milady. I'll let myself out."

He left the room. A quick check of my computer monitor confirmed he'd exited the building, gotten into his car, and driven away.

A speculative light played in Rogan's eyes. "I always liked Milady more than Constance."

"I'm not Milady or Constance," I told him, getting up. "I'm Captain de Treville. I'm the voice of reason that's trying to keep you two from doings criminal things without any regard for the law or the lives of others."

He smiled. A potent, heated mix of need and lust warmed his eyes. It should've banished the darkness that had made its nest there, but it didn't. He was eyeing me from the back of his dragon cave, tired, haggard, dangerous, but willing to throw it all aside for my sake. It made me want to run my hands down the hard, corded strength of his shoulders. I could slide my legs over his, straddle him right there in the chair, and make him forget everything. Let him make me forget everything, if only for a few minutes. He would smell like sandalwood. His skin would be hot under my tongue. He would grip me and the strength of those arms and the feel of his fingers on my body would carry me away, into the place where only pleasure existed.

Some men seduced by words, others with gifts. Connor Rogan seduced by simply looking. The sad thing was he wasn't even trying. He was just looking at me and wishing we were naked together.

And if I didn't stop fantasizing, he would pluck the impressions from my mind and run with them.

"Go home, Rogan."

"You stopped calling me Mad a while ago," he observed.

"I called you Mad mostly to remind myself who I was dealing with." I leaned my butt against the desk.

"And who would that be?"

"A possibly psychopathic mass murderer who can't be trusted."

No reaction.

"And now you call me Rogan. What are you reminding yourself of now?"

"That you're mortal."

"Planning on killing me?" An amused light flashed in his eyes.

"Not unless you become a direct threat. Are you planning on becoming a direct threat?" I winked at him.

He laughed quietly. There, that was better.

"Are you going home?"

"No." Steel tinted his voice.

I sighed.

"Is this about the overpass?"

"Yes."

"I handled it."

"I know," he said quietly. "Troy survived because you were in that car."

If I hadn't been in the car, Troy wouldn't have been attacked in the first place, but now didn't seem like a good time to discuss that. "Then why do you want to stay?"

"Because Cornelius, Matilda, and you are now here under one roof. This is what we call a target-rich environment."

"The bad guys could take care of their problems with one well-timed explosion," I said.

He nodded. "My presence might be a deterrent. If not, I'm good in explosions."

"I remember."

I could argue but what would be the point? He wouldn't hurt me or my family, and I felt better when he was here. I was responsible for my family's safety and for Cornelius and Matilda, and I needed all the backup I could get. I just had to deal with the fact that when I climbed into my bed tonight, he would be sleeping somewhere downstairs. Probably on the air mattress, since Cornelius and Matilda had the guest rooms.

"Won't Bug miss you?"

"Bug's never far away." Rogan showed me his phone.

"I'll have to sell it to my mother," I said.

"I discussed it with her before waking you up," he said, matter-of-fact. "She thinks it would be prudent."

Wow. My mother was so concerned about our safety she'd invited Mad Rogan to stay at the house. That knocked me back a bit.

"Maybe this isn't such a good idea. I don't know if I'll be able to sleep knowing that you're prowling in my house while I'm in my loft."

He rose, his face serious and harsh. "You will. You'll fall asleep fast and sleep soundly until morning, and then you'll get up and have breakfast with your family because

I'll be prowling in your house tonight. And if anyone tries to interrupt your sleep and end your life, you have my word that they'll sleep forever."

That was the most romantic thing anyone had ever said to me. He meant it and he would make every word of it come true.

I made my mouth move. "Okay. I'll see you in the morning."

I'd barely closed my bedroom door behind me when someone knocked.

"Come in."

The door opened and Leon slipped through. My youngest cousin was still in the lanky-teenager stage. Skinny, dark-haired, olive skinned, he reminded me of Ghost Elves from the recent fantasy blockbuster *Road to Eldremar.* I could totally picture him jumping from some ancient tree with two curved knives and blue war paint on his face. For a while we thought he might turn out to be really tall and once he hit his height, he'd fill out, but he'd stopped two inches short of six feet and so far showed no signs of adding bulk to his slight frame.

"If this is about Mad Rogan . . ."

He lifted his laptop and held it open for me. A dark background ignited on the screen, simulating deep space, and in the middle of it a beautiful nebula blossomed, made of luminescent threads, each spider-silk thin and weakly glowing with bands of different colors. Ah. The Smirnoff rubber-band model. I remembered doing that in high school. Magical theory was a core class and it hurt.

"I can't do it," Leon said.

After the day I'd had, homework was the last thing I wanted to do right now. "Leon, you really need to do your own homework."

"I know." He dragged his hand through his dark hair. "I tried. I promise, I really, *really* tried."

Leon had two settings: sarcastic and excited. This new sad Leon was puzzling.

I sighed and sat down in my recliner. The chair was a necessity. I ended up taking work into my bed way too much, and my last laptop had leaped to its death in protest when I fell asleep and it slipped off my bed. From that point on, bed was strictly for TV watching, reading, sleeping, and having frustrating thoughts about certain telekinetics. Work was done in a recliner chair. It was comfortable like a cloud but it still made me feel like an old lady.

I studied the nebula. "Tell me about it."

"This is a computer model of the Smirnoff rubber band theory," he droned out.

"Your enthusiasm is overwhelming. What does the theory say?"

"It says that a space-time continuum is acted upon by many different factors. The influence of these factors is too great for any small change to affect the state of a continuum. It says that our reality is like a tangle of rubber bands. If you pull one out, the state of the tangle isn't significantly affected. So if you went back in time and shot Alexei I, for example, World War II would still happen. Instead of Imperial Russia invading Poland in the 1940s, somebody else would've invaded, like France or Germany. Concentration camps and anti-Jewish ethnic cleansing would still happen. The rubber band theory is the complete opposite of the chain-link theory, which says that events are directly precipitated by each other, so if you go back in time and kill a mosquito, we'd all evolve gills or something."

Good enough. "And your assignment is?"

"Prove or disprove rubber band theory as it relates to

the introduction of the Osiris serum." Leon pantomimed throwing up and pointed at the model on the screen. "Okay, so I know it should change. There is no way it wouldn't change. If there was a huge plague, the world wouldn't stay the same, right? Magic is like a plague. It's affecting everything, so the events wouldn't be the same. It's too big of a factor. But I can't make it work. Okay, so let's say everything that glows blue is magic, right? I tried to pull all of the threads of the same color out to make a nonmagic model and nothing. Look, I let it run for ten years. Look."

Leon clicked some keys. The screen split in two. On the left side the original nebula glowed with a rainbow of colors. On the right a new nebula formed. All of the blue threads vanished from it, but the shape of the new nebula remained the same.

"You're ninety percent there," I told him. "It's a space-time continuum, Leon."

"I know that."

"So what are you forgetting?"

"I have no idea. Nevada, just help me, please. Please."

I typed in new parameters. "You're forgetting to take your time."

On the screen the time counter rolled forward, dashing through decades. The nebula on the left remained unchanged, but the one on the right stretched, turned, evolving into a new odd shape. The counter clicked. One hundred years. Two hundred years. Five hundred. It came to a stop at a thousand. Leon stared at a completely different constellation of threads.

"You didn't run it long enough," I told him. "It's like two roads branching from each other. At first they are close and going almost in the same direction, but the farther you go, the more they split. In the beginning magic didn't change much. But with each generation it transforms our world more and more. Think about it. Without the magic we wouldn't have Houses or Primes. Some things would probably stay the same, because some strings remained relatively untouched for a short while, but others would be completely different. Inevitably all strings will be affected, and the further we go, the more different the world will be."

He landed on the bed. "How long did it take you?"

"Three days. I was frustrated and tried different things one by one, until I realized how it works."

"Two weeks," he said. "I've been doing it two weeks. Do you know how long it took Bern?"

"I have no idea."

"Four minutes. I checked the school log. He holds the record."

I sighed. "Leon, Bernard is a Magister Examplaria. He recognizes patterns. Code and encryption talk to him the way tanks talk to Grandma Frida. He probably figured it out within the first thirty seconds and then spent the next three and half minutes trying to find alternative solutions for fun."

"I can't do it." Leon slumped, deflated. "I tried to do what Bern does and I just can't. I'm a dudomancer."

Not this again. "You're not a dud."

"I have no magic."

Magic was a funny thing. What Catalina did and what I did was somewhat in the same area, but Arabella's magic didn't just come out of left field, it came out of the grass on the other side of the fence of the left field. Everybody in our family had magic, except for my dad, but Leon wasn't directly related to him. His mom was my mother's sister. All indications said that Leon had magic as well. It just was taking its sweet time demonstrating itself.

"Your talent will show up," I said.

"When, Nevada? At first it was all 'when he turns

seven or eight,' then 'when he passes puberty.' Well, I'm past puberty. Where the hell is my magic?"

I sighed. "I can't answer that, Leon."

"Life sucks." He took his laptop. "Thanks for the help."

"You're welcome."

"About Mad Rogan . . ."

"Out!"

"But—"

"Out, Leon!"

He stomped out. Poor kid. Leon so desperately wanted to be special. He wasn't strong and large like his brother. He didn't have Bern's magic talent. He didn't excel academically like Bern did. Bern was a wrestling star in high school and a lot of people had come to his matches. Leon ran track. Nobody cared about track except for people who did it. Some people in his place would've hated their older brother, but Leon loved Bern with an almost puppy-like devotion. When Bern succeeded at something, Leon nearly burst with pride.

When he was little, I used to read baby books to him. One of them was about a puppy lost in the forest, with a picture of a small golden puppy among tall dark trees. Both Leon and Arabella inevitably bawled when we came to that part. Behind all of that sarcasm, he was still that little sensitive kid with big eyes. I just wished his magic would show up already.

Chapter 7

I sat in near absolute darkness. Around me the cave stretched on, deep, deep into the black. Watching me. Breathing cold that seeped into my bones. The jungle waited around the bend of the brown wall. Something stalked within it, something with long vicious teeth. I couldn't see it or hear it, but I knew it was there, waiting. Other shapes rested next to me, swathes of deeper blackness. They knew it too.

The cave breathed. Something was biting my legs and I knew it was ticks and I should pick them off, but moving seemed too hard. I was too tired.

The sniffers were out there, waiting for the faintest splash of magic. Desperation had passed. Emotions too. We were numb animals now, trying to get from point A to point B. Animals who didn't speak, who communicated with glances, and who moved as one.

A watery green light to the left announced someone had sacrificed a glowstick. The shapes around me shifted, drawn like moths to this pathetic ghost of a real fire, starved, filthy, stretching hands to each other looking for some human touch in the nightmare.

A smaller shape scuttled to the side and fell under

*someone's knife. Another squeaked and died. Rats. At
least we'd eat tonight . . .*

I sat upright in my bed. The shreds of the nightmare
floated around me, melting. I groped for the lamp on the
night table and flicked it on with trembling fingers. The
welcome electric glow flared into life. My phone next to it
told me it was almost two in the morning.

I wasn't in a horrible cave. I was in my bedroom.

I felt clammy all over. I'd had nightmares before, but
this was different. Oppressive, chilling, and hopeless.
My room didn't seem real, but the cave was. It was very
real and it waited for me just beyond these walls. I was
trapped.

I shuddered.

Pulling the blanket to my chest and clenching it didn't
seem to fix my freak-out.

I peered around the bedroom with wide eyes. There
was no way I could go back to sleep. There was no turning off the light either. My stomach growled. I'd gone to
bed without dinner. I'd been too tired to eat.

Okay, sitting in bed and shivering really didn't accomplish anything. What I needed was to get out and go
downstairs to our clean modern kitchen, and drink a hot
cup of chamomile tea and eat something that didn't look
like a rat. Possibly a cookie. Cookies were as un-ratlike
as you could get.

I pulled the blanket back, put on a pair of yoga pants,
and opened my door, half expecting to see the cave walls.

No cave. No secret enemy with terrifying teeth waiting
in the darkness. Just the familiar warehouse.

I tiptoed down the ladder and went along the hallway
toward the kitchen. The above-the-table lamp was on and
warm electric light pooled at the doorway. Rogan sat at
the table, a laptop open in front of him. He leaned forward, his chin resting on his chest. His eyes were closed.

He dwarfed the chair. He was so well proportioned it was easy to forget how big he was. His shoulders were huge and broad, his chest powerful, his arms made to crush and rip his opponents.

His hair wasn't really long enough to be tousled, but it looked unbrushed and messy. Dark stubble touched his jaw. He'd lost some of that killer efficiency that made him so terrifying. He was human and slightly rough. I could picture him looking just like that, stretched out on a bed, as I climbed in there next to him.

Mad Rogan in his off mode. All of his titles—Prime, war hero, billionaire, major, butcher, scourge—lay at his feet, discarded. Only Connor remained, and he was so unbearably sexy.

I could just turn around and go back the way I'd come, but I wanted him to open his eyes and talk to me. My mother taught me that former soldiers could fall sleep anywhere, in any position. And they didn't react well to being surprised.

"Rogan," I called from the door. "Rogan, wake up?"

He awoke instantly, going from deep sleep to complete awareness in a blink, as if someone had thrown a switch. Blue eyes regarded me. "Problems?"

"No."

I walked into the kitchen. Electric kettle or single-use coffeemaker? Coffeemaker was faster. I took a cup out of the cabinet, dropped the tea bag into it, and watched as the coffeemaker poured hot water over it.

He checked his laptop. "What are you doing up? I thought we agreed that you would rest."

"I had a nightmare." I extracted the jar of cookies from the pantry and brought it and my tea to the table.

He straightened, squaring his shoulders, stretching slightly. The chair couldn't have been comfortable.

"What are you doing?" I peeked at his laptop. A shot of

the video with the Suburban passing our Range Rover, ice frosting the road behind it. He must've been going frame by frame through it, trying to see some clues he missed.

"Bug is really good at this sort of thing, you know," I told him.

"I know." He pushed the laptop away. Drowsiness still hid in the corners of his blue eyes.

A cup of coffee sat in front of him. I stole it.

"I wasn't finished with that."

"It's cold. I'll warm it up so you will have something to drink. You can't eat cookies without a drink." I stuck the mug into the microwave. "Why aren't you asleep on your air mattress?"

"I was working. What happened in your nightmare?"

The microwave beeped and I took the cup out and placed it in front of him.

"I was trapped in a cave. It was cold and dark. Something scary was waiting outside and then someone killed a rat, and I knew we were going to eat it."

I shuddered and sipped my tea. It was almost scalding, but I didn't care.

"I'm sorry," he said.

"It's not your fault." I opened the plastic cookie jar, extracted a fat chocolate chip cookie, and offered it to him. He snagged it and bit into it.

"Good cookies."

"Mhm." I broke my cookie in half and bit one piece. There are times in life when sugar turns into medicine. This was one of those times.

"Did you make these?"

"Ha. I wish. It was probably Catalina. I can't cook."

He frowned at me. "What do you mean, you can't cook?"

"Well, I can make good panini, but that's about it. The way I look at it, someone has to put the food on the table and someone has to cook it. I'm the put-it-on-the-table type."

He was looking at me oddly.

"Can you cook, Mr. I-Am-Prime?"

"Yes."

"Don't you have people for that?"

"I like to know what's in my food."

I propped my elbow on the table and leaned my chin on my hand. "Who taught you to cook?" He wouldn't tell me, but any little glimpse into him was worth taking a chance.

"My mother. One summer when she was six, her family was celebrating her older sister's birthday back in Spain. Her sister loved cream puffs so the caterer brought a tower of cream puffs drizzled with chocolate and strands of sugar. It was the best thing my mother had ever seen up to that point."

His voice was quiet, almost intimate. I could just sit here and listen to him talk all night.

"As adults were putting candles on the tower, her five-year-old cousin stole a cream puff and ate it. My mother was outraged, because the cream puffs belonged to her sister, so she slapped him. His sister, Marguerite, took offense to the slap. They had a brawl right there on the lawn. Half of the children started fighting, the other half cried, and everyone was sent to their rooms without dessert. The tower was covered with plastic, because their mother was determined to still have the celebration once everyone calmed down. The cousin died half an hour later."

My heart dropped. "Poisoned."

Rogan nodded. "They were involved in a long feud with another House."

"They targeted the children?"

"Children are the future of any House. When my mother was fourteen, she killed the person responsible. She collapsed their summer villa."

Somehow that didn't surprise me.

"My mother cooked all of my food herself from ingredients she grew or purchased. So I eventually learned to make my own. Who do you think made that enormous stack of pancakes Augustine had to eat for his initiation?"

"Did you put anything weird into those pancakes?"

"No. That wouldn't be fair." He grinned at me. It was a sharp, amused grin that made him appear wolfish. "The real question here is would you like me to cook something for you?"

"Like what?"

"What are you in the mood for?"

Sex.

Rogan leaned forward, muscles rolling under the sleeves of his T-shirt. His face took on a speculative expression. There was something slightly predatory about the way he focused on me; it wasn't the fear of being in the presence of a man who posed real danger. It was the feeling of being in the presence of a man who was about to try to seduce me. Anticipation zinged through me. Had he actually plucked the impression of my lust out of my head? Maybe it was just a coincidence.

He reached over.

I tensed.

His fingers slid so close to mine, I thought for a moment we touched. He stole the remaining half of my cookie and looked at it.

"That's mine," I told him.

"Mhm."

"There is a whole jar of cookies."

A light sparked in his eyes. "I want this one."

"You can't have this one. Give it back." I held out my hand.

He examined the cookie and slowly raised it to his mouth.

"Connor, don't you dare."

He bit the cookie and chewed it. "I took your cookie and ate it. Are you going to do something about it?"

I was playing with fire. Fine. He ate my cookies, I'd drink his drink. I reached for his coffee. It slid out of my reach and settled next to him.

"Not fair."

"This isn't about fair. This is about delicious cookies."

"In that case, that will be your last." I grabbed the jar and put it in front of me. It shot straight up and hung above us. My half-empty teacup took off like a rocket and landed on the far end of the island. *Okay, enough is enough.* This was my kitchen.

I jumped up and marched around the table.

He surged up and his arms closed about me, catching me. His touch was light, but I knew with absolute certainty that there was no getting away. He had me.

Only two thin layers of fabric separated me from him. I wasn't even wearing a bra. My breasts brushed against the hard wall of his chest. My hands rested on his shoulders. A low, insistent feeling began to build between my legs. I wanted to be touched and stroked.

He was looking at me like I was the most beautiful thing in the world.

"What are we doing?" I asked. My voice came out quiet.

"You know exactly what we're doing."

His breathing deepened. Need and lust swirled in his eyes. I searched their depths for the familiar icy darkness, but it was gone. I had chased it away. He was focused on me completely and I drank it in. Oh, I wanted him.

I slid my hands up his arms, feeling the hard cables of muscle tense and bulge under the pressure. He made a low male noise but didn't move. His body was hard with tension against mine, but he didn't move an inch.

It dawned on me that he was waiting for me to decide.

"You're being very patient."

"I can be a good dragon, when the occasion requires it."

I licked my lips. His gaze snagged on my tongue.

I had to decide. I couldn't stand it any longer. Either we did this, or I needed to march back upstairs. I was a grown woman, damn it. I'd almost died less than twelve hours ago and he was here, protecting me, making sure my family survived the night. He didn't have to do it. Maybe he was a sociopath, but if he was, for some reason, I mattered to him. In this moment, right now, he belonged to me.

"This one time, maybe you shouldn't be."

"I shouldn't be what?" he asked.

"Maybe you shouldn't be so good."

He spun me around. My back pressed against the kitchen wall. His big muscular body caged me in. His blue eyes laughed at me. "How bad am I allowed to be?"

"I don't know. Let's find out."

"Try not to scream." He winked at me.

His magic touched my skin just above the knee, a familiar heated velvet pressure. His arms stroked mine, pinning them against the wall. *Try not to scream, huh. Aren't we full of ourselves . . .*

The pressure burst, prickling my skin with raspy heat. Oh my God.

I gasped and his mouth sealed mine, stealing the sound. The taste of him flooded my senses, overloading me. I wanted my hands on him, but he held me tight, pinning my wrists against the wall with his left hand.

His magic stroked my skin and slid sideways, to the sensitive spot on my inner thigh just above my knee. It felt rough, a little like a burn, a little like pain, and a lot like pleasure. It lingered and slid up, higher and higher, setting my sensitive skin and nerves on fire. My head spun. I wanted sex. I wanted him inside me, right now. I wanted to feel the full length of him stretching me and feel his body shudder on top of mine.

I moaned into his lips. He kissed me, pillaging my mouth, the slick heat of his tongue taking over, and I teased him with my tongue, nipping at his lower lip. My breasts felt heavy and full; my body turned pliant. He was all hard muscle and rigid strength, and I stretched myself against him, seducing, enticing. He groaned.

The magic spilled over my inner thigh and licked the sensitive lips around my clit with its velvet tongue. Pleasure washed over me. I cried out. He caught it with his mouth, smothering the sound.

The heat was building between my legs, a crazy mix of pain and ecstasy. I was breathing too fast and I wanted more of him.

Please. Please, more. Please.

"Shhh, baby," he whispered into my ear, his voice rough with desire. He kissed me again and again, trailing a line of kisses down my neck. Each touch of his lips sent bursts of electric shocks through me. His gaze roamed my body. "You're so beautiful. You have no idea."

I wanted to see more of him. "Let me go, Connor," I whispered.

He hesitated for a moment and released me.

I pulled his shirt off and looked at him, taking in the solid strength of his shoulders, the powerful chest, and the flat hard lines of his stomach in a single supercharged second. The sheer physical power of him was overwhelming. He had the kind of body that made women sigh because they knew they would never be able to touch it. And here it was, all mine. Not a fantasy. Not an image on the screen. Right here, the reality.

His hands caught my T-shirt. He pulled it off, picked me up, and slid my ass onto the kitchen table, sliding between my thighs. My nipples were cold and as he pulled me to him, they mashed against the heated wall of his chest.

I wrapped my arms around him, feeling the muscles of his back roll in response to the pressure of my fingers. I was so far gone I felt like I was drunk.

He was kissing my throat, trailing a line of heat down my neck. I found his lips and kissed him, quickly, deeply. I was in a hurry.

"Say my name again," he growled into my ear.

The magic licked me, each stroke pushing me higher and higher. My skin burned in its wake as if slapped. It was beyond anything I'd ever tried, but it felt so good. Aaaaah . . . Please, please, please please please . . .

"Say my name, Nevada."

"Connor."

The magic drenched me, wringing pleasure from me. I felt on fire. I dug my nails into his back. This was sweet torture and I didn't want it to end. He bent down, his rough fingers teasing my nipples. His mouth closed on one tight aching bud and he sucked.

I arched my back against the liquid tease of his tongue. More. More.

We were about to have sex on the kitchen table. Some part of me insisted I should care, but it was so hard to hear it.

I found his belt, undid it, and reached inside.

Oh dear God. I might need two hands.

He made a harsh male noise and I slid my hand up and down the shaft of his cock, pumping the smooth skin . . .

His phone screeched.

"Fuck!" Rogan grabbed the phone. "What?"

A brisk male voice spat out the words, loud enough that even I heard it. *"Semi and four ATVs coming fast."*

Shit. ATVs, light armored vehicles, served as the armed forces' version of a Jeep. They carried personnel and each sat four people and sometimes a gunner, which meant more than a dozen attackers were coming our way. We were about to have company. I grabbed my shirt and threw Rogan's at him. He caught it with one hand. "Which direction?"

"They just turned onto the west access road."

The access road let trucks roll up to the back of the warehouses. We used it for tanks and armored vehicle transport. They'd hit us from the motor pool side.

"Correction, not a semi. A tanker truck."

Better and better.

"ETA?" Rogan barked.

"Sixty seconds."

Rogan ran for the motor pool, pulling his shirt on.

I ran to the alarm console and hit the internal panic button. A loud metallic screech rolled through the warehouse. I pressed the intercom's button. "A tanker truck and four ATVs coming at us from the west access road."

I ran for the motor pool. The two industrial garage doors were up, the light of the street lamp spilling through the rectangular bays. Rogan strode into the pool of light and went down the street. Unarmed.

I keyed the correct sequence into the laptop and the feed from four cameras flared up. I pushed the intercom. "I'm in the motor pool."

Grandma Frida burst through the door in her yellow rubber-ducky pajamas.

"Grandma's here," I added.

"In position," my mother reported.

"I'm up," Bernard said from his post in the Hut of Evil.

"We have Matilda and Cornelius," Catalina reported.

I heard the roar of a tanker truck picking up speed. Out of time.

I need stopping power. I grabbed an AA-12 shotgun from the weapon cage, unlocked the ammo cage, and slapped the twenty-shell drum containing high-explosive Frag-12 shells and grabbed a grenade.

Out of the corner of my eye, I saw Grandma Frida yank the tarp off of Romeo. Romeo's real name was M551 Sheridan. He was a light armored tank. He carried nine anti-tank Shillelagh missiles, and Grandma Frida kept him in perfect health.

I sprinted to the garage door and stuck my head out. The truck tore toward us on the access road, making no effort to slow down. An oblong cistern loomed behind the green cab. There was no telling what the hell was in that cistern. At this speed, the truck could ram the warehouse and rip through the walls like paper and whatever it was hauling would spill over.

I couldn't let it get to the warehouse.

Behind me Romeo growled into life. It required a four-person crew to effectively operate—a tank commander, a loader, a gunner, and a driver. By the time Grandma swung it around, the tanker truck would have hit us.

Rogan strode down the road. Apparently he'd decided to play chicken with the tanker.

I ran after him. If I could toss a grenade under it, I'd derail it before it reached the warehouse.

The tanker roared toward us.

Twenty yards between the tanker and Rogan.

Fifteen.

"Get out of the road!" I yelled.

Ten yards.

"Connor!"

The truck smashed into empty air. Its hood bent, crushed by an invisible hammer, and tore. The black engine parts bulged out, as if the truck was trying to vomit, and disintegrated from the impact. The top part of its cab folded on itself. Its windshield exploded in a thousand shards, spilling over the exposed motor.

Holy crap.

The tanker truck still revved, trying to push its way forward. Its tires spun, spitting acrid smoke, and burst like two loud gunshots.

Behind us the tank engine growled. I glanced over my shoulder. Romeo tore out of the garage bay and turned left, away from us and the truck, going around the corner to the other side of the warehouse. The attack force must've split.

The truck's engine snapped, crying and screeching, and began to turn back in on itself, folding. The metal popped, groaned, snarled, folding tighter, and collapsing backward, from the front of the hood toward the cab.

I stopped in spite of myself as my brain tried to make sense of what I was seeing.

He was rolling the truck up like a half-empty tube of toothpaste.

A loud thud echoed through the night. Grandma Frida fired Romeo.

Rogan took a step forward. The truck slid back.

Another step. Another slide.

The cistern exploded. The blast wave punched me. I flew back as a colossal ball of fire roared up, blossoming against the night sky, brilliant white in the center, then yellow, then deep ugly orange. I curled into a ball trying to shield my head. The pavement slapped my back and side. Ow. Something in my spine crunched. Chunks of burning pallets clattered around me.

Gasoline didn't burn when shot. You could unload a full magazine into a car with a full tank and it would just sit there. They must've rigged the cistern to remotely detonate. That huge fireball had been meant for my family.

A piece of wood smashed against my arms, burning. Shit. I kicked the chunk of a broken pallet off of me and jumped to my feet.

The street was empty, except for the massive fire. Where was Rogan? Was he dead? *Please don't be dead . . .*

The fire growled like an animal. Wind howled and the fireball snapped up, shaping into a tornado of flames. The tornado spun and slid sideways like some crazy colossal spin top. The light of its fire illuminated the warehouse across the street, and I saw Rogan pressed into the narrow alcove next to the AC units.

The tornado edged closer to him.

If the whirlwind of flames found him, he'd burn alive. The mage controlling the tornado had to be down the street in one of the ATVs that had been following the tanker truck.

I jumped the concrete barrier separating me from the twin squat buildings of OKR Industries and dashed through the narrow gap between them. Thunder cracked behind me. The air smelled of ozone.

The gap ended. I glanced around the corner. In front of me, two people in tactical gear and armed with automatic weapons stood on the edge of the street, hidden from Rogan by the front OKR building. The third, in the mage pose—arms bent at the elbow, palms up—floated three feet above the pavement. An aerokinetic.

Behind them, on the street, one ATV was a crushed mess, with a chunk of the truck's cistern sticking out of its smashed windshield. Past it, thick steel bars blocked the street. I was one hundred percent sure they hadn't been there when I drove home.

"He has to be near that building. Swing it more to the right," a man next to the mage said, his voice accented.

I took a deep breath, steadying myself. I should've brought the rifle instead.

"That's it. Cook him."

I braced myself, put the shotgun to my shoulder, and

fired. The automatic shotgun barked, spitting death. An AA-12 combat shotgun fired three hundred rounds per minute. Each three-inch cartridge in the drum held a tiny warhead that armed itself three meters after it left the muzzle and exploded on impact.

I put two rounds into the mage before he realized what was happening. The high explosive ripped his body apart, tearing through flesh. He didn't even scream. He just fell, but I was already swinging the shotgun around at his friends. Five rounds left the muzzle. The other two bodies jerked and went down without a word, turned into human meat.

The other side of the street erupted with gunfire. Bullets buzzed, biting chunks from the building around me. I ducked back into the gap. Five rounds for two people at that range was overkill. My adrenaline was too high. I had to calm down or I would panic and then I'd die.

I grabbed the grenade, jerked the firing pin out, and hurled it across the street. The loud boom of the explosion echoed through the night. I leaned out and ducked back in as a bullet grazed my shoulder, like a red-hot bee. *Didn't get them. Damn it.*

To the right of me, the wind mage twitched on the ground, convulsing. He should've been dead. How was he not dead?

The fiery tornado swung into my view, zigzagging wildly all over the parking lot. It veered toward me. Unbearable heat stole all the air, as if a bonfire had exhaled into my face. It hurt to breathe. I backed away through the gap.

The mage still twitched. I raised the shotgun and fired. The round took him in the head. The fire loomed over me and rained down. I sprinted back out of the gap toward my home and burst into the parking lot.

Behind our warehouse, on the other side of the building, lightning cut the sky, flashing again and again, answering a steady staccato of gunfire. On the street, the remnants of the tanker truck burned, the orange flames fighting with the darkness.

Shots ripped through the night. I spun around. It was probably the same people who'd shot at me from across the street when I took out the mage. They weren't shooting at me this time. They couldn't see me behind the building, so Rogan had to be the target.

A twisted chunk of truck cab shot down the street, as if launched from a cannon. Metal clanged and the shots died. Ha!

I turned and saw him pressed against a building across the street. He slumped over. Shot? Fear gripped me. No, no blood. Not shot. Tired. Rogan was spent.

Shadows leaped over the remnants of the cistern, illuminated for half a second by the flames. Hairless, wrinkled, about four feet tall, they didn't look human. Nor did they look like any animal I had ever seen. Their legs bent backward, like the hind appendages of some demonic grasshopper, while the front of their bodies curved up, ending in two muscled arms equipped with two claws longer than my hand and a dinosaur head with round yellow eyes and a forest of teeth.

Holy crap.

The front creature let out a gleeful bloodthirsty screech. As one, the pack spun toward Rogan's hiding place.

Oh no, you don't.

I jerked my shotgun up and fired.

The first round took the leading creature in the stomach. It kept coming. I squeezed the trigger and kept firing. The Frag-12 rounds chewed through the monster flesh, shredding their bodies. Strange intestines spilled out. An awful sour stench polluted the air. The creatures fell, one, two, three . . . Seven rounds gone.

The leading beast was too close to Rogan. If I aimed for it, I'd hit him. The creature leaped almost ten feet, flying at Rogan, his black claws poised to rend into flesh. Rogan sidestepped like his joints were liquid. A knife flashed in his hand. He dodged and buried his knife in the beast's side. The creature flailed, ripping a gash across Rogan's chest. Rogan kept stabbing with brutal efficiency, sinking the blade into the wrinkled alien body again and again, slashed its throat, and dropped it aside, his knife bloody.

Only twenty yards separated me from the last three creatures. They turned and charged me. I fired twice. The shotgun clicked, empty, the drum spent, one beast unmoving on the ground.

The first beast leaped, claws raised like sickles. I jumped aside and swung the shotgun like a club. The shotgun connected, but the beast was too huge. I might have hit it with a fly swatter for all the good it did me. The creature whirled.

A chunk of metal smashed into its side, sweeping it off its feet. Rogan.

The second beast rammed into me, its claws locking onto my shotgun. I hit the pavement with my back and clamped the shotgun with both hands, trying to keep it between us. Across the street Rogan was running to me.

The dinosaurian jaws gaped open. The monster reared, about to plunge for the kill.

A dark lean body flew above me. Bunny's teeth flashed and locked onto the creature's throat. The Doberman swung its body, throwing all of its weight into the bite. The wrinkled flesh of the beast's neck tore. Bunny landed on the pavement, snarling. I scrambled upright.

The monster shuddered, dazed, shook its head . . . The creature's skull exploded with red. My ears almost didn't register the shot.

Mom.

Two more shots cracked, one, two, with barely a pause. The first took the last creature in midleap as it tried to carve Rogan's chest. The other shot took down someone out of my view.

The night was still.

Rogan stood ten feet away from me, looking like he hadn't gotten enough blood on his hands. The sudden silence was deafening.

It was over.

"Sixteen people," Rogan's right-hand man in charge of the warehouse defense crew reported.

His name was Michael Rivera and he had the athletic build of an MMA lightweight fighter—he could pass for a normal man until he flexed and then you realized that he could break your bones with his bare hands. Rivera was in his mid-thirties, Latino, with medium brown skin, dark hair, and an absurdly jovial, kind smile. When he grinned, his whole face lit up. Since he was smiling at eleven corpses neatly laid out in a row on our street, the smile was alarming.

Rogan watched with a dispassionate face. He'd promised me that if anyone disturbed my rest, they would sleep forever. He'd kept it. A long gash snaked its way across his chest, currently covered by a bandage. The wound had looked shallow, but there was no telling what sort of bacteria and poison rode on that creature's claws. I'd gotten away with a gash on my thigh and some scrapes on my lower back. The medic that had cleaned and treated our wounds hovered protectively near Rogan, ready to spring into action but trying to stay out of his direct line of sight.

My sisters and cousins stood just outside, huddled together. Arabella covered her mouth with her hand. Catalina's eyes were huge. She looked completely freaked out. Bernard was solemn enough for a funeral. Leon, for some bizarre reason, seemed excited, like he'd just ridden a roller coaster. My mother leaned in the doorway. Grandma Frida had ducked into the motor pool for something and was taking her time coming back.

Cornelius knelt by the corpses of the beasts, lost in thought. Matilda sat on the side, on some pallets, with Bunny. When I objected to her presence in view of the dead bodies, Cornelius patiently told me that they were dead and couldn't hurt her and that this was her heritage and she needed to know. She didn't seem disturbed by it, which in itself was enough to unsettle anyone with a conscience.

"Eleven dead here," Rivera said. "Two burned up in the ATV Mrs. Afram shot with her tank. We're gathering the body parts. Two we can't recover until equipment gets here because Major dropped a truck engine on them and we can't move it. Then we have seven MCMs."

"Seven what?" I asked.

"Magically Created Monsters," my mother said. "It covers all nonhuman combatants of unknown origin."

"These are not Earth animals," Cornelius said. "This is something pulled from the astral realm by a summoner."

Great. Just great.

"Of these eleven, three magic users," Rivera continued. "The summoner, the fulgurkinetic, and the aerokinetic."

"Elementalist," Rogan corrected. "An aerokinetic would've made the tornado, but couldn't twist fire into one."

Elementalists were rare. They controlled more than one element, usually air in conjunction with water or fire. They almost never reached the rank of Prime, but even at Average level, they were dangerous as hell.

It finally sank in. Someone really had tried to kill my family. They had come in with professional soldiers, military equipment, and heavy-hitter mages. Nausea swelled in me. My stomach tried to clench and empty itself. Now was so not the time.

An armored car rounded the corner behind us. Two of Rogan's people got out and dragged a man into view, half carrying, half walking him.

"And number sixteen," Rivera said, his voice precise. "Who tried to flee in the last ATV. We got ourselves a coward. We love cowards."

"Why?" Leon asked.

"They talk," Rogan said. His voice sent icy shivers down my spine.

They dropped the man in a heap on the ground. Dark-skinned, bleeding, he was somewhere between thirty and fifty. With all the soot covering his face it was hard to tell.

I glanced at Cornelius.

"Matilda," he said. "Please go inside."

"I'll keep an eye on her," Catalina said. Her voice squeaked. She picked Matilda up and took off inside at a near run.

"Leon, Arabella, inside," my mother said.

"But . . ." Leon began.

"Now."

They went into the warehouse.

The man stared at me, his face twisted with fear.

"What's your name?" I asked.

He pressed his lips together.

"I can compel you to respond," I said. "I really don't want to. Please just answer my questions."

Sweat broke out on his forehead and ran down, leaving a clean track in the soot. I pushed with my magic. Strong will. He looked tough, like he had been through more than one interrogation before and it had just made him harder. He wasn't posturing and he wasn't making any promises. He just stayed silent. This one would need a careful interrogation. Antonio had needed a punch; this man required a scalpel.

Rivera glanced at Rogan. Rogan shook his head.

"Chalk?" I asked.

Rogan reached into his pocket and pulled some out.

"Why didn't you draw any circles when the truck was coming?" I asked.

"Because they would've veered off course," Rogan said. "They had a plan. I wanted them to stick to it."

Because nobody would expect one man to stop a tanker truck. A Prime in a circle was another matter. I crouched and drew an amplification circle on the ground: small ring around my feet, larger one around that, and three sets of runes in between. Rogan watched with a pained expression. Primes practiced circlework since birth. My circles made his brain hurt.

I straightened and held the chalk out to him. "Thank you."

I pulled the magic to myself and shot it into the circle. It reverberated back into me as if I had bounced on a magic trampoline. I kept bouncing. One, two, three, each jump stronger than the last. Four. Should be enough.

My magic snapped out and clamped the man in its grip. My voice gained inhuman strength. *"Tell me your name."*

Rivera's eyes went wide. All around us Rogan's people took a few steps back.

The man froze, gripped tight by my magic.

"Rendani Mulaudzi."

"What is your profession, Mr. Mulaudzi?"

"Mercenary."

His breath was coming in shallow puffs. I'd been practicing on my family. My sisters were only too willing to cooperate. It was a game. They tried to keep from telling me the truth and I learned how to do it carefully. This man's will was strong, but Arabella's was stronger. Sometimes she passed out rather than break, and before she did, her heart rate sped up and she started to hyperventilate. I'd have to watch him.

"What is the name of the company that hired you for this raid?"

"Scorpion Protection Services."

"How long have you worked for Scorpion?"

"Six years."

"What were you before?"

"Recces."

"South African Special Forces," Rogan said.

No wonder he was strong-willed. He wasn't that young either, which meant he must've done at least a few years in the military and then survived six years as a mercenary.

"Where is Scorpion headquartered?"

"In Johannesburg."

South Africa. He was a long way from home.

"How big is Scorpion?"

"It has four tactical teams, sixteen to twenty members each."

"How many teams are involved in this mission?"

"One."

"Were you hired specifically for this mission?"

"Yes."

"Who hired you?"

"I don't know."

"Who would know?"

"My team leader."

"What is his name?"

"Christopher van Sittert."

"Do you see him among the dead?"

"Yes."

Of course. It couldn't be that easy, could it? "Point to him, Mr. Mulaudzi."

He pointed to one of the corpses.

"What was the objective of this mission?"

"To eliminate the following targets: Nevada Baylor, Cornelius Harrison, Penelope Baylor, Frida Afram, and Bernard Baylor within twenty-four hours of arrival."

I'd never been number one on anyone's hit list before. "What about the minors present in the house?"

"Their lives were left to our discretion. We weren't paid to kill them."

"Were you planning on killing the children?"

"I don't know."

The question had been too general. "Did you personally plan to kill the children?"

"Nevada," Rogan said softly.

I raised my hand, warning him off. This was important to me.

"Not unless they presented a threat."

"Do you bear any personal animosity to the targets you listed?"

"No."

I glanced at Rogan. "Before we go any further, he is a mercenary; he was hired to do a job and he failed. He is now unarmed and a prisoner."

Rogan's eyes were dark. "You don't want me to kill him."

"No. I would like you to send him back to Scorpion wrapped up like a Christmas present. If their whole team disappears, they will have to send someone to investigate. I don't want them coming back. This way, they don't have to wonder. He'll tell them that they came here armed and ready to kill, and we let only one of them live. They're mercenaries. I want them to understand that it isn't cost effective to continue this fight."

"Be careful," Rogan said. "You're thinking like a Prime." I waited.

"Very well," he said. "We'll ship him back to his friends."

"What do you want to know?" I asked.

"Ask him when he was hired."

"When were you hired?"

"December 14th."

Cornelius hired me on December 14th. That seemed really fast.

"Doesn't make sense," Rivera murmured. "Johannesburg to Houston is at least a twenty-hour flight."

"Where were you when you received the orders for this mission?" I asked.

"Monterrey, Mexico."

"What were you doing there?" The pauses between his replies were getting longer and longer. I would have to let him go soon.

"We had an alternative mission in Montemorelos. We were rerouted."

"Montemorelos to Houston is a two-hour trip. They pulled them off a job," my mother said. "They needed a team from out of town that couldn't be traced to any existing House. The Scorpion team was likely the closest."

"Describe your actions since arriving to Houston, Mr. Mulaudzi."

"We arrived to Houston airport via Aeromexico Flight 2094. We proceeded to the base of operations."

Rogan raised his hand. "Was the base set up by them or third party?"

I repeated the question.

"The base was prepared by a third party. We were issued weapons and gear and attended the briefing showing recon of the warehouse and the surrounding area. We formed a battle plan. We waited until the optimal time and executed the plan. The attack failed."

No kidding.

"What is the address of this base?"

He gave the address in Spring, one of the little towns

Houston had gobbled up as it grew, about forty minutes north of us. Rivera took off at a run. Three of Rogan's people peeled off and followed him.

"Anything else?" I asked Rogan.

He shook his head.

I let the mercenary go. He collapsed on the ground and rolled into a ball, covering his face. His body shook and an unsettling low sound came from him. He was sobbing. I had opened his mind with my magic can opener, scooped out the contents, and displayed them for all to see. It was a deep violation of his person.

People were staring at me, their eyes brimming with fear. A couple of them gripped their weapons in alarm. I had horrified the professional soldiers. I looked at my mother. Sadness softened her face, her mouth slack.

It hit me. I was the monster on the street. Without me, they would've questioned and even tortured this veteran mercenary. They would've done it with the understanding that he would resist and he wouldn't have faulted them for it, because in their place he would've done the same. There was a twisted kind of professional courtesy about it all. But me, I didn't torture. I broke his will without even breathing hard. Each one of them could see themselves in the mercenary's place. I could make them tell me all their secrets and that was more frightening than Rogan stopping a massive tanker truck at full speed.

I'd never felt so alone in my whole life.

Rogan stepped between me and them, his eyes full of something. Whatever it was—pride? Admiration? Love?—I held on to it like it was a lifeline. He understood. At some point in his life he had stood just like that, while people stared at him in horror, and he must've felt alone, because now he was here, and he was shielding me from their judgment.

"You're amazing," Connor Rogan said and smiled.

For some unfathomable reason Bernard had let Leon operate the remote cameras during the attack. They had an almost 180-degree rotation on their mounts and you could point them with precision, which was exactly what Leon had done during the fight. I was now in the motor pool, watching the recorded feed on Grandma Frida's computer. Rogan and Cornelius both stood next to me, watching over my shoulder.

Leon had decided that the video needed narration and provided running commentary as it was being recorded. Apparently, he found the whole thing incredibly exciting.

The camera panned to capture two ATVs approaching from the north.

"Oh yeah, we got ourselves a badass killer vehicle," my cousin's voice came from the speakers. *"We're so cool, we're so cool, we're going to roll up and kill everybody. Wait, what? Oh no, is that a tank? It is a tank. It's headed straight for us. Run, run, run . . . Too late. Hehehe."*

The front ATV exploded, taking a missile from Romeo straight on. The second vehicle swerved and screeched to a stop on a narrow side street next to the automotive shop, out of Romeo's sight. People in tactical gear jumped out and ran into the night, looking for cover.

Leon zoomed in on the man in his forties on the right, who'd crouched by the ATV. *"I'm a veteran badass. I've seen bad shit. I've done bad shit. I've survived five months in a jungle eating pinecones and killing terrorists with a pair of old chopsticks. I'm one bad motherfucker."*

Behind me Rogan laughed.

"I've got two days to retirement. After I kill everyone here, I'll go to my retirement party. They'll serve shrimp on crackers and give me a gold watch, and then, I'm going to have my midlife crisis and buy a Porsche and . . . Oh shit, my head just exploded."

Either my mother or someone on Rivera's team had found the mercenary's head. Blood and brains splattered on the ATV.

The camera swung wildly to the right to a woman advancing toward the warehouse. She had gone to ground by the oak, hidden by the low stone wall bordering the tree.

"I'm death. I'm a ghost. I'll find you. You can run, you can hide, you can beg, but none of it will help you. I'll come for you in the darkness like a lithe panther with velvet paws and steel claws and . . . wait, brains, wait, where are you going? Why are you all leaking out of my head? Don't leave me!"

I put my hand over my eyes.

"Oh no, look—my feet are twitching. That's so undignified."

I would kill Bern for letting him do this. And then I would have a serious talk with Leon.

"Your cousin has an interesting sense of humor," Cornelius noted.

"I'm Mr. Ripped," the computer announced in Leon's voice. I didn't even want to look anymore. *"I live in the gym. My teeth have biceps and my biceps have teeth. I chew up weights and shit out lead bricks."*

Rogan's face turned speculative.

"Don't," I told him.

"In about three years or so, I could use him. He's demonstrating a very specific moral flexibility . . ."

"I'll shoot you myself," I told him.

Grandma Frida tore into the motor pool from the street, followed by an Asian woman in her late twenties. The woman wore Rogan's team's tactical gear. My grandma wore her "talk to the hand" face. She also carried a can of spray paint in her hand.

"What is it, Hanh?" Rogan asked.

"She marked all of the ATVs with her initials!" Hanh declared.

"Because they're mine," Grandma Frida growled.

"She doesn't get all the ATVs."

Rogan's face took on a very patient look.

"Yes, I do. I tagged them, they're mine."

"Just because you tagged them doesn't mean they're yours. I can walk into this motor pool and start tagging things left and right. That doesn't make them mine."

"Aha." My grandma picked up a huge wrench and casually leaned it on her shoulder. "How are you going to tag things with broken arms?"

"Don't threaten me." Hanh turned to Rogan. "She can't have all of them."

"Yes, I can," Grandma Frida put in before Rogan could open his mouth. "The enemy attacked our position; it's an emergency, and since I'm the acting platoon sergeant for this family, I'm requisitioning my Class VII supplies. They're on our land."

"Those three ATVs are on your land. The one down on the access road is on our land," Hanh said.

"Nguyen, let her have the ATVs," Rogan said.

Hanh opened her mouth to argue and clamped it shut.

"Ha!" Grandma Frida pointed her wrench at Hanh.

"Grandma . . ." I started. "If that other vehicle is on their land . . ."

Wait a minute.

I pivoted toward Rogan. "What does she mean that ATV is on your land?"

Hanh froze.

Rogan looked like he wanted to strangle somebody.

"Rogan?"

He was thinking of a clever way to phrase his answer.

"Did you buy property adjacent to this warehouse?"

He closed his eyes for a second, then looked at me, and said, "Yes."

"How much property did you buy?"

"Some."

I stared at him. "Could you be more specific?"

"Everything between Gessner, Clay, Blalock, and Hempstead."

Dear God. That was almost two square miles of industrial real estate and our warehouse was sitting smack in the middle of his land. Every day I drove past these businesses and nothing seemed different.

"When did you buy this land?"

"I started the day Adam Pierce was arrested."

"Why would you do this?"

"Because you live in the middle of an industrial jungle, Nevada." His face was hard. "You have a number of small roads, you have industrial traffic going through here, and there are about a thousand places one could hide a strike team. I bought it because there is no way to effectively secure this location."

"And you've secured it?" I had diagnosed him as a control freak long ago, but this was going too far.

"Yes. Now this area is patrolled, equipped with structure defenses, and secured by armed personnel."

"No, Rogan. Just no."

"The only reason these people came in on that particular road was because I allowed it. I shut down all nonessential roads at night. I made sure that stealth wasn't an option. They were forced to punch through and come in hot, rather than use covert tactics and slit your throats while you slept. Even so, an assault of this scale is difficult to control. That's why I stood there and presented a convenient target. Now we have a solid lead."

So that's where the spiked barricades came from. I

should've known. When you worked for Rogan, he made sure you were defended. He went so far as to make you immune to financial pressure from outside sources: his companies provided your car loan, your kids' college loans, your mortgage . . .

Oh no. No, he wouldn't.

My voice could've frozen the air in the warehouse. "Rogan, do you own my mortgage?"

"Not personally."

"Damn it!" He couldn't have touched our business. Augustine would never sell, so he went after my home instead.

"Nevada, it's in a trust. I don't personally own it. One of my companies owns it. I can't foreclose on it and I can't sell it. The terms remained exactly the same."

"You had no right to buy my mortgage!"

"I had every right. It was right there. Anybody could've bought it and used it as leverage."

"You and I'll never be financially equal; I get that. But you can't just buy up chunks of my life. For anything between us to work, I have to be able to say no to you. If you own my house, I lose that ability. I lose my independence."

"That's ridiculous."

"There is no such thing as a simple meeting now. Any communication from you will be an invitation from a man who owns my house."

"Have I used it as leverage? Have I mentioned it? Did I wrap it up with a pretty ribbon and offer it to you on a silver platter and said, 'Here is your mortgage, sleep with me?'"

"You didn't have to. It's enough I know you could."

"So now you're blaming me for the things I could theoretically do?"

"I'm blaming you for the thing you already did. You

bought every business around me and then you bought my mortgage. For any kind of relationship to work, I have to have a choice to walk away from it. You're taking that ability away from me. You know I would do anything to keep the roof over my family's head."

"That's not even logical," he said, his voice precise and sharp.

"Oh? Then why didn't you tell me about it?"

"I did tell you when you asked."

"Let's look at the sequence of events: you proposition me, I tell you no, you buy my mortgage. The fact that you don't tell me about it just reinforces the fact that you may have used it as leverage. Because you would, Rogan. You will use every resource at your disposal to win."

"I don't want to win." He locked his jaw. "This isn't some idiotic competition between you and me to see if I can wear you down. I didn't tell you because I knew you would react just like this."

"You knew it was the wrong move."

"Wake up," he growled. "Tonight sixteen trained killers came here to murder you. They had military-grade weapons and equipment. They would've driven a tanker truck into this place, detonated the charges, and shot all of you as you ran out with your skin on fire. Do you honestly think that your seventy-three-year-old grandmother in an aging tank, your mother with a permanent injury and a sniper rifle, and a cage full of guns can protect you? This is House warfare. You were vulnerable. You were vulnerable physically and financially. I eliminated those vulnerabilities."

His magic flared around him, raging, and met mine. Our powers collided.

"I didn't ask you to eliminate them. They were not yours!"

"Your normal existence is over, Nevada. It was over

when you took Harrison's contract. The first time you popped on these people's radar, you were forced to go after Adam Pierce. This time you voluntarily put yourself in the crosshairs. They can no longer ignore you. This isn't about ethics, laws, or noble adherence to the rules. This is about survival. I didn't tell you about it because you desperately cling to the illusion that you're still a normal person living a normal life, and I tried to preserve it for you, because I wanted to keep your head above the river of shit and blood as long as I could."

"I waded into that river on my own. I don't need your help. Get off my property," I ground out.

Rogan marched through the open garage door to the middle of the street, turned toward me, and spread his arms. "I'm on my property now. Is everything fine now? Did all of your problems disappear and none of this happened?"

"I'm going to shoot him," I squeezed through my teeth.

"No, that would be murder," Grandma Frida told me, her voice soothing. "You've had a long day. Let's put your magic away. You know what you need? A nice cup of chamomile tea and a tranquilizer . . ."

I turned and marched out of the motor pool. It was that or I would explode.

Chapter 8

It was morning and my mother made breakfast. Various animals ate from different bowls on the floor, all with the exception of Bunny, who dutifully sat by Matilda's side and tried his best not to drool at the smell of bacon. As I watched, Matilda quietly dropped a piece on the floor. Bunny wolfed it down and resumed his vigil.

My mother had her patient face on. Catalina cut strawberries on Matilda's plate. Arabella made odd patterns in her pancake with the tines of her fork. Leon, bright-eyed and bushy-tailed enough for me to want to strangle him, shoveled bacon into his mouth. Bern devoured his food in a methodical fashion. One day he would drop all pretense and just divide his plate into a grid. Everyone looked tired. Nobody talked.

Bern had done an audit of our finances. Mad Rogan owned our mortgage. He also owned our car loans and our business line of credit. We'd received paperwork regarding the change in ownership for all those things, but our mortgage had already been sold once, so my mother simply shrugged and filed it. A small college loan Bernard had taken out last year in addition to his scholarship was the only thing Rogan left alone, probably because it came through a federal financial aid program and couldn't be acquired.

"We can pay off the vehicles," Grandma Frida said. "I let that girl have the last ATV, so we've got two and a burned-out wreck, but the two vehicles are in decent condition with only some damage. They're state of the art. I have the buyers lined up. We can unload them for about three hundred thousand each."

"We should keep one," Mom said. "We may need it the way things are going."

Grandma Frida made big eyes and tried to inconspicuously point in my direction.

"Keep one," I said, struggling to swallow my pancake. Overnight the red welts on my neck had matured into a spectacular bruise. My throat hurt. "It doesn't matter. We still owe a million four hundred thousand on the mortgage."

I had reached a seething point last night. Eventually my anger boiled over, and now only quiet determination remained. Rogan owned our mortgage. I would just have to work very hard and take it back from him. There was no other way to do it. We were Baylors. We paid our debts, and when life knocked us down, we picked ourselves up and punched it in the teeth. Sometimes that hurt more, but we still did it.

"A million and four hundred thousand? That's almost the original price of the warehouse," Arabella said. "We've been paying on it for seven years. How is that possible?"

"Interest," Catalina said with a distant look that manifested when she did complicated math in her head. "With the 4.5 percent interest and finance charges, that's about right. I can crunch the exact numbers for you."

"That's not fair. Buying on credit sucks," Arabella declared.

"We would have to be attacked about three more times

before we can pay the mortgage off," I said. "We'd need six more ATVs to sell to buy Rogan out."

Leon speared his strawberry with a fork. "I, for one, welcome our new Mad Rogan Overlord. I'm eager to learn and prove to be a valuable member of his team."

"Shut up," Catalina, Bernard, and Arabella said at the same time.

Leon squinted at them. "Maybe he'd let me have a gun, unlike some people."

"You don't need a gun," Mom snapped.

"Do you even know where that overlord line is from?" Bern asked.

"A TV show."

"No, you idiot, it's from a movie called the *Empire of the Ants*. Look it up." Bern's phone chirped. He looked at it. "It's Bug. Okay, so, two things. One, I have the video of the mercenary dude being loaded on the plane to Johannesburg, alive, like Rogan promised. Do you want to see it?"

"No." Rogan was a controlling overbearing asshole, but when he gave his word, he kept it.

"Two, this morning I made a door in Scorpion's server and Bug spent the last hour waltzing around in their confidential files. Scorpion was hired through an intermediary and paid by electronic transfer. Rogan's people found the intermediary. He was paid in cash by an unidentified man."

"How much?"

"Half a million."

"We're expensive, yus!" Arabella said.

"I left Scorpion a little present," Bern said. "Bug activated it a couple of minutes ago, before hightailing it out of their servers."

"What's the present?" I asked.

"When they try to access their confidential files, they

will find a marathon of *Hello Kitty's Paradise*. All twelve
years of it in the original Japanese."

"I like Hello Kitty," Matilda said.

Cornelius cleared his throat. "I feel partially responsible for this situation."

Matilda reached over and petted his arm. "It's okay,
Daddy."

Everything stopped as all of us collectively struggled
with an overload of cute.

"Thank you," Cornelius told her. "But I'm responsible.
I knew what was to come, or at least I suspected, yet I
minimized that risk in our initial conversation."

I sighed. "You didn't minimize anything. I was aware
of the risk when I took the job. The responsibility for everything that happened is on me."

"Your outrage over Rogan's actions is well warranted,"
Cornelius said, obviously choosing his words carefully.
"But the danger of your family being harmed or put under
pressure is very real. He isn't wrong."

I dropped my napkin on the table. "I know he isn't
wrong in his assessment, Cornelius. I'm upset because he
refuses to acknowledge that I'm also right."

"If he'd come to you with all of it, you would never
have agreed to the purchase," Bernard said.

"Probably not, but at least I would've had a choice."

"What choice?" he said.

"I don't know." I got up and went to rinse my plate.

"Are we going to school today?" Leon asked.

"No," my mother said.

"Great." Leon smiled. "Then I'm going to go outside
and see if I can get a gun. Since my own family won't let
me have one, I'll have to beg strangers."

"What's wrong with you?" Catalina asked.

"Do you think guns are just lying around outside?"

Arabella asked. "Or did someone plant a gun tree in our parking lot?"

"Have any of you looked outside?" Leon asked. "Since the sunrise, I mean."

Bern poked his phone. "He's right. I think we should look outside."

I got up and marched down the hallway, through the office, and to the front door, my entire family behind me. I pushed the door open.

An armored transport rolled past us, carefully staying on the other side of a white line someone had painted on the pavement around our property. Across the street, a team of military-looking people installed an M198 Howitzer. A mobile howitzer that resembled a tank roared down the street in the opposite direction. To the right, an observation tower was going up, put together by another military-looking crew. Two severely groomed people in tactical gear double-timed it past us. The one on the left was leading what looked like an abnormally large grizzly on a ridiculously thin leather leash. The grizzly wore a leather harness marked "Sergeant Teddy."

My mother's mouth hung open.

Grandma Frida elbowed my mom in the ribs. "Pinch me, Penelope. It's Fort Sill."

I opened my mouth but nothing came out.

A trim woman about my age approached the white line and stopped. Her straight dark hair was pulled back into a ponytail. Her skin was a rich medium brown with an olive tint, her eyes were dark, and her features pointed at both African and possibly Latino heritage. She wore a beige pantsuit.

"Melosa Cordero with a message from Mad Rogan," she said. "Permission to enter?"

This was ridiculous. "Sure."

She stepped over the white line.

"The major regrets that his presence makes you uncomfortable; however, he wants me to inform you that Baranovsky's shindig is tomorrow, so he respectfully suggests that you go shopping. I'm to accompany you. I'm authorized to make purchases on his behalf."

"That won't be necessary." Rogan wouldn't be paying for anything else of mine if I could help it. "You're free to go. I'll buy my own dress, Ms. Cordero."

"Please call me Mel. He said you would say that. I'm to tell you that—" She cleared her throat and said in a deeper voice, obviously quoting, "This is strictly business. Don't throw a tantrum, Nevada. It's not like you."

A tantrum, huh? I made a heroic effort to keep my mouth shut. I was reasonably sure that if I opened it, I'd breathe fire and melt her face off.

"He said that if you got this look on your face, I'm to tell you that I'm an aegis," Melosa said. "I'm ranked as Significant and I'm a trained bodyguard. My mission is to shield you and Cornelius. I'm also to remind you that the safety of your client is your first priority."

I pulled out my phone and texted Rogan.

Thank you so much for providing us with an aegis. So kind of you.

My pleasure. Is there anything else I can do for you?

As a matter of fact there is. Make a fist and hit yourself with it.

Is this the part where I tell you some ridiculously condescending line about how attractive you are when you're angry?

Do you actually have a death wish?

Are you going to do something about it?

Argh.

"Cornelius?" I asked. "Your agreement with Rogan is terminated once we discover the identity of your wife's killer?"

"Yes," he said.

"Good." Because once that contract was over, I would make Rogan eat every single word of this message. I had no idea how I would do it, but it would happen.

"If I may," Melosa said. "We have a saying in this business. Don't look a gifted aegis in the mouth."

"What was your last assignment?" my mother asked.

"I was guarding the Argentinian finance minister," Melosa said. "I was pulled from that detail last night, but I'm in operative condition. Equzol is a hell of a drug."

"I feel like I missed something. We're going to Baranovsky's art gala?" Cornelius asked, his face puzzled.

That's right. He'd slept through it. I told him that my personal "relationship" with Rogan wouldn't interfere with this investigation. I would keep my word, no matter what it cost me.

"Come inside," I told Melosa. "There are pancakes and sausage. Feel free to have some while I bring Cornelius up to speed."

Briefing Cornelius took a lot longer than I'd anticipated and by the time I was done, my throat was in serious pain. He took it well. He and Melosa watched the video of the overpass incident, and then Cornelius declared he would be coming with us from now on.

Which was how all three of us ended up going to see

Ferika Luga together. Cornelius said that his sister frequently shopped there for formal attire, and since I had no idea where to buy a suitable dress, I decided to trust his judgment. I also dipped into my emergency budget. I wouldn't be wearing a dress Rogan bought me.

Since my Mazda was gone I abandoned all pretense of blending into the traffic and took one of the captured ATVs instead. ATVs weren't made for comfort or for city traffic. We stood out like a sore thumb, and by the end of the trip, I'd need a butt replacement. The day had started on a high note so far. I couldn't wait to see how wonderful things would get from now on.

As we drove out of the neighborhood, we passed a crew installing an electric fence along Clay Road.

"Did Rogan move his headquarters somewhere around here?" I asked.

"Yes," Melosa answered. "It's not cost effective to protect two different headquarters."

"Where is it located?"

"I'm not at liberty to say."

I finally understood why he was called Mad Rogan. It wasn't because he was insane. It was because he drove you nuts with sheer frustration.

We had to make a detour into an older neighborhood, where Cornelius disappeared down a narrow street with another mysterious sack.

"What's in the bag?" Melosa asked.

"He won't tell me. For some reason I thought it might be body parts, and now I can't get rid of that thought."

"It's not body parts. The bag would be lumpy."

"That occurred to me as well."

While we waited for Cornelius, Bug emailed me Forsberg's autopsy report. No traces of foreign particles had been discovered; however the wounds contained traces of frozen tissue. Someone had frozen Forsberg's eyes and the brain behind them, turning it into mush. Somehow I wasn't surprised. Sadly there was no way to narrow it down. The Assembly's visitor logs were handwritten and kept confidential. Even Rogan couldn't gain access to them.

This mysterious ice mage was really getting on my nerves.

Ferika Luga was a short, plump woman of Native American heritage. Her shop occupied one of the business suites in a high-rise, sandwiched between an accounting firm on the floor below and an Internet start-up on the floor above. Cornelius mentioned that she saw clients by appointment only, so he had called ahead. I don't know why I had expected a retail space, but there was none. The front of her workspace was a simple open room with a row of chairs at one end, floor-to-ceiling window on the right, and a wall of mirrors on the left.

Ferika looked Melosa and Cornelius up and down and pointed to the chairs. "Wait here. You—come with me."

I followed her to the back, through a door, into a dressing room with a round platform in the middle. A large mirror occupied one wall. Through the open door on my left, I could see a sewing workshop and rows and rows of dresses in plastic, hanging on a metal rods suspended from the ceiling.

"You're going to the Baranovsky's dinner." Ferika faced me. "What do you want people to see? Don't think, say the first thing that pops into your head."

"Professional."

"Think about it. Picture yourself there."

I pictured myself on a shiny floor. Rogan would be there in all of his dragon glory. I'd need a spear and a helmet.

"What is it you do?"

"I'm a private investigator."

"Are you going to hide that thing on your neck?"

"I haven't decided yet."

The older woman crossed her arms, thinking. "How did you get it?"

"A man tried to kill me."

"Since you're standing here, he didn't succeed."

"No."

"Wait here."

She disappeared between the racks of clothes. I looked around. Nothing caught my eye. The floor was plain chestnut-colored wood. The ceiling had lots of white panels. The mirror offered my reflection—the bruise really was a wonder.

"How long have you worked for Rogan?" Cornelius asked.

The wall, apparently, was paper thin, because he hadn't raised his voice, but I heard him clearly.

"A long time," Melosa said. "You might say I'm one of the original employees he hired after separating from the military."

"In your experience, does he often become infatuated?"

Where was he going with that?

Melosa cleared her throat. "I'm not at liberty to discuss my employer's personal life. And even if I was, I wouldn't. The major has earned my loyalty. I would take a bullet with his name on it. He is entitled to his privacy and I'll safeguard it, so I suggest you choose a different line of questioning."

Well, she'd shut him down fast.

Ferika returned, accompanied by a younger woman carrying a black dress. "Put this on."

I stripped and slid into it as she watched. It was surprisingly heavy. Ferika's helper zipped the back, held out her hand, and helped me step back onto the platform. I looked into the mirror and held still.

The silhouette was timeless: two thin straps supporting a sweetheart cleavage that left my neck and most of my chest bare, close fitted waist, and a skirt gracefully falling into a train, not long enough to become cumbersome and allowing me to move fast if I had to. The fabric of the dress, black silk tulle, would've been completely sheer if it wasn't for the thousands of black sequins embroidered into it. The complicated pattern curved around and over my breasts, lined my ribs and hugged my hips, finally fracturing into individual whorls just below mid-thigh. They slid down the sheer tulle skirt like tongues of black flame, melting into nothing near the hem. The dress didn't look embroidered; it looked chiseled out of obsidian, like some fantasy bodice of a Valkyrie. It looked like armor.

"How much is it?"

"Fifteen thousand."

"I can't afford it."

"I know," Ferika said. "You can rent it for one night for ten percent of the cost. The shoes and clutch will be complimentary."

Fifteen hundred dollars for one night and I wouldn't even own it. Technically this was a necessary expense and I would bill Cornelius for it, but just because I had the ability to bill things didn't give me the license to be careless with my client's money.

The look on Rogan's face when he saw it would be worth it.

"Shoes," Ferika said.

The assistant placed a pair of black pumps in front of me. I stepped into them. They fit perfectly.

"Hair."

The assistant moved behind me, released my hair from the ponytail, rolled it into a crown around my head, and expertly pinned it in place.

Ferika held out her hand. I took it and stepped off the raised platform, and she led me out into the open space.

Cornelius blinked. Melosa's eyebrows crept up.

"It's fifteen hundred for a night," I said. "Yes, no?"

"Yes," Cornelius and Melosa said in one voice.

It was Friday evening. I sat in my office, trying to get some peace and quiet while staring at the pictures of magical heavyweights likely to be at Baranovsky's party. Augustine had emailed them to me segregated into two helpful categories: will kill you and can kill you. This was going to be one hell of a soiree.

The doorbell chimed. I tapped my laptop to bring the view of the front camera. Bug's face greeted me. He stuck his tongue out, crossed his eyes, and waved his laptop at me.

I got up and opened the door. "What, you're not going to ask me if you can enter my territory?"

"Pardon me, Your Divine Princess Majesty." Bug executed a surprisingly elegant bow with a hand flourish and began backing away, bowing. "Pardon this lowly wretch, pardon . . ."

"Get into my office," I growled.

"What the hell, Nevada? No, I'm not going to ask permission." Bug came in and landed in my client chair. "Nice digs."

"Thanks," I sat in my chair. "What's up?"

He opened his laptop, tapped a key, and pushed it toward me across the table. "Any of these assholes look familiar?"

I stared at the row of faces, all men ranging from about fifteen to sixty. "Ice mages?"

"Mhm."

I scrutinized them one by one. "No."

Bug sighed and took his laptop back. "Are you sure of what you saw?"

"Yes. I'd recognize the smile for sure. He showed me his teeth before icing the road." I showed him Augustine's list. "He isn't on there either."

"Shit," Bug said, his face sour. "It's that thing again. We've been dealing with it since Pierce. You think you have a lead and then poof"—he made a puffing motion with his fingers—"it melts into nothing and all you have is frustration and the fart noise your face makes when you hit your desk with it."

Fart . . . what? "We'll find him. As long as we keep investigating, he'll show himself sooner or later."

Bug looked behind him, leaning to get the better view of the hallway. "Got something else to show you."

He came around the desk, leaned on it next to me, and tapped his laptop. The security video from last night's shooting came on, complete with Leon's awesome voice-over.

I grimaced. "Yeah, I know. My cousin got excited. Look, he is fifteen. He thinks he's immortal."

"No." Bug's face was completely serious for once. "Watch."

The recording zoomed in on an older mercenary. *"I'm a veteran badass,"* Leon's voice said. *"I've seen bad shit. I've done bad shit. I've survived five months in a jungle eating pinecones and killing terrorists with a pair of old chopsticks . . ."*

"Where was he while this was happening?" Bug asked.

"In the Hut of Evil. I mean, in the computer room."

". . . Oh shit, my head just exploded."

The camera panned to the right to a woman crouching by the oak.

"I'm death. I'm a ghost. I'll find you. You can run, you can hide, you can beg, but none of it will help you.

I'll come for you in the darkness like a lithe panther with velvet paws and steel claws and . . . wait, brains, wait, where are you going?"

I sighed.

"Oh no, look—my feet are twitching. That's so undignified."

Maybe there was something wrong with Leon. I should give him more work to do. That would keep him from being bored and trying to get guns. "Whatever it is you want me to notice, I don't see it," I told Bug.

"How does he know who will die next?" Bug asked. "He pans the camera to them in the exact sequence they are killed."

That couldn't be right. I rewound the recording. Older male mercenary, an athletic female mercenary, bodybuilder mercenary, thin mercenary, a large female mercenary . . . Five targets in the precise order they were killed. In each case the camera panned to the victim and Leon started his narration before the shot ever rang out.

Oh crap. I put my hand over my mouth.

"If your mother called out the shots, it would make sense," Bug said. "But two of these were popped by our guys. At first I thought he was a precog." He rewound the video to just after the first female mercenary died. "Look, you see here he swings the shot to the left first?"

I followed the camera as it tilted to the left, focusing for a second on the lamppost as if Leon was waiting for something. The camera tilted up, catching a glimpse of the window in the building across the street and moved to the bodybuilder mercenary.

"He didn't do it in any of the other cases, so I went to talk to our guys." Bug typed on the laptop. The image of the street filled the screen.

"We had a guy here." He tapped the window with his finger.

"Is that the window in the video?"

He nodded. "The skinny guy that got killed after the bigger dude is here." Bug pointed at the spot by a warehouse, shielded from the view by the low stone wall. "The guy in that window didn't have a direct shot at the thin guy. So for shits and giggles, we put a dummy in the spot where the skinny guy was." He clicked a key and the screen showed the street from a different angle with a mannequin crouching by the wall, a canvas bag on his head.

"Why did you put the bag on his head?"

"You'll see in a minute. This is the view from the sniper's window." The screen split in a half. "No shot."

"Yep."

The sniper sighted the spot on the lamppost, where Leon had zoomed in before, and fired. The bag on the mannequin's head tore and a thin trickle of sand spilled out.

"Ricochet," I whispered. Leon wasn't a precog. He'd evaluated the potential targets and positions of the shooters, calculated the trajectory of the bullet, and waited for it to happen. When it didn't, he moved on to the next most likely target. And he did all this in a split second.

"I don't know what this is," Bug said. "It's some sort of wonderful whatthefuckery I've never seen before. But I thought I should tell you."

Leon would never have a normal life. There was only one path open to his kind of magic.

I looked at him. "Please, don't tell Rogan."

"I'll have to tell him if he asks me about it," Bug said. "But I won't volunteer. Does Leon know?"

I shook my head.

"It's your call," Bug said, picking up his laptop. "But a word of advice. From personal experience. When you keep people from doing things they are destined to do, they go crazy. Don't let him go crazy, Nevada."

Chapter 9

It was six o'clock on Friday evening and I was sitting in our media room in a fifteen-hundred-dollar-a-night dress, holding a tiny evening bag containing my phone, and trying not to move. Arabella had done my makeup. Catalina had rolled my hair into a suitably messy crown on my head and pinned it in place with a black metal hair brooch. My shoes were on. I had gone to the bathroom before I got dressed, I hadn't eaten anything that would give me gas, and I was probably dehydrated, because Murphy's Law guaranteed that if I had a drink in my hand, I would spill some of it on my nice dress.

I was ready to go. Grandma Frida and my mom were keeping me company until Augustine showed up.

I had spent the last several hours memorizing names and faces from Augustine's list and my poor brain buzzed like a beehive. Several of the men in the photographs were blond. I had stared at them for an hour, trying to match their features to the smudged blur I had seen through the rain-speckled window of the Suburban. I failed.

On TV the talking heads speculated about Senator Garza's murder. The police were still sitting on the details of the investigation and the rabid intensity of the earlier commentary had died down to annoyed declarations that sounded suspiciously like whining. The press so desperately wanted the story, but there was only so much speculation you could come up with, and starved of information, they were ready to admit defeat and move on to more exciting topics.

The pictures of Senator Garza came on the screen again. Young, handsome, politician's haircut, and probably politician's smile. He'd been murdered, and somebody had to answer for that.

"Poor family," Grandma Frida said.

Leon ran into the room. "Neva—"

He stopped and stared at me.

"Yes?"

"Nevada, you're pretty." He said it with a sense of wonder, as if he had discovered some alien life-form.

"And normally I'm . . . ?"

"My cousin," he said, loading a lot of *duh* into his voice. "There's a limo outside. Two limos."

I held out my hand and Leon helped me stand up.

"How do I look?"

"You look good," Mom assured me.

"Break a leg!" Grandma Frida told me. "Take lots of pictures!"

I stepped out of the media room. Cornelius was waiting for me. He wore a black tuxedo that hugged his body and set off his handsome features. He looked sharp and elegant, a man who belonged in the world of fifteen-thousand-dollar dresses. I felt like a little girl playing dress-up.

Cornelius offered me his arm. I rested my fingers on his forearm and we walked through the hallway to the door.

"This is like going to the prom," I said.

"I didn't go to mine," he said. "Did you?"

"I went to my junior prom. My date's name was Ronnie. He joined the Marines and was due to ship out two weeks later. He showed up high as a kite and proceeded to cheat on me with weed the entire evening because it was his last chance to let loose. I got fed up and ditched him thirty minutes after we got there." I had gleefully skipped the prom my senior year.

"I promise not to abandon you," he said.

"Between you, Augustine, and Rogan, there is no danger of that."

Cornelius opened the door for me and I stepped out into the night. Two limousines waited. Augustine stood by the second limo. He wore a tuxedo as well and it fit him like a glove. I took a second to come to terms with it. Wow.

"Nevada, you look perfect. Harrison, good evening."

"Good evening," Cornelius echoed.

The driver of the first limo, a tall blonde woman, stepped out and held the door open. "Mr. Harrison."

"Are we arriving separately?" I asked.

"Yes," Cornelius said. "I'll be arriving in the limo of my House."

And I would be going with Augustine as his employee. Just as well.

"I'll see you there."

His limo slid into the night. Augustine held the door open for me. I sat very carefully.

He shut the door, walked around, got in next to me, and we were off.

"The bruise is a masterful touch," Augustine said.

"The two of you said Baranovsky prefers unique."

"It's certainly that. It draws the eye. Together with the dress it's a powerful statement. Have you noted that Rogan tried to dissuade you from attending?"

"Yes." Where was he going with this?

"Rogan is, at the core, an adolescent," Augustine said. "Driven, dangerous, and calculating, but an adolescent nonetheless."

No. Rogan was anything but. He sought to maintain control over his environment, his people, and most of all himself. On the rare occasions his emotions got the best of him, the glimpse of his true nature was so brief I still hadn't been able to completely figure him out. There was nothing impulsive about him.

"Adolescents are ruled by their emotions," Augustine continued.

You don't say. If only I had some adolescents in my life with whom I had to deal on a daily basis.

"Abandoning your family obligations and running away to join the army is a teenage move," Augustine said. "It is one peg above dramatically declaring that you didn't ask to be born."

Given that Rogan was nineteen when he joined the army, the teenager criticism wasn't exactly fair. I finally understood why Rogan had joined. He was trying to escape the predetermined path of all Primes: go to college, attain an advanced degree, work for your parents, marry a spouse with the right genes, and produce no less than two and no more than three children to ensure succession. The path that Augustine himself had studiously followed with exception of finding a spouse.

"My point is, occasionally Rogan has an emotional reaction and acts accordingly. He had an emotional reaction to sharing you with the rest of the world. I don't know the nature of his fascination. Perhaps it's personal. Perhaps it is professional interest. I don't believe you realize how valuable you are, but Rogan does and so do I. And I don't like to lose."

He flicked his thumb across his phone. My clutch let out a melodious tone I set specifically for this event. I opened it and checked my phone. A new email from Augustine waited in my email box. I tapped it.

A contract. *Agreement between House Montgomery . . .* He was offering me employment, but not with MII. With House Montgomery. This was new. *Base Salary. Employee shall receive a Base Salary in the amount of $1,200,000 per year . . .*

That couldn't be right.

Payment. Base Salary shall be payable in accordance with the customary payroll practices of the Employer . . .

Adjustment. On November 1st of each year during the Term, (i) Employee's Base Salary shall increase by no less than 7%; (ii) The Company shall review the Employee's performance and may make additional increases to the Base Salary in its sole discretion.

What was the term? I scrolled through it. Ten years.

Augustine Montgomery had just offered me a contract that guaranteed a payment of one million two hundred thousand per year for ten years with an annual 7 percent increase and bonuses based on performance.

I could buy Rogan out. I could pay off our mortgage. I could guarantee my sisters' education. I could . . .

What was the catch? There had to be a catch.

Noncompete Covenant. For good consideration and as an inducement for Company to employ Employee, if such employment is terminated for any reason during the Term, the employee shall not engage directly or indirectly, either personally or as employee, associate partner, partner, owner, manager, agent, or in any other capacity in any business within the Unites States and its protected Territories involving private investigation, security services, or personal interrogation for a period of ten years. Any private security or investigation businesses currently owned by the Employee must be dissolved prior to employment.

If I took this contract, Baylor Investigative Agency would cease to exist. And if I quit or was fired for any reason, I wouldn't be able to support my family.

Augustine smiled at me. Funny; from this angle you couldn't see his shark teeth at all.

If I took this deal, all of my years of hard work would be gone. The agency was my father's legacy, but it was also so much more than that. It was a testament to our perseverance as a family.

As my dad's health rolled downhill, the business had dwindled to nothing. He couldn't work. My mother was focused on taking care of my father. When I thought back to that time, it was muted in my memories. Dark and oppressive, as if filmed through a blue filter by my brain. There was time before Dad got sick and then there was time after he died. Between that lay awful memories I was trying to forget in self-defense.

I couldn't help Dad. I had made things worse. I had read a letter from his doctor, and he caught me and asked me to not tell anyone. I kept his secret for far too long. Had I spoken up sooner, he might have lived longer. When he was sick, I couldn't reassure my sisters and cousins. Anything I could've said would have been a lie. We all knew the awful truth from the start. Dad was going to die. We fought for weeks, not years.

In that time, the only thing I could do was to step up and try to earn a little bit of extra money for us. I stepped onto the sinking ship that was Baylor Investigative Agency and plugged the holes one by one. I fought for every new client.

I ferreted out every crumb of work we could get. And slowly the business started moving. It stumbled, lurching forward, but it was no longer standing still. Then, after Dad died, we all desperately needed something to hold on to. We were like runners who had run a long, grueling race, crossed the finished line, and didn't know how to stop running. We needed a focus and the agency became that. It kept a roof over our heads and put food on our table. My sisters and cousins hadn't asked for an allowance in the past three years because they earned it through the family business. If things ever went wrong for them in their adult life, the business would be there to provide some income. It would never make them rich, but it would pay the bills. It was there for all of us. It thrived now, living proof that we stood together as a family. We were all proud of it. My father had hoped it would take care of us and it did, in so many more ways than just money.

If I took Augustine's offer, all of this would disappear. Yes, I would earn more money. Crazy money, the kind I would never see otherwise. But instead of earning their own money, the rest of the family would now depend on my handouts.

I wanted to get away from Rogan. I wanted it so badly. With this, I could.

What would I be doing for this money? Probably the exact thing my parents had fought so hard to keep me from doing: working for Augustine as a living lie detector. Making people curl into fetal positions on the floor as they wept after I violated their minds.

"That's a very generous offer," I said.

"No, it's a fair offer. I'm a businessman, Nevada. I always watch my bottom line. This offer isn't modest, but it isn't generous either. It is, in my estimation, adequate and fair compensation for the valuable service you will provide to House Montgomery. Compensation which, I might add, will increase. There is so much I could do with your talent, Nevada. You have my word that I'll never attempt to emotionally manipulate you. You have my word that I'll never threaten your family or attempt to purchase all of your loans without your permission in some underhanded attempt to influence you."

He had looked into my finances. Of course. He owned a private detective agency, after all. And he had looked into them so he could do the exact same thing that Rogan had done. Except Rogan had beat him to it.

"I offer a professional alliance, Nevada. A mutually beneficial partnership. If you scroll down, you will see a sign-on bonus. It will take care of your immediate debt obligations and permit you to put a down payment on a reasonable residence, should you choose to move out of the warehouse and begin a more independent lifestyle. Again, I'm not doing it as a charity. I'm doing it because I would like you to be professionally happy. In my experience, happy employees mean a stable, healthy business."

He smiled again. "I understand that right now things are chaotic and this is a big decision. Take all the time you need. There is no expiration date on this offer."

I smiled back at him, trying to show no emotion except light amusement. "You're confident Rogan won't offer me more?"

"He may offer you more. The question is, what will you be expected to do for that money?"

I raised my eyebrows at him.

"I didn't mean a sexual engagement," Augustine said. "Rogan may try to seduce you, but unless his personality has undergone a very drastic change, he'll never pressure you into a sexual relationship against your will. Do you know what Rogan does for a living?"

"A great many things, from what I understand."

"No, he owns many things. There is a difference. I also

own a great many things, but I run MII. It's my day-to-day business. Rogan is a warlord in a very real sense of the word. His people are mercenaries. He does have one of the best private armies in the world, I'll give him that, and on the surface he does fun things with it like hostage rescue, security detail for aid workers, and stabilizing operations. However, we're both adults. You know as well as I that the most profitable operations are rarely white knight affairs. Even more interesting is what he does in the city of Houston."

"He owns a private security firm, from what I understand," I said.

"He owns Castra. It's an ancient Latin word for *military fort*. Every day Roman legionnaires would march twenty miles in full gear and then they would set up camp and build fortifications of dirt and timber around it before going to sleep. Castra is a shelter in an inhospitable land, a wall of protection impenetrable to outsiders. Rogan's Castra provides security to Houses. Do you need to meet with your rival? Don't trust him or your own people? Are you afraid of an ambush? Castra will secure the site for you. They are elite, expertly trained, and incorruptible. They are the reason why Rogan knows every major player in the Houston underworld and why he is well informed about most major feuds between the Houses. He takes time to cover his tracks really well. I know of it because I was involved in a complex transaction between two parties, secured by Castra, and I recognized one of his people."

It didn't surprise me. Rogan had said before that when he wanted someone found, his people brought that person to him within hours. That wouldn't be possible without an extensive network of contacts among the shadier side of Houston, and one didn't get those contacts by being an altar boy.

"Does he know you know?"

Augustine shook his head. "I wasn't present as myself. With me, your work would be legitimate and legal. I can't promise that once in a while you won't run across a situation that will compromise your principles, but such situations would be an anomaly, not the norm. What kind of work would you be doing for Rogan? Who would you question for him?"

All valid points. Except Rogan didn't want to hire me. He wanted me, in every sense of the word. He wanted me to be with him. It was more than lust. I wasn't quite sure what it was yet.

Augustine smiled. "It might pay to consider your options carefully."

The limos slid up the curving driveway past lush gardens and beautiful granite terraces.

"Where are we?" I asked.

"Piney Point Village," Augustine said.

Piney Point Village was officially the wealthiest place in Texas. Like many of the neighboring communities, it started as a small city that had been gobbled up by Houston's sprawl. I had cause to briefly visit it last year in connection with a runaway case. Part of the Memorial Villages' wealthy bedroom community, Piney Point restricted businesses of any kind within its borders, employed an urban forester, and regulated everything, including the format of the For Sale signs. According to the census, the tiny municipality had only three thousand residents. The taxable value of real estate they owned totaled two billion dollars.

The limo slid into a roundabout, circling a breathtaking fountain. At the other end of the parking lot a huge white mansion rose from the trees. From here the massive building resembled an eye. A large round tower sat in the center, like an iris, guarded by towering white columns supporting a circular balcony above. Two curved wings stretched from the tower, gracefully couched by the greenery. Arched glass doors and windows glowed with inviting amber light. I could almost hear some luxury home Realtor's voice: *"Built in an elegant fusion of Italianate, French, and early Disney styles, this magnificent estate offers a thousand bathrooms for all of your executive Cinderella needs . . ."*

"How big is this house?"

"Thirty thousand square feet," Augustine said. "Baranovsky built it specifically for the gala a few years ago. The tower houses the central ballroom, the right wing has a restaurant space and a presentation auditorium, the left contains the living quarters. He rents it out as a corporate retreat when he isn't here."

The limo slid to a stop. *Here we go.*

"No worries," Augustine said. "You will do well. Be yourself, Nevada."

The driver opened my door. Augustine walked around the limo and held out his hand. I leaned on him and stepped out of the car. He offered me his arm. I shook my head. The point was to make a statement and stand out. Being attached to Augustine as his date would cause most people to overlook me. We walked up the wide staircase to the arched entrance between towering Corinthian columns. A man and a woman, both in severe dark suits, waited by the entrance. Augustine made eye contact with the woman and held up a small card.

She inclined her head. "Mr. Montgomery. Welcome."

"Good evening, Elsa."

The man raised a scanner. Red laser dashed across the card.

The male guard touched his headset. His voice sounded

in two places at once, from his mouth and from the speaker somewhere within the house. "Augustine Montgomery of House Montgomery and guest."

They probably knew my name, weight, and shoe size. But next to Augustine, my name meant nothing. I became "and guest," and that was precisely how I liked it.

We stepped through the arched entrance onto the granite floor polished to a mirror shine. White walls rose high, decorated with long banners showcasing the various exhibits of the Museum of Fine Arts, Houston: a woman in an impossibly wide mother-of-pearl dress with an equally wide hairdo and the caption "Habsburg Splendor: Pieces from Vienna's Imperial Collections"; a ceramic statue of a man in a round helmet sitting cross-legged with his hands resting on his knees, labeled "Ballplayer: Arts of Ancient Mexico"; and an insane-looking plastic bracelet in orange and red, with a pattern of black dots encircled with white and multicolored spikes, marked "Ronald Warden's Enigmatic Jewelry."

A wide door offered access to the ballroom directly in front of us, giving us a glimpse of the main floor and the crowd inside—women in bright dresses and men in black. Two suspended staircases with elaborate iron railings swept up on both sides of it, leading to the upstairs floor and two additional doors.

Augustine headed straight for the ballroom. I lifted my chin and walked next to him like I belonged here.

"Why not just hold the gala at MFAH?"

"Baranovsky is a Prime. We like to control our environment. Follow my lead. We'll walk in and then we'll simply drift."

We walked through the door and I had to concentrate on walking instead of stopping in midstride and gaping. The vast circular room gleamed. The floor was white granite with elaborate flourishes of malachite-green inlay.

The walls were polished white marble with flecks of green and gold. A wide marble staircase at the other end of the circle offered access to an inside balcony that ran the entire circumference of the ballroom, punctuated by doors, which probably led to the outside balcony. Seamless floor-to-ceiling windows soared on both sides of the balcony, caged by columns. Here and there small groups of plush chairs and tables were tucked in near the walls. Houston's magical elite stood, sat, and strolled, conversing. Laughter floated. Diamonds shone. Waiters glided through the gathering like ghosts, carrying trays of delicacies and wine.

True to his word, we drifted. People looked at us. I glanced at Augustine. Somewhere between the front door and ballroom, he'd become stunning. He was usually handsome—his illusion affording him an icy perfection—but now he'd transformed into a Greek demigod. A living, breathing work of art, superhuman in its beauty. Women looked at him, then invariably at me, their gazes snagging on the bruise on my neck.

Augustine led me to the left. A waiter ghosted over to us, offering champagne. Augustine took a flute, but I waved mine off. The last thing I needed was to get drunk. We kept strolling, bits of conversation floating to us.

"You look divine . . ."

"Lie," I murmured under my breath.

". . . so lovely to see you . . ."

"Lie."

". . . would have never thought her capable of such a direct action . . ."

"Lie."

"I hate these gatherings."

"Lie, lie, lie."

Augustine laughed quietly.

A woman thrust herself into our way. In her forties,

with a carefully structured blond hairdo, she wore a turquoise dress. A man who had to be either her son or a lover half her age accompanied her. Dark-haired and handsome, he was overgroomed and slightly effeminate. Too much eyebrow tweezing. I didn't recognize either face, so they probably wouldn't murder me.

"Augustine, my dear, what a delight."

Lie.

"Likewise, Cheyenne," Augustine said.

Lie. Clearly this wasn't a close friend.

"We've been admiring your lovely companion," Cheyenne said. Both she and her boy toy looked at me and for some reason I was reminded of hyenas baring their fangs.

"So interesting," the boy toy said. "Perhaps she can settle our dispute. See, Cheyenne here contends that a woman should retain some hint of her natural state, while I firmly believe that a female body should be bald from the eyebrows down. Care to opine?"

Aha. Clearly he was some kind of idiot. I had no time for that nonsense. I looked directly at him, holding his stare for a full five seconds, then deliberately turned my back to him. Augustine and I walked away.

"Well done," Augustine whispered.

"Who were they?"

"Nobody important."

An elegant African American woman was making her way toward us. She wore a pink dress, not the overwhelming bright pink of Pepto-Bismol, but the gentle pastel pink a mere shade redder than white. The dress, slightly looser than a mermaid shape, hugged her statuesque frame. A half cape spilled from her shoulder, giving her a regal air. From the distance she looked ageless, but now, close up, I could see she was probably twice my age.

Augustine bowed his head. "Lady Azora."

"May I borrow you for a moment, Augustine?" She glanced at me.

Augustine also glanced at me.

"Of course," I said.

"Thank you, my dear," Lady Azora told me.

They strolled away.

I turned so I could keep them in my view without staring at Augustine's back. A man emerged from behind a group of people. African American, in his mid-thirties, he moved with an athletic grace, walking until he stopped next to me. Or rather loomed. He had to be three or four inches over six feet tall. Every tuxedo and suit in this place was custom-made, but his must've taken a couple of extra yards to accommodate his height and broad shoulders. His hair was cropped very short, and an equally short goatee beard and mustache traced his jaw, cut with razor-sharp precision. Our stares met. An agile intellect shone from his dark eyes. One look and you knew that he wasn't just intelligent, he was sharp and shrewd. He wouldn't mow down his opposition. He would disassemble it.

The man bent his head slightly toward me. His voice was deep and quiet. "Do you need help?"

I had no idea what he was talking about.

"Do you need help?" he repeated quietly. "One word, and I'll take you out of here and none of them can stop me. I'll make sure you have access to a doctor, a safe place to stay, and a therapist to talk to. Someone who understands what it's like and will help. "

The pieces clicked in my head. The bruise. Of course. "Thank you, but I'm okay."

"You don't know me. It's difficult to trust me because I'm a man and a stranger. The woman speaking with Augustine is my aunt. The woman across the floor in the white-and-purple gown is my sister. Either of them will vouch for me. Let me help you."

"Thank you," I told him. "On behalf of every woman here. But I'm a private investigator. I'm not a victim of domestic abuse. This is a work-related injury and the man who put his hands on me is dead."

The man studied me for a long moment and slid a card into my hand. "If you decide that the injury isn't work related, call me."

Augustine turned toward us.

The man gave him a hard stare and walked away. I glanced at the card. It was solid black, with the initials ML embossed on one side in silver and a phone number on the other.

"Do you know who that was?" Augustine asked.

"No."

"Michael Latimer. Very powerful, very dangerous."

"He wasn't on my list."

"He was supposed to be in France for the next month. What did he want?"

There was no harm in telling him. "He thought I was a victim of domestic violence. He offered to help."

"I had no idea he cared." Augustine narrowed his eyes. "Interesting."

Men and women drifted by us as the announcer kept reciting a measured litany of names. So-and-so of House so-and-so. So-and-spouse of House Whatever. I saw Cornelius next to a woman who could have been his sister. He looked at me in passing as if he had no idea who I was and I returned his gaze in the exact same way.

Minutes drifted by.

I turned and saw Gabriel Baranovsky on the second floor above us talking to an older Asian man. Two large men with shoulders so broad they looked almost square in their expensive suits waited calmly nearby. Bodyguards.

According to our background check, Baranovsky was fifty-eight. He wore the years well. His build, slender, almost slight, pointed to a man who was either a habitual runner or had an iron will when it came to food. His dark hair fell in a loose wavy mane, framing an angular intelligent face with a long nose, narrow chin, and large eyes. I had studied his picture from the files. You couldn't tell from here, but he had remarkable eyes, light brown like whiskey and possessing a kind of sorrowful, wise expression. The rest of him was perfectly ordinary, but the eyes elevated his face, transforming him into someone unusual, someone you would want to talk to because you were sure he would have something unique to say. The eyes of the man who looked into the future. No wonder he collected women.

And he wasn't looking at me at all.

The announcer's voice faltered and for once I tuned into it.

"Connor Rogan of House Rogan."

The floor around us became still and quiet. On the second floor Baranovsky pivoted toward the door, frowning. The pause lasted only a couple of moments, the slow drift of bodies and hum of conversation resuming, but now the voices were lower and the seemingly casual movement had acquired a definite direction as the attendees tried to clear the middle of the floor without looking like they were tripping over their feet.

Rogan walked into the hall. He wore a black suit, but the way they looked at him, he might as well have marched into the room in full armor. He'd shaved and brushed his hair, but the circles under his eyes betrayed the fact that he probably hadn't slept last night. A scowl hardened his face. He looked like he would murder anyone who got in his way.

One half of me wanted to punch him in the face for

buying up my debts. The other half wanted to march into his path and chew him out for not sleeping. If this was love, then love was the most complicated emotion I had ever felt.

He saw me. Surprise flickered in his eyes and for a moment he was too stunned to hide it. The dress was worth every penny.

Rogan altered his course. Across the room Michael Latimer watched him quietly. The crowd's reactions split. Most faces turned worried. A few others, men and women both, watched him the way Latimer did, not afraid but ready. They were all predators who'd agreed to play nice for one night and now they weren't sure if the beast with the biggest fangs in the room would follow the rules.

Rogan crashed to a halt before me and held out his hand without saying a word. I didn't dare to check if Baranovsky was watching but damn near everybody in the room was. Their stares pinned me down like daggers.

In for a penny, in for a pound. I put my hand in his.

He turned smoothly, sliding my hand down to rest on his elbow. We walked together up the stairs. I felt lightheaded.

If I tripped now, I would never live it down.

We reached the top and Rogan turned left, away from Baranovsky, and back along the second floor. Ahead an open door led outside to a balcony framed with planters of roses, their fat blossoms a dark red, almost purple. Rogan walked through. The cold evening air washed over us in a rush.

I remembered how to breathe.

"Did you have to be so obvious about it?" I ground out.

"I warned you." His voice was cold, his face distant. He was looking me over. "You wanted to catch his attention."

I turned away from him and looked at the garden below. No man should have a garden blooming in winter but somehow Baranovsky had managed. Shrubs with yellow blossoms framed the whorls of garden paths; tall spires of unfamiliar plants with white triangular flowers beckoned; and roses, lots and lots of roses, in every shade from white to red filled the flower beds. Between them small gazebos offered a place to rest and enjoy the view. Bright canvas canopies, triangular and stretched tight into slightly curved shapes, like sails of some galleon, shielded parts of the walkways between them. The rest of the house curved into the distance, hugging the garden's edge.

Rogan said nothing. Fine. We could just stand here and say nothing.

A gust of wind came. I hugged my cold shoulders. Evening gowns weren't designed for dramatically running out onto strange balconies in the middle of winter nights.

Rogan pulled off his jacket and draped it over my shoulders.

I brushed it away. "Don't."

"Nevada, you're cold."

"I'm fine."

"It's a damn jacket," he growled.

I squinted at him. "What's the catch?"

"What?" Irritation vibrated in his voice.

"What's the catch with the jacket? What will it cost me? You keep chipping away at my independence every time you try to 'take care' of me, so I'd rather know the price in advance."

He swore.

"Colorful, but not very informative." My teeth chattered. I clamped them together and my knees started shaking. Great.

"Take the jacket."

"No."

We stared at each other. It was good that stares weren't swords or we would've had a duel right here on the balcony.

"You can go back now," I told him. "I'm sure he'll come and see what all the fuss was about if you leave."

"I'll leave when I'm damned good and ready."

Judging by the set of his jaw, he wouldn't budge and he was too big for me to shove him off the balcony into the roses down below. Although it would be tempting to try.

"I know about Castra." *Let's see him deal with that one.*

He didn't react. "How?"

"Augustine made your people during one of the exchanges they secured."

"Ah." He grimaced. "Augustine started taking interest in my affairs after Pierce's idiocy. I've invested in a canine unit to account for that possibility. He may change his appearance but he can't change his scent. It seems I didn't do it soon enough."

"What deals do you secure? Who are your clients? Drug dealers? Murderers?"

"Murderers, yes. But only if their name is attached to a House. I've never secured a drug transaction. I know of the underworld, and it knows of my people. We pass each other like two strangers on the street, aware but never interacting, and that's the way I like to keep it."

True. "Why do you do it?"

"Information," he said, his voice matter-of-fact. "I exist outside of Prime society by choice, but I know more about them than those who are entrenched in it. Information gives me power, and when necessary, I use it."

Another gust of wind hit me. If Baranovsky didn't show up in the next two minutes, I'd freeze to death.

Rogan glanced at the garden. A canvas canopy tore from the rest, shot toward us, and wrapped the balcony

on the left side, shielding us from the wind. In response a
dark shadow shifted behind the window on the third floor,
about five hundred yards from us, across the garden. Rogan's gaze checked the window and he turned away. He
saw it too. We were being watched, probably by someone
with a sniper rifle.

"This is exactly what I'm talking about. I refused your
jacket, so you went over my head. You aren't taking my
wishes into consideration. At all."

"You want to be cold?" He stared at me.

"Yes." And that sounded stupid. I sighed at myself.

"Nevada, we both know that you're freezing. I can hear
your teeth clicking. If you're doing this to prove a point, I
already understand it. This is childish."

I faced him. "It's not childish, Connor. You're trying
to take over my life. You do things for me, even when I
specifically ask you not to, because you feel you know
better. I'm desperately fighting for my independence and
my boundaries, because otherwise there will be no me
left. There will be just you and I'll become an accessory."

Rogan turned and half closed a mirrored door behind us.
The glass caught my reflection. The black dress sheathed
me like armor. My blond hair crowned my head. The look
on my face brought it home: there was something defiant
and almost vicious in my eyes. I barely recognized myself.

I didn't like it.

Rogan moved to stand behind me, his resolute face
tinted with regret. "What do you see?"

"I see me in a leased dress."

"I see a Prime."

True. He meant it. Breath caught in my throat. Deep
down I had known it. I just didn't want to deal with all the
things that title meant.

His voice was quiet. "This isn't you playing dress-up.
This is you, Nevada. This is what you truly are."

Why did he sound like he was hammering nails into his own coffin?

"You must've realized it by now. It can't be that much of a surprise," he said, his voice quiet. "Augustine knows it too. He isn't an idiot. Sooner or later he'll try to lock you into vassalage. He'll try to offer you a deal, probably what will seem like a great sum of money attached to handcuffs and a chain. In reality, whatever he offers you will be a pittance. If he could lock you in, your value to House Montgomery would be enormous. Your value to any House would be beyond measure, especially if you don't know what you are and you submit, allowing yourself to be controlled and used."

Like offering me over a million dollars to walk away from everything I'd built. My instincts had been right, but the trap did prove so tempting.

Rogan stepped toward me and gently draped the jacket over me. The heavy warm fabric felt heavenly on my icicle shoulders. He loomed behind me, grim and slightly scary.

"Your debts are like this jacket, Nevada. A small favor that costs nothing. You don't yet realize how infinitesimal their total amount is, because you're still clinging to the illusion of being ordinary. Soon you'll make that money in a blink. You're an emerging Prime and it's a dangerous time for you. People will use you, manipulate you, pressure you. Everyone will want a piece of you. I simply shielded one of your pressure points until you were ready to shield it on your own."

If I took everything he said at face value, it meant that he was guarding me. Protecting me. If he expected anything in return, he hasn't said what it was. But nothing in the world of Primes was free.

"What other measures have you taken for my safety?" I asked.

"You know everything I've done."

True.

"I didn't do it to control you. I did it because you were vulnerable."

"Did anyone attempt to purchase my mortgage from you?"

"Yes."

True. "Who and when?"

"A boutique bank, yesterday. My people are tracking it down. We'll know who's behind it in the next twenty-four hours."

I had a strong feeling it would lead back to House Montgomery. "Why do you care what happens to me, Rogan?"

"It amuses me." Neither his voice, nor his face betrayed any delight.

"Really, Connor?" I turned and looked into his eyes. My magic licked him and liked the taste.

"If you do this to a member of a House, it's a declaration of war," he warned, his eyes dark. "Keep your magic to yourself."

"Then answer the question so I don't have to go to war with you."

Rogan turned and walked away, leaving me standing wrapped in his jacket.

I pulled the jacket tighter around myself and looked back at the garden. If we had calculated correctly, Baranovsky would approach me.

Measured steps broke the silence behind me. Someone walked out onto the balcony and leaned on the rail next to me. I turned my head. Baranovsky looked at me with his remarkable eyes. In the hallway, the two bodyguards waited, far enough to not obviously intrude on the conversation but close enough to shoot me in the head and not miss. I pretended not to see them and turned back to the garden.

"Enjoying the brisk air?" Baranovsky asked.

"Yes," I said. I wanted to babble to ease off the pressure, but the more we spoke, the less mysterious I would seem.

We stood in silence.

"A woman of few words," he said. "A rarity."

I raised my eyebrows at him. "You're too sophisticated for that remark."

A self-deprecating smile stretched his lips. "What makes you think that?"

"You're a collector. You value each item in your collection for its unique charm. A broad generalization, especially one so ham-fisted, would be out of character for a connoisseur."

His eyes narrowed. He was looking at the bruise on my neck. "And you believe me to be one?"

"You had an affair with Elena de Trevino, a woman with perfect recall, who can reproduce every wrong thing you have ever said to her."

"One could say every woman possesses such power."

I shook my head. "No, we only remember things that emotionally wound us. Elena remembered everything."

Baranovsky shook his head, smiling. "This is a dangerous conversation."

"You're right. You should save yourself and gracefully retreat."

"Who are you?" he asked, his voice holding a note of wonder.

Got him. Now I just had to keep him. "And guest."

"I'm sorry?"

"That's how I was announced. And guest, one of many. Nameless, anonymous, here for one night, and then gone."

"But hardly forgotten."

I looked back at the garden.

"Do you know why I'm drawn to roses?" he asked.

"You like their thorns?" He couldn't possibly be this lame.

"No. Each seedling is unique. Two seeds from the same cross, originating from the same two parent plants, will show variation in color, in the shape of petals, in the whorls themselves, even in how long the bloom will last."

"See? A connoisseur of dangerous women and flowers with thorns."

"You're making fun of me," he said, still smiling.

"Only a little."

He offered me his arm. "Walk with me."

I shook my head. "No."

"Why not?"

"Because you're right—this conversation is too dangerous for you."

"Should I be worried about Rogan?" A mischievous light sparked in his eyes. Gabriel Baranovsky liked walking a tight rope.

"You should be worried about me." I gave him a sad smile and for once actually meant it. "I'm a monster of a different kind. I think some would prefer Rogan over me."

"What do you do?"

Wouldn't you like to know? "Do you miss Elena?"

"Yes."

Truth. My magic wrapped him, saturating the air but not touching. I could almost sense the hesitation in his words, something he was trying to hide. His will was strong, but unlike Rogan's steel-hard determination, Baranovsky seemed flexible. Almost pliant. I could try to nudge him toward the right answers. Not enough pressure to compel a direct reply, but just enough to keep him talking more than he would have otherwise. I had never done it before.

If he sensed my magic, he would have me killed. Baranovsky wasn't a combat Prime, so he would rely on more conventional means of security and he would have a great deal of it, because currently his house was full of people who shot lightning from their fingertips and belched fire. I knew for sure there was one sniper in the window. There were likely to be more in the garden. If I grabbed him with my power and made him tell me what I wanted to know, I'd never make it out of this gala alive.

"We were more than lovers," he said. "We were friends."

"Does it bother you that she died?" I kept pushing, trying to stay subtle, but keeping him on the balcony with me.

He leaned back on the rail and let out a sigh. "It's the way of our universe. A never-ending chain of cannibalism: the stronger prey on the weaker only to become prey in return. The only way to win the game is to not play."

"Do you know why they killed her?"

"No."

Lie. Outright, direct, bold lie. He knew.

"Did you know Elena?" he asked.

"No," I told him. "I met her husband."

I focused on him so completely my voice sounded like it was coming out of a stranger's mouth.

"Ah." He'd sunk a world of meaning into that one sound.

"Elena is dead. Someone has to pay for it," I told him. My magic slid tighter around him.

His smile fled. "A bit of advice. Don't go digging in that grave. I don't know what hold you have on Montgomery and Rogan, but they won't risk themselves for your sake."

In my head, somehow, he was glowing, an almost silvery figure with a dark spot to one side of his silhouette, on the left side of his skull. He was hiding something in that spot and I needed to get at it. I was concentrating so hard my head threatened to burst.

"She came to see you before she died."

"You know too much about this." He was staring at me carefully.

Gently, delicately I pulled the noose of my magic around him, tethering him to me. I pushed him, steering his answers to the place I wanted him to go.

"Did she leave anything with you?"

The spot turned darker. Yes, yes she had. What could she have given him?

"A memento of your relationship, perhaps?" The vision of the freckled soldier tossing a USB drive out of the window flashed before me. "A USB drive containing documents meant to be released after her death?"

"That would be terribly cliché, wouldn't it?"

Sweat broke on my hairline. Blood pounded through the veins in my head. "She's been dead for days and you haven't gone public. Are you scared, Gabriel?"

"She gave me nothing."

Lie.

He smiled, a casual easy grin. "And you and I are not on a first-name basis."

I smiled back. "Did you look at it?"

Nothing.

I needed to nudge him, just a little tiny bit, so he wouldn't feel it. Just a tiny bit . . .

The dark spot faded slightly in response to my magic.

"As I said, she left me nothing. And if she had, if such a thing existed, I would have the good sense to put it somewhere safe from the outside world. Somewhere it would stay buried."

"You looked at it." I smiled wider. Circles swam before my eyes. I could barely see. "Where would it be buried?"

The dark spot faded completely for a moment.

"It's safe in my bedroom."

My hold on him slipped.

Baranovsky frowned. "My dear, as I said, if it existed, I would've destroyed it long ago."

He didn't even realize what he'd told me while under the influence of my magic. If that was accurate, then his memory of this conversation would be completely different from mine.

Baranovsky shrugged, his expression disappointed. "This conversation started out promising but sadly devolved into minutiae. I have no time for banality. Enjoy the rest of the party."

He turned and walked away.

Get off the balcony before you get shot.

I forced myself to slowly walk into the hallway, resisting the urge to sag against the balcony rail. My chest hurt. My stomach too. Circles swam before my eyes.

Breathe. Breathe, breathe, breathe . . .

I kept walking, without really seeing where or what was happening until I came to a staircase. Rogan caught up with me. I leaned on his arm and he walked me down into the ballroom. He was practically carrying my weight on his arm.

"Easy," he said under his breath. "One step at a time."

"I'm going to fall over and embarrass both of us."

"You won't fall over. I'll keep you up."

I leaned even more onto his rock-solid arm. I had to keep walking.

"Did you overextend?" Rogan asked, his voice controlled.

"A little."

"Does Baranovsky know?" He was asking if he needed to fight his way out of the gala.

"He didn't feel it. I was very careful, which is why I'm having trouble walking. She gave him a copy of the USB. He said it's safe in his bedroom. Exact quote."

The stairway ended. I tried to turn right toward the door, but Rogan turned left taking me with him.

"Where are we going?"

"To find Augustine."

"Why?"

"Because Baranovsky maintains a workstation in his quarters. It's not connected to the Internet and can't be hacked from the outside. Any document uploaded to it is safe."

"How do you know that?"

Rogan smiled, a narrow parting of lips. "I bribed his cleaning crew. There are few people more motivated than a parent with a child accepted into an Ivy League college and no way to pay for it."

"Can you use them to get at his computer?"

"No. It's too risky. That's why we have to find Augustine."

Augustine was an illusion Prime. He could assume any form. "You want Augustine to become Baranovsky, go to the bedroom, and get the data from his computer?"

"Exactly."

"You'll get him killed," I murmured.

"He once walked around CIA headquarters for three hours, passing fingerprint and retina scanners." Rogan's mouth quirked. "Until they figure out how to do an instant DNA check, no facility is secure from Augustine. This will be child's play."

Ahead, Augustine stepped up from behind a group of people and began making his way to us.

"Connor," a woman called from the left.

Rogan glanced in the direction of the voice. His face softened and he halted. "Rynda."

A red-haired woman smiled at Rogan. She was about his age, slender, willowy even, with a heart-shaped face framed by loose waves of copper hair, a flawless complexion, and bright grey eyes, so light they almost glowed silver. I recognized her instantly. Her name was Rynda Charles, Rynda Sherwood now, after she married, and at some point in the distant past Rogan had been supposed to marry her. He'd mentioned it once in a casual conversation and I had looked her up.

"It's nice to see you," Rynda said. "Doesn't seem like your scene."

"It's not," he said. "How are Brian and the kids?"

"Great." She smiled again. She had a dazzling smile, the kind that lit up her whole face. If you put us side by side in identical dresses and let ten people into the room, they would flock to her, while I would be left standing alone. That was perfectly fine with me. I didn't want anyone's attention.

It hit me like a ton of bricks. I wanted Rogan's attention. I was jealous, and my jealousy was a full-blown monster with needles, fangs, and claws. In my mind, Rogan was mine.

Crap. When did this even happen?

I chanced a quick glance at them. They were talking to each other with the easy familiarity of old friends. They looked good together. Rogan—huge, hard, and wrapped in broody darkness—and Rynda: sweet, light, almost delicate. And here I was, the third wheel, wanting to slap that sweet delicate smile right off Rynda's face.

"Jessica is in the first grade and Kyle will be starting school next year," Rynda reported. "Can you believe it? I'll be all alone."

"Feeling abandoned already?" Rogan asked.

"Yes. I know it's completely irrational."

I glanced in Augustine's direction. *Rescue me. Please, before she notices I exist and I make a fool of myself.*

He was moving toward us, but not nearly fast enough for my liking.

"Who is your companion?" Rynda asked.

"Nobody," I said.

Rogan glanced at me, surprised.

"We're not together," Rynda said. "We never were."

If I could've disappeared into thin air, I would've. "I'm sorry, I think you misunderstood the nature of our relationship. Mr. Rogan isn't my date. I work for House Montgomery, and he was simply kind enough to escort me. I think I see Augustine over there. Excuse me."

I tried to separate myself from Rogan, but he slid his arm around my waist. I wasn't going anywhere without drawing attention to myself.

Rynda peered into my eyes. "No, stay, please. I'm sorry, I didn't mean to make you uncomfortable."

"I'm not uncomfortable," I told her. "I simply didn't want to intrude."

"You're not intruding," Rogan said.

And the exact thing I didn't want to happen happened. Both of them were now focused on me.

I glanced back at Augustine, desperately hoping he was close. For some reason he turned almost in mid-step and was walking to the left. In his place an older woman who looked like a carbon copy of Rynda except twenty years older was marching toward us.

"Your mother is coming," Rogan said.

"I know. Can you hear the 'Ride of the Valkyries'?" Rynda sighed. "You probably should run."

"Too late," Rogan said.

Mrs. Charles stopped next to us and raised her eyebrows at me, then glanced at Rogan as if he was some dirty homeless person come to beg for change as she exited her limo.

"It's too late for regrets, Connor."

Rogan's face had snapped into his Prime expression, cold and tinted with arrogance. "It's a pleasure to see you too, Olivia."

"No, the pleasure is all mine. It's been over a decade. My daughter is radiant. Her husband is successful and both of her children are likely to be Primes. And you're a recluse, reduced to escorting your former college friend's employee." She spared me a look. "Couldn't you have done something about her neck? I'm sure Augustine would do you this small favor. Or have you managed to ruin that relationship as well?"

"Enough, Mother," Rynda said.

Rogan regarded Olivia with mild interest, as if she were an odd insect.

"No, I don't think so." Olivia's stare could've cut like a knife. "I'm quite enjoying my revenge. Fifteen years of financial planning and genetic forecasts ruined, because he wanted to play soldier."

She turned back to me. "Let me explain things to you, my dear. If you ever hope to make something of yourself, you will walk away from this man as fast as your feet will carry you. You stand here, in what is probably a borrowed dress, and you think that because your hand is on his arm, you're Cinderella with a head full of dreams and he's your wonderful prince."

"Mother!" Rynda snapped.

"In reality, you're an adornment, like a scarf that happened to complement his outfit. He doesn't care about you beyond the fleeting benefit you can provide. And when he is done, he'll discard you in the back of his closet, where you will linger, forgotten and still hoping, while your dreams wither and die one by one."

Her magic rose behind her like a nest of invisible snakes slithering to me. Her voice reverberated through my skull, reaching deep into my mind.

"You better run, my dear. Run fast and hard, and never look back. Go on."

Her magic crashed against me, a powerful hard surge pushing me to leave, and broke against my own. A psionic.

I could've stared into her eyes and fired back. Her will was strong, frightening even, but so was mine. And if I won, I'd make her spill every dirty secret she had on this floor. I wanted to so badly.

Instead, I turned around, broke free of Rogan, and hurried off, seemingly in the random direction that would take me to Augustine.

Rogan laughed quietly behind me.

You idiot, I'm pretending to run for my life. Don't ruin it.

Rynda's voice was brittle. "Are you happy now?"

"I'll be happy when he dies alone," her mother said.

"Always a pleasure, Olivia," Rogan said, his voice amused.

The crowd ignored me, concentrating on Rogan and Olivia. Nobody openly watched, but most glanced at them, some with interest, others with alarm. Baranovsky viewed the show from his favorite spot on the second floor by the stairs. He was sipping champagne from a flute, his face wearing an amused expression.

Augustine stepped into my way. I pretended to bump into him.

"What's going on?" he asked.

"I'm very publicly fleeing Olivia Charles and her magic," I whispered to him. "I'm distraught. You should calm me down somewhere out of sight, where nobody will realize that two Baranovskys is one too many."

"Of course," Augustine said, putting a protective arm around my shoulders. "Let's go this way."

Rogan said something to Olivia, but we were too far to hear.

Augustine led me to the side, aiming for a hallway. "What would this second Baranovsky be doing?"

"Getting a copy of Elena's USB from the computer in his bedroom."

"Splendid," Augustine said. "This will be fun."

Behind us glass shattered. I whipped around.

Gabriel Baranovsky clutched at his throat. Blood poured from his neck, shocking against his pale skin. He stumbled, poised above the stairs, like some odd bird about to take flight, and plunged down. His shoulder crunched, connecting with the steps. His body flipped, his head bouncing off the red carpet, slid, and came to rest midway down the staircase, his unseeing eyes staring straight at the ceiling.

The two bodyguards pointed guns at the crowd.

Nobody screamed. Nobody rushed to help.

The silence was deafening.

The entire mass of people turned as one and marched toward the exit, streaming past the guards, out of hallways, and down the stairs. Instantly bodies flooded the space around us, all moving in the same direction.

I tried to fight my way to the hallway, but Augustine grabbed my hand and pulled me toward the exit. "No! They'll lock down the mansion! We'll be trapped here for hours."

Damn it.

The security personnel charged into the room, cutting the crowd in a half. Cornelius appeared by my side. "We have to go!"

In the middle of the human current, Rogan turned and began striding against the flow of bodies forcing his way in our direction. He probably couldn't even see us.

"Rogan!" I called out.

Ahead a tall blond man turned his head. Our stares connected. He smiled.

I had seen that smile before through the window of the Suburban.

"Rogan!" I jerked my phone out of the clutch and held it up, pressing the camera icon to activate burst mode. The phone clicked in staccato, taking a dozen shots of the crowd in rapid succession.

The blond man turned and melted back into the crowd.

Behind us metal groaned as the security gates began clanging into place. "Remain calm!" a clipped voice announced from the speakers.

The crowd double-timed it toward the doors.

Rogan emerged from the mass of bodies.

"The guy from the Suburban!" I told him.

"Where?" he snarled.

I stabbed in the direction of the exit. I couldn't even see him anymore. Too many people between us and the doors. We'd never catch up to him.

Rogan raised his hand.

The wall to the left of us exploded. Chunks of marble littered the floor, spilling outside into the cold rainy night.

"Exit stage left," Cornelius murmured next to me.

I kicked off my shoes, hiked up my dress, and scrambled over the rubble out of Baranovsky's mansion.

Chapter 10

$\mathcal{T}$he glamorous Houston elite was evacuating at full speed. Several wind mages took off into the night sky while circles ignited with blue fire as the teleporters popped out of existence, leaving their arcane footprints on the pavement. Helicopters hovered overhead, cars streamed out of the parking lot. Chaos reigned. I spent ten minutes in the pandemonium, looking for the ice mage, before Rogan practically dragged me away and loaded me into his armored SUV. Cornelius and Augustine both jumped in with us and the SUV took off.

I scrolled through the images on my phone. I had taken thirty-two pictures. Of those, three showed the mage as he smiled, turned, and looked away. I got three quarters of the face, a profile, and the back of his head. The shots were lousy, his features blurry, but it should be enough for Bug.

I tried to email the pictures to myself. No signal. Damn it.

"Give me your phone, please," I asked Rogan.

He handed it to me. I zoomed in on the best shot of the mage, took a picture of my phone with Rogan's, and handed it back. Just in case.

Rogan stared at the image and shook his head. I passed my phone to Augustine.

"He looks familiar." Augustine frowned. "I've met him, but I can't recall when or where." He offered the phone to Cornelius.

"I don't recognize him," Cornelius murmured, his gaze boring into the mage. "Do you think he killed Nari?"

"We don't know that," I said, jumping in there before anybody else had a chance to say anything or Cornelius decided to leap out of the car and go back to look for the ice mage. "We know that an ice mage was involved. We know that this ice mage tried to kill me. We don't know anything else."

"But there must be a connection," Cornelius insisted.

"There probably is one." I was trying my best to sound calm and reasonable. "Remember, I promised you proof. We must be certain before we take action."

Cornelius squeezed his hand into a fist. "He might still be back there."

"We'll get him," I promised.

"We have his face," Rogan said, his voice reassuring. "There is no place he can hide now."

An hour later we piled through the doors of Rogan's HQ, located in a large two-story building a street away from our warehouse. Judging by the open first floor, it might have been some sort of industrial building, but it was now filled with vehicles and people. We got out and crossed the floor to the left, climbed the stairs, and emerged onto the second floor, elevated high above the concrete expanse of the first. This space was wide open as well. A metal frame had been erected in the middle of it, holding nine computer screens and braids of cables. In front of the screen Bug sat in his chair, with Napoleon sleeping on what looked like a dog-sized padded throne of red fabric decorated with gold fleur-de-lis. He saw us, but decided our presence wasn't incentive enough to bestir himself.

"I have a face for you," I told Bug.

He exploded out of his chair. "Give!"

I handed him the phone.

He plugged a cable into it. My pictures filled the screen. "Which one?"

I pointed at the mage.

Bug dropped into his chair. His fingers danced over the keyboard with the agility of a virtuoso pianist. Faces filled the nine screens, blinking in and out of existence.

Around the frame, couches and chairs waited in a ragged horseshoe. A huge industrial fridge stood against the left wall next to a counter that supported three coffeemakers, each with a full carafe. Coffee!

Augustine landed on the leather couch, his pose effortlessly elegant. "I have state-of-the-art facial recognition software at the Montgomery building."

"Bug is faster," Rogan and I said at the same time.

Cornelius stared at the screens. Rogan moved to stand by Bug's shoulder and spoke to him in a low voice. Probably bringing him up to speed on our wonderful adventure.

I texted Bern. Everything okay?

Yes.

I waited for more information. Nothing. Perfect Bern. Sometimes my cousin took things too literally. How are the kids, Mom, and Grandma? How are you?

We're fine. You missed fried-rice night. I had to hold Matilda's cat so she could clean his eyes. Leon is still trying to get a gun. Aunt Pen says she'll take him for target practice once this is over. Grandma Frida wants to know when the wedding is.

Never.

I'll tell her that.

"Found him!" Bug announced.

A portrait of a man in his thirties filled the screen. He seemed to be about five years or so older than Rogan. Dark blond hair cut short on the sides and fashionably longer on top of his head, brushed back from his face. A light stubble added a mild roughness to his jaw. His features were handsome and well formed, and he clearly didn't bother with illusion, because he was smiling in the picture, the same quiet, sly smile I had seen an hour ago, and the crow's feet in the corner of his light hazel eyes stood out. In the picture he wore a tuxedo and a bow tie.

"David Howling," Bug said. "Of House Howling."

"That can't be right," Augustine said. "House Howling is a fulgurkinetic house."

Howlings didn't freeze things. They shot lightning.

My phone chimed. A text message. I checked it. Grandma Frida.

How is it going with your boyfriend?;);) ;)

Not my boyfriend!

"Is David Howling registered?" Cornelius asked.

"Average fulgurkinetic," Bug reported. "Says here he tried three times to pass as Significant, but failed."

"Run the genealogy," Rogan said.

Bug played another melody on the keyboard. The middle screen blinked, presenting the family tree of House Howling, listing the current head of the House, spouses, and children.

Richard Howling II

```
                    ┌─────────────────────────────────┐
Valorie Howling (Styles)                    Diana Howling (Collins)

├── Richard Howling III                      └── David Howling

└── Jolina Howling (Roberts)
```

"Run Diana Collins," Rogan ordered.

House Collins appeared on the screen.

Bug's voice was precise and loud. "Diana Collins is registered to the New York branch of House Collins as aquakinetic Prime with psychrokinetic specialization."

Psychrokinetic stood for "ice mage."

"A dark horse," Augustine said, his perfect face wrinkling with disdain.

I'd heard of dark horses, mostly because a lot of romance and action fiction involving Primes centered around them. Primes divulged just enough information about their capabilities to maintain their status, often hiding their secondary talents. Dark horses carried it a step further. They didn't register as Primes at all, pretending to be less than they were so they could do shady things to further their family's interests. "So it's a real thing?"

"Regrettably, yes," Augustine said. "House Howling is a fulgurkinetic family. All of their enterprises are tied into it. Instead of registering an ice Prime who couldn't really add anything to the family, they kept David on the back burner. He probably received a very specialized training."

"He's an assassin," Rogan said, matter-of-fact. "A good

one. Bug, I want surveillance on his house. Find his vehicle. I want to know where he is at all times."

"Baranovsky was drinking champagne when he died," I thought out loud. "Could Howling have frozen the liquid in his throat?"

"Very likely. He didn't simply freeze it. If he'd done that, Baranovsky would've simply choked on an ice cube. He must've made the liquid into a flat sharp blade and slit the throat from inside out." Rogan stared at the screen, a calculation taking place behind his eyes. "Forsberg's brain showed signs of ice damage as well."

"It's an insidious practice," Augustine continued, disgust plain in his voice. "And much more rare than the movies will lead you to believe. It requires a huge sacrifice on the part of the dark horse. They can never admit their Prime status or reap any of the benefits it affords. They are always viewed as lesser by their peers. I've known only two dark horses in my life and in both cases, it didn't end well for them or their families."

I kept thinking back to Baranovsky drinking. I could picture it in my head, him standing there with a champagne flute, watching . . . watching Rogan and Olivia Charles. Olivia Charles, who'd given me a mental push to flee. What was it Rogan said about manipulators? They were often registered as other specialties, a psionic being a favorite.

"Rogan, how is Olivia Charles registered?"

"A psionic Prime." He clamped his mouth shut. His gaze gained a dangerous edge.

"What is it?" Augustine looked at him and at me.

"We've been played," I said. "Olivia Charles created a diversion and while everyone focused on Rogan and her drama, David Howling cruised by Baranovsky and turned the champagne in his throat into a solid block of ice. They used us."

"That's a heavy accusation, Ms. Baylor," Augustine said.

Funny how I was Nevada until I dared to accuse one of their own. "Nari and the other lawyers were killed by an ice mage and a manipulator working together. Rogan, if Olivia was a manipulator, would anyone know?"

"Olivia Charles is a fourth generation Prime." Augustine leaned forward. "She is mean as a snake if she doesn't like you, but her reputation is beyond any contestation."

"Would anyone know?" I repeated, searching Rogan's face for an answer.

"No," he said, his voice grim. His face told me he was contemplating violence, and a lot of it.

"Whoa." Augustine raised both hands. "Let's back way, way up, past the line of insanity. We're not talking about some loose cannon spoiled child like Pierce or a dark horse from a second marriage who is barely known in society. We're talking about someone with a spotless record and vast connections in our community. My mother hates Olivia Charles, but when Olivia invites her to a luncheon, my mother makes an effort to attend. Before you even consider going after Olivia, you have to have bulletproof evidence of her guilt. If you videotape her stabbing someone with a butcher knife and then play it before the Assembly, half of the people will swear it was a fabrication and a quarter would claim she was drinking tea with them when the stabbing occurred. If you accuse her of anything without evidence, you will be crucified. I'll have to disavow any connection with you. You will never land another client of any prominence." He turned to Rogan. "And you will lose the last shreds of your standing."

"I don't care," Rogan said.

"You should care." Augustine slid his glasses back up the bridge of his nose. "You have nothing. You have hypothesis and conjecture. This course of action won't just affect you."

Bug cleared his throat.

"This will affect me, our families, and even Rynda. This is the kind of accusation that must be made with exceptional care. Not only that, but it makes no sense for Olivia to be involved in this mess. She is at the pinnacle of her life. She has power, wealth, and influence. Why would she jeopardize it?"

Bug cleared his throat louder.

"What?" Rogan asked.

"Voilà." Bug tapped the key. The front of Baranovsky's mansion filled the middle screens, filmed through the haze of rain and bordered in dark wet leaves.

David Howling stood to the side, smoking, that familiar smile on his face. He seemed to be perpetually calm and happy.

A limo slid into place before the front staircase. The driver dashed to the passenger door, opened an umbrella, and swung the door open, holding the black umbrella above it. Olivia Charles stepped out, walked up the staircase, paused for a moment before security and went inside. Fifteen seconds later David flicked his half-finished cigarette aside and followed her in.

Augustine's face turned white. "Dear God."

And it proved nothing. They didn't look at each other. They didn't say anything to each other. Everyone in the room knew it wasn't a coincidence. Howling had waited outside to make sure she arrived. And we could do exactly nothing with that knowledge.

"He's right," I told Rogan. "We have no direct evidence."

"Then we should get some," he said. "We need that USB drive."

He looked at Bug.

"How?" Bug asked. "Baranovsky has a DaemonEye security lock on his network. I would have to get the kid to crack it, but even if Bern opens all the cyber doors, it won't do us any good. You can't hack something that's not connected to the Internet. You have to physically access the computer. Someone has to walk in, get the computer, or at least the hard drive, and walk out with it. Every security person Baranovsky employed is likely at that mansion right now, not to mention cops who are swarming within the place. That house is locked up tighter than a clam with lockjaw. By now the gap in the wall is probably repaired and if it isn't, it's guarded like Fort Knox."

"How did you film that footage?" Cornelius said behind me.

I almost jumped. He'd been so quiet I'd forgotten he was there.

"A drone transmitting the feed from its camera." Bug waved his arm. "A fifty-thousand-dollar drone, which, by the way, I lost because some asshole wind mage knocked it out of the sky just as I tried to recover it. The last thing it transmitted was a tree, up very close."

"If I understand correctly, you don't need the entire computer." Cornelius rested his elbow on his bent knee and leaned his cheek on his fingers. "You just need the hard drive."

"Yes." Bug spread his arms. Napoleon decided that things had gotten exciting enough to warrant his input and barked once to underscore the point.

Rogan glanced at Augustine.

"I suppose I could try to impersonate one of the security personnel," the illusion mage said. "Assuming we kidnap someone with access to Baranovsky's inner sanctum. That will take time and research."

"What about a short-range teleporter?" I asked. Teleportation was a last resort. It usually didn't go well, but among the three of them they had to know at least one mage capable of it.

"Too risky," Augustine said. "The place is crawling with security. And two-thirds of human teleportations, unless the teleporter is a Prime, end up with the teleported party resembling an undercooked meat loaf."

"Find out who is securing the mansion," Rogan said to Bug. "Let's see if we can throw money at them."

"I'll need another drone," Bug said.

"Ferrets," Cornelius said.

All of us looked at him.

"Ferrets?" Augustine asked.

"It's a domesticated form of European polecat," Cornelius said. "Closely related to weasels, minks, and stoats."

"I know what a ferret is," Augustine said, obviously making a heroic effort to be patient. "I'm asking how ferrets would help us retrieve the computer."

"I assume the mansion has laundry facilities?" Cornelius asked, a mild expression on his face.

"Yes," Bug reported.

"Industrial dryers?"

"Most likely."

"And you only require a hard drive from the computer?"

"Yes," Bug said.

"In that case, I can extract those things for you provided you can attach a very small camera and a radio receiver to a ferret harness. I have to be able to talk to them and I must see what they see. I have several harnesses at Nevada's warehouse, but my camera needs to be replaced and I haven't gotten around to it."

"You want to send in harnessed ferrets through a laundry vent?" Augustine clearly had difficulty coming to terms with that idea.

"Yes," Cornelius said.

I blinked. "Wouldn't the vent be secured by an alarm?"

The three of them looked at me as if I'd suddenly sprouted a second head.

"It doesn't make sense to secure a laundry vent," Rogan explained. "It's too small and it opens into a dryer."

"I'm curious, what are you picturing exactly?" Augustine asked. "A crisscrossing pattern of red laser beams and ferrets in harnesses slithering through it like ninjas?"

Ugh. He needed some of his own medicine. I dropped some cold into my voice. "Mr. Montgomery, contrary to what popular entertainment would like you to believe, laser beams are neither red nor visible under ordinary circumstances. I would think a man in charge of an investigative firm would know that."

Augustine flushed. "I do know that, which is why I asked the question in the first place."

I plowed on ahead. "Lasers wouldn't make an optimal choice for securing a dryer vent anyway, because air carrying dryer lint would create false positives and would eventually clog the mirror system. For the same reason, heat sensors or movement sensors are out, but the exhaust could be secured by a pressure sensor. How paranoid is Baranovsky? I don't want Cornelius' ferrets to die. It would be painful for him."

Cornelius reached over and squeezed my hand. "Thank you for thinking of me."

"I'm more paranoid than Baranovsky," Rogan said. "My laundry vents aren't secured. But I'd imagine there is a metal grate over them."

"Does anybody else find this whole idea of a ferret heist mildly absurd?" Augustine looked around the room.

"Grates are not an issue," Cornelius said.

"Can your animals handle screws?" Augustine asked.

Cornelius met his gaze. "Let's assume that I spend as much time training my animals and honing my magic as you do practicing your illusions."

"How confident are you that this will work?" I asked Cornelius.

He smiled at me.

"Let's do it," Rogan said.

Rogan owned a surveillance truck. From the outside, it looked like a medium-sized RV. Inside, it was a high-tech wall of computer screens, equipment, cables, and various monitors. I sat in my black leather seat, which could rotate 270 degrees when unlocked and came equipped with a seat belt and a hiney warmer, and watched the night-vision camera feed on the main screen as two ferrets and a slightly larger creature Cornelius called a Chinese ferret-badger loped their way through the brush. The Chinese ferret-badger was adorably fluffy and I got to pet him and feed him some raisins before Bug put him into a harness that supported a camera and a communicator. Two side monitors provided similar feeds from the ferrets. Cornelius and Bug sat in front of them, both wearing headsets with mikes.

"I can't believe you put cameras on ferrets," Augustine said on my left.

"You put cameras on drones," Cornelius responded.

"Yes, but drones are supposed to have cameras. This is . . . unnatural."

Cornelius spared him a smile.

On the screen the drizzle still soaked the ground. It was the kind of night when cold seeped into your bones. I leaned closer in my seat, grateful to be dry and warm. While they had put the harnesses together, I'd made a brief run home, where I switched out of my beautiful and thoroughly rain-soaked dress into a prosaic T-shirt and jeans. My hair was still put up, but the makeup had to go. I felt more like me, but there had been something magical about that dress, about being at the gala, and walking with Rogan up to the balcony. Something that reached back through my adulthood to an almost childlike belief in magic and wonder. When I thought back to this evening, I should've remembered Baranovsky, the man I had spoken to only minutes before he died, murdered in his own mansion. Instead I remembered the feel of Rogan's fingers on mine and his face when he said, "I see a Prime." He said it as if he'd dreaded it. It bothered me. It bothered me more than Baranovsky's murder.

Was I getting used to death? I hoped not.

According to Bug and his surveillance staff, David Howling had never made it home. He had vanished off the map somewhere between Baranovsky's mansion and his house in River Oaks. Neither Bug nor his two surveillance helpers were able to locate him. When Bug plucked Howling's cell phone number out of some Internet ether and called it at Rogan's directive, the number was no longer in service.

The brush ended. The three little beasts paused. In front of them, twenty yards of open ground stretched. Past it loomed the walls of the mansion's northern wing, where according to Rogan's informant, the laundry room was located. Some ornamental shrubs and rose bushes wound between the walls and the brush. The laundry vent was likely concealed behind the greenery.

Cornelius flicked a switch on his headset, his voice clear and friendly, as if he were speaking to a group of small children. "Look left."

The cameras shifted as the beasts looked left in unison. "Look right."

The cameras obediently swung right. All clear.

"Run to the wall."

The three beasties dashed across the open ground, under the rose bushes, and to the wall.

Cornelius concentrated, his gaze focused, his voice intimate and almost hypnotic. "Harsh scent. Yellow poison scent. Find it."

"Poison scent?" Rogan asked.

He'd moved to stand next to me and suddenly I was acutely aware that he was standing only inches away. I wanted him to reach out and touch me. He didn't.

"Bleach," Bug said softly. "He had them smell paper towels soaked in bleach. The scent lingers on clothes even in the dryer."

The beasties dashed left, rounded the corner, and stopped before a square foot-wide vent secured by a metal grate.

"Use the small tooth," Cornelius intoned. "Open the burrow."

"I'm in a Disney movie," Augustine said, his face disgusted.

One of the ferrets reached over and pulled a tiny screwdriver out of the ferret-badger's harness. The beast raised it up and put it into the screw. The other ferret squeezed it and the electric screwdriver whirred quietly, pulling the screw out. The screwdriver slipped. The ferret patiently repositioned it again.

Augustine blinked.

It took them almost five minutes, but finally the screws came loose and the three furry burglars hooked their claws into the grate and pulled it out.

"Balu, enter the burrow. Loki, enter. Hermes, enter."

The badger squirmed into the vent, with the ferrets following it. Lint dust floated in the air as they moved. One of the ferrets sneezed adorably. *Please don't get killed, little beasties.*

Cornelius' burglars double-timed it through the air vent. Abruptly the metal tunnel ended in a T-section, with the perpendicular tunnel running left and right. They must've had more than one dryer attached to it.

"Loki, wait. Hermes, wait."

The two ferrets obediently crouched down.

"Balu, charge."

The badger shot forward and smacked into the T-section's wall. The entire tunnel quaked. A dent bent the soft metal.

"Again."

The beast rammed the wall ahead. The view from its camera turned, shaking. The tunnel sagged. The weight of the badger had strained the connection between the wall and the semi-rigid metal duct running to the dryers. A narrow gap formed between the duct and the length of the dryer vent.

"Open the hole," Cornelius intoned. The ferrets hooked their claws into the gap.

Rogan watched, an odd expression on his face.

Three minutes later Loki, the lighter ferret, squirmed out of the hole and pulled off the clamp, disconnecting the duct.

Rogan lifted his cell to his ear and said quietly, "Margaret? Look into putting pressure sensors into our dryer vents . . . Yes. Dryer vents."

Augustine was typing something on his phone, his face unreadable. *Serves you right.*

The burglars dashed into the house, navigating the vast mansion and following commands as Cornelius patiently talked them through their heist. Bug had been right. The place swarmed with security personnel and detectives. Once, just before the ferrets ducked behind a curtain, Hermes' camera caught a glimpse of Lenora Jordan, the Harris County district attorney. In her late thirties, with medium brown skin and a mane of hair twisted into a careless bun, she strode through the house with a scowl on her face. Baranosvky's murder was big enough news to drag her out of bed and she clearly wasn't happy about any of it. A team of haggard-looking people in professional clothes trailed her, watching her every move. Most likely those were Baranovsky's lawyers. He must've made provisions for his death.

Lenora Jordan was my hero. When I was growing up, I'd wanted to be just like her.

Slowly, foot by foot, the furry beasts made their progress into the depths of the house.

I was so tired. It'd been a long night. *If I just closed my eyes for a moment, I'm sure nobody would mind . . .*

Rogan's hand skimmed my back as he leaned forward to glance at my face. "Coffee?"

I jerked awake. "Yes. Thank you."

I should've said no. Ugh.

He stepped away and returned with coffee, cream already in it.

Augustine raised his eyebrows at him. "You really are trying."

Rogan gave him a flat stare. Lesser men would've fled for their life, but Augustine was clearly made of sterner stuff.

"Congratulations, Nevada." Augustine allowed himself a narrow smile. "I do hope you appreciate the full gravity of this momentous occurrence. Mad Rogan actually physically moved his body to bring you a cup of coffee instead of simply floating it to your lap. The manipulation is so blatant it's painful to watch. Sadly for him, I'm still a better employer."

Rogan paused by him. "If you need any pointers on how to properly treat a woman, I can give you a lesson later."

"Please." Augustine held up his hand. "Spare me. Do you honestly think that she is dumb enough to fall for that? What's next? A picnic under the stars? Just how underhanded are you planning on being in your hiring process?"

Pot, kettle. "Thank you, Rogan," I said. "The coffee is delicious."

"You haven't even tried it," Augustine pointed out.

"The coffee is delicious," I repeated and sipped. It tasted divine, probably because it had at least half a jar of sugar in it.

"We reached the computer," Bug reported.

Baranovsky's personal computer was a tower of alien design, complete with weird plastic scales. The ferrets dismantled it in under a minute, plucked the hard drive out, dropped it into a plastic baggie they pulled out of Hermes' harness, and began the long trek back to the laundry. The coffee wore off somewhere between the first and second floor. I pulled my legs to me and tried to nestle deeper into the seat. I had spent too much magic today. I needed to learn to pace myself.

I hung on through the narrow escape through the staff rooms and the mad dash across the rain soaked forest. Finally, the screen showed the truck. Rogan opened the door and the wet beasts dashed inside and swarmed over Cornelius' lap, chirping and screeching like there was no tomorrow.

Cornelius' face lit up. He smiled, the first genuine smile I had ever seen on his face. It was a beautiful smile, filled with simple powerful joy. Loki thrust the drive in the baggie at him, hitting Cornelius in the face with it. The animal mage took the drive, handed it to Bug, and petted the furry beasts. I exhaled. Something had gone right. I was sure we would pay for it later, but for now, I could sit here and just watch Cornelius with his animals.

Soon the beasts calmed down, the ferrets overjoyed at offerings of cooked chicken, while the ferret-badger munched on plums. Cornelius slumped in his seat, exhausted.

"That was incredible," I told him.

"Thank you. The biggest problem is keeping the ferrets on task. They are like hyperactive toddlers."

"Found it," Bug announced.

The screen ignited, showing a nighttime recording of a man in a light trench coat exiting a high-rise. A taller man in a suit followed him closely. A bodyguard.

The angle of the video was much too low for a street surveillance camera. Somebody was recording it from a car. I'd done it hundreds of times and my videos looked just like that.

The bodyguard and the man waited for a moment. A car pulled around the corner and the headlights illuminated the bodyguard and the man in the trench coat. Breath caught in my throat. Senator Garza.

The car slid to a smooth stop. The bodyguard opened the door.

Lightning ripped from the corner of the screen, its feathery tendrils clutching the bodyguard, Senator Garza, and the vehicle and binding them into a single glowing whole. The lightning burned and burned, the two men jerking in its lethal embrace. The front of the car melted. Fire burst from the rear, popping the tires.

The lightning blinked and came back again. Slowly, shakily, the camera panned left. A lone man stood on the street, older, dark-haired, wearing a business suit, his hands raised in a trademark mage pose, arms bent at the elbow, palms up. The camera zoomed in on his face. His features were slack, his expression almost serene, but his eyes furious, churning with the pain and despair of a man not in control of his own body.

The lightning died. The camera panned back. The car burned, a charred wreck. Garza and the bodyguard sprawled on the sidewalk, their bodies smoking.

The view switched back to the man. He stared at the two bodies, a horrified expression on his face, then turned and fled.

"I know him," Augustine said, his voice sharp. "It's . . ."

"Richard Howling," Rogan said. "Controlled by Olivia Charles. House Howling killed Senator Garza."

It was obvious now, and putting together the pieces seemed like an afterthought. I did it anyway, just so I didn't miss anything.

"For some unknown reason, Olivia Charles wanted Senator Garza dead. Most likely, he stumbled onto their scheme and became a threat. They needed to take him out and do it in a way that wouldn't come back to them."

"So they kill two birds with one stone," Augustine said. "Olivia used her magic on Richard Howling, forcing him to kill Garza, which eliminates the threat and potentially implicates Richard Howling."

"But why use Richard Howling?" Cornelius asked. "If she could impose her will on Howling, she could've taken control of Garza's bodyguards."

"It must've been a concession to David," Rogan said. "It's unlikely that this is the first time he killed for them."

Augustine nodded. "Richard's sister is married to a different House. With Richard out of the picture, David becomes the only viable choice as the head of the Howling House. Like I said, dark horses never turn out well. They tend to hate their handlers."

"Everything was going well," I continued. "Except Olivia and David didn't know that Forsberg had Garza under surveillance. When Forsberg realized what was on the recording, he tried to use it to his advantage. He turned it over to his legal team with instructions to make a deal either with Garza's people, with Howling, or with someone else. Olivia found out, and she and David Howling killed everyone involved to keep the recording from getting out. Why would Forsberg have Garza followed?"

"Because Forsberg was a Steward," Rogan said. "There are a number of factions within the Assembly, but the two largest are the Civil Majority and the Stewards. The Stewards are pro-mage and the Civil Majority is pro-people."

"That's an oversimplification," Augustine said. "The Stewards see themselves and the Houses as the primary guiding force of human society. They reject the current democratic model and advocate for greater power and influence of the Houses. Simply put, they want to rule. The Civil Majority takes its root from the quote by Johanna Hemlock, a nineteenth-century philosopher and Prime. The Civil Majority seeks to limit House involvement in politics."

"What's the quote?" I asked.

"In a country ruled by a civil majority even the smallest minority enjoys greater protection than a majority living in a country where power is hoarded by select few," Cornelius said.

"That sounds almost altruistic," I said. "Don't take it the wrong way, but Houses are not known for giving up power."

Augustine sighed. "No, it's not altruism. It's self-interest. Our policy of noninvolvement has been working really well so far. We're wealthy and secure, and we have a lot to lose. Garza was the darling of the Civil Majority. Matthias Forsberg was an active member of the Stewards. The Stewards likely conspired to torpedo Garza's rise to power, so Forsberg must've put him under surveillance, hoping for some dirt from which the Stewards could've manufactured a scandal."

I rubbed my face, trying to brush the drowsiness off.

"So Olivia and her people obtained the recording," Rogan said, "and now it's an unexpected bonus. What do they do with it?"

"Blackmail is an obvious choice," Augustine said. "Howling controls the Moderates, the third-largest faction within the Assembly. This might be about Assembly elections."

"No." Rogan pushed from his seat and began stalking back and forth like a caged tiger. "These people want destabilization. Chaos. The surveillance recording wasn't supposed to exist, but it does and they have a copy of it. If we hide the recording and they choose to sit on their copy, Richard Howling becomes their puppet. If we forward the recording to Lenora, she will have to arrest Richard Howling. There would be a public outcry over Garza being murdered by a head of a House. David still gets what he wants. If they release their copy ahead of us, David again gets his House and the DA's office will look incompetent. There will be a huge wave of public outrage."

"Doesn't matter what we do, they win," Augustine said. "This isn't just usual House politics. This feels like a seismic shift within the power structure, one I'm not sure we have the combined power to oppose. Rogan, are we on the wrong side of this?"

Rogan pivoted to him. "They murdered civilians and nearly demolished downtown, which would've killed thousands more. They will never be the right side. I intend to win this war."

"I know that." Augustine's face was tired. "I just wonder if history will view us as heroes or villains."

"Depends on who writes it," I told him. "We have to take it to Lenora."

Rogan studied me. "Why?"

He knew perfectly well why. "You said yourself, these

people are interested in chaos. You can't create chaos unless you rile up the public. They will release the video, they will do it somewhere it can't be contained—like the social networks—and they will stoke the outrage. It will look like the DA's office deliberately hid the fact that a beloved senator and champion of the people was murdered by a Prime. I don't understand why they haven't released it already."

"They're waiting for the right moment," Rogan said.

"And that's exactly why the more time Lenora has with the video, the better."

"We'll talk to Lenora's office in the morning," Rogan said. "I'll need time to pull together paperwork."

He knew I was right so why the hell was he stalling?

"Are you going to apply for a Verona Exception?" Augustine said, a calculating look in his eyes.

"Yes."

"You will require the cooperation of House Harrison." Augustine turned to Cornelius.

"What is the Verona Exception?" I could look it up on my phone but I was too tired.

"It's named after the Capulet and Montague feud," Cornelius explained. "*Romeo and Juliet* begins with the Prince of Verona issuing an ultimatum to both families promising to put to death the next person who rekindles the feud. Then he walks off stage and washes his hands of it until their actions force him to return."

"A Verona Exception means filing a claim against House Howling with the DA's office," Rogan said. "Troy is my employee and so are you by virtue of my agreement with Cornelius. Howling attacked you both, made no effort to offer any reparations, and can't be reached by normal means."

"But you don't know that." My brain was so slow and tired, and when I pushed it to make rational thoughts, it threatened to collapse. "You haven't called the head of his House."

"I'll call Richard in the morning," Rogan said. "He'll disavow any knowledge of the incident. He doesn't want to be involved, which is why he made David into a dark horse in the first place."

"A Verona Exception effectively states that this now becomes a matter of open warfare among specific members of these three Houses," Augustine said. "By granting the Verona Exception, the DA's office will acknowledge that enough evidence exists to warrant retribution from House Rogan and House Harrison and empower them to enact this retribution, provided they don't demonstrate gross disregard for civilian welfare."

"So it allows them to wash their hands of it and let us fight it out?" I asked.

"Yes," Rogan said.

It made sense. The DA's office had some magic users on staff, of whom Lenora Jordan was the most dangerous, but if they got involved every time two Primes fought, the result would be catastrophic for police personnel.

"It's standard procedure," Rogan said. "The DA gets involved when the safety of the public is at stake. I'll need a sworn affidavit from you and dispensation from House Harrison stating that they allow Cornelius to engage."

"That may be a problem," Cornelius said quietly. "We have a small House. We act cautiously and we don't get involved. My parents maintained this policy for years and now my sister preserves it."

The same sister who had sent a card and some flowers when she learned her youngest brother's wife had been murdered.

"I'll speak to her tomorrow," Cornelius said.

Tomorrow might be too late. If that video hit the Internet, there would be riots. I didn't almost die about ten times trying to save Houston from being burned only to see it tear itself apart.

I turned to Bug. "Can I have a copy of the video, please?"

He glanced at Rogan.

I pretended to sigh. "This is getting tiresome. Rogan and my employer signed a contract, and that contract goes both ways. If we have to share evidence with you, you have to share evidence with us, especially since my employer obtained it. I would like a copy of the video, please. Email would be great."

"Do as she says," Rogan said. He was smiling. I had no idea what was so funny.

My phone chimed announcing a new email.

"Thank you."

"Take your time, Cornelius," Rogan said. "Like I said, paperwork takes time and Lenora may not even see us tomorrow considering the Baranovsky mess. This is a delicate matter."

"If my sister refuses, I'll proceed on my own, but our case would be stronger with us both."

I got up. "Where is the bathroom?"

Rogan pointed to a door in the far wall.

"Thank you."

I got up, walked into the bathroom, and shut the door behind me. Was there conflict of interest? I had promised Cornelius that I would give him the name of his wife's murderer, but I had made it abundantly clear that I wouldn't kill that person for him. Cornelius' agreement with Rogan technically had nothing to do with me. It only specified mutual cooperation and bound Rogan's hands.

No, there was no conflict of interest. I was in possession of a video showing the murder of two citizens. It was my obligation under the law to report it. I texted Bern. This is very important. I'm going to email you something.

Can you find a way to send it to Lenora Jordan so it won't be traced back to us?

No answer. It was three in the morning.

I'm sorry to wake you, but this is really important. Please wake up. If I blew up his phone, the beeps would wake him up.

Sorry.

Wake up.

Sorry again.

Wake up.

A reply popped onto the screen. I'm up. On it. Are you okay?

Yes. Thank you so much.

I exhaled. He would find a way to do it.

I put my phone away and looked at myself in the mirror. There were bags under my eyes and they weren't Prada. I was so tired all of a sudden, I could barely stand. I had to get out of this bathroom, because the floor was beginning to look nice and inviting.

I washed my hands, came out, and sat on the couch. They were still talking about something, but I could no longer follow. My eyes were closing. I tried so hard to keep them open, but someone had attached weights to my eyelids. Augustine said something I couldn't quite hear. Rogan answered and then the world turned soft, warm, and dark, and I sank into the welcoming blackness.

Chapter 11

*T*he tantalizing scent of freshly brewed coffee drifted over to me. I opened my eyes.

The ceiling didn't look familiar. I wasn't in my house. That meant I was . . .

I sat straight up. I was in Rogan's command room, on one of his huge black leather couches. Someone had put a pillow under my head and a blanket over the rest of me. At the far end of the room, Rogan poured coffee into a large black mug. He wore a white T-shirt and black pants. The T-shirt molded to his biceps. He looked like he'd spent the last hour working out and had just taken a shower.

He saw me and grinned. It was an evil kind of grin and all of the alarms blared in my head.

"What time is it?"

"Ten past nine."

Terror shot through me. "Morning?" *Please don't say morning.*

"Yes."

"Oh no. Did you tell my family where I was?"

"No."

I exhaled.

"But I imagine Cornelius did when he went back to your warehouse."

Ugh. I lay back on the couch and pulled the blanket over my head. I would never live it down. Grandma Frida and my sisters would be merciless. *"So you spent the night with Mad Rogan? How was it? When is the wedding?"*

The blanket moved down, revealing Mad Rogan standing over me, way too close for comfort. He looked even larger from this angle, which was a neat trick considering he was already huge. He had shaved, his jaw completely clean. I liked stubble better. It made him . . . more human. Now he looked every inch a Prime, except for a narrow red gash on his cheek.

I see a Prime . . . Prime or not, Rogan and I still weren't equal. We probably would never be.

"Where is everybody?" I asked.

"We're waiting on the dispensation from Cornelius' sister. There was no point in waiting here, so everyone went home." He smiled a wicked smile, as if I were a delicious lamb who'd somehow wandered into his wolf den. "Except you."

I sighed. "You might not want to count on that dispensation."

"I gathered they're not close."

"His sister hadn't seen Matilda since she was a year old."

"Are you afraid of what your family will think?" he asked, drinking his coffee.

"I'm not afraid. I'm mentally preparing myself for a vigorous defense. You should've woken me up."

"You overextended yourself," he said. "Your body needed rest."

"I just closed my eyes for a moment."

"You passed out," he said, a grin tugging at his mouth. A man had no business being so handsome first thing in the morning.

"I did no such thing."

"Did you know you snore?" he asked.

"I don't."

"You do. It's adorable." He winked at me.

I threw a pillow at him. It stopped a couple of inches from his face and streaked back to its spot on the couch. He crouched by me. The distance between us suddenly shrunk. His coffee mug moved to the side table.

"You know what I think?" he asked. His gaze snagged on my hair. He reached over and touched one blond strand. "I think your family will expect that you stayed over here and you and I had unforgettably dirty sex."

My mind went straight to the gutter.

"Especially after they see your hair."

I pulled my hair out of his fingers. "What's wrong with my hair?"

"It's the special style called the morning after."

I touched my head. Last night's hair spray, rain, and my pillow had clearly conspired to create a once-in-a-lifetime mess on my head. My hair felt like it was standing straight up.

Rogan was looking at me and in the depths of his blue eyes, I saw the same icy darkness. Not again.

"Did you call House Howling?"

"Not yet," he said. "Why? Would you like to watch?"

"Maybe."

"Kinky beast."

"Rogan!"

He smiled at me. It was the kind of smile that blazed a trail from your heart to your mind and popped into your head the next time you wondered why you put up with a man who made you want to punch things.

"You look sexy in the morning, Nevada." His voice caressed me, his magic dancing on my skin, setting off tiny explosions of desire.

"Stop," I warned. The magic caress vanished.

"It would be a shame to disappoint your relatives."

"I make it a habit to disappoint them on a regular basis." I reached over and gently touched the skin under the gash. "How did this happen?"

"Got nicked yesterday in the crowd." His voice deepened slightly.

I was still touching him, his skin warm under my fingertips. The faint scent of sandalwood swirled around me. He held completely still, as if worried I'd take my hand away.

"I thought Olivia might have clawed you. She isn't your biggest fan."

He smiled. "You noticed."

"You seemed to like Rynda. Why didn't you marry her?"

"Because I like her too much."

That stung. I pulled my hand back slowly. I shouldn't have started this conversation.

Rogan sat on the floor next to me and rested his arm on his bent knee. "When I was three, my father survived his sixth assassination attempt. He was attacked by a manipulator. My mother killed the assassin, but it fueled my father's obsession to compensate for our weakness. You can't kill what you can't see. If only we were telepathic and telekinetic. Then we'd feel the killers coming. He'd tried to make a telekinetic-telepath hybrid with me and failed. He was determined to succeed with my children, so he started shopping for my bride."

"You were three."

"He was a long-term planner. Rynda is a powerful telekinetic and an empath. My father would've preferred a telepath, but to get telekinesis and mind manipulation in one Prime is very rare. They almost never occur together. He feared that if I married a telepathic Prime, our child would lose telekinesis. Rynda's father is a telekinetic, her mother is a psionic, so her set of genes was perfect for his purposes. The tentative engagement agreement between our families was reached when I was three and she was two. That was the first time she attempted to levitate an object and succeeded."

"What did she levitate?" I asked in spite of myself.

"Her parents were arguing and she tried to put a pacifier into her mother's mouth to make her be quiet."

I pictured Olivia's face with a pacifier in her lips and snickered.

"Rynda was always a peacemaker. She likes when things are calm."

"So you knew you would marry her your entire life?"

"Yes." He nodded. "And for most of my childhood and adolescence I was okay with it. Marriage was something that would happen far away in the future and I liked Rynda. Especially after puberty."

Jealousy stabbed at me with sharp little needles. "Rynda *is* beautiful."

"Gorgeous," he said. "Elegant, refined, exquisite, ravishing . . ."

Now he was just baiting me. I pretended to study my fingernails.

"I get it that you're heartbroken that she had another man's children. That's okay, Rogan. Don't feel bad. I'm sure you'll find somebody who'll take pity on you . . . eventually."

He laughed quietly. "You're prickly this morning. I could get used to this."

"Don't. Are you going to tell me the rest of this story or should I just go home now?"

"Alright. When I was sixteen, Rynda came to a party at our house. I don't remember now what the occasion was, but I had caused my mother some grief and she was still recovering from it. I was a difficult teenager."

"You don't say." I rolled my eyes.

"I was sixteen." Rogan shrugged.

"What did you do to make your mom mad at you?"

He sighed. "Earlier that summer my father and I had gotten into an argument, and he told me that if I didn't like the rules of the house, I should go live in a cardboard box on the street. I did. I walked out with the clothes on my back and nothing else. It took them almost three weeks to find me."

"Where did you go?"

"Downtown," he said. "I didn't think anything bad could happen to me. I slept on the street, ate at a soup kitchen, and got into a couple of fights with other homeless guys. Then I found people betting on fights under an overpass and beat up a couple of guys for money. I made fifty bucks and got my head bashed in by a guy who could magically harden his fists. A man tried to pick me up with promises of vodka and pizza. I didn't like the look in his eyes, so I got into his car to see what would happen. Turned out he was fond of strangling. It didn't end well for him. I never managed to find a cardboard box to sleep in. I slept in the park under some bushes until my father's security people tasered me, pumped me full of sedatives, and delivered me back to my house."

I just stared at him. He wasn't lying.

"So when I woke up in my room, my mother chewed me out. She told me she'd worried. She told me I had no right to scare her like that. It was infinitely worse than sleeping on the street. By the time the party rolled around, we had resolved our family conflicts, so when Rynda asked my mother where I'd been for the past three weeks, my mother told her. Rynda started crying."

"Why?"

"She picked up some residual traces of stress and fear from my mother. It upset her. She was sitting there, tears rolling down her cheeks, and asked my mother how she could put up with me. My mother told her that I was a gifted child and gifted children do extraordinary things. Rynda said that in that case she didn't want gifted children. That's when I knew I couldn't marry her."

"Because she didn't want gifted children?"

Connor leaned closer and smiled again, but it didn't reach his eyes. "No. Because I didn't love her. Marriages among Primes are rarely based on love, but Rynda would know that I didn't love her. It would always hurt her. And, selfishly, I realized that being with Rynda meant being alone. She wanted family, children, and stability. Safety. I didn't know exactly what I wanted, but I knew I didn't want that. I would take risks and it would crush her. And if I smothered my will and submitted to the marriage, I would always have to be cold to her. I could never let her feel the full extent of my anger, fear, or worry, because it would be cruel."

Rogan's personality was like his magic: a powerful typhoon that swept away everything in its path. I had seen the extent of his rage and the intensity of his desire. When he focused on you, he did so completely and you felt privileged to be the object of his attention in spite of yourself. A true relationship required honesty. When he was scared, or raging, or helpless, he would have to calm down and pull his feelings inward before he went home. He would have to lie to her.

Rogan had never lied to me. It hit me like a ton of bricks. Occasionally he worded his replies carefully, but he had never lied to me except for the time on the balcony, right after we watched his people being murdered. He'd lied on purpose, knowing I would react. He could've refused to answer my questions. Instead he always told me the truth, even when he knew I wouldn't like the answers.

"Something wrong?" he asked.

"No," I lied. "Go on with the story."

"Not much left. I officially broke off the engagement at eighteen. They held on to hope for another year, but when I joined the military, it was clear that all bets were off. Rynda married her now husband within six months. He is uninterested in politics and risky games, and by all indications he loves her."

"Do you regret it?"

"No. She's happy and I need somebody else. Someone who doesn't crack under my pressure."

True. "That's a tall order."

His face turned thoughtful. "Do you remember that big speech I made in your garage?"

"Which one?" I sighed. "You've made several. I'm contemplating installing a personal soapbox with your name on it."

"The one where I said you would beg to climb into my bed?"

"Ah. That one. How could I forget? I kept waiting for you to pound your chest like a silverback gorilla."

"Forget what I said—"

A speaker came on and Bug's voice resonated through the room. "Nevada, wake up. Bern says call him back right now. It's urgent."

I grabbed my phone from the side table. Someone had turned the ringer off. I dialed Bernard.

"Yes?"

"Montgomery is on a video call in your office," he said. "He's pissed off. I tried to tell him you'll call back, but he's holding the line open."

Something bad had happened.

I jumped off the couch and spotted my shoes on the side. I pulled them on. Rogan watched me.

"Trouble?"

"Probably."

"Do you need help?"

"No." Augustine knew where I was. He didn't call here, which meant whatever new emergency had occurred was for me and me alone. I would handle my own affairs.

I looked up at him. He was back to the familiar icy Prime, intense, hard, and lethal.

"If I become a Prime, will you be my enemy, Rogan?"

"No," he said. "You have nothing to fear from me."

"I'll hold you to it."

I dashed into the warehouse. A blue Honda CR-V was sitting in my parking lot. Bern met me at the door.

I pointed to the Honda. "Do we have a client?"

"No." Bern's face took on that collected expression that usually meant he was about to methodically recite a sequence of events that led to the Honda being in the parking spot and would probably start his story right around the Great Flood.

I held up my hand, hoping to stave off the flow of information. "Later. What the hell is Augustine pissed about?"

"This might be it." Bern held up his tablet. A headline crossed it: "The Question of the Lady in Green: Should Primes Do More?"

Just what I needed. I landed in my office chair, pulled my hair back the best I could, and pushed the key on the keyboard.

"Yes?"

Augustine's perfect face was so cold it might as well have been carved of a glacier. "Congratulations, Lady in Green."

Damn it.

"Your altruism bore rotten fruit. I told you so."

"It's one lousy article, Augustine."

"I'm not talking about the article."

I leaned back and crossed my arms on my chest. "Will you please speed this up?"

"Victoria Tremaine's people contacted my office. She is on her way to Houston to see me. She's asking for the identity of the Lady in Green."

I sat up straighter. Ages ago when I first realized I was a truthseeker, I looked up truthseeker Houses. There were three in the continental United States, and House Tremaine was the smallest and the most feared. It had only one Prime: Victoria Tremaine. She was near seventy and people hid when they heard she was coming. She didn't just pull the truth out of her victims; she could lobotomize them and frequently did. Rich and feared, she wielded unprecedented power. I remembered looking at her picture—a tall aristocratic woman with vicious eyes—and thought she looked like some evil witch. The kind that had a noble title and ordered you skinned alive if you happened to spill a drink while serving it to her.

"I have no desire to upset Tremaine," Augustine said. "Neither do I want her anywhere near my office, but I can't simply not see her. You have this one opportunity to tell me why she would be interested in you."

"I have no idea."

"Make sure you figure it out. If you need protection from Tremaine, you must sign the contract I offered you. My House will defend its own. You have . . ." He checked the computer screen. "Twenty-two hours."

The screen went black. I looked at Bern. He raised his arms.

If Augustine met Victoria Tremaine, she would pull my identity out of his head. I was a baby Prime, and I'd managed to get Baranovsky to admit things to me. Victoria had a lifetime of practice. Why would she be interested?

A terrible suspicion ignited in my head. If Rogan was

right, and I was a Prime, my talents had to come from somewhere. Spontaneous manifestations of Primes without anyone in their immediate family possessing a lot of power were extremely rare.

"Is Mom home?"

Bernard nodded. "Nevada, about the car . . ."

"Later."

I got up and walked through the hallway into our house and to the kitchen. My mother was at the sink, rinsing a plate. Arabella lounged at the table, playing with her phone.

My mother took in my hair. "Eventful night?"

"Is there any reason Victoria Tremaine would be interested in me?"

My mother's face turned white. The plate slipped out of her hands and shattered on the floor.

"Mom!" Arabella jumped up.

"Leave the room." Her voice turned cold and harsh.

Arabella blinked. "Mom, what's wron . . ."

"Now."

My sister took off, her eyes opened wide. Mom fixed Bern with a thousand-yard stare. He retreated without a word.

My mother slowly wiped her hands with a towel. Her face turned rigid and calculating. I had only seen that expression once, when she had become a total stranger and ended her PI career. Fear squirmed through me.

"What did you do?" she asked, her voice eerily calm.

"I saved a little girl. Amy Madrid."

"Who knows?"

"Augustine and his secretary. Mom, you're scaring me."

"Is Victoria on her way to the city?"

"Yes."

"When is she arriving?"

"Tomorrow."

My mother hung the towel on a rack with methodical precision. "Listen to me very carefully. You have to wipe Augustine's mind."

"What?"

"You have to wipe Augustine's mind. Fry him if you have to."

I recoiled. "Do you have any idea what you're asking me to do? Even if I did know how to do it—and I don't—it would turn him into a vegetable."

"You can do it," my mother said with complete confidence.

She'd turned into someone I didn't recognize.

"I know him. He is a human being. I can't just break his mind. I won't."

"Then I'll kill him."

"Have you lost your mind?" my voice squeaked.

"Wipe his mind, or I'll kill him."

"Mother! That's not what we do. It's not who we are. Dad wouldn't—"

"It's not just about you." A hint of emotion finally broke through my mother's expression. "You have a responsibility to your sisters! If the Tremaine bitch finds you, she'll kill me and your grandmother. Arabella will end up in a cage, and you and Catalina will end up serving her for the rest of her life. Is that what you want? You have to protect your family."

I opened my mouth but no words came.

Mom's bottom lip trembled. She moved across the kitchen and gripped me into a fierce hug. "I know. I know it's hard. That's okay. I'm asking too much. Don't worry, baby. I'll take care of it. Forget it ever happened."

I broke free. "Why is she after us?"

"She's your paternal grandmother."

The hair on the back of my arms stood on end. I dropped into a chair.

"She couldn't carry a child to term, so she did . . . things and your father was born. She wanted a son who was a Prime. Your dad had no magic. None. She always neglected him, but while she was waiting for his talent to manifest, she would pull his mind apart every day, looking for the evidence of magic. When she realized that he was completely normal, the indifference turned to hate. He ran away from her as soon as he could. She needs you desperately, because without another Prime, her House will die with her."

Oh my God.

"Don't worry," my mother said. "I'll . . ."

No, she wouldn't. Like Rogan said, this was House warfare. I was the oldest Prime in my family. I'd made this mess. This was my responsibility. I held up my hand, my own voice dull. "No. I'll take care of it."

"Nevada . . ."

"I'll take care of it, Mom. I'll take care of it by tonight. Promise me you will wait. Promise me."

"I won't do anything until you tell me," my mother said.

I got up, held my head high, and went to my room to clean up.

I took a shower, dried and brushed my hair, and put on my work clothes, moving on autopilot. I should've been freaking out, but somehow I couldn't muster any emotion. All I had was a cold methodical rationale. It was what I needed.

Victoria Tremaine was my grandmother. In retrospect it made sense. My father's reluctance to speak about his family, his insistence that I was very careful with my magic, and my mother's distrust of Primes. If Victoria Tremaine was my mother-in-law, I wouldn't trust Primes either.

Victoria Tremaine had no heirs. Certainly no Prime heirs. That was an established fact. If she realized I existed, she would move heaven and earth to make me part of House Tremaine. She would do it by holding my sisters hostage. Of the three of us, I was the only truthseeker. It would be slavery for the three of us.

I couldn't let her meet with Augustine. She would crack him like a walnut.

I couldn't wipe Augustine's mind either. This was not what we did. It . . . it went against everything I stood for. Yet I would have to do it to save my family. It was that, or my mother would kill him.

I couldn't see a way out of it. I had to take care of my family.

I walked down the stairs. Catalina marched out of the media room to intercept me. Matilda followed her, mimicking my sister's movements. Any other time I would've found it comical.

"What's going on? Arabella said Mom went crazy . . ."

"Mom is going through a rough time right now. Don't worry. It will all get straightened out by tomorrow."

"What rough time? Why? You look like you're going to kill somebody."

Funny choice of words. "Nobody is getting killed."

"I hate when you treat me like a child."

I looked at her for a moment to make sure she understood. "People are trying to kill us. Mom is freaking out. Augustine is freaking out. I'm trying to fix it. It would help if you didn't freak out at me too."

She fell silent. I kept walking.

"Where are you going?"

"To make a plan."

I stepped out of the warehouse and paused by the Honda. It looked perfectly generic, at least three years old. I would ask Bern about it when I came back. I left the warehouse, walked two blocks over, and stopped on the sidewalk in front of Rogan's HQ. This wasn't my wisest move, but I had nowhere to turn. I dialed his number.

"Yes?" he answered.

"I need your advice," I said. "I'm in front of your HQ. May I come in?"

"Yes."

I walked in past the soldiers, who all stopped talking as I passed them, and climbed the stairs. Rogan was waiting for me. He surveyed my work clothes with his familiar focus.

"I don't want Bug to hear us, if that's possible."

"It's possible."

Rogan led me to a door in the far wall and held it open. I walked into a small office. A desk, a couple of chairs, and a bookshelf filled with notebooks and manuals. Rogan closed the door and sat on the corner of the desk.

I swallowed. Everything in me rebelled against sharing the information, but I had no choice. He already knew I was a Prime. He said he had no intentions of fighting me.

"Victoria Tremaine is my grandmother."

The five words fell like bricks and lay between us.

His eyebrows crept up a fraction of an inch. "I had expected House Shaffer. Tremaine is a surprise."

"She's coming to see Augustine tomorrow. If she finds out I exist, she'll destroy my family. My mother will kill Augustine unless I wipe his mind."

"A predicament." Rogan's expression was nonchalant, as if he were playing a particularly convoluted game of chess. "Do you want me to rescue you?"

It was tempting. So tempting. "No. I want advice."

Pride flashed in his eyes. "You're turning into a dragon."

"I have no choice. I own this. Even if my mother tried her best, I don't believe she could get a shot at Augustine."

"I agree. Very well." He leaned back. "Victoria Tremaine is despised and feared and knows it. She travels with an aegis, a cloaker, and a telepathic shielder. Her body and mind are superbly protected at all times and if she is under attack, the cloaker will make her disappear in a fraction of a second. She is an extremely difficult target. You can't eliminate her. Your mother knows this, which is why she focused on Augustine."

I nodded. I had gathered as much.

"Augustine is the closest thing to a friend I have among members of the Houses. He has a much younger sister and a brother. His father is dead and he is their caretaker. Don't mistake his professional interest in you for friendship or camaraderie. If he thinks for a moment that you pose any danger, no matter how slight, to his siblings, he'll kill you. From a Prime's point of view, you owe him nothing."

"Rogan, I can't just wipe his mind."

"Can't or won't?"

I sighed. "I'm not sure."

"Yes, you are." His gaze was merciless.

"I can." I could break Augustine. I had been on the verge of breaking a mind before, when interrogating the mercenary and when practicing on my sisters. I knew precisely where that wall lay, and I had worked my hardest to never approach it.

"Augustine has a strong will. If I attack Augustine's mind, let him feel it, and push it too far, he'll cripple himself trying to fight me. It will take time, minutes, possibly an hour, so it's not a good combat power, but it will leave his psyche shredded. I could do it. But I won't."

"Yet you have to protect your family."

"Yes."

"This is what I was trying to avoid when I urged you to not go to Baranovsky's gala," he said. "It happened anyway, sooner than you or I would've liked. I thought we might have more time. The question now isn't what you should do. You know what you should do. The question is, what can you live with?"

"Would Augustine willingly open his mind to Victoria Tremaine?"

"He'd rather die," Rogan said without any hesitation. "Augustine is intensely private. A man who never shows the world his real face would never allow intrusion into his inner sanctum."

"Would he be open to the idea of protection?"

"By you? You would have to convince him that he is powerless before a truthseeker. Be very careful, Nevada. If you make that demonstration too personal, he'll turn on you. Go after something that's confidential but without emotional baggage. He must not feel that his deepest secrets have been violated."

That would be a very delicate dance, and even if I could get what I wanted, I wasn't sure I'd be able to do it.

"What are you planning to do?"

"I'm planning to apply the lessons Adam Pierce taught me." I shook my head. And if I failed to pull it off, my life would collapse and Augustine could spend the rest of his life with a feeding tube, not sure where or who he was. No pressure.

"Let's say this problem is resolved," he said. "What then? Victoria Tremaine doesn't give up. She won't simply turn around and go home empty-handed. She'll continue her pursuit. This is only a short-term solution to a large looming problem."

I made my mouth move. "I realize that."

"What's the long-term strategy?"

"I don't have one."

He frowned. "Does your immediate family have more than one living Prime?"

He was asking about my sisters. "Yes."

"Is that other mage a truthseeker?"

"No."

Surprise reflected in his eyes. "But you're sure they can qualify as Primes?"

"Yes."

"Then your best option is to petition for the formation of your own House. It would require you and the other Prime to admit to your magic in public. The qualification process and House formation is very fast, less than forty-eight hours, once all the proper forms have been submitted and the date of the trials has been set. Should you become House Baylor, you're granted immunity from aggression from all other Houses for a period of three years. It is a cardinal rule not even Victoria Tremaine can break. It's put in place to protect the emergence of new magic, which is good for everyone, and is a cornerstone of our society."

House Baylor. I would be throwing myself and my sisters into shark-infested waters.

"This is the best course of action for you." A muscle jerked in his face, then his expression relaxed as if he'd purposefully willed himself into neutrality. "You asked for my advice. Become a House."

Too bad there wasn't enough time to do it now. It would've solved the Augustine problem. No, I needed to think about this. Becoming a House had to be the last resort.

"One more point. Once you're formally registered as House Baylor, this . . . whatever it is between you and me has to end."

Whatever it is? I leaned back, putting one leg over the other. "Why?"

"As the head of a fledgling House, your first responsibility is to secure the future of your family. You have to make the connections and secure alliances so when the three-year period runs out, you're anchored and well-defended against any attack. Your best bet is to cement such an alliance through marriage. It will assure protection and the future of your House. There are services available that will map your DNA and suggest the match which would most likely result in children with Prime truthseeker talent, someone from one of the truthseeker Houses, or someone with a complementary discipline like manipulator to compensate for your lack of combat magic. You and I are not compatible. Our magic comes from entirely different realms. It is clear that despite my father's efforts, our bloodline doesn't mesh well with mind-domination mages. Should you and I produce offspring, they may not be Primes."

Ah. So that's where he was going with this. "Mhm."

Rogan's voice was eerily calm. "You think you won't care about it, but you will. Think of your children and having to explain that their talents are subpar, because you have failed to secure a proper genetic match. It will matter, Nevada."

"If you say so. Right now I'm more concerned with Augustine."

"Don't worry. You will persevere. Things have a way of working out."

He said it with utter confidence. Rogan wasn't the kind of man to leave things to chance. Unease crept over me. I might have just done something very stupid.

"Rogan, I want to be completely clear. I came only for advice. Don't act on my behalf."

He smiled back at me. The civilized mask tore, and I saw the dragon in all of his savage glory, teeth bared, eyes cold. He would kill Augustine if I failed.

"Don't," I warned him. "He's your friend. You don't have that many."

He kept smiling. I had no power. Nothing to counteract the promise of murder I saw in his eyes.

"You promised."

"I didn't."

Damn it. I should've made him promise before I said anything. "I'll never speak to you again."

"That would be terrible," he said.

"I don't want this. I don't want Augustine's death. You're doing that thing again when you think you know what's best for me and you insist on it in spite of my wishes."

"We Primes tend to be assholes that way."

"I'm a Prime too."

"Yes, but I'm Mad Rogan."

Of all the stupid, bullheaded, idiotic things . . .

"If something were to happen to Augustine, you would bear no responsibility for it," he said.

"But you will."

"I know what I am," he said.

"Connor . . ."

"Rogan," he corrected. "Mad Rogan."

The man who told me the story about running away when he was sixteen and the Prime here and now couldn't be the same person. "You're scaring me."

"Good," he said. "You're catching on. This is the world you're walking into. It's a place that requires people like me, capable of doing evil things so people they love survive."

He hadn't just said that.

I was in love with Connor Rogan. And he was in love with me.

I got up and walked toward him. A step. Another step. One more, and I was in his personal space, standing too close. He towered above me. Barely an inch of space separated us. I raised my chin and looked into his eyes. I saw cold determination and nothing else. He was keeping it all hidden.

He wanted me badly enough to kill his friend to save

me, but he'd told me I was a Prime. He was telling me to become a House now, fully convinced that he was severing any hope for a relationship at the root, because he believed it to be in my best interests. Being a Prime had ruled his life and he thought that becoming one would trump everything else for me.

"If you had a child, somebody like Matilda, and that child wasn't a Prime despite all the proper genetics, would you still love that child?"

"Of course."

"Would you protect her and take care of her? Would you teach her and try to make sure she has a happy life?"

"Yes."

"Good to know."

His eyes narrowed. "What does that mean?"

"It means you won't kill Augustine, Rogan. You will let me handle it."

His magic spun out, surging in a wild typhoon, potent enough to send you screaming. It twisted around us and met the cold wall that was my power. The line of his jaw hardened. *That's right. This is me not cracking under your pressure.*

Power suffused his voice. The dragon was staring me straight in the face, his eyes full of fire and scorched earth. "And why would I do that?"

"Because killing your friend would hurt you and I wouldn't like that."

His magic raged, but mine persevered. I held his gaze.

"Respect my wishes, Rogan. And I'll respect yours."

I turned on my heel and walked out, straight through the torrent of his magic warping the reality around us.

Chapter 12

I needed power. When you were a mage, there was only one way to bump up your power reserve. Which was why I walked into Grandma Frida's motor pool carrying a box of chalk and my arcane circle book. She saw my outfit of spandex shorts and a sport bra and her eyebrows crept up. I would've stripped naked if I could to maximize the power gain, but my room and bathroom were the only places that allowed me to parade around in the nude. My room had a bumpy bamboo floor that wouldn't take the chalk well, and my bathroom had tile. My circlework wasn't anything to write home about to begin with, and I wanted a level surface.

I picked a spot in the corner out of the way and opened the book to the charging circle page. It looked complicated enough to break my brain. Greater Houses combined the charging circles with a special ritual called the Key, perfected with each new generation. I had watched Rogan perform it once. He had drawn a constellation of arcane circles on the motor pool's floor and moved between them with lethal grace, his hands striking like a weapon, his kicks breaking bones of invisible opponents, as his body absorbed the magic. I had no House and no

Key, so I would stick to the single charging circle. I had tried it once before and it worked.

I crouched and began drawing on the concrete floor. It would be tempting to use tools, but every source I ever consulted said that using anything except chalk and a firm hand would diminish the power of circle. Whether it was true or just a magic legend didn't matter. I couldn't afford to take chances. I had called Augustine and set our meeting for eight o'clock. It would take me half an hour to get there, so if I started now, I could get at least eight hours of charge. The benefits of charging tapered off with each hour you spent in a circle, and eight hours would nicely top me off.

The blue Honda was parked in the middle of the motor pool and Grandma Frida was messing with its engine.

"Whose car is this?"

"Yours," she said. "Your not-boyfriend's people dropped it off. There is a note." She handed me a small card.

I opened it. *Sorry about the Mazda.*

"Are you going to pitch a fit about it and demand that he takes it back?" Grandma squinted at me.

"No. Maybe later." I'd need a car this evening.

I crouched, trying to meticulously replicate the design from the page on the floor. Ugh. It looked like a five-year-old was drawing it. Why the hell was it so complicated anyway? More importantly, why hadn't I learned the circlework years ago?

"So, how is it going with Mad Rogan?" Grandma Frida asked, wiping her hands with a towel.

"Good." *A circle inside a circle inside a circle . . . Kill me, somebody.*

"You're still fighting?"

"No."

Three circles on the outside. Three smaller circles on the inside.

"You're concentrating so hard I can see the steam coming out of your ears."

"Mhm."

"Have you done the deed?"

I paused my drawing and looked at her. Really?

Grandma Frida held the towel between me and her like a shield. "Whoa, the stare."

I went back to drawing.

"I just want you to be happy."

"I'll be happy when everyone who is trying to kill us is dead."

"You sound like him." Grandma Frida's voice faltered. "Nevada, Penelope has been up in her crow's nest for an hour. She barely said two words to me this morning and she looks like she is preparing for a funeral. Now you look like you need to punch something. Honey, what's wrong?"

What's wrong? That's a great question. Rogan is in love with me, but he doesn't want to act on it because I'm a Prime who will sooner or later form her own House. My mother has been lying to me for years and I don't even know if all of those times she and Dad urged me to hide my talent was for my benefit or just so we wouldn't be discovered by my other, psychotic, grandma. She's coming to town, and both Rogan and my mother want to murder Augustine. We know David Howling helped kill Nari, but we don't know where he is and we don't have the evidence to attack his co-conspirator. And tonight I have to convince the one person who spends all of his time trying to take advantage of me that it's in his best interest to let me screw around in his psyche. Other than that, things are great.

"I'm just tired," I said. "I have some things I need to do tonight."

"I don't believe you."

I almost snapped, *You don't have to,* but her bright blue

eyes were so filled with worry that I bit that reply back
before it even started. I wouldn't be mean to my grandmother.

"Is there anything I can do?" Grandma asked.

"I would take a hug," I said.

Her face fell. "Okay, now I'm really worried."

"Do I get a hug or not?"

Grandma Frida opened her arms. I came over and
hugged her, inhaling the familiar comforting scent of
machine oil, and for a short moment I turned five and the
world was simple and bright. She patted my back gently.
"I put a new computer guidance system into Romeo. You
just tell me who to shoot, okay?"

"Okay." If only I could fix my problems with Romeo.
My life would be so easy.

Someone stood outside of my circle. I opened my eyes
slowly. A sheen of sweat slicked my body. The inside of
the circle steamed slightly, as if I was in a sauna. Matilda
crouched by the line of chalk. Her menagerie of pets
sat around her, the cat and the raccoon on one side, and
Bunny on the other.

We didn't say anything. We just looked at each other.

Matilda patted Bunny. He got up and padded away,
his claws clicking on the hard floor. A few moments later
he returned, carrying a small pink sleeping bag. Matilda
straightened it out, climbed into her bag at the very edge
of the circle, and curled up, looking at me with her big
brown eyes. The animals lay down by her, the cat and raccoon by her feet and the big Doberman on the other side
of her. She stretched one hand toward the circle, close but
not touching the fragile chalk line, and watched me.

For a long while we stayed that way until her eyes
closed and she fell asleep.

The next time I opened my eyes, Cornelius walked into the room. A woman followed him, short but wearing high heels, her hair the same silvery blond as his. A shimmering dress, dark grey with a bateau neckline, sheathed her trim figure. Expertly applied makeup highlighted her soft brown eyes and the sharp arches of her eyebrows. Two black panthers followed her on velvet paws.

I must've charged for so long that my poor brain had developed hallucinations.

"There she is," Cornelius said quietly, nodding at Matilda.

The panthers stared at me with golden eyes. I braced myself for the inevitable clash between Bunny and the panthers. It never came. The three beasts studiously ignored each other.

I rocked forward, trying to get on my feet. My butt and legs had fallen asleep and tiny electric needles of blood flowing back into the muscles stabbed into my thighs.

"Please, don't get up on my account," Cornelius' sister said.

Cornelius stole a metal mesh chair from the security desk and rolled it over to his sister. "Please."

She carefully swept her dress with her hand and sat. The panthers settled at her feet.

"Just so we're all on the same page, everyone sees the panthers?" I asked quietly.

"They're real," Cornelius' sister said. "Although mostly there for the sake of appearances. I attended a business event before I came here, and I wanted to remind the other parties involved that I'm a Prime. I couldn't leave them in the car. They get snappish without supervision and claw at leather upholstery. If you're really in need of protection, dogs are best. Medium to large size, nothing too bulky. You want an athletic dog that can charge and jump but with enough mass to knock an attacker off their feet. Dobermans, Belgian sheepdogs, Rottweilers . . ."

She stroked the head of the left panther with her fingertips. The massive beast raised his head just like an overgrown house cat and leaned into her hand. "Dogs will die to protect their owners without a moment's hesitation. Cats have to be convinced it's their problem."

She glanced at Bunny. "My brother was always the most pragmatic of the three of us."

Cornelius smiled. "I have someone besides myself that I have to protect, Diana."

She glanced at Matilda. A shadow crossed her face. She seemed ill at ease. "Why does she lie like that?"

"Nari was an empath." Sadness saturated his voice, threatening to roll over into despair.

"I didn't know that," Diana said.

"Her magic was weak. She never bothered registering. Still, it helped—whenever she had a trial or a jury selection, she'd spend the night like this, in the circle. Matilda missed her, so she would come and sleep next to her."

I looked at Matilda's hand, stretched to the circle. So tiny. Her mother was gone forever, so she'd come and slept next to me because it was familiar and for a few seconds when she was between the dream and reality, she might think I was her mother, alive and waiting for her in the circle. Someone reached into my chest and squeezed all the blood out of my heart.

Diana shifted in her seat. "This isn't what we do, Cornell. Rogan, Howling, Montgomery—those are the big names. Harrison doesn't belong among them. You're asking me to sanction something that would put all of us in danger. It won't bring your wife back. She was . . . a spouse."

"Disposable," Cornelius said.

"I didn't say that."

"But you meant it."

"She was a human," Diana said quietly. "I never understood your devotion to her. It is—"

Matilda sat up and stared at me, blurry eyed.

Oh no. Please don't cry, little one.

Her lower lip trembled. She turned to look at her father and her aunt. Diana blinked, suddenly taken aback. Matilda rose, walked over, and climbed into Diana's lap. Prime Harrison sat utterly still. Her niece hugged Diana, snuggled up close, and rested her head on her aunt's chest.

Diana swallowed and wrapped her arms around the little girl to keep her from sliding off. "What is this?"

"Your niece is grieving," Cornelius said. "She feels your magic and it's familiar. She knows you're family and a woman, and she misses her mother. She wants comfort, Diana."

Matilda sighed quietly. Her body relaxed.

"This is almost like . . . binding."

"It's more," Cornelius said. "When an animal binds with us, there is a simplicity to their needs. Meet them and you earn devotion. With a child, it's infinitely more layered and complicated, but it is wonderful, because this love is freely given. There is no bargain. Sometimes, if you're very lucky, you're loved and the one who loves you expects nothing in return. She trusts you, Diana, and she doesn't even know you."

Diana looked at Cornelius. "Why don't we have that?"

"We did. Do you remember the strawberry syrup?"

She groaned and squeezed her eyes shut. "That was my favorite shirt. I loved that shirt."

"But you didn't tell Mother I did it."

"You had enough to deal with. You had to spend your

days with that little Pierce monster . . ." Diana sighed. "I suppose you're right. We grew up."

"And now we're a family in name only."

She winced. "That is surprisingly painful to contemplate."

The clock on the wall showed quarter to seven. I needed to get dressed. I rose and stretched slowly. They didn't notice.

"When was the last time you saw Blake?" Cornelius asked.

"In person?" Diana frowned. "He usually emails. Six months? No, wait, a year. I ran into him at that abominable NCBA dinner last December."

I got the push broom and scrubbed the chalk lines off the floor.

"Two years for me," Cornelius said.

"He lives half an hour away," Diana said.

"I know."

Diana craned her neck to glance at her niece. "Is she asleep?"

"Yes," Cornelius said.

I headed for the door.

"Tell me about it again," Diana said behind me. "About your family. Tell me about your wife."

Two hours past sundown, Houston's downtown showed no signs of slowing down. Ragged clouds drifted across a deep purple sky, framing a huge silver moon glowing above skyscrapers. The tall business buildings stretched to it, studded with lights as the office workers surrendered their evening to the electric glow of computer screens. The city was a turbulent ocean, its buildings rocky spires thrusting from the streets as the glowing rivulets of traffic wound among their base. And the asymmetrical triangle of the Montgomery International Investigations HQ, all twenty-five stories of it sheathed in cobalt glass, was a shark swimming through it all to bite at me with razor teeth.

"Are you sure you don't want me to go in with you?" Melosa asked. I had found her waiting by the car when I left the house. She'd insisted on coming with me and considering the hot water we were in, I would've been an idiot to say no.

"No. I'll be fine."

"Okay." Her tone plainly said she didn't approve but she couldn't do anything about it.

I walked into the familiar ultramodern lobby and took the elevator to the seventeenth floor. The gleaming stainless tube desk that served as Lina's workspace stood empty and her purse wasn't on the chair. Augustine's secretary was out. That was okay; I remembered the way to his office well enough. I walked through the vast space, a sloping expanse of blue windows on my left and frosty white interior walls on my right. I was in the corner of the shark fin, in Augustine's lair, and House Montgomery spared no expense in creating its elegance. It always felt slightly sterile to me, too clean, too devoid of personal touches, but the view was breathtaking. During the day the glass tinted the office a gentle blue, as if you were at the bottom of a shallow sea, but at night the glass melted into the darkness, all but disappearing, and the city spread below, bottomless and glowing with lights.

Ahead a wall loomed, frosted with feathery white. A section of the glass had been pushed aside, and through the gap I saw Augustine at his desk, reading something on his tablet. I reached the door.

"Come in," he invited without raising his head.

I stepped into the office and sat. He kept reading. Augustine was reminding me he was my boss.

Gently, softly, I let my magic out. It began to grow through the office, spreading in thin tendrils, branching and growing, like the roots of some massive tree. I held it back, letting it barely creep forward. I had to take my time.

Finally, Augustine raised his head.

"I had a few questions about my contract," I said.

Surprise flickered in his eyes and turned into speculation. He put two and two together. The impending arrival of Victoria Tremaine scared me and I was considering picking up his option of a decade of servitude in return for the protection of House Montgomery.

"Very well. I'll do my best to answer."

I pulled out a printed contract and a camera. Augustine's eyebrows rose.

"I prefer to do it on paper, so I can write notes," I said. "And I would like to record our conversation, if you don't mind."

"I should be insulted that you believe me capable of going back on my word, but I suppose I'll compliment you on your prudence instead. Let's begin."

I pushed the record button on the camera. "Paragraph I, 'in the interests of House goodwill.' Could you give me more details on the specifics of goodwill? It's rather vague as written."

"The goodwill of a House is a layered concept. On one hand it represents the relationships House Montgomery has with its customers and clients. Such goodwill is evidenced by repeat contracts with existing clients and referrals to new clients. A less specific aspect of House goodwill involves our reputation, name, and location. House Montgomery stands for confidentiality. We're a local House with solid ties to the community and a proven history. In our line of business, trust is essential, and as a House Montgomery vassal, you will be held to a high standard . . ."

My magic crept forward. I asked a question, he offered an answer, each exchange reinforcing the pattern, and with each answer I claimed a little more of him, until he was completely shrouded in my power.

"Paragraph V, 'financially labeled.' What does that mean?"

"Where?" Augustine scrolled on his tablet.

"Here." I offered him a piece of paper and let my magic spread a little more. The more I distracted him, the better.

He focused on the paragraph, his lips moving silently. "It's a typo. It should say financially liable." He grimaced. "My apologies."

"No problem." I corrected the right paragraph.

"I detest sloppiness. I've stressed it before that a spell check is no substitute for human attention. The more eyes reviewing the contract the better."

He was volunteering information he didn't have to disclose. He was ready and I couldn't keep him here indefinitely. Now or never.

"How will I be compensated for my services?"

Augustine opened his mouth.

I gave him a slight nudge.

"By direct deposit into your bank account."

"What bank would that transfer be coming from?"

"First House."

"Could you tell me the routing and account number?"

This was a gamble. If he needed to look that up, he might pause. But Augustine was almost pedantic in his attention to detail.

"Certainly." He named the two strings of numbers. I wrote them down.

"Do you access that account online?"

"Yes."

"What is your username and banking password?"

"JulienMont. LoT45B9!n."

"Who is Julien?"

"I am. It's my middle name. I quite detest it."

"Paragraph XII, line three guarantees me three weeks of paid leave. Can I take them at once or separately?"

"Whatever way you choose."

I began pulling my magic back. Two more questions, and I released him completely. Augustine was frowning. He must've felt something, but couldn't quite put his finger on it.

"I believe that covers everything," he said finally. "All that remains is your signature."

I leaned back. "I won't be signing the contract, Augustine."

He stared at me. "That's a mistake. Did Rogan make a better offer?"

I shook my head. "No. This has nothing to do with Rogan. We both know what you're offering me is a disproportionately small compensation to my ability to aid your House. I understand where you're coming from. Having a vassal Prime would be a great asset to House Montgomery."

His eyes narrowed. "You believe you're a Prime?"

"It would save some time for the purposes of this discussion if you treated me like one." Maybe he would listen to me. Maybe I could convince him and then I would take my camera and he would never have to confront what was on it.

A condescending smile played on his lips. "I'll humor you. Go on."

"Tomorrow Victoria Tremaine will walk into your office. She'll crack your mind like a walnut. There is nothing you can do to stop it. If she chooses to be subtle, she'll leave you with the capacity to reason. If she doesn't like the way you look, the cut of your suit, or the color of your office walls, she'll lobotomize you."

Augustine's eyes narrowed. He took off his glasses. "This is adorable."

Nope. We'd have to do this the hard way.

"I was attempting to be magnanimous in my offer. Thus far, I have been exceedingly patient," he continued. "You did show me the error of my ways, so let me give you this last bit of advice free. You spent some time in Rogan's and my own company, and you believe you know how things between Houses operate, so you presume to take it upon yourself to explain it to me as if our roles were reversed and I was an ignorant dilettante."

Here we go.

"You may or may not be a Prime. Your powers and abilities are open to debate. You're an amateur with an inflated evaluation of your own abilities and importance. I have been a Prime all my life. I'm the head of a robust House with four living Primes, I run a multimillion-dollar international enterprise, and I have impeccable standing in the community. Victoria Tremaine is an old hag whose House is in decline."

Okay, he'd moved from fact to complete exaggeration. I really made him mad.

"If I don't feel like entertaining her presence, I won't see her. If I do choose to allow her that courtesy, she'll mind her manners and will do absolutely nothing to jeopardize her safety or I'll have her ejected onto the street."

I flipped the top piece of paper on the contract stack and pushed it toward him.

"The very idea that she would walk in here and I'll simply tell her the contents of my mind is preposterous. Your presence in my office is preposterous. I have had enough."

"Look down."

Augustine glared at me, then at the paper. On it in neat numbers I had written out the routing and account numbers followed by his username and password.

"How did you get this?" he snarled.

"You told me."

Augustine grabbed the camera, rewound the recording, and watched himself recite his password. His face lost all color. He held the rewind button and listened to himself again.

He dropped the camera and lunged across the table. I had no time to move. His hands clamped my shoulders and he jerked me to my feet. A furious grimace distorted his face and his features rippled as if the illusion threatened to slide off his face. "What else?"

"I took nothing else. Except your middle name, Julien. Feel free to check the record. I would let go if I were you. I have shocker implants and I don't want to use them."

He released me.

I sat back into the chair. "Dealing with Primes is new to me. I did manage to learn some things, including that Primes never divulge the full extent of our talents. Truthseekers are among the rarest of Primes. What most people believe to be our primary talent—determining if someone lies to us—is in fact a passive field talent. It's a side-effect of being a truthseeker, something that we do casually with very little effort."

Augustine was staring at me. Anger and worry warred in his eyes.

"Do you know how Rogan realized I was a Prime? Someone had tried to kill my grandmother. I thought it was him and so I locked him with my will and I forced him to answer my questions."

I could only maintain that hold for a few seconds, because bending Rogan's will was like trying to contain a tsunami, but for those few vital seconds I'd broken him.

I had never before seen a man's mouth literally hang open. It was deeply satisfying.

"You're right. I'm a new Prime. But Victoria Tremaine isn't. I'm here to tell you that everything you heard about her is true. Every horror story and ugly rumor you've caught—assume she can do it. She hates my family and she'll go to any length to hurt us and she is capable of horrible things."

That conveniently skirted the full truth but wasn't exactly a lie.

"If you refuse to see her, she'll wait until an opportunity to be within earshot of you presents itself and destroy your mind. If you tell her everything you know, she'll rummage in your head anyway looking for more. She doesn't care about your Prime status, your connections, or the size of your business. She goes after what she wants and she gets it."

Augustine finally closed his mouth. His eyes turned dark. "Why are you here?"

"Because I want to shield your mind."

"You want to hex me?" He clenched his teeth. "Hexes take weeks."

"No. I want to create the appearance of a hex. When I opened Mr. Emmens' mind to find out what Adam Pierce was after, I got a good look at how it was structured. The hex forms barriers within your mind, tapping into the very essence of your magic, and then wraps it all in a hard shell, rooted deeply in your psyche. If you use brute force to smash the shell, you will kill the mind that fuels it. You can only peer under it, carefully and slowly, guessing at the contents. The stronger the magic user, the harder it is to break the hex. If you let me, I'll imitate this shell in your mind. You're a Prime with a huge magic reserve and the shell will appear to be impenetrable. If Victoria Tremaine probes your mind, she'll encounter the shell. Breaking it wouldn't be an option—you would die and take your secrets with you. Probing further would require too much time and preparation, likely a magic circle and some knowledge of the answer to the question she is asking. She's looking for my identity, which is a very specific piece of information. She can't just sit and pick at your brain indefinitely. You would feel it. She'll realize that it's out of her reach."

"How long will this fake shell last?"

"A few days." It was a guess on my part. The book I'd been studying claimed that a false wall could last up to a couple of months if done correctly. Given that I had never attempted it before, a few days was a more likely estimate. "And I'll need your help to make it. You have to open your mind and want for the shell to be formed in the first place."

"Have you ever done this before?" he demanded.

"No."

He leaned back, exhaling frustration. "What are the risks?"

"I could damage your mind."

"What does that mean, Ms. Baylor?"

"I don't know. But it is the only scenario I can think of that doesn't end with you dead," I said.

"Will I be assassinated if I decline?"

There was no point in lying. "Yes."

"Why do you care? Wouldn't it be easier to simply murder me?"

Because I wouldn't be able to sleep at night. Because that's not who I am. He wouldn't understand. I had to give him a reason he could wrap his mind around, something calculated that would spare his pride. "Because should there ever be a House Baylor, it will need powerful allies."

Minutes stretched.

Augustine put his glasses on the table. "Rogan called me half an hour before our meeting."

I'd asked him not to kill Augustine. I didn't ask not to call. "What did he say?"

"He said that when you make a sequence of wrong choices, eventually you're left with no choice at all. I thought he was speaking about Howling at the time. I realize now he managed to meld a rebuke and a death threat into a single sentence."

Augustine faced me, his gaze direct.

"We're sitting here because of my hubris. I made a sequence of poor decisions. I allowed you to interrogate a serial killer against my better judgment, knowing that you were circumspect about your magic and realizing the full extent of your possible exposure. I did this because Cornelius is my friend and our respective social positions precluded me from offering him a handout and would've prevented him from accepting one, but I wanted you to take his case. I also allowed my name to be connected to that interrogation, because the idea of being associated with a truthseeker appealed to me. Then I made a deliberate choice to offer you an unfair contract. I could've treated you as what you are—a young, talented Prime with a rare skill set—but I chose instead to attempt to take advantage of your inexperience. Then, I resorted to manipulation to win a pissing match with Rogan, even though I had realized at that point that while my interest was purely professional, he was emotionally invested. And so here we are. You, my former employee, would like to violate my mind, and if I don't allow it, my best friend will murder me."

"Augustine . . ."

He held up his hand. "Please. I've known Rogan a lot longer than you. I understood the phone call. I've miscalculated this gamble and badly. I'm being saved by your inexperience and the fact that you haven't yet learned to eliminate problems with a brutal preemptive stroke. If this situation occurred five years from now, I would be dead."

"Augustine . . ."

"It's quite humbling. I have worked and schemed, and I've managed to manipulate myself into a place where I have no choices left to me. I suppose there is a lesson in there somewhere." He opened the top drawer of his desk and put a piece of white chalk on the table. "Do it. Let's get this over with."

An hour later I walked into the night. Cold wind cut right through my clothes. Fatigue wrapped around me, pulling me down to the ground like an anchor. I had sunk all of my reserves into the shell on Augustine's mind. And now I would have to drive home. I didn't want to drive. I wanted to lie down right here on the pavement and close my eyes. It looked kind of soft and inviting. Definitely better than staying upright . . .

Okay, I needed to get home.

I surveyed the parking lot. A lone Honda waited in the parking spot. Rogan leaned against it.

I walked over. "Where is Melosa?"

"Home by now." He held the passenger door out to me. The thought of taking the keys briefly flashed before me. No. As tired as I was, I'd probably wrap the Honda around the nearest tree. I slid into the passenger seat. He got in next to me and drove out of the parking lot.

His magic filled the cab, brushing against me, the beast with sharp fangs, ready to lash out. For once I didn't pull away. I had none of my own left. It curled around me like one of Diana's panthers—dangerous, volatile, but for the moment calm.

The city rolled past my window. I was turning into someone else. Augustine said in five years I would've just killed him. A few months ago it had seemed like an impossibility, something I would never do. Now I could see the slippery slope of decisions that would lead me there. They all would be hard decisions, made for the sake of a friend or for the protection of my family, and each one would come a little easier until the things I promised myself I'd never do would become the default. Would I even recognize myself in five years? I was looking into my future and all I could see was a black hole and a woman in a dress like armor.

Tension radiated from Rogan. A grim coldness gripped his features, petrifying them into a harsh mask, like the faceplate of some ancient helmet. The magic intensified, wrapping tighter around me. Visions of blood and ash swirled before me, and beyond them, a harsh cold darkness . . .

I reached out and put my hand on his arm. He startled and glanced back at me.

The interior of the car wavered and another place pushed itself into my mind. A lodge, all soft electric light, amber wood, and glass, beyond which white mountains rose, the sharp lines softened with snow and the velvet cushioning of distant trees. Winter ruled outside, cold and severe, but inside, within the lodge, comfortable warmth saturated the air. I sat on a huge bed, the sheets silken and soft under me. A white blanket wrapped around me, soft as a cloud, and so deliciously warm. I smelled hot chocolate. I felt completely and utterly content. My life and all its problems remained far behind, and here, at the edge of the world in the snowy wilderness, I didn't have to worry about anything.

I stirred and the illusion rippled. I was still in the car, Rogan was driving, and my hand still rested on his muscular forearm. He was projecting. It had to be a memory, probably from childhood. I didn't know if he was doing it on purpose or if it was an unconscious side effect of him remembering it, but I had a choice. I could reject it and stay in this car, miserable and feeling sorry for myself, or I could let myself sink into the place where I was safe and warm while winter raged outside. I held completely still and welcomed it.

We didn't say anything until he parked before our warehouse. The lodge melted into thin air. I unbuckled my seat belt. I would have to go inside and explain to my mother that she wouldn't have to kill Augustine. I would have to explain what I'd done. It seemed so daunting right now.

Rogan turned the car off and reached out. His fingers wrapped around my hand, reassuring and trying to forge a connection between us.

"Did you send me the books?" I asked quietly.

"Yes."

I leaned across the seat and kissed him. Time stopped and for a few blissful moments there was nothing except Connor, intoxicating and irresistible, the taste of him, the scent of him, the raw male power in his arms, and the tender seducing touch of his lips . . . And then I was out of the car and gone before the power of that kiss wore off.

Chapter 13

1 opened my eyes to the blinking lights and loud beeping of my alarm. I slapped it down and swiped my phone off the night table. Three text messages: Rogan, Diana Harrison, and the third from an unknown number. I clicked Rogan's first.

> House Howling disavowed David. Lenora will see us this morning at eight. You and I are going alone. Cornelius' dispensation specified that he must stay behind to protect Matilda.

So Cornelius got his blessing after all, but not exactly in the way he wanted. I clicked his sister's text message. My brother rarely draws attention to himself. Don't underestimate Cornelius. He's a dangerous mage and he loves his wife enough, still, to sacrifice every animal he bonded with in her name. I hold you personally accountable for the safety of my niece.

Great. She'd known me for a whole five minutes and she already held me accountable.

I clicked the last text message. A picture of David Howling, smiling, holding a drink with his left hand and shooting with the index finger of his right. *I've played this game before*. I typed back, Cute.

Come on, text me back.

Nothing. Probably used a burner phone.

You'd think there would be some savagery in David's eyes. Some indication that he was a cold, calculating killer, but no. They were warm and calm, their color a very pale hazel. His face was relaxed, his smile genuine. *What makes you tick, David?*

The message was sent to me, but it was really for Rogan. I forwarded it to him.

The response was instant. Cute.

Ha! Evil minds think alike.

Someone knocked. "Who is it?"

"It's me," Catalina said through the door.

"Come in."

My sister stepped inside and carefully closed the door behind her. Her face was pale, her lips pinched together. "What happened?"

She sat on my bed and offered me a tablet.

"Is that Matilda's?"

She nodded. "Matilda has an email address. Her mother would send her cute cat pictures from her work. She knows how to check her email and this showed up this morning."

I glanced at the tablet. A video clip. Okay. I tapped it.

David Howling's smiling mug filled the screen. "Hello, Matilda."

Oh, you sonovabitch.

"I heard your mommy had to go away."

Fury punched me.

"Do you miss your mommy? I'm so sorry that she went away. It's not right when mommies just go away like that. But don't be sad. You will see her very soon. I'll make sure of it."

He pointed his index finger at the screen, winked, and pretended to shoot. The video stopped.

The world had gone red and for a second I couldn't even see.

"She is four years old." Catalina's lips trembled with barely contained rage.

"Has Cornelius seen this?"

"No."

"Talk to Bern and tell him to scrub that email out of Matilda's email box and off the server. This was designed to make all of us lose it and do something rash."

Cornelius was already not in a good place. This email could push him over the edge.

Catalina grabbed the tablet. "You kill him, Nevada. Kill him, or I will. He isn't touching one hair on Matilda's head."

"I will," I promised her.

Thirty minutes later, showered, dressed, and suitably armed, I climbed into the passenger seat of Rogan's Range Rover. Melosa nodded at me from the back seat. Normally I'd hide my gun in a canvas bag or a purse. Today I didn't bother. My Baby Desert Eagle rested in a hip holster. Its magazine held twelve rounds, .40 S&W, and I'd brought two spare magazines, in the interior pocket within the lining of my jacket.

We drove downtown in silence, Houston sliding past our windows under an overcast sky. Lenora Jordan's new HQ was a far cry from the marble elegance of the old Justice Center. Rogan had leveled it while trying to save Houston. The new Justice Center had been raised by one of the larger Houses as a business high-rise and bought by the city of Houston three days before it was set to open.

The new Justice Center was built with polished sunset-red granite, its facade a complex pattern of rectangles and triangles of insulated tinted glass. When the sun caught it just right, the entire building glowed, its tint changing with the time of day and color of the sky. Sometimes it was fiery orange, sometimes almost purple, and sometimes red. It stabbed at the clouds, a sharply cornered, massive obelisk taking up the entire block between Travis and Capitol streets. A meaner, leaner, harder tower, a monument to Houston's resolve, daring any enemies to take a shot at it. People called it the Spire. The name fit.

As Rogan slid the Range Rover into a parking space two blocks away, the Spire loomed above the city, and the overcast sky turned it a reddish purple, the color of a fresh bruise. A bad feeling came over me. I wished we could have brought more backup. Unfortunately, this part of the downtown was a no-escort zone by mutual agreement between the Houses. We'd brought Melosa, who could be viewed as our driver, but that was it.

Theoretically the restriction made the downtown safe. Practically, we had been attacked only a few blocks from the old Justice Center and the no-escort policy didn't exactly fill me with confidence.

"Good luck," Melosa said.

Yeah. I hoped we wouldn't need it.

We walked to the building without incident, I surrendered my firearm to security, then we crossed the Spire's cavernous lobby—polished white marble floor and red granite columns rising to a dizzying height. We selected the right elevator and let it carry us to the twenty-third floor without incident. Lenora Jordan's gatekeeper, a Native American woman about forty or so, gave us a long once-over and nodded toward the door. We stepped into her office and I almost did a double take.

Nothing had changed. Same massive bookcases, same leather visitor chairs, same deep red curtains. Even the massive desk of reclaimed wood looked the same. It wasn't just like her old office. This was an exact duplicate of it, as if the collapse had never happened.

Lenora Jordan sat in her chair, typing on her computer. The first time I'd met her, I couldn't remember how to breathe. Lenora was the hero of my adolescence. Incorruptible, powerful, confident, she bound criminals in magic chains and dragged them to justice. As Rogan once said, Law and Order were her gods and she prayed to them sincerely and often.

Maybe it was because this was the third time we'd spoken, or maybe too much had happened, but I couldn't muster any hero worship. Instead I noted faint lines around her mouth and a touch of puffiness around her eyes. Her curly black hair was still perfect and the makeup enhancing her deep brown skin was still flawless, but fatigue smudged the perfection. The Harris County DA was working overtime.

"Yes?" she asked without raising her head.

Rogan took out his phone, flicked his finger across the screen to start the recording of Senator Garza's death, and held it between Lenora's eyes and her computer screen. She snapped the phone out of his hand. Recorded moments ticked away. Lenora's gaze sharpened. She focused on the video like a bird of prey, a powerful eagle ready to strike.

The video ended.

"Do you want to be made aware of this?" Rogan said.

Lenora raised her head. Fury drowned her eyes. All of the hair on the back of my neck stood up. Oh wow.

"I'm aware of it now," she snapped.

Rogan placed a USB drive on her desk. Lenora took it and placed it into her desk drawer.

"How did you get this video?"

"Before his death, Gabriel Baranovsky indicated to Ms. Baylor that Elena de Trevino, an employee of House

Forsberg, shared this recording with him. He and Elena were lovers. He intended to make the video public and shared it with Ms. Baylor."

Looking at Rogan, I could've never guessed he'd just lied.

"That's a nice lie." Lenora pinned me with her stare. "What really happened?"

"Baranovsky admitted to having the video but he was assassinated before we could get to it," I said. "So we used a covert team of ferrets to break into the house and retrieve it from his computer."

Lenora stared at me. I felt two inches tall.

"Ferrets?"

"Yes."

"To be accurate, two ferrets and one ferret-badger," Rogan said.

She closed her eyes and slowly opened them. I wondered if she was counting in her head, trying to calm down.

Rogan opened the black zip-up folder he was carrying and put a piece of paper in front of Lenora. "This is a copy of the police report indicating that four attorneys of House Forsberg were killed in Hotel Sha Sha on December 13. Among them were Elena de Trevino and Nari Harrison, wife of Cornelius Harrison, the third scion of House Harrison."

Another piece of paper.

"This is a mutual cooperation agreement between House Rogan and House Harrison in an effort to discover the identity of the parties responsible for the death of Nari Harrison."

The papers just kept coming.

"This is a copy of a police report indicating evidence of psychrokinetic activity at the scene of Nari Harrison's and Elena de Trevino's murders.

"This is a sworn statement from me, Connor Rogan, head of House Rogan, describing the evidence in my possession that indicates an egocissor and a psychrokinetic combined efforts to bring about said murders. This is a sworn statement from Abraham Levin, my employee and chief of surveillance, in support of my assessment."

I had no idea Bug's real name was Abraham Levin.

"This is an incident report and sworn statements from Troy Linman, an employee of my House, and Nevada Baylor, a contractor hired by House Harrison to pursue an inquiry into the death of Nari Harrison. These statements describe an unprovoked attack by the third scion of House Howling, David Howling, with the purpose of killing Mr. Linman and Ms. Baylor.

"This is a declaration of feud and a petition for Verona Exception from House Rogan and House Harrison with intent to bring David Howling, and all parties found to be acting in concert with him, to justice."

I made a mental note to never try to fight Rogan with paperwork.

Lenora Jordan flipped through the stack of papers. "Do you know the identity of the manipulator working with David Howling?"

"We have a suspect," Rogan said.

Lenora thought about it. Rogan had drawn a clear line: a manipulator was involved in the death of Senator Garza; Elena de Trevino had been in possession of surveillance footage of said murder, which she shared with Baranovsky; Elena and Nari Harrison were murdered by a manipulator and an ice mage; when we tried to investigate the murder, an ice mage tried to kill us, and that ice mage was David Howling. To get to the manipulator, we had to get David Howling. I wasn't a lawyer, but even I could see that while we had enough to declare a feud, Lenora didn't have enough to go to court. The video of

Garza's death was stolen and confirming its authenticity would mean arm wrestling with House Forsberg. Even if the video was authenticated and presented to the court, it offered no evidence of ice mage activity. For all intents and purposes, the death of Garza and David Howling's attack on us could be completely unrelated incidents.

Lenora pulled the petition to her and signed it: "Petition for Verona Exception granted. The principals will provide full disclosure and will make every reasonable effort to detain the accused parties so they can be questioned by law enforcement. Don't screw this up, Rogan."

We left the massive lobby and exited onto Milam Street. While we'd spoken to Lenora Jordan, the clouds had torn, and now narrow rays of sunshine stabbed through the grey. Tall buildings turned the street into a canyon with a current of cars at the bottom. We turned left, walked to the end of the block, and made a right onto Rusk Street, moving against the flow of traffic. In this part of Houston, streets ran one way, crossing at 90 degree angles. Rusk channeled traffic southeast, Miriam ran perpendicular to it to the southwest, and I didn't see anything suspicious in either direction. So far so good.

Ahead, on to the corner of Louisiana and Rusk, Melosa leaned against the Range Rover, her arms crossed, her face grim. Leon stood next to her, with an I-didn't-do-anything-and-I-don't-know-why-this-is-happening expression on his face. How . . .

"I'm going to kill him," I squeezed through clenched teeth.

"Does he drive?" Rogan asked.

I accelerated. "No, he doesn't drive. Do you think we'd let him have a car? He must've snuck into your car."

"There was no time," Rogan said.

"He's talented." And once I reached him, I'd pull his legs out.

Rogan gripped my shoulder and jerked me back. A carmine bolt of lightning exploded on the pavement in front of me. The air popped, punching my eardrums with an invisible fist. An enerkinetic.

I pulled my gun.

Another crimson burst rocketed toward us from above. A metal subway sign tore from the building and shot up to intercept it. The lightning splashed against it, spattering like glowing blood, fizzling. Ahead the street lamp turned as if cut at the base and flew straight up, snapping the tethers of electric cables.

Behind us brakes screeched. I spun around, my back against Rogan's.

Creatures galloped toward us down Rusk, dodging the individual cars. Four feet tall and corded with steel muscle, they moved like giant cats, sprinting to kill their prey.

"Incoming!" I yelled.

"Melosa, get him out of here!" Rogan barked, his voice carrying clear across the street.

I chanced a glance back. Melosa grabbed Leon. The blue bubble of the aegis shield snapped into existence around her and she dragged him away, running down Louisiana Street.

Above us the red energy pounded against the subway shield, tearing it to pieces. The lamp post shot up and turned horizontal, sweeping the roof of the short two-story building.

The first beast leaped up onto a taxi and skidded over the cab. From the throat down it resembled a lean lioness sheathed in spiky purple-blue fur, splattered with black rosettes, each marked with a spot of red in the center. Thin furry tentacles thrust from its shoulders. The tentacles whipped and moved, flexing independently of each other, sampling the air like whiskers. Four small red eyes studded its head, each in a ring of black. It had no ears and no visible nose, only a lipless mouth filled with fangs.

The beast posed for a moment on top of the taxi, unsure where to take its next leap. Its mouth hung open, too wide, unhinging like it was the maw of a snake. The thin membrane of its cheeks glowed with red.

I sighted and fired.

The first two bullets ripped into the beast's face. Pink mist flew from its skull. It leaped forward and charged me.

I exhaled and fired again, in a tight burst. Three, four.

The red clusters of enerkinetic magic rained on the pavement around us like crimson hail, exploding with an electric hiss.

The fourth bullet punched a hole between the creature's eyes. Its momentum carried it forward another few feet, then it collapsed, head into the ground.

The second beast shot out from between the cars. I fired in twin bursts.

Five, six.

It kept coming. I had thirty bullets left. I had to be precise.

My heart still pounded, my blood still thudded through the veins in my head, but I left it behind, aware but separate from it, almost as if it was happening to someone else. The target was all that mattered.

Seven, eight. Nine, ten.

The beast skidded to a halt and collapsed.

The red lightning splashed near me. Two creatures jumped into the open—one on the car, the other next to it on the ground. I fired twice, emptying the magazine into the creature on the right. It howled, an eerie high-pitched whine that didn't come from any animal originating on Earth, and charged.

I ejected the magazine, slapped the new one in, all in one fluid motion, then raised my gun and squeezed the trigger. The bullets punched into the beast's skull, one after the other, hitting the precise spot between its eyes. One, two, three, four . . .

It kept coming.

Five, six . . .

The light faded in its eyes. It was still running, but it was already dead. I swung to its sidekick. It was huge, a full four inches taller than the rest. I sighted and fired. The gun spat thunder. Bullets punched the beast's face. It didn't even slow down.

A man screamed and plummeted to the pavement from above, landing in the beast's path. Rogan had found the enerkinetic.

The beast dodged and sprinted forward. Ten yards.

The two final shots rang out. I'd emptied my Desert Eagle.

Eight yards. It would tear me to pieces.

I ejected my magazine.

Six yards.

I slapped the new magazine into the gun. My last one.

Five. The beast leaped, its fangs bared, the fingers of its massive paws spread, the red claws ready to rend and tear.

The lamppost slammed into the creature from the side, impaling it and driving it into the glass front of the dark building to my left. Glass shattered.

"You're allowed to ask for help," Rogan said.

A wave of magic washed over me, a disturbing echo of a huge magical reserve expended all at once. Not good.

Down Rusk, the few cars that had failed to flee slid aside, as if pushed by some massive force. A round dent appeared in the pavement, as big as a manhole cover. Another. A third. Something massive and invisible was walking toward us.

Rogan moved his hand. A chunk of building broke off from the right and sliced through the empty space where the creature would be. It passed through empty air without any resistance and streaked back and forth, up and low, as Rogan tried to smash the invisible giant. How the hell do you fight something that has no body? It could hurt us, but we couldn't hurt it.

Thud! A pothole.

Thud! Another.

Thud!

The next would land on a blue SUV. A woman cringed inside. Rogan jerked the vehicle out of the way and the invisible foot thundered into the asphalt instead.

I could try to shoot it, but there was no telling where the bullets would land if there was nothing to stop them. We were smack in downtown, with thousands of people around us.

A mere half a block separated us from the transparent giant.

Rogan smashed the chunk of the building into the spot where the giant's next step would land. The invisible force punched straight through it. A car raced down Miriam Street and fishtailed, trying to avoid the potholes. Rogan waved his hand and the vehicle swerved left, out of the invisible apparition's way.

"Too many civilians," he growled. "We can't do this here."

I backed away. "It doesn't want civilians. It wants us."

We needed open space. What was even around here? Tranquility Park was two blocks away, but it was bordered by a stone wall, with only a few open entrances. However, next to it was Hermann Square, a spot of flat, wide-open ground in the canyon streets of downtown. "Hermann Square."

Rogan turned. "Come on."

We turned and sprinted for the Range Rover.

The steps accelerated behind us, pounding the pavement in an urgent staccato. Thud, thud, thud.

I had to run faster, damn it. Faster!

The air burned my lungs. We dashed into the parking lot, and I spun around. Whatever chased us was still invisible, but the building to the left, a wall of black glass, reflected the street. A fractured image flickered in the multitude of glass panes as the invisible giant pounded its way toward us.

I squinted, unable to look away. It was enormous and pallid, shambling forward on two massive legs, dripping rolls of fatty tissue. The legs supported an oblong wrinkled body, hairless, with stubs of forelimbs. It had no neck. Its body just bent forward like a question mark, and at the end of that question mark, a round black mouth gaped, filled with rows and rows of triangular clawlike teeth, like some nightmarish intestinal parasite thirty feet tall.

Oh my God.

"Nevada! Get into the car!"

I jumped into the passenger seat, snapping the seat belt closed. "Go! Go now!"

Rogan tore out of the parking lot. Going down Rusk would bring us toward the monster, not away from it. There was only one direction to go—northeast on Louisiana.

I looked behind us.

"Is it following?"

A section of the building twenty feet up shattered, showering the pavement with black glass. Thud! A dent in the pavement.

"It's following. Do you have a plan?"

He made a left onto Capitol. Here the traffic still flowed, oblivious to what was happening a block away. Rogan glanced at the building on our right. A row of windows on the third floor exploded. The traffic did its best to scatter.

"It would help if I knew what it was," he said.

"It looks like a giant maggot."

"Can you see it?"

"I can see its reflection."

The creature thudded its way onto Capitol. Where were the cops? There was an army of cops downtown. The Spire and city hall were blocks away.

"Use your phone," Rogan said, his voice clipped.

I swung back and snapped a shot with my phone. The awful giant tapeworm appeared on the small screen in all its revolting glory. I thrust the phone at Rogan.

"Crom Cruach. It's a Prime-level summon, and some-one is cloaking it."

"But why couldn't you hit it?"

"Because it doesn't have a material body in our world. They didn't summon the actual creature, only its magi-cal footprint. It's still within its own arcane realm. What we're seeing is a magical echo."

"If it doesn't have a body, then how is it damaging the street?"

"It's made of arcane magic. When the magic comes into contact with our reality, it creates damage."

Rogan expertly cut off another car.

"So can it hurt us?"

"Oh yes."

"How do we kill it?"

He flashed a grin, sharp and fast, like a sword coming out of a scabbard. "We kill it with water. It's in our world because a summoner is keeping it here through a magical bond. Water disrupts the bond. If we drench it in water, it will manifest in the flesh or disappear."

Hermann Square Park had a huge rectangular fountain.

Rogan made a sharp left onto Smith. The entire left

side of the street was blocked by construction barriers as the workers bore into the pavement in front of the Department of Public Works. We barely had two lanes to work with, but they were clear. Rogan stepped on the gas. The Range Rover roared, accelerating, the stone wall of Tranquility Park sliding past us.

I reached into my pocket and found a piece of chalk. We'd probably need a circle . . .

Ahead five children waited on the sidewalk, all elementary school students holding hands, a single middle-aged woman with them. The theater district was just down the street. That was all we needed, panicking kids. A hell of a time for a school trip.

The older woman turned her head. Pale brown hair, attractive face with high, pronounced cheekbones, pale pink lipstick, wide eyes under high arches of eyebrows plucked to thread-thin lines, and the look in those eyes . . . The look of deep, intense satisfaction. Kelly Waller. Rogan's cousin.

The children walked into the street, holding hands, a human barricade that blocked our way.

"Rogan!" I screamed.

We were going too fast. He'd never stop in time.

Rogan threw the wheel to the right. The Range Rover punched through the narrow opening in the Tranquility Park's wall. I caught a glimpse of a concrete picnic table. The Range Rover smashed into it with a sickening crunch. The airbag punched me in the face. The momentum jerked me forward, the seat belt burning my shoulder. The heavy car flew, airborne for a torturous moment, and plunged down, rolling into the grass. We stopped upright, the air bags hanging limp from the dash. I tasted blood in my mouth.

"Nevada?"

"I'm okay."

Rogan snarled like an animal and yanked his seat belt off, his face inhuman, aggression rolling off him like heat.

I had to get out of the car. I clicked my seat belt, jerked the door open, and stepped onto the grass. White chalk lines burst into cold flame around us. We were inside an arcane circle, so huge it had to be thirty yards across. The symbols pulsed once, the fire surged, and then something reached down my throat with slimy cold hands, grasped my insides, and tried to rip them out of my mouth.

The ground vanished. I flailed in midair, suspended in some primordial darkness, agony twisting and breaking me, wringing my bones, and then the blackness tore and I collapsed on an ice-cold floor, the pain a fading echo in my joints. My breasts hit a rough cold surface. I was naked. Rogan fell next to me and rolled to his feet, naked.

I blinked, trying to clear away tears.

The street was gone. Houston was gone. Instead a football-field-sized stone cavern surrounded us. All around, slender concrete columns stretched in neat rows to support a stone ceiling three stories above us. Round electric lights illuminated the space, glowing with yellow radiance at the top of the columns.

Arcane lines burned with turquoise around us. We were inside a circle—the most layered and complex circle I had ever seen—drawn on the concrete floor. Inside the circle, that floor was bare, but outside of the lines it was white with frost. A narrow foot-wide channel of power made of perfectly straight lines fed the circle. I raised my head. Ten feet away the channel of power widened into a second, smaller circle. In the middle of it, naked and covered with blue glyphs, sat David Howling.

"Hello," he said and smiled.

It was cold. It was so unbearably cold. I got off the floor and hugged myself, trying to hoard what little heat my body had. Next to me Rogan stood, his shoulders squared, his feet apart, the muscles of his thighs tight as if he were ready to leap forward. Looking at his face, I could hear David's bones breaking. Unfortunately, he was all the way over there, and we were here, trapped inside the circle.

It was a hell of a circle too, complex and twisted. The base of it had to come from Pùbù, a higher-level circle named after the Mandarin word for *waterfall*. Pùbù started as two circles, one large, one small, connected by a narrow channel of power about eighteen inches wide. The smaller circle fed the larger one, the channel focusing and magnifying the mage's power, like a lens. David had modified it, adding another row of glyphs, a second border, and odd constellations of smaller circles branching out from the outer boundary.

"Here we are," David said.

Rogan's magic stirred, building slowly, like a hurricane about to be unleashed. I forced myself to stand still. He was about to let himself go and do the thing that had earned him his terrifying nicknames.

"I wouldn't advise that," David said, his voice casual. "Look around you, Rogan. This place should look familiar. Let me jog your memory. You're a Crownover Raven, like me. History of Houston Houses, a required course for high school graduation in the Crownover Academy? The obligatory cistern-viewing trip, spiced by the lecture on John Pike and Melissa Crownover's duel? Any of it ring a bell?"

Rogan looked around. His magic died as if snuffed out. I looked at him.

He shook his head, his face grim.

"For the lovely lady's benefit," David said, "this cistern is one of many underground water reservoirs the Houses of Houston built after 1878. This particular cistern belonged to House Pike. It's located only a proverbial stone's throw from Buffalo Bayou, and is sitting under what is now Pike University, approximate capacity at this hour about three thousand students. Give or take."

Memories of a crumbling downtown floated before me, the buildings around us shattering as pulses of Rogan's power fractured them while he floated within the circle, his face otherworldly and serene. When Rogan used the magic that made him the Butcher of Merida, it didn't just generate a null field. It punched a hole in reality. Nothing could touch him within that circle, but his power would pierce straight through the rock and the campus above us. The first pulse of his magic would crumble the ground above us, and the next would trigger a collapse. Even if I managed to stop Rogan again, as I had done before, by the time we were done, the campus would be in ruins, partially buried, and the waters of Buffalo Bayou rushing into the depression would drown the survivors. We would survive. Nobody else would make it.

The temperature dropped. I shivered. So cold.

Rogan stepped close to me, wrapping his big body about mine. The warmth of him felt so good, and I locked my arms around him. I didn't want him to die.

"This wasn't my idea," David said. "I prefer quick, precise kills, but apparently there are some specific plans for your corpses. I'm instructed to kill you without any obvious wounds or damage to extremities and your faces, which eliminates my usual range of weapons and leaves us with hypothermia. Unfortunately, teleportation transports only living things. Thus we find ourselves here, naked, with no shreds of dignity left. I don't like confrontations, and quite frankly, this entire situation is rather distasteful. This space is quite large, so I'll need another twenty to thirty minutes. As deaths go, this one is long, but the pain lessens the closer you are to expiring. It will be easier once confusion sets in. At some point you might even feel warm. I've had people dance in delirium before. They went into the Great Beyond never knowing they were leaving. Try to relax."

If only I could get my hands on him, I'd wipe that smug smile right off his damn face.

Rogan stroked my back. The harsh expression on his face told me everything I needed to know. We were trapped. The inner boundary of our circle cut us off from the rest of the world and from David. Nobody knew where we were. No help was coming. We would die here, naked, while David Howling looked on and smiled.

The cold was unbearable now. My teeth chattered. My knees wanted to knock together.

I shifted from foot to foot and stepped on something hard. Pulling away from Rogan and the warmth physically hurt. I crouched down, hugging my knees, as if trying to keep warm, keeping my body between David and whatever I'd stepped on. I felt around with my hand and found the familiar shape. The piece of chalk I had clutched in my hand as I had gotten out of the car. I almost cried. Instead I stood up and wrapped my arms around Rogan again.

"Inconsiderate of you," Rogan said, looking at David. His voice was calm.

"I did the best I could. Teleportation is tricky business," David said. "Nobody wanted you to end up as a human version of the Wisconsin cannibal sandwich. If it came to it, they would accept such a death, but it certainly wasn't ideal. Teleportation required a place that was relatively close and large enough to absorb the teleportation echo, while I required an isolated, enclosed area with high moisture located somewhere where your penchant for urban destruction wouldn't be an issue."

"Still, the risk was too high. Over fifty percent of tele-portations fail."

David shook his head. "Neither of you had any major surgeries requiring inorganic components. I did take a chance on Ms. Baylor not having breast implants. Fortu-nately for all of us I was right, otherwise things would've gotten quite messy. The only wild factor was whether or not you would drive over the children, but after the in-cident at Antonio de Trevino's house, I was reasonably certain you would do everything in your power to avoid it. Principles make us predictable. We all have the lines we don't cross. Yours simply happened to be one of the more obvious ones."

"Compounds of organic origin," I said. My voice sounded hoarse.

"I'm sorry, what?" David asked.

"Teleportation doesn't affect living things. It affects compounds of organic origin."

"Yes, but I fail to see your point. Even if one of you wore something made of pure cotton or silk, it would only prolong your death by a couple of minutes."

I fixed him with my stare and offered Rogan the chalk. His eyes shone. He kissed me, hard, gripping me to him. It wasn't a kiss, it was a declaration of war and I reveled in it. He let go of me.

"How do we get out of this circle?" I asked him.

"We kill him," he said.

"Good. Let's kill him and go home."

"I thought you'd never ask." Rogan turned and studied the circle, chalk in his hand.

"Well, this is an exciting development." David's smile remained glued in place, but his eyes betrayed a hint of doubt.

Rogan stared at the lines, his gaze calculating. His lips were turning blue.

He would figure it out. If anyone could, he would be the one.

The cold seeped into my bones. My breath flittered from my lips, a pale cloud of vapor, carrying the precious warmth with it. I was so tired, but my heart was racing, and I couldn't get it under control. My stomach begged for food, as if I hadn't eaten for days. My body realized I was freezing to death and desperately sought a source of fuel to warm itself.

Rogan turned to me. "Do you remember what you told me in the elevator?"

I'd told him several things in the elevator.

"Does that promise still stand?"

What promise? What did I say? He had grabbed Cornelius; I told him to let go of my client; he had, and then I said . . . *Try that again and I'll shock you into oblivion.*

"Yes," I told him.

He pointed to a spot opposite and a little to the left of where the channel leading from David to us joined our circle. "Stand here."

I moved to the spot. He hugged me to him, quickly let go, crouched, and drew a perfect semicircle around my feet, cutting me off from the rest of the interior space. I had barely a foot and a half around me. Rogan stood up, his eyes meeting mine. I wanted to reach out and touch him, but the chalk line separated us and I could feel the first hints of power trickling through it.

"Trust me," Rogan said.

I nodded.

"It's pointless, you know," David said. "You can't break this circle. Even if by some miracle you could, it would accomplish nothing. Some changes are as inevitable as the rising of the tide."

Rogan went down to one knee and began to draw. "You've made a concerted effort to destabilize Houston.

What is it you want?" His voice was casual, as if we were having lunch somewhere.

"Me personally or us as collective?"

"Both."

"Personally I get to witness the public destruction of House Howling."

"Hate your brother and sister that much, huh?" My teeth clicked. It was hard to talk. The temperature dropped again.

David shrugged. "It's the usual story. Man becomes a widower; man marries a much younger woman; the children from the first marriage see her as the evil usurper of their mother's memory and make her life a living hell. House Howling wasn't a pleasant household. As to the collective wants and needs, you should've figured it out by now."

"Enlighten me." Rogan sectioned off the circle, drawing perfect lines toward one side. I couldn't stop trembling. The sheer power of will he had to use to keep his hand from shaking was frightening.

"History repeats itself," David said. "You were usually good at history, Rogan. I sat behind you in Classics in your freshman year at Harvard. Professor Cormack was teaching it. The one who started every first lecture with 'What you need to understand is ancient Greeks were predominantly homosexual.'"

Rogan kept drawing, creating a network of lines and glyphs on the floor.

"You don't remember me. I stayed in the background while you were busy being young and brilliant."

"I don't," Rogan said.

"I didn't think so." David smiled. The cold bit at me. "You do remember the lessons, however. Rome—corrupt, rich, and disorganized, a republic that ruled the world yet couldn't rule itself. Its senators fighting for power in vicious political squabbles; the policies of compromise forgotten in favor of personal gain. Its armies pledging their loyalty to their generals rather than to the republic they were meant to serve. Its population torn between the Optimates, supporting the traditional rule, and the Populares, playing for the favor of the unwashed mass of plebs. Mob violence, treachery, murder."

"Mhm." Rogan wrote a string of glyphs along one of the lines and turned on his toes, drawing a perfect circle around himself.

David craned his neck, tilting his head to the side as he studied the lines.

Rogan sat cross-legged within the circle he had just made and drew two smaller circles, connecting them to the boundary with precise straight lines.

"Intriguing. Theoretically possible, but practically you'll run out of power," David said. "You'd have to break my hold first."

"We'll see."

"You're trying to save the girl. Whatever path you choose, you're still dead, Rogan. That much magic expended that quickly comes with a price."

Rogan closed his eyes, his face serene.

"It's a race then." David grinned. "Let's see if I can freeze you first."

I couldn't help with whatever it was Rogan was doing, but I could keep David occupied. As long as David kept talking, he'd be splitting his attention between killing us and thinking. "What's the point of the history lesson?"

"Like so many before us, we're Rome," David said. "The Houses concern themselves only with personal gains. The concept of true civil service is all but forgotten. Of those who are given much, much is required, and we're falling short. We're adrift without any purpose or direction. We believe in nothing and don't belong to anything. There is honor in service. In standing for something larger than yourself."

Dizziness came over me. I fought to keep from swaying.

"Every Rome has its Caesar," Rogan said.

"Indeed," David said. "We do as well."

"So this is the plan?" My words came out garbled. I had to strain to make my lips move. It felt like my feet were turning into chunks of ice. My skin hurt, every muscle underneath awash with icy agony. "Throw Texas into chaos and use it to create a dictatorship? Do you think Texas will just stand for that?"

"By the time we're done, they'll welcome anyone who promises stability with open arms. And our Caesar is beyond reproach. A person of true honor."

Keep him talking. "Even if you manage to do it here, the United States won't stand for it."

"It's a slippery slope," David said. "Our republic offers an illusion of freedom. You'd be surprised how many people would trade it in for certainty."

"And you think this justifies killing innocent people."

"Yes," David said.

"Even children?"

"If necessary. The birth of a new nation is never gentle. If you're referring to Matilda, I take no pleasure in child murder. I promise that when I tie up that loose end, it will be very quick."

That bastard. "And Olivia Charles is okay with you murdering a little girl? Does she have any regrets or guilt over killing Matilda's mother?"

"Olivia comes from an old House. She knows what's required of her and she does it. Whether she feels guilt over killing Nari Harrison, I don't know."

I had my confirmation. Olivia Charles had killed Matilda's mother. If I survived this, I would bring Cornelius the name of his wife's murderer.

Rogan opened his eyes and planted his palms in the two small circles in front of him. Power punched through the circle like a huge gong being struck, melding the new and the old into a unified whole. White light burst from Rogan, running down the chalk lines like fire along the detonation cord, and crashed into the turquoise of the main circle.

David gritted his teeth. His shoulders shook.

The white and turquoise struggled, two waves trying to overwhelm each other.

Every muscle in Rogan's body went rigid. David's face shook with strain, as if lifting a weight that was too heavy. He groaned.

Rogan snarled, baring his teeth. A grimace wrinkled his face. His power coursed through the arcane lines, a raging torrent.

David jerked; his arms flung back.

White light claimed the circle, smothering the turquoise.

"It won't help you." David got to his feet, biting out the words like a pissed-off dog. "Do it! I outweigh her by fifty pounds and I'm a trained killer."

The hard cords of muscles on Rogan's arms trembled and the flow of magic halted. Slowly, ever so slowly the power reversed its course, as if Rogan had thrown a rope and was now pulling it in. I didn't even know this was possible. If he kept pulling on the magic . . .

"Do it!" David dared. "I'll kill her."

Rogan's spine curved; his massive shoulders hunched forward in a classic rowing pose. His back shook with strain. He locked his teeth and pulled, straightening. The lines of the circles spun in different directions. The smaller circle containing David slid across the floor toward me, taking the ice mage with it. I forgot to breathe. It was like the main circle had become a bobbin and David a dangling thread. The bobbin turned, winding the thread, and bringing David closer.

"I'll squeeze the life out of her with my bare hands," David snarled.

Blood dripped from Rogan's nose. He pulled again. David slid closer.

I had shockers, but he was a Prime. He was stronger, faster; he had training, and I was half dead. But I was angry. I was so angry.

"You'll get to watch her die. The last thing you'll see before all that magic you spent puts you under will be my hands on her throat."

He was doing to Rogan exactly what he'd tried to do to Cornelius. *No. You don't.*

"I'll break her. You'll hear her bones snapping."

My teeth clicked from the cold. "Hurry up. We don't have all day."

David's eyes gleamed. "Ready to die?"

"Matilda got your email," I told him. "You sent a death threat to a little girl. You're a piece of shit. Look at me. Look at my eyes. Do I look scared?"

David blinked.

"You're a wart," I told him. "You need to be removed. I'll do it and three months from now nobody will remember your name."

It was so cold it hurt to breathe. The world wavered. *Don't black out. Not now.* Rogan was almost out of magic. If he didn't black out, I wouldn't either.

If I failed, I died. Rogan died. Howling would kill Cornelius and little Matilda just to cover his tracks. He would kill a child and keep on going with his life like it didn't matter.

Rogan cried out, his voice pure agony. The spell spun one last time. David hurtled toward me. His circle came apart, absorbed by the larger arcane design, and suddenly we were in the same space, about eight feet across. He charged toward me, his fist thrusting like a hammer. I tried to dodge, but his knuckles smashed into my chest. Something crunched. A sharp burst of pain tore through my insides. I forced myself through it and lunged at him, throwing all of my weight at him, aiming for his neck. He must've expected me to go down, because he barely managed to dodge. My hand locked on his forearm. Agony swelled in my shoulder and rolled down my arm to my fingertips.

David Howling screamed.

He flailed in my hands, spit flying from his mouth as my magic pulsed from my fingers into his body, a whip of pain shocking him like a live wire. He screamed again and punched me, hammering his fist into my shoulder, my head, my side, wherever he could land it in a desperate rush to knock me off him. I hunched my shoulders, trying to hide from the barrage, and hung on. Blood filled my mouth. His hand slapped my face, his thumb trying to gouge my right eye. I jerked away, my fingers still locked on his wrist. Only one of us was getting out alive. I wouldn't let him kill me. I wouldn't let him murder anyone else.

Glowing worms swam before my eyes. I had to let go or the shockers would kill me.

I unlocked my fingers. He stumbled back, foam dripping from his mouth, his eyes insane, and I raised my foot, leaned back, and kicked his kneecap. He howled, spun away from me, and dropped down to one knee. I had seconds before he shook it off and strangled me. I jumped on top of him, grabbed his head, and pushed it straight down on his neck. His vertebrae locked and I twisted.

Nari's terrified face flashed before me. *I've got it. I won't let him hurt your daughter.*

Bones crunched with a dry pop. I let go and David fell facedown, his head jutting at an odd angle.

A strange sound echoed through the cistern and I realized it was Rogan laughing.

Around me the power of the circle melted, the lines once again mere chalk, and I saw him on his back on the floor.

My feet didn't want to move. I staggered over and dropped by him. His eyes were open. His chest barely rose.

"Connor?" I turned his face toward me. "Connor, talk to me!"

"A wart, huh?" His voice was weak. "Good speech."

"I read it in some fanfiction on Herald." I was so tired. I just wanted to sit here for a little bit. But sitting meant death. "Come on, we've got to get you up. We have to get out of here."

"You go," he said. "Get help. I'm good here for a bit."

Lie.

I glanced up. David was dead, but his magic had done its damage. The floor was white with frost. We were already past the point of being cold. We had to get out of here or we'd die.

"No, you're not. The cistern will take hours to warm up."

"I'll be fine."

Lie.

"Go get help. The faster you get someone here, the better my chances. I'll be fine."

Lie.

"You're at your limit," I said. "You will freeze to death before I can get back."

"No."

Lie.

"Stop lying to me!"

He raised his hand and stroked my cheek with his fingers.

"Listen to me."

"We have to get out of here!"

He focused on my face and for a moment the old Rogan with steel-hard eyes resurfaced and melted back into Connor. "That nightmare you had with the cave and the rat, it wasn't yours. It was mine. I don't know why or how, but you attuned yourself to me. You're sensitive to my projections. You pick them up even when I don't concentrate on sending them to you."

I tried to pull him upright, but my arms were so weak.

"I project when I'm under stress. The moment I pass out, my mind will react and try to purge all this shit from my head so I can rest. I'll project while unconscious and you're exhausted. You have no defenses. If you're still here, you won't be yourself. You'll be me. You won't know where you are or what you're doing. I need you to go now, Nevada."

"No."

He was looking at me like I was the only thing that had ever mattered. "If you don't survive, none of this is worth it to me. I love you."

"No."

"Yes. This was never about both of us getting out. Leave. Now."

"Don't you pull this hero bullshit with me. Get up. You're Mad Rogan. Get up."

"God damn it," he snarled. "Get the hell away from me."

"Get up or I'm dying here with you. I'll lie down right here on the floor."

"Get out of here!" He tried to sit up. His eyes rolled back in his head. I grabbed him before he hit the floor. He was heavy. So heavy. He slumped over me, limp.

Tears wet my cheeks. "Connor, please. Please. I can't carry you. Please wake up. I love you. Don't leave me."

His skin was cold. He stopped breathing. Oh God.

Panic slapped me. I pushed him back and put my head on his chest and heard the beating of his heart, distant and weak, but steady. I pressed my cheek against his nose. A faint flutter of air escaping warmed my skin. Still alive. I straightened. He wasn't waking up. Think. Think . . .

David didn't teleport here, which meant he had to have clothes. I got up and stumbled about looking for clothes, a bag, anything.

The cistern tore in front of me, the concrete columns vanished, and jungle breathed into my face, bright violent green. I fought it with everything I had. *This isn't real.* The hazy concrete columns swung into view. I forced myself to move. There! A duffel bag by one of the columns.

Something was coming for me. I could hear it moving through the vivid growth. Something with long needle teeth, with a bite that burned like ice and turned your skin blue and black with necrosis. It was close. I had to hide.

Bag. Stay with the bag. Bag. Bag. Bag.

I reached it and dropped on my knees. Clothes— T-shirt, underwear, jeans, windbreaker—car keys, a gun, phone. Yes! I swiped the screen. Password locked.

I was out in the open and the thing with needled teeth was staring at my back. Its gaze bore into me. I had to get out. I had to hide.

I tapped Emergency Call. No signal.

The thing was coming for me. Rogan was lying in the open, in the middle of a clearing. I had to get him out before it found him.

I grabbed the bag, slung it over my shoulder, and staggered to Rogan. I pulled out and tied the windbreaker over his hips. It would make him easier to drag.

The jungle wasn't real. It wasn't real. I hooked my arms under his armpits and heaved. My feet slid on the frost and I fell on my ass. Why was this happening? *I just want out. Help me, somebody, I want out of this nightmare. I just want for this to end.* I could shoot myself. Just finish it. I had a gun.

If I killed myself, who would walk them out of the jungle?

I clawed my way through the visions flooding my brain. At the right wall, thirty-five yards away, a door broke the uniform concrete. I had to get us to that door. I crawled back up and heaved his huge body to me. He moved an inch. I would take an inch. An inch was closer to the door than before.

I was warm. Dear God, I was warm. That meant I was dying.

There were stairs.

I couldn't do stairs. He was too heavy.

Daniela would fix him. Daniela fixed everyone and everything, except a bullet to the head.

The mage hunters were coming. I could hear them breathing. I got my gun and waited.

Get to higher ground. Radio for pickup.

Jimenez was waiting upstairs with his knife. His face swam before me, hazy, his eyes two bottomless pools of darkness. "It's not him. He would have broken by now. This is a career officer. Take him to the back and shoot him."

I still had six rounds left.

Get to higher ground.

They were coming for me. Their voices floated down to me.

No. No, I didn't come all this way for them to kill us now.

Something bit me. My body gave out. I crashed down. The mage hound's maw loomed over me, all slimy serpentine tongue and thin sharp teeth, and swallowed me whole.

Chapter 14

Che sheets were so soft and warm it was like being wrapped in a heated cloud.

I was alive. I smiled.

Rogan!

I sat straight up in bed. I was in a large room with a single hospital bed.

"Hello? Is anybody there?"

The door swung open and Dr. Arias strode into the room. About forty, over six feet tall, Daniela Arias was huge: broad shoulders, powerful legs, and muscular arms. Her features, large and attractive, were handsome rather than pretty, but right now her face was a cool professional mask. I'd met her before. She was Rogan's private physician.

"Is Rogan alive?"

"In better shape than you."

Relief washed through me. I slumped back on the pillow. He lived. We both lived.

"What happened?"

She pulled up a chair. "You dragged him out. Somehow, you managed to pull him thirty yards across the floor and up two flights of stairs. His back and ass are one long bruise with a helping of concrete road rash, so his dreams of being a nude model are shattered for a while."

I'd laugh, but her face told me it wasn't a good idea.

"The reservoir's door had an excellent waterproof seal, which is what saved you. The air outside of it was at a normal temperature. You got up to the second landing, where you got a signal and you called 911 and told them that you needed a pickup because Cazadores were coming. They thought you were delusional, but we were monitoring the 911 calls."

"How?"

"Your cousin and Bug, from what I understand. After Rogan and you disappeared and his tracking went dead, they snapped to it. Rivera's team was dispatched Downtown, to mop up, and my team sat, waiting for any sign of you. As soon as we caught your call, we went to you. We've dealt with Rogan falling unconscious before, so we knew what to expect. You had a gun, so we tasered you, and then we did all the things you normally do when you're trying to save someone's life. Here we are, almost twenty hours later. You have two broken ribs. Howling did a number on your face, so you won't be modeling in the near future either. I've notified your family that you're safe but otherwise occupied. I figured you needed some downtime. Your cousin is fine. Melosa got him out. The summon disappeared after you teleported out, so Houston is fine as well."

"Rogan's cousin? She walked children onto the street to block our way. That's why we crashed."

She shook her head. "She disappeared."

Of course, she did.

Daniela handed me a mirror. Bruises covered the right side of my face. A lump swelled on my right shoulder. I looked like a boxer at the end of a final round of a hard title match.

"It doesn't hurt," I told her.

"Oh, it will," she said. "Once the painkillers wear off."

"Where is Rogan?"

"He decided to give you some space."

That wasn't an answer. I reached for my blanket.

"I understand that your first instinct is to dramatically jump out of bed and rush over there," Daniela said. "It's a good plan, except you're so medicated you'll have trouble making it to the bathroom, let alone driving. Why don't we sit here and chat a bit?"

"Do I have a choice?"

Her eyes were hard. "Not really."

"Okay."

Daniela cleared her throat. "I have a nephew. Sweet kid. Martin's twenty-four now. He did his four years in the army, earned his college tuition, and enrolled in UNC. He wants to be a geologist. He says he likes rocks because they don't shoot back at you."

It sounded like a joke, but again she didn't smile.

"He got himself expelled a month ago. You know that horror movie where the guy in a pig mask chases kids across college campus. Screamer-something."

"Screamer-Dreamer." Living in a household with three teenagers made me a horror movie expert. It was a stupid cheap flick, but for some reason it had caught on and there were memes of Piggy, the killer, all over the Internet with witty sayings plastered over them.

"A campus radio station was pranking people live on the air. They had a guy dressed in a pig mask and some sort of black shroud. He'd hide behind something, burst out with a big plastic knife, and chase people around. They were filming it for YouTube."

Yep. Sounded just like something college kids would do. I knew exactly where this story was going.

"The pig guy charged Martin, and Martin took the

knife away from him and hit him. He didn't just hit him
once. He went for the knife hand first, dislocated the guy's
shoulder, and then punched him four times in the head in
less than two seconds. It took three people to pull him
off. I asked him about it. He said something just snapped
inside him. He saw a threat and reacted. He isn't a violent
kid. Never been in a civilian fight before. He felt terrible
about it. He apologized. The college expelled him and
there were serious charges, until Rogan's lawyers moved
in and had it dropped down to a misdemeanor. Still, it
will be on his record forever. He's going to a private university in January."

"Piggy should've played dead," I said. "If he stopped
moving, Martin would've stopped hitting."

"Probably," she said. "The kid who had the bright idea
to scare people with his knife didn't expect to be hospital-
ized, because civilians typically don't try to kill you when
you scare them."

"It was irresponsible either way."

Daniela sighed. "We have rules in our society. Don't
steal. Don't hurt others. Don't kill. That's the big one.
We take these kids, some of them barely eighteen years
old, tell them that rules no longer apply and then we drop
them into the war zone. Fight or flight is a constellation
response, a perfect storm within your body. It makes you
faster, stronger, hyperaware, but all of it comes at a cost.
Soldiers in combat are running a biochemical sprint,
except for them it's a marathon that doesn't end. It wears
the body down and it carves new neurological pathways
through your brain. It changes you. Permanently. Then
you finally come home and people expect you to set all
that aside and immediately remember what it's like to be
a normal person."

Daniela leaned back.

"My nephew, Martin, is a relatively well-adjusted veteran. He simply needs time and a little help to re-attune himself to the civilian world. The switch that moderates the severity of his response needs to be recalibrated. Some people don't understand that."

I understood it. I knew all the statistics and I'd seen the hysteria firsthand. When Mom snapped, the assistant DA assigned to her case called her a ticking bomb and waved around the PTSD flag, which Mom didn't have. He made it sound like she would go on a shooting rampage any minute. In reality, most veterans were a danger to themselves rather than others. The suicide rate among vets was 50 percent higher than in the rest of the population.

"Like I said," Daniela continued. "Martin was a sweet kid. You know who else was a sweet kid before the army got a hold of him? Connor Rogan. I knew him at the very start of his service. He was so young. Full of himself, a little cocky, and idealistic. The brass realized early on what they had, so they guarded him like the Hope Diamond and controlled everything he saw. We used to call him BL—Bubble Lieutenant. They built this bubble of patriotism around him. Everyone he interacted with told him he was a hero, that he was serving his country, saving lives, and doing the right thing. They would bring him out, tell him how many thousands of lives would be saved if he did what they ordered, then he'd crush a city, and they'd whisk him away before we combed through the ruins. He knew there were casualties, but he never saw the dead bodies. He was an officer in name only. When they promoted him to captain, we had a good laugh."

Daniela's voice broke. She held her hand up for a moment, then continued.

"After about two years of this, he became their ultimate weapon. Just a rumor of his presence in an area changed the conditions of engagement. During that summer the command received reports of a superweapon being built in the Maya Forest, thirteen million acres of jungle that stretch all across Belize into the Yucatan. It was some sort of superbomb that could level a city and then poison everything around it with radiation, and the Mexican military was desperate enough to use it. I never got all the details—above my clearance—but whatever it was had to be convincing, because our command got together a strike team and attached Rogan to it. The plan was to covertly paradrop into Campeche, get Rogan to target, and once the facility was destroyed, get picked up. Ten seconds into the paradrop we knew we were fucked, because they were shooting at us while we were still in the air."

She paused. Her eyes turned haunted.

"Captain Gregory died before his boots ever hit the ground. Top, our master sergeant, died after Rogan started mowing down the jungle and they dumped napalm on us. Once we got clear, we ran across a Cazador tower."

Everyone knew what Cazadores meant. A special forces unit of Mexican military, Cazadores hunted mages. They were elite troops—scary, efficient, and lethal.

"It was a trap," I guessed.

"Mhm. They wanted Rogan so badly they built a fake factory in the jungle hoping to lure him in, and we served our greatest weapon to them on a silver platter." Daniela's face was grim. "They flooded the jungle with Cazadores and their hounds. Except they weren't really hounds. They were these things they pulled out of the astral realm."

"I saw them in Rogan's memories." I fought a shiver.

"Then you understand. You see one, it will give you nightmares for a lifetime. We learned the rules fast. Cazadores had sniffers, mages sensitive to magic. Any use of it by us brought another air strike. Any attempt at radio communication brought an air strike. Any sighting of one of us brought dozens of troops. There would be no pickup. If we called for help, we'd die.

"Rogan had a choice. He could radio in, and if he used his full power, he'd survive within his null field long enough to be rescued. But he would be the only one who got out. Or he could try to walk out of the jungle with us. He chose to walk out. He became the senior officer after Gregory's death, and Heart, our staff sergeant, became the senior NCO. You haven't met Heart yet, have you?"

"I don't think so."

"Trust me, you would remember if you did. We were supposed to have been out in forty-eight hours. We had food for five days. People think the jungle is paradise, filled with fruit and game. Let me tell you, the jungle is hell. There is nothing to eat, there is nothing to kill, especially when you can't shoot. Insects come at night, relentless, draining you dry. Howler monkeys follow you and scream and scream and scream every day and night. There is no clean water. We ate snakes. We ate worms."

The dark cave flashed before me. "Rats," I said.

"Yes. Some nights the Cazadores were so close, there was no fire, no light, just the jungle and the hounds, always near, always listening and waiting. Rogan could've pulled the plug anytime. Instead he stayed and he took care of us. When Hayashi went down with infection, there was no way to get the stretcher through the growth, so we built a frame out of wood and strapped it to Rogan. He carried Hayashi for two days on his back."

It didn't surprise me. Not even a little.

"To get off the mountain we had to clear a Cazador camp, and we couldn't walk around it. Rogan walked into it and let them take him so they would send a scout team out in the direction he came and we could sneak past. We went around the camp and had to wait until the next night to come back for him. They had him for fourteen hours. We heard him screaming."

She swallowed.

"They only had prewar images of Rogan and by that point, after five weeks in the jungle, he looked a decade older. He gave them Gregory's name and so they tortured him for a while, until Jimenez, the man in charge, decided that if Rogan were a Prime playing soldier, he would've broken by then. Jimenez finally ordered him shot. You probably saw Rogan's dog tags. They're not his. He killed Jimenez when they cut him down off the torture rack and took his tags. It's his reminder that he survived."

The tags were probably lost now, disintegrated by the teleport spell. Rogan would have to find something else to remind him that he was alive.

"We spent nine weeks in the jungle, fighting and starving, as the Cazadores bled us like wolves bleed an injured deer. Twenty-four people went in. Sixteen came out."

Bug had said that Luanne was one of sixteen. Now it made sense. The sixteen who had walked out with Rogan.

"It's my professional opinion that Connor Rogan died in that jungle," Daniela said. "The war took Connor, crushed him down to powder, and reformed him into Mad Rogan. He had to become that to survive. I told you that my nephew Martin will adjust to civilian life with some help. Mad Rogan will never adjust. His world is black and white. There are enemies and allies."

"And civilians," I added.

Had Rogan put her up to this speech? No. Rogan wouldn't have made her do it. Rogan took care of his own dirty work. Dr. Daniela must've taken it upon herself to spell things out for me.

"He does recognize noncombatants, although his definition of *civilian* is shaky. He won't kill children. He tries not to take a life unless the person presents a direct threat, but if he chooses to kill, he does it. There are only two Primes in House Rogan: him and his mother, and she has no interest in involving herself. He has us, and we'll do anything for him. We all tried to go our separate ways, yet we all ended up right back here. We're good at what we do, but none of us are Primes. Rogan has to rely on himself and he likes the way he is. He thinks it keeps him sharp and alive, and he's probably right. He doesn't feel he needs to change and he doesn't want any help."

"You're not telling me anything new," I said. "I already know what he's like. I've seen it."

"Then you know there will be no normal with him. There will never be sweetness and light."

You might be surprised. "I know."

"Love makes you helpless," Daniela said. "You think about the object of your affection all the time. Your happiness or misery depends on another person's mood. You give up all power over yourself, hand it to the person you love, and trust that they will be gentle with it. Do you know what Major hates most of all?"

"Feeling helpless?"

"He'll go to great lengths to avoid it. I don't even know if he is capable of maintaining a relationship in the traditional sense. He'll never change, Nevada. The best you can hope for is that he alters some of his behavior out of respect and consideration for you, but he won't think that what he does is wrong. He's ruthless and when he devotes himself to something or someone, that devotion is a frightening thing that doesn't always survive collision with reality. Take my advice. Walk away."

"No."

"He isn't here. He left you here and went home because he knows that you need time to think. He left the door open for you, so you can make a clean break. No guilt, no pressure. You can still meet someone normal and have a happy life."

"Are you done?" I asked.

"Will talking more do any good?"

"No. I heard what you had to say. Thank you for worrying about my well-being." I pulled my blanket back and swung my legs sideways.

"What will happen when you tell him someone aggravated you and he throws that person off the roof?"

"He won't. He'll trust me to handle it, because the only way I'll ever respect his wishes is if he respects mine."

"Walk away," Daniela said again.

"Did Rogan ask you to give me this speech?"

"He didn't have to. I take care of him. We all take care of him. I don't want to see him hurt. I don't want you to be hurt."

I faced her and I let whatever it was that made me Prime show in my eyes.

"I've sat here and listened to you talk for an hour. I heard you, I understand, and I'm done. I'm going to get up, get my clothes, and get dressed. Then you will arrange for a car to take me to where Rogan is. If you try to stop me or impede me in any way, I'll shock the shit out of you. Do we understand each other, Dr. Arias?"

I took a deep breath and rang the bell on the front door of Rogan's house. After I'd gotten out of bed, Rogan's people had panicked. Well, *panicked* might have been too strong of a word. They sprang into action with agitated efficiency. A pair of sweatpants and a T-shirt were brought to me, and by the time I walked out of the building, a car and a driver were waiting for me, with Melosa in the passenger seat, followed by another vehicle filled with armed personnel. They delivered me to Rogan's front door and beat a strategic retreat.

I did get a chance to ask Melosa about Leon. Apparently he had a feeling that something bad was going to happen to me and Rogan, so he stole a Glock out of our gun cage and caught a ride Downtown. His plan was that Melosa would shield him, while he heroically shot all of our enemies to pieces. Melosa admitted that he was so crushed when he realized that aegis shield worked both ways, that she almost felt sorry for him.

I waited, feeling stupid. Rogan was somewhere inside the house. Here I was, wearing some sweatpants and a wrinkled white T-shirt. My hair was probably greasy. The right side of my face was one big ugly bruise. I . . .

The door swung open and I saw Rogan standing in his living room.

It finally hit me. We'd both survived. We were both alive and he was standing there, and he was the most handsome man I had ever seen. I looked into his eyes and the iced over darkness stared back at me.

No. He was mine. There was a dragon under that ice and I would bring him out.

I walked across the threshold. The door stayed open behind me. He was giving me an escape route.

"You found me," he said.

"You didn't hide very well. And I'm a PI."

"Nevada, nothing's changed."

His expression was detached, his voice almost casual. He'd locked his emotions behind a steel wall of his will. *Too late, Rogan. I remember the way you looked at me in that cistern.*

"Sooner or later, you will become a House," he said.

"So you told me."

"Genetics and children will become important."

"Children are always important."

"I can't share, Nevada. I won't."

"Share what?"

"Share you," he said, his voice harsh. Something wild was trying to claw its way out of him. The cold mask was breaking. "I can't be with you knowing that you will go back to another man, whether you love him or not. It's beyond me. It wouldn't end well."

"That's good, because I don't want to share you either."

"I've given all the warnings I can give," he said. "All in or all out, Nevada. Decide."

"You're a fool, Connor." I slipped out of my shoes and took a step toward him.

The door behind me slammed shut.

Fire flared in his eyes and burned through the darkness. It was more than lust. More than need. Nobody else ever looked at me like that.

Anticipation gripped me.

He strode toward me, confident, unhurried, a dragon in his domain.

"Am I trapped?"

"You walked into my lair." He circled me, stalking.

The first drop of his magic fell on the back of my neck, hot and soft like velvet. Breath caught in my throat.

"I gave you a chance to escape."

The magic slid over my spine, setting every nerve aflame.

"You didn't take it." He was behind me.

A quick feather-light touch brushed over my shoulders and dashed down my hips. I turned. He was standing a couple of feet away.

"Now you're mine."

I moved, and my t-shirt and sweat pants fell off me.

I gasped.

He pulled off his T-shirt, his huge golden body hard, and waited. Giving me one last chance to walk away.

I closed the two steps between us. My breasts mashed against his sculpted chest. The heat of his powerful body burned me. He wrapped his hand in my hair and claimed my mouth.

Magic dripped onto my lower thighs, like molten honey,

soft and hot. It pooled on my skin, heating up, the sensation so intense, the pleasure of it was overwhelming. My body turned supple. My breasts ached, suddenly too heavy.

He smelled of sandalwood. The taste of him in my mouth was making me crazy.

An insistent heat built between my legs. I leaned into him, rubbing myself against him, inviting, enticing, trying to seduce.

He let out a short male growl. His hand closed on my ass and he pulled me on to his hips, supporting my weight like it was nothing. The hard length of his cock strained against my aching core. His tongue thrust between my lips again and again, ravaging my mouth. My head was spinning. I wanted to feel his steel-hard shaft, wrapped in silken skin. I wanted his pants off and my panties to disappear. I wanted him to thrust himself inside. Waiting for it was torture. My hands locked on the powerful muscles of his back and I shifted my hips, grinding against him.

The velvet heat slid up the inside of my thighs, ever so slowly. Inch. Another inch. Oh please. *Please.*

He let me take a breath. We were face to face. His eyes were dark and feral.

"Are you going to warn me not to scream?" I asked.

"Scream all you want," he said.

"You seem so confident you could make me . . ."

The delicious heat dashed up my thighs and slipped inside of me, straight to the aching center. Molten honey drowned my clit. Pleasure burst in me. I cried out.

He carried me across the room, deeper into his house.

A heavy wooden door burst open in front of us. A massive bed occupied the room—tall, solid, its headboard ancient and scarred. He tossed me onto the bed. The door slammed shut behind me.

I was in the dragon's cave, on the dragon's bed, and he thought he caught me. But he was wrong. I caught him.

Connor loomed over me. His pants were gone. He was huge, naked, and corded with muscle. And hung. Oh dear God.

He reached over and pulled off my panties. His gaze roamed my body and his eyes told me he loved what he saw.

I wanted him so much. The anticipation was killing me. It made me shiver.

"Are you cold?" he asked, his voice deceptively calm.

The magic splashed onto my collarbone and rolled lower. Its velvet pressure cupped my breasts. My nipples turned hard. The intoxicating heat slid over them, turning ache into bliss.

I moaned. He was on top of me, his big hands caressing me. His mouth closed on my left nipple and sucked, his tongue painting heat on top of his magic. It was almost too much to take.

His head and magic moved lower, dragging moans out of me.

He kissed my stomach.

He pushed my legs apart.

I wanted to grab his head by the hair and drag him to my aching center, but he pinned my arms down by my sides.

He tongued the inside of my right thigh.

The wait was agony.

His magic crested, spilling into the crease between my legs. The velvet heat squeezed ever so gently and released, washing over me and pulling back, faster and faster. His mouth closed over me. His tongue danced across my clit.

I screamed.

He licked me, again and again, his magic stroking me. I writhed under him. My legs shook. The bed was gone, the room was gone, and all I could do was wait, tense and hot, centered on him and my need for release. It felt like if I didn't come now, I would die.

My body shuddered with the first pulse of my climax.

The universe exploded.

The orgasm rocked me, but that usually fleeting moment of ecstasy didn't end. The exaltation built and built, overwhelming, pleasure so intense, so complete, I had no idea my body was capable of it. I couldn't even breathe. My eyes snapped open and I saw him. He was above me, his eyes wild and drunk. He felt it, I realized. He felt my pleasure and he was sharing it.

Finally, the ecstasy released me, fading in pleasant aftershocks.

I slumped on the sheets, exhausted, my face damp with sweat. The magic pressure eased, still there, but featherlight now.

He was next to me, his hand stroking my side.

So that's what sex with a tactile was like.

He blinked, clarity returning into his eyes and turning into lust. There was something hungry, and harsh, and male in the way he looked at me. He grabbed my hips and dragged me over to the center of the bed.

The velvet touch of magic between my legs grew warm, then hot, so hot I could barely stand it. It pulled me out of my drowsy bliss into awareness.

He paused over me, muscles tight on his chest and stomach, blue eyes dark, and pulled me to him, lifting my legs onto his shoulders. His warm fingers stroked my skin as he ran his hands down the length of my legs, his touch sending shivers through me.

The last echoes of the orgasm finally faded.

He planted his hands on my thighs and thrust into me.

Oh my God.

I cried out, tilting my hips, trying to take in the whole length of him. He thrust again and again, hard, relentless, dominant, every slide of his cock sending a jolt of pleasure I could feel all the way in the base of my neck. His magic seared me. All of my nerves were on fire. I gasped with each stroke. I was hot and so wet, and he kept pumping, his magic caressing my body in a steady rhythm.

Pressure began to build inside of me.

He pushed my legs apart, wrapped them around his back, and then he was on top of me. I writhed under him, trying to match his rhythm. His muscular golden body caged mine, all those muscles contracting tight, devoted to a single movement.

Ecstasy drowned me. My body contracted, trying to milk his shaft. Climax shook me again.

He growled, holding still. His eyes told me my orgasm was rolling through him and it was about to drag him under into his own release. He fought against it and pulled back.

Wave after wave of pleasure rocked me. I couldn't even move anymore. I just lay there, limp and shaking, until it faded.

His lips were on my neck. He kissed me and pulled me on top of him, and then I was straddling his hips. He was looking at me as if I were the most beautiful woman in the world.

I reached for his hands, locked my fingers with his, and rode him. We moved in perfect rhythm, making love as if our bodies were meant to be together.

His magic wound around me. I leaned into it, my shoulders back, letting it claim me.

He was thrusting into me.

I felt the climax build. It broke like a wave. I shuddered, feeling the hardness of him inside me, and slumped on his shoulders, boneless, breathing deep, done. Sated and happier than I had ever been in my life.

He locked his arms around me and emptied himself

inside me with a short rough growl. A burst of pleasure consumed me, so intense everything else paled before it, and I realized I was feeling the echo of his orgasm.

We stayed like that, pressed together, arms around each other.

Slowly Rogan lowered me onto the bed. I curled into a ball and he wrapped himself around me and pulled a sheet over us. I wanted to stay awake, to enjoy the feeling of him holding me, but instead I yawned and fell asleep.

When I woke up, the first thing I felt was Rogan next to me.

He nuzzled my neck, his hand stroking my stomach. "Are you alive?"

"The jury is still out." I tried to smile. Pain shot through my face and I winced. "Ow."

"Did I hurt you?"

"No, the painkillers wore off." I tried to gently turn over and instead managed to hurt my whole right side. "Ow." I finally flopped on my back.

He reached over carefully and brushed the hair from my face. Anger stirred in his eyes. "I'm an asshole."

"You just now figured that out?"

"I should have waited."

I gave him my best come-hither look. My puffy eyes probably made it look really stupid. "That wasn't your decision."

"Yes, it was."

"What was the alternative? Leave me standing naked in your living room? Because shoes were only the first step. My clothes were coming off."

"The alternative would've been not jumping you and dragging you into my bedroom like some sort of Neanderthal."

I kissed him. "Foolish, foolish Rogan."

"Don't start," he warned me.

"You realize that you will never be able to hear me say that without thinking about sex?"

He shook his head. "Sorry to burst your bubble, but that changes nothing. Anytime you say anything, I think about sex. Anytime I see you, I think about sex."

I caressed his face. "Am I that sexy with my bruised face and messy hair?"

He kissed me, his touch light and tender. "Yes."

"Let me see your back," I said.

He sat up and turned. His whole back was raw. He looked like somebody had dragged him across a stretch of asphalt behind a car.

I groaned. "I should've put some clothes on you."

"You should've left me." He turned around and leaned closer to me. "The next time I tell you to leave me, you will go, do you understand?"

"No. I'll do whatever I think is right." *The next time . . .*

"What?" he asked.

"Will there be a next time?"

"There might be," he said. "This mess isn't finished. It's a dangerous game and we're in it now. There is no backing out."

The memory of him limp in the circle came to me. I remembered my hands on David Howling's head. It was too much. I covered my face with my hands.

"Don't," he said quietly.

"Rogan, I snapped a man's neck with my bare hands. I don't even know how I did it."

"Well," he said. "You did it well. Too well even."

I stared at him.

"It was quick," he said. "He didn't suffer nearly enough. If I had gotten my hands on him, I would've made it last. Instead I lay on the floor, unable to move, and watched him hit you."

I slid even closer to him. He moved to the other, less injured side of me, and pulled me to him. I lay with my head on his carved arm.

"I don't want it," I said.

"Don't want what?"

"The life of a Prime. I don't want it."

"Too late." He kissed my head. "No choice now."

We'd gone through all that, and Olivia Charles was still free. As long as she remained free, none of us would be safe, and Cornelius would still be waiting for justice. We had to end it.

But even if we ended it . . . David had mentioned Caesar. Olivia wasn't Caesar. When David mentioned her name, he did it matter-of-factly. When he said *Caesar*, his voice was filled with awe.

"Did Bug get anything off David's phone?" I asked.

"It was brand new and Howling was careful about texts and calls—all went to burner phones. The texts are interesting. This thing reaches very far. At least six Houses are involved, likely a lot more. And the moment we walked into Lenora's office, the video hit the Internet." His lips stretched.

"Then why are you smiling?" It was a disaster. We'd gone through all that, had nothing to show for it, and whoever was behind it all still got his civil unrest.

"I'm smiling because I emailed the video to Lenora the night we got it. I beat you and Bern by about ten minutes."

I sat up. "What?"

"Don't act so shocked. I knew you would send it to her the moment you asked for a copy of it."

I stared at him.

"I might be a dragon, but you're a paladin." He put his hands behind his head, looking unbearably smug.

"Why don't you just tell me the whole thing?" I asked.

"Originally these people had two options: they could continue to blackmail Howling or they could release the recording of his actions and incite civil unrest. Once they realized that we had the recording, they would release their version. You were right. If you want to destabilize the existing power structure, you have to incite the public to action. It was just the matter of timing it to cause the most damage. They were waiting for the right moment and, since Howling decided to wink and smile at you across the room to make sure you saw him, I realized that that moment was tied to us. We were annoying, because we kept digging. We had to be neutralized. They had plans for you and me. Or rather for our corpses. We were to be the fuel to their bonfire."

Mad or not, Rogan was a war hero and a man who'd saved the city from Adam Pierce. Houston was proud of its homicidal, terrifying son. If they released the video of Garza's murder, and then dumped us somewhere in a public location, dead, naked, discarded like trash, the message would be clear. *We killed your representative and now here is your hero, stripped naked, humiliated, and dead. He couldn't protect himself or the woman with him. If this could be done to him, think what can be done to you.* That's why Howling had to resort to hypothermia. They wanted us killed by magic but be instantly recognizable and they wanted people to know we died slowly and suffered.

Houston would have rioted for sure.

Rogan reached over and ran his fingers down my arm.

I exhaled slowly. We'd come so close to the edge of disaster.

"So, after you fell asleep after the ninja ferret heist, Lenora called me on my private line. Augustine, Lenora, and I talked. She had to bring Richard Howling in safely.

We assumed that he was being watched, so Augustine volunteered his services. That day Richard Howling went to work as usual, and then he split. One Howling went up to his office and the other was smuggled out by Houston PD. Then that first Howling simply vanished."

"What's in it for Augustine?"

"Augustine, despite all his ruthless corporate maneuvering, always tries to stay on the right side of legal and on the right side of the DA's office, Lenora in particular. He justifies it by claiming it's good for business. In reality, he has these annoying things called principles."

"Augustine?"

"I know, shocking." Rogan grinned at me.

I kissed him. "What happened next?"

"We needed to buy Lenora time to move all of her chess pieces into place. The fact that Olivia and Howling targeted Baranovsky meant they knew the video existed and that he had a copy of it. Either they bribed someone or most likely, it was the matter of a simple logical deduction. Elena de Trevino had access to the video and if she wanted insurance, she would've given a copy of it to the most powerful person she knew for safekeeping."

Made sense.

"After our appearance, I knew they would watch us. One doesn't go to see Lenora without evidence, so the moment we made that move, they would put two and two together and realize that we either have the recording or know where it is. So, I delayed as much as was realistic, and then you and I went to visit Lenora in broad daylight. She put on a show for the benefit of whoever was listening. Meanwhile, Howling was secured, and Lenora's second-in-command, Atwood, called a press conference. By the time the video hit the social networks, he was in the middle of the speech explaining how badass they were. Olivia's firecracker fizzled out. There is still outrage, but not nearly as much of it as they hoped."

"You could've told me all this from the start," I said.

"You were trying to decide what to do about Augustine. It didn't seem like the best time."

"So what now?"

"It turns out that domination forges a link between the dominator and the person whose mind they are hijacking. Richard Howling named Olivia Charles as the dominator who forced him to murder Garza. Olivia has disappeared. That Verona petition Lenora signed specifies that we are free to pursue David Howling and all known associates implicated in the assault, which gives us a clean shot at Olivia, if we can find her. The DA's office would like Olivia Charles alive, but they will understand if circumstances make it impossible."

"So we have to find Olivia."

Rogan bared his teeth, looking predatory. "Howling's people bugged my car. A very sophisticated piece of equipment. Looks like a tack. We rolled over it and our tire picked it up. Howling tethered his phone to it, so he'd know where we were at all times. He didn't realize that every time he accessed the app, it recorded his location."

I laughed.

"David spent a lot of time on a ranch outside of Houston, owned by Dedalus Corp. Bug is still untangling exactly who is behind it. It's a fortified compound. Sixteen hours ago Olivia Charles arrived there with armed guards and a pile of suitcases."

"When are we going?"

"Tomorrow," he said. "There are a lot of people in the compound. It will be a long fight."

"I'll need to go and see my family," I said.

"I'll take you."

"But not now."

"What would you like to do now?" he asked.

I turned over, leaning on his chest. "I would like you to convince me that this is real and we're alive. Do you think you could do that, Mad Rogan?"

His magic slid over me. His blue eyes darkened. "Yes."

Chapter 15

I sat in the media room of our warehouse. My head buzzed. I'd taken some of the awesome painkillers Daniela sent home for me. They killed the pain, but brought a slight feeling of dizziness and I kept wanting to spin to the right.

My family dealt with my new purple face about the same way they dealt with the fact that Mad Rogan had kissed me in front of everyone before leaving to his HQ across the street. Nobody said a thing.

I missed him. He'd been gone for less than two hours and I missed him. That was just sad.

I formally told Cornelius that Olivia Charles was the person who'd pulled the trigger and murdered his wife. David Howling helped, but it was Olivia who took over the minds of Rogan's people. Cornelius equally formally thanked me and offered to release me from my contract with a full payment.

"No," I told him. "I'll see it through."

"Okay," he said quietly.

He and Matilda then went off to the kitchen. He was cooking her something special for dinner.

My mother was going over the plans for the assault.

Both of my sisters sat in the room quietly. Leon studied the image of the ranch on TV. It had been recorded from the air. Cornelius and Bug had attached a camera to Talon's harness.

The building rose out of a clearing like a foreboding Spanish fortress, and that's exactly what it was: a massive rectangular structure complete with observation towers, thick walls, and sheltered passageways. Bug reported both M240G and SAWs, M249 machine guns.

"How much armed personnel?" my mother asked.

"They estimate close to a hundred," I said. "Some former soldiers, some private security forces, and some civilian employees."

"Why doesn't Rogan just collapse it?" Leon asked.

"Because it would kill everyone inside. You don't just destroy a fort filled with people. You give them a chance to surrender." The buzzing in my head made it hard to concentrate. "Some of them probably have no idea what they are involved in."

"But it would be safer," Leon said.

"That's what bad guys do. We're not bad guys." At least some of us were not. I wasn't that sure about myself anymore. "Also Cornelius' contract specifies the right to confront Nari's killer. Basically, we can't kill Olivia Charles."

"Contracts are important." Leon nodded.

I looked at my mother.

"Leon," Mom said. "A man is a man because he has a set of principles. He has lines he doesn't cross. It shows discipline, commitment, and willpower to do the job. A man is someone who can be relied upon because he holds himself to a higher standard. That's how you get respect. You need to sit down and figure out where your lines are, or you will grow up to be one of these assholes everyone despises because they would strangle their own relatives for money." She looked at my two sisters. "The same goes for you. I said man because I was talking to him, so take the same speech, put woman in it, and use it to come up with some guidelines for yourself."

Nobody said anything.

Catalina cleared her throat. "Nevada, can I talk to you?"

"Sure."

"In your office."

I forced myself off the couch, walked to my office, and sat into my chair. Catalina and Arabella followed me.

"There are over a hundred people in that building?" Catalina asked.

"Yes."

"And they are armed?"

"Yes."

My sister squared her narrow shoulders. "Then I'm coming."

"Absolutely not."

"What if you get shot?" Catalina crossed her arms on her chest. "What if Rogan or Cornelius get shot? Or one of their people?"

"We're all adults. We . . ."

"I'm not losing you because of this thing. These people came here and tried to kill us. They tried to murder Matilda."

"Which is fucked up," Arabella volunteered.

"Language," I told her.

She shook her blond head. "Oh, shut up, Nevada, you swear like a fucking sailor."

"I'm twenty-five," I growled.

"Well, I'm fifteen and I have more to swear about than you."

"If I go," Catalina yelled over the two of us, "nobody will have to get shot!"

"No," I told her.

She faced me. "Yes."

"You can't control it."

"Yes, I can." She raised her chin. "I'm better at it."

"Oh yeah?" I tilted my head. "Can you disengage?"

"Some," she said.

"She doesn't have to disengage," Arabella said. "I'll get her out."

"You will get her out in front of a bunch of people, all of whom will see you. Have you two lost your minds?"

"It doesn't matter anyway," Arabella said.

"We know," Catalina added.

"Know what?"

"Mom told us about Tremaine," Catalina said. "We know about the other grandmother."

I rubbed my face. They had a right to know, but I really wished Mom would've waited. Silence lay between us like a big heavy brick.

"What will happen if she finds us?" Arabella asked.

"Bad things." I didn't want to elaborate.

"How are we going to protect Mom?" Arabella asked. "Also, she thinks that I'll end up in a cage."

Decades with no information and then all the information at once. Thanks, Mom. "Mom will be okay and nobody will put you in a cage. Once this is over, we'll form a House."

They stared at me. They looked so different—tall willowy Catalina with long dark hair, and short athletic Arabella with blond curls. How the hell they managed to have an identical expression on their faces, I would never know.

"Our own House?" Arabella asked.

"Yes. If we form a House, she can't touch us for three years. That's enough time to get established."

"We won't be forming any Houses if you're dead," Catalina said, her voice flat. "I'm coming, Nevada. You can't stop me."

"Yes, I can. You're a minor."

Catalina raised her chin. "I'm a Prime."

"So am I."

"Yes, yes, we're all special," Arabella said. "But she is right. What if you get shot? Who will take care of us? Who will bring us sushi?"

"I'm doing this," Catalina said. "I'm not letting them hurt you or Cornelius, or Matilda, or anybody else. My way nobody has to get hurt."

That's what I must've looked like eight years ago, when I told my parents that they wouldn't be selling the family firm. That I would take it over and keep it afloat. And I did. I'd been seventeen too.

She was right. If she got involved, we'd cut casualties and injuries down to a bare minimum.

"Fine." I leaned back. "You'll do this and then you'll do your best to disengage." I turned to Arabella. "You will get her out. You won't hurt anybody. You will grab your sister and get the hell out of there. No heroics."

She made a high-pitched squeak. "Okay, boss lady!!!"

"We're not telling Mom about this," I said. "We're not dropping hints and we're not making cute comments."

Catalina and I looked at Arabella.

"I won't say anything."

"Okay," I said. I hoped I wouldn't regret it.

They left my office and I called Rogan. He answered immediately. "Yes?"

"We probably won't need to besiege the fort. My sisters will be coming."

He didn't answer for a long moment. "What should I plan for?"

"A strike team big enough to contain Olivia Charles. But we won't need to storm the castle."

"You sure about this?"

"Yes."

"You don't sound thrilled."

"I'm not." This probably wasn't a good time to explain all the difficulties Catalina's magic caused. "All we need to do is get Catalina to a gathering of people large enough within the fortress. The more people, the better. Trust me?" I hadn't meant for it to sound like a question.

"Okay," he said.

Silence stretched. I wanted to see him so badly.

"Where are you?" he asked.

"In my office. Where are you?"

"Outside your front door."

My heart sped up. I got up, lowered the blinds in my office, locked the door between the business hallway and the rest of the house, and opened the front door. He took the phone from his ear and came inside. We walked into my office. I shut the door behind us, and then his arms closed around me and tomorrow disappeared. He kissed me, long and eager. Memories of him lying next to me naked swirled in my head. I kissed him and kissed him, nibbling on his lip, licking his tongue, stealing his breath . . .

My phone chimed. I ignored it.

His phone beeped.

The intercom came on, Bern's voice spilling from it. "Nevada, where are you? I need to talk to you. This is urgent."

Rogan's phone beeped again, then again, then emitted a high-frequency electronic whine. He growled and put it to his ear. "Yes?"

A tiny voice on the other end said something urgent. Rogan rolled his eyes. "Yes. Yes. No. Handle it. Yes."

He turned the phone off and tossed it on the table. It went off again. He stared at it as if it were a snake.

"Take it," I told him.

He turned to me. No trace of Mad Rogan remained in

his face. There was just a man and he was frustrated as hell. "When this is over, any place. Anywhere you want."

"Is that lodge in the mountains real?"

"Yes."

"Take me there," I told him.

Ten minutes later I walked into the Hut of Evil to find both of my sisters standing over Bernard's computer.

My cousin's face was pale. "Augustine sent this over."

He clicked a key and a video filled the screen, showing the ultramodern interior of Augustine's MII office. The camera sat just behind and to the right of Augustine. The door stood open. The normally opaque glass walls sectioning off his workspace were now transparent, and from this vantage point we could see all the way down to the receptionist's desk. Lina was gone. Instead a young man occupied the chair, busily working on his computer. I'd never seen him before and he probably didn't know I existed.

A tall woman strode into the hallway, her face lined with age. She held herself ramrod straight, her silver hair carefully styled, her dark brown eyes challenging anyone in her way. Two bodyguards followed her, dressed in suits, both square jawed with identical short haircuts and identical expression.

Augustine stood up. "Good afternoon, Mrs. Tremaine. To what do I owe the honor?"

She stared at him, her eyes measuring him with the deadly precision of a raptor sighting her prey. Icy claws gripped my spine. *This is it.*

Victoria Tremaine turned without a single word and walked back the way she'd come.

I wore a Scorpion bulletproof vest, a helmet, an urban assault outfit, and boots. Rogan's people offered me a light machine gun but I stuck with my Baby Desert Eagle. It made me feel better.

We'd gone to ground in the Texas scrub on the edge of the perimeter fence bordering Olivia Charles' fortress. Ahead a lone guard sat in a booth.

I felt like a turtle. How in the world had my mother and grandmother worn this gear for years?

Next to me Arabella, wearing the same outfit I did, pursed her lips together and took a selfie. Ugh.

"Do you remember the exit route?" I asked.

She nodded. "We go north, quick sprint, five miles over the brush, to Rogan's helicopter. I got it. Stop worrying."

A limo slid down the road and stopped before the gate.

"Are you sure this will work?" Cornelius asked.

"Yes," I told him.

Cornelius worried me. He'd brought no animals and no weapons that I could see. His face was calm, his eyes distant. Something odd was taking place in his head.

"It's just that your sister is so shy," he murmured. "I've been at your house for a week and she barely spoke to me."

The limo's window rolled down. I couldn't see into it from this angle, but I knew who was inside. Melosa in the driver's seat, ready to snap her aegis shield up at a moment's notice; my sister in the passenger seat; and Rivera in the back, armed to the teeth.

The guard said something.

Come on, Catalina. You can do it.

The gate swung open. The guard left his booth and stood next to the car.

"Okay." I got up to my feet.

A few yards down, Rogan stepped out from behind a tree. If things went wrong, he planned to level the booth and the guard with it. I brushed the twigs from me and trotted to the limo. Around me Rogan's strike team—

six people he'd handpicked—fell into place. Cornelius shrugged his shoulders next to me.

Rogan joined us. We jogged to the limo, where the guard waited. He saw us and winked. His face shifted and Augustine's familiar perfection took his place. "You brought children, Rogan? This is a new low for you."

"What are you doing here?" Rogan asked.

"I wouldn't miss this. What—and let you have all the glory and information to yourself?" Augustine pushed his glasses up the bridge of his nose. "Shall we?"

The limo moved ahead. We followed it.

A second checkpoint loomed ahead.

"Is it a real soldier this time?" I asked.

"Yes."

The limo stopped, the window rolled down, and I felt magic shift in the distance, a mere splash of it, like a raindrop in the night. The soldier left his booth and walked next to the limo. We rolled on up the road to the guardhouse at the doorstep of the fortress. They saw us. Weapons snapped up.

The soldier waved at the guards. The limo stopped again. The guards put away their weapons and joined the second soldier.

"What is your sister, exactly?" Augustine asked.

"You'll see." There was no name for it. No talent like this had ever been recorded. But it wasn't something you would ever forget. "Just don't look at her directly once she starts."

The soldiers unlocked the massive front doors, then one of them wandered over to the side of the limo and opened the door. Catalina stepped out. The soldier waited behind her, his face relaxed, attentive like a bellhop at a luxury hotel. Melosa got out of the car. Her eyes were wide like two saucers.

Catalina turned and waved at us. I sped up, trying to close the distance. An older man in a grey uniform with a bearing of a soldier smiled at us.

"Are you her friends?"

"Yes," I said.

"That's so nice. Come on, I'll show you inside. It's lunchtime."

Catalina squared her shoulders and stepped into the fortress. Two sentries rose from their seats. The older soldier waved at them. "Come with me."

We walked through the narrow hallway, turned right, turned left. My mouth tasted like a copper penny. I should've never let her do this. Ahead an open door revealed a large cafeteria.

The strike team around me put in their earplugs and halted. We'd gone over this maneuver during the planning stage. If they walked into that mess hall, we'd have no strike team left. Rogan, Cornelius, Arabella, Augustine, and I followed Catalina in. I'd told them it was a bad idea. They'd decided they would do it anyway.

At least sixty people sat at the tables, eating. Everyone stopped and looked at us.

My sister smiled. "Hi!"

"Hi?" a woman said from the nearest table. "Who are you?"

"I'm just a kid."

Every pair of eyes watched her.

"I go to Cedar High. You wouldn't believe what happened to me in algebra class yesterday."

Rogan looked at me.

"Watch," I mouthed.

"I was sitting at my desk and Dace Collins just broke up with his girlfriend."

Sixty people in the room and not a single one was eating. They held completely still.

"He did it right in front of the whole class. She cried. It was so uncomfortable. I didn't know what to do."

The room fell silent.

"Dace Collins is an asshole," a man on the left said.

"Yeah, what the hell?" a young guy on the right said. "What kind of a little punk does a thing like that?"

"You don't worry, sweetie," the first woman said. "Don't stress out about it. He isn't worth it."

"How dare he put you in that position? You shouldn't have to feel embarrassed for him and his girlfriend," another woman said. "Do you want us to go and get him for you? Because we'll go right now."

The older soldier nodded at the crowd. "Jake and Marsha, go get a vehicle out of the motor pool, find this Dace, and bring him here. We'll have us a little talk and teach him how to treat a lady."

"No, no, that's okay," Catalina said. Getting Dace Collins would've been a tall order, since he was a character on *Liars*, the latest teen soap opera. "Would you like to hear the rest of the story instead?"

"Yes," several voices said at one. "Yes, please."

They moved toward her, forming a tight semicircle.

"That's close enough," she said.

They didn't want to stop, but they obeyed.

"I really want to tell you the rest of the story, but can we get the rest of the people here? They might want to hear what happened."

The older soldier spoke into his radio. "All personnel report to mess hall immediately. I repeat, all personnel, report to mess hall immediately." He looked at Catalina, his face and smile soft. "They will be here right away."

"Oh good. Please sit down."

They sat on the floor as one, devotion shining on their faces. Next to me Cornelius tried to bend his knees. I grabbed his arm and hauled him upright.

"My friend is going to make a hole in that wall right there." Catalina pointed to the far wall. "So we have more light."

"That's a great idea."

"Yes, more light never hurts."

I nudged Rogan. He raised his hand. A gap sliced through the far wall, cleaving a twenty-five-foot hole in the reinforced concrete.

"Bigger," I murmured. Arabella would need a fast exit.

The gap grew to forty feet.

"Bigger."

The wall exploded.

"Thank you!" Catalina said.

"You're so nice," one of the soldiers told Rogan. "I'm glad she has nice friends like you."

"Is that your brother?" a woman wanted to know.

"No, it's my sister's boyfriend."

"You have a sister! That is awesome. I have a sister too."

More people poured into the mess hall. An athletic man with a long scar across his face led the charge. He saw us and narrowed his eyes. "What the hell is going on here?"

"She's telling a story," the older soldier said. "You've got to hear this, Gabe. It's a hell of a story."

"Have you all lost your damned minds?"

"Welcome, Gabriel," my sister said. "Welcome, all of you."

Gabriel's eyes softened. He raised his hand. A shy smile tugged at his hard face. "Hi."

"I was telling you about Dace," Catalina said. "Yes. Dace is one of those neither-here-nor-there guys. He isn't smart and he isn't athletic. He just kind of bums around the school and tries to look edgy . . ."

They stared at her with rapt attention.

"We have to go," I murmured.

Rogan startled, as if coming awake.

"Wait," Augustine said. "I want to hear the end of this."

"No, you don't."

"No, really, this is fascinating," Cornelius whispered.

Rogan locked his right arm on Augustine's shoulder, his left on Cornelius, and dragged them out the door.

"You've got this?" I asked Arabella.

She nodded. "They won't get her."

I walked out and shut the door behind me. The strike team had closed ranks and kept walking, herding Augustine and Cornelius down the hallway. We were twenty yards away before either of them stopped looking over his shoulder.

"What was that?" Augustine asked, stunned.

"Love," I told him. "They love her."

"Is that why Matilda likes her so much?" Cornelius asked.

"No. Catalina never uses her magic on those close to her. Matilda likes her because my sister is nice and takes care of her. We have about thirty minutes. The longer they stay near her, the more they love her. Eventually they'll want to touch her. They'll want a piece of her clothes or better yet a chunk of her hair or a finger. She can't stop it. In twenty minutes Arabella will have to get her out of there, or they will rip her apart."

"But what about Arabella?" Cornelius asked.

"She and I are immune. She is our sister. We already love her as much as we can."

We ran through the narrow passageways, going through the place room by room. As soon as we cleared the mess hall hallway, Cornelius began to hum to himself. It was an incessant, almost hypnotic tune. It didn't sound like any song I'd heard before. Maybe all this pressure had finally made him lose his mind.

Three people jumped us. The strike team took down two, while Rogan collided with the third and broke him like a rag doll. The man slumped on the floor, breathing fast, his right leg bent at an odd angle. I crouched by him.

"Where is Olivia Charles?"

The man's hands curled into fists. He strained, but my magic was too strong. "Down the hallway to the bottom floor. She is in the room at the end of the hall."

We left him in the hallway, sobbing.

Eight minutes later we reached the room, a vast empty space, its walls and floor completely black. I had seen a room just like it before, at MII. It was painted with chalkboard paint. A half-finished circle marked the floor, the piece of chalk lying discarded next to it. Olivia Charles was nowhere in sight. We spread through the room. No doors besides the one we had come through.

Rogan's radio came on. "SWAT is en route," Bug reported. "Three vehicles."

Lenora Jordan must've gotten tired of waiting. I turned to Rogan and kept my voice low. "We have to find Olivia now. SWAT can't see Arabella. They will try to kill her."

"She's here," Cornelius said.

He was standing by a wall. Rogan and I moved to stand by him.

"Are you sure?" Rogan asked.

"Yes," Cornelius nodded, his eyes clouded. "She's here."

Rogan looked at the wall. It trembled.

Colin, a short dark-haired man, snapped his gun up. Rivera gripped him in a headlock, before Olivia forced him to do anything else.

I faced the wall, gathered my magic, and struck at the mind behind it.

Power punched me, gripping my mind in a steel vise and wrapping me in pain. All I could do was hold it at bay.

Colin stopped struggling and clamped his head.

Out of the corner of my eye I saw Rogan on the floor by my feet. He was taking off my left boot, then my right.

"Sir?" Rivera said. "You could break the wall, sir?"

"Never disturb two mental mages locked in a duel," Augustine said. "If you kill one, the other might end up with no mind."

The vise squeezed my mind, red hot.

I just had to hold. As long as she held on to me, she couldn't get to anyone else.

My bare feet touched the floor. Rogan moved around me, drawing.

She was crushing my mind like a nut.

Magic snapped into life under me. It was like landing on the surface of a pond, but instead of water, its surface was pure power. Rogan had drawn an amplification circle. I sent my magic into it, surrendering a little more of myself to the pain, and it bounced back into me, making me stronger. Magic coursed through my veins. I bounced again, and again, and again. Five. Any more and I'd expend too much.

I snapped the vise. It shot back and clamped my mind again, turning into shackles.

The room vanished. I stood in a vast dark cavern. Light pooled in a circle around my feet. My hands were glowing, a pale almost white light with a faint touch of yellow. To my side, I saw other shapes: a pale gold that felt like Cornelius, a brilliant blue beacon that had to be Rogan, and a conflicting clash of pale white and grey that must have been Augustine. Before me another humanoid shape stood in a similar circle, her light pulsing with violet. Beyond us in the distance, two more shapes waited, one pale and light yellow, like me, and one knitted of pure furious red. Catalina and Arabella.

What is this? Where am I?

The enemy magic squeezed me, trying to crush me.

I snapped the shackles. The violet presence recoiled and struck again, wrapping invisible chains around me, trying to tether me. I reached deep inside me and let the magic explode. It tore out of me, a powerful flood of light.

My body shook under the strain. She was wrapping her will around me. I felt myself unraveling, retreating further and further into the center of myself.

The light of my sisters waned.

I had to win. I would win. I had to know who the invisible puppeteer was, pulling all of the strings behind the scenes. I had to meet Caesar, because if I failed, he would keep sending people after my family. I had to know.

More chains spun out of the darkness, trying to contain me.

No. You won't bind me. You can't control my mind. I'll be free.

I pushed. I had to win.

The first chain snapped, breaking. Then another and another.

Nobody controls me except me.

The chains broke. The other glowing figure screamed. My magic reached out and gulped her in a single swallow. The cavern exploded around us, shattering.

I opened my mouth and let my magic speak. *"How do I open this door?"*

"There is a panel on the left side," Olivia Charles' wooden voice replied from some hidden speaker. "The code is 31BC."

The year the Roman Empire was born.

Rogan opened the panel and entered the code. Something clanged within the wall. It slid aside a couple of inches and stopped.

"Why didn't the door open?" A low gnawing ache began within me. My magic still wasn't at one hundred

percent after I had drained myself down to nothing shocking David Howling. I was about to run out of power.

"I've disabled the mechanism from the inside."

"We're out of time." Rogan raised his hand. "Are you clear?"

I let go, pulling my magic back to me. "Yes."

The section of the wall trembled. Hairline cracks split it with a thunderous snap. The separate chunks of the wall shivered and streaked between us in a controlled starburst, revealing a small room. Inside it within an amplification circle stood Olivia Charles. Her gaze fastened on me. "You!"

"Me."

Her gaze shifted to Rogan. "Enjoy your pitiful triumph. It won't last."

I reached out and looked into her mind. Crap.

"She's been hexed," I said. "She has what we need, but it will take a lot of time to pull it out."

"How much time?" Rogan asked.

"Days." It would take me that long to regenerate enough magic to take her hex apart.

"No," Cornelius said in his eerie voice, his word suffused with emotion. "She murdered my wife."

Conflict churned in Rogan's eyes. We needed Olivia. We needed her badly.

The muscles on his jaw locked.

He'd promised.

Rogan opened his mouth. "I stand by my word. She is yours."

"Let her go," Cornelius told me.

I released her. Another moment and I would've lost my hold.

Cornelius looked at Olivia, his face pale. "You took Nari's life away from her. You took my wife away from me. You took the mother from my child."

Olivia sneered at him. "What will you do, you pathetic little man? You're not even a Prime. Will you summon a litter of puppies to lick me to death? Go on. Show me."

"When my grandfather came to this country," Cornelius said, "he took a new name, one that would be familiar to his new countrymen."

Olivia crossed her arms on her chest.

"Our real last name isn't Harrison. It's Hamelin."

A low sound like the noise of a waterfall came from behind us, insistent and oddly disturbing.

"We're not named for the place where we were born. We're named for the place where years before Osiris serum was discovered our ancestor became infamous for his magic."

Cornelius opened his mouth and sang a long wordless note. A black wave burst into the room. It shifted and moved, charging forward, not uniform, but made of thousands of tiny bodies.

Olivia Charles screamed, terror raw in her voice.

Cornelius' voice rose, commanding and beautiful. It reached right into your chest, took your heart into a cold fist, and held it still. The wave surged between us and swarmed Olivia, burying her body. She shrieked and flailed, but the rats kept coming, thousands and thousands of them, until she became a swirling mound of fur. There was nothing I could do but stand there and listen to her being eaten alive while the Pied Piper of Houston sang like an angel, mourning the love of his life.

I sat in my office and watched the correspondents on *Eyewitness News* lose all cool over a still shot of Olivia Charles' skeletal remains. How they had gotten it, I had no idea. Houston PD had that scene wrapped up tighter than a straitjacket. By the time we exited the building, my sisters were gone and the majority of the fortress guards with them. SWAT found them later, wandering through the brush, weeping, and telling stories of the girl and a thing that stole her. Nobody could adequately describe the thing, only that it was huge and monstrous, which was just as well. We'd dodged the bullet.

Lenora demanded Rogan's and Cornelius' presence for a debriefing and mounds of paperwork. I wasn't invited, for which I was grateful. I went home, hugged my sisters, ordered pizza, and fell asleep on the couch before it arrived. It was afternoon now—I had slept straight through the morning and would've slept longer, but Grandma Frida got worried and put ice on my face to make sure I "wasn't in a coma." It was time to settle with my client, who was due to walk through my door at any minute. He'd spent the entire day today moving out.

I hadn't heard from Rogan. No calls, no messages, nothing. It was less than twenty-four hours without contact, but I had the most unsettling sense of déjà vu. He couldn't disappear on me again.

As if on cue, Cornelius walked through the door separating the office from the rest of the house and knocked on the glass wall of my office.

I clicked off the broadcast on my laptop. "Please, come in."

He came in and sat in the chair.

"How do you feel?" I asked him.

He thought about it. "Relieved. The anger is gone. All I have left is grief. Thank you for everything you've done."

"You're welcome. I'm glad that you're relieved."

"If I can ask, why the change of heart?" Cornelius said. "You were adamant before that you didn't want to contribute to the killer's death."

"David Howling sent a death threat to Matilda."

Cornelius sat up straighter. "Why was I not told?"

"Because it was designed to throw you off balance. I was concerned about your mental state. You weren't sleeping and you kept carrying mysterious sacks into odd places."

"They were grain sacks," Cornelius said. "Rats need a lot of food to grow from a mischief to a swarm."

"Mischief?"

"That's the proper term for a group of rats. A pack of dogs, a murder of crows, a mischief of rats. They are misunderstood creatures. In reality, they are intelligent colony animals. Studies have proven that rats will feed caged companions before eating, themselves, for example. But people have an instinctual fear of them, so I kept the exact method of my revenge to myself. And no, I wasn't unhinged."

"It was my call and I made it."

He nodded. "Please continue."

"When Howling confronted Rogan and me in the circle, he assured me that he didn't enjoy child murder and that he would tie that loose end with minimal pain."

Cornelius locked his jaw. "Did he?"

"I realized that as long as he and Olivia Charles lived, your daughter wouldn't be safe. I also realized that Olivia would never permit herself to be captured and interrogated. I don't know why, but their devotion to this new Caesar is absolute. When Howling spoke about his new vision, his face lit up. They truly believe they are patriots. Patriots don't turn state's evidence. They become martyrs. I could wash my hands of it and let you and Rogan do the heavy lifting or I could come and help. I chose to help and I'll live with my decision."

I opened the file and handed him the bill. "This is your final bill."

He looked at it for a moment. "That's it?"

"Yes. You will see the final breakdown of hours and expenses below. The dress charge has an explanation. Due to the circumstances beyond my control, I was unable to return the dress in a timely manner, so I was charged an additional fee of two thousand dollars. Because these circumstances happened as the direct result of the investigation, the surcharge was passed onto you. With your $50,000 deductible applied, your final bill comes to $7,245 even."

Cornelius pulled out his checkbook and wrote a check to me. Usually I didn't deal with checks, but I had no doubt that his would be good.

"Thank you."

I signed the receipt and passed it to him. He looked at it. "Somehow it just doesn't seem like enough."

"You could pay more, if you want, but I suspect you may need that money. What will you do now?" I didn't add "since your wife is dead." Nari had been their primary breadwinner.

"I'll find a job," he said. "I was hoping to ask you for one."

"Me?"

"Yes. I've seen what you do. I believe I would be an asset."

I blinked. Nobody outside my family had ever asked me for a job before. If I could get him, I'd dance with joy. Between the birds, the cats, and the ferrets, we could expand our surveillance while minimizing the risk. We'd take in twice as much money.

If. That was a huge if.

"I would love if you worked for us."

"I sense a but," he said.

"You're a member of a House and your magic is incredible. I can't possibly pay you your worth."

"How do you normally handle your payroll?" he asked.

"It depends on the case. Bernard is paid by the hour.

He doesn't typically see a case through from the beginning to the end. Usually his services are required on an as-needed basis. Sometimes my sisters take individual cases and earn commission upon successful resolution. The firm takes thirty percent of the fee, the contractor takes seventy. We provide dental and medical."

"I would work on commission," he said.

"It wouldn't be that much money to begin with."

"I have a cushion," he said. "In fact, you provided me with one. I came into the office prepared to write a check for half a million."

"I thought I explained our fees."

"Yes." He smiled. "But I didn't expect you to stick to that arrangement."

"Well, this is one point you will have to take into consideration. What you quote to the client is what you get. We have rules. Rule One, we stay bought. Once we're hired, we don't switch sides. Rule Two, we don't break the law unless there are extremely unusual circumstances. Rule Three, at the end of the day we have to be able to live with our choices."

Cornelius considered it.

A loud thumping came from outside. When Rogan finally did show up, I would have to discuss the whole turning-this-area-into-an-army-camp thing. At some point I would have to return to normal business without all this racket. If he showed up. Worry squirmed through me. Maybe he'd changed his mind.

No. This was just anxiety talking.

"Agreed," he said. "When can I start?"

It was Wednesday. I'd need at least a few days of downtime.

"Next week," I said.

"Until next week, then."

He got up and offered me his hand. I stood up and shook it.

"I'll let myself out."

He left and I sank back into my chair. We'd just acquired our first permanent employee.

I heard the door open. The thumping noise blasted into the room. This really was too much.

"Nevada!" Cornelius called, trying to out-scream the mechanical roar. "I think this is for you!"

What now? I got up and stepped into the hallway.

An odd-looking military helicopter sat in the middle of the intersection, its spinning blades blasting the street with man-made wind. Rogan was walking toward me.

What . . .

He closed the distance and grabbed my hand. "Come on."

"Come on where?"

"You said you wanted to see the lodge." He grinned.

"I have no clothes."

He winked at me. "You won't need clothes."

Heat warmed my cheeks. "I need to tell my family . . ."

"You can call them from the air."

"But . . ."

His blue eyes laughed at me, warm and light. "Come with me, Nevada."

I clamped my mouth shut and ran with him to the helicopter.

Epilogue

Nevada rolled a heap of snow into a ball. Her smile practically glowed. He'd never seen anyone so happy to play in the snow. It was a wonder the stuff didn't melt around her. She was like spring, warm and full of life and promise. When she was with him, he couldn't feel the cold.

They'd had three blissful days of nothing but snow, good food, hot fire, and even hotter sex. He could stay in this lodge forever. He knew they couldn't, and thinking about going back brought dread. It would be like coming back to a war.

Relax, he told himself. She's right here, safe and happy. Her family will want to see her on Christmas, and he would have to take her back, but for now they could play in the snow.

He had already bought her present.

The snowball hurled through the air and hit him in the chest.

"Really?"

"Bring it," she called, her eyes shining.

He raised his hand, shaping the magic around him. A barrage of snowballs broke free from the snowy bank behind him, streaked across the air, and pelted her. He kept the hits gentle, breaking the snowballs a fraction of the moment before they hit her. She stumbled and landed on her back in the snow, laughing.

"Not fair!"

"I'm Mad Rogan. I don't do fair."

His phone chirped. He took it out and flicked his finger across it. A message from Bug.

Cold gripped him.

He didn't see Nevada until she was on top of him. She knocked him off his feet and landed on his chest. Her lips closed on his, and he kissed her, while his mind feverishly cycled through a dozen different strategies.

"What is it?" she asked.

"What?"

"You were here with me and now you're not. What is it, Connor?"

He opened his mouth to tell her it was nothing, greedy for a few more hours of bliss, and then remembered who she was.

"Bug identified the shell company that tried to buy your mortgage."

Nevada pushed her hat back. "And?"

"We thought it was Augustine. It's not. The shell corporation belongs to House Tremaine. Your grandmother knows, Nevada. We have to go back. Your family is in danger."

Keep reading for a sneak peek of

———

WILDFIRE,

———

the thrilling conclusion to
the Hidden Legacy series

Available August 2017

When life hits you in the gut, it's always a sucker punch. You never see it coming. One moment you're walking along, worrying your little worries and making quiet plans, and the next you're rolled into a ball, trying to hug yourself against the pain, frantic and reeling, your mind a jumble of scared thoughts.

I paused with my hand above the lock's keypad. This morning I was at a mountain lodge playing in the snow with the most dangerous man in Houston. Then Rogan's surveillance expert texted him, and here I stood, six hours later, my hair a mess, my clothes rumpled from being under a heavy jacket, in front of the warehouse that served as my family's home. I would have to go inside and break the ugly news, and nobody would like what was going to happen next.

The main thing was not to panic. If I panicked, my sisters and my cousins would too. And my mother would do her best to talk me out of the only logical solution to our crisis. I'd managed to keep a lid on my emotions all the way from the lodge to the airport, during the flight on the private jet, and through the helicopter ride from the plane to the landing pad four blocks away. But now all my fears and stress were boiling over.

I took a deep breath. Around me the street was busy. Not as busy as it had been a few days ago, when I was helping Cornelius Harrison, an animal mage and now an employee of the Baylor Investigative Agency, find out who murdered his wife, but still busy. Rogan's views on security were rather draconian. He was in love with me and decided that my home wasn't assault proof, so he'd bought two square miles of industrial real estate around our warehouse and turned it into his own private military base.

Rogan's people wore civilian clothes, but they weren't fooling anyone. They didn't wander or stroll. They moved from point A to point B with a definite goal in mind. They kept their clothes clean, their hair short, and they called Rogan Major. When we made love, I called him Connor.

A dry, popping sound came from the street. The memory of Olivia Charles' bare skeleton punched me. I heard the crunch her bones made as they clattered onto the concrete floor. A wave of anxiety drowned me. I let it wash over me and waited for it to recede. Finding Nari's killer had been an ugly and brutal mess.

I didn't want to walk back into that world. I just . . . I just wanted a little bit more time.

I made myself look in the direction of the sound. An ex-soldier was coming my way, in his forties, with a scarred face, leading an enormous Kodiak bear on a very thin leash. The bear wore a harness that said SGT. TEDDY.

The ex-soldier stretched his left arm and twisted, as if trying to slide the bones back in place. Another dry crunch, sending a fresh jolt of alarm through me. Probably an old injury.

The bear stopped and looked at me.

"Be polite," the soldier told him. "Don't worry. He just wants to say hi."

"I don't mind." I stepped closer to the bear. The massive beast leaned over to me and smelled my hair.

"Can I pet him?"

The soldier looked at Sgt. Teddy. The bear made a low, short noise.

"He says you can."

I reached over and carefully petted his big, shaggy neck. "What's his story?"

"Someone thought it would be a good idea to make very smart magic bears and use them in combat," the ex-soldier said. "Problem is, once you make someone smart, they become self-aware and call you on your bullshit. Sgt. Teddy is a pacifist. The leash is just for show so people don't freak out. Major is of the opinion that fighting in a war shouldn't be forced on those who are morally opposed to it, human or bear."

"But you're still here," I told the bear.

He snorted and looked at me with chocolate-brown eyes.

"We offered him a very nice private property up in Alaska," the ex-soldier said. "But he doesn't like it. He says he gets bored. He mostly hangs out with us, eats cereal that's bad for him, and watches cartoons on Saturdays. And movies. He loves *The Jungle Book*."

I waited for the familiar buzz of my magic that told me he was pulling my leg, but none came.

Sgt. Teddy rose on his hind legs, blocking out the sun, and put his shaggy front paws around me. My face pressed into the fur. I hugged him back. We stood for a moment, then the Kodiak dropped down and went back on his walk.

I looked at the ex-soldier.

"He must've felt you needed a hug," he said. "He stays in the HQ most of the time, so you can come and visit him."

"I will," I told him.

The ex-soldier nodded and followed the bear.

I punched my code into the lock. I had been hugged by a giant, super-intelligent bear. I could do this. I just had to walk in, call for a family meeting, and tell them that Victoria Tremaine, my evil grandmother, found us, and if we didn't do something to protect ourselves right now, our family was doomed. It was almost dinnertime anyway. On a Sunday, everyone would be home.

I opened the door and walked into the small office space that housed Baylor Investigative Agency—a short hallway, three offices on the left, a break room, and conference room on the right. The temptation to hide in my office almost made me stop, but I kept going through the hallway to the other door that opened into the roughly three-thousand-square-foot space that served as our home. When we sold our house trying to raise money for my father's hospital bills, we moved our family into the warehouse to cut costs. We'd split the floor space into three distinct sections: the office, the living space, and beyond it, past a very tall wall, Grandma Frida's motor pool, where she worked on armored vehicles and mobile artillery for Houston's magical elite.

I took off my shoes and marched through the maze of rooms. Faint voices came from the kitchen. Mom . . . Grandma. Good. This would save me time.

I walked into the kitchen and froze.

My mother and grandmother sat at our table. A young woman sat next to my grandmother. She was willowy and beautiful, with a heart-shaped face framed in waves of gorgeous red hair and eyes so grey, they looked silver.

Ice gripped my spine.

Rynda Charles. Rogan's ex-fiancée. Olivia's daughter.

"Do you remember me?" she asked. Her voice was breaking. Her eyes were bloodshot, her face so pale her lips seemed almost white. "You killed my mother."

I opened my mouth. Nothing came out.

Mom made big eyes at me and nodded toward the table. I dropped my bag on the floor and sat.

"Drink your tea," Grandma Frida said, pushed a steaming cup of tea toward Rynda.

Rynda picked it up and drank, but her gaze was fixed on me. Desperation in her eyes turned to near panic. Right.

I closed my eyes, took a deep breath from the stomach all the way up, held it, and let it out slowly. One . . . Two . . . Calm . . . calm . . .

"Nevada?" Grandma Frida asked.

"She's an empath Prime," I said. "I'm upset, so it's affecting her."

Rynda stared into her cup.

Five . . . Six . . . Breathe in, breathe out . . . Ten. Good enough.

I opened my eyes and looked at Rynda. I had to keep my voice and my emotions under control. "Your mother killed an entire crew of Rogan's soldiers and four lawyers, including two women your age. It was an unprovoked slaughter. Their husbands are now widowers and their children are motherless because of her."

"A person is never just one thing," Rynda said. "To you she might have been a monster, but to me she was my mother. Grandmother to my children. They have no grandparents now."

"I'm sorry for your and their loss. I regret that things went the way they did. But it was a justified kill." Dear God, I sounded like my mother.

"I don't even know how she died." Rynda clenched her hands into a single fist. "They only gave me back her bones. How did my mother die, Nevada?"

I took a deep breath. "It wasn't an easy or a quick death."

"I deserve to know." There was steel in her voice. "Tell me."

"No. Why are you here?"

Her hand shook and the mug danced a little as she brought it to her lips. She took another swallow of her tea. "My husband is missing. I need your help."

Okay. Missing husband. Familiar territory. "When was the last time you saw . . . ?" Rogan had said his name one time, what was it? ". . . Brian?"

"Three days ago. He went to work on Thursday and didn't come back. He doesn't answer his phone. Brian likes his routine. He's always home by dinner." A note of hysteria crept into her voice. "I know what you'll ask: Does he have a mistress? Did we have a good marriage? Does he disappear on drunken binges? No. No, he doesn't. He loves me and the kids. He comes home!"

She must've spoken to the APD. "Did you fill out a missing persons report?"

"Yes. They're not going to look for him." Her voice turned bitter. She was getting more agitated by the minute. "He's a Prime. It's House business. Except House Sherwood is convinced that Brian is okay and he's just taking a break. Nobody is looking for him, except me. Nobody is returning my calls. Even Rogan refuses to see me."

That didn't sound right. Rogan would never turn her away, even if I pitched a huge fit about it. I'd watched the two of them talking before. He liked her and he cared about her. "What did Rogan say exactly?"

"I came to him on Friday. His people told me he was out. He was out on Saturday. I asked to wait and they told me it was a waste of time. They didn't know when he would be back. I may be naive, but I'm not an idiot. I know what that means. Two weeks ago, I had friends. I had my mother's friends—powerful, respected, and always so eager to do Olivia Charles a favor. Two weeks ago, one phone call and half of the city would be out looking for Brian. They would be putting pressure on the police, the mayor, and the Texas Rangers. But now everyone is out.

Everyone is too busy to see me. There is an invisible wall around me. No matter how hard I scream, nobody can hear me. People just nod and offer platitudes."

"He didn't stonewall you," I said. "He was out of state. With me."

Silence fell, heavy and tense.

"I shouldn't have come here," she said. "I'll get the children and go."

"That's right," Grandma Frida said.

"No," Mom said. I knew that voice. That was Sergeant Mom voice. Rynda knew that voice too, because she sat up straighter. Olivia Charles was never in the military, but three minutes of talking to her had told me that she had ruled her household with an iron fist and had a very low tolerance for nonsense.

"You're here now," Mom said. "You came to us for help because you had nowhere to turn and you're scared for your husband and your children. You came to the right place. Nevada is very good at tracking missing people. Either she'll help you or she'll recommend someone who will."

Grandma Frida looked at Mom as if she had sprouted a pineapple on her head.

"Right," I said. I may not have personally murdered Rynda's mother, but I made that death possible. And now she was a pariah, alone and scared. She lost her mother, her husband, and all of the people she thought were her friends. I had to help her. I had to at least get her started in the right direction.

"Can I talk to the two of you for a damn minute?" Grandma Frida growled.

"One moment," I told Rynda and got up.

Grandma grabbed my arm with one hand, grabbed Mom's wrist with her other hand, and dragged us down the hallway all the way to the end, as far from the kitchen as we could get.

"Children?" I glanced at Mom.

"Your sisters are watching them. A boy and a girl."

"Have the two of you lost your damn minds?" Grandma Frida hissed.

"She isn't lying," I said. "Her husband is really gone."

"I expect that of her!" Grandma Frida pointed at me with her thumb, while glaring at my mother. "But you ought to know better, Penelope."

"That woman is at the end of her rope," Mom said. "How much do you think it cost her to come here? This is what we do. We help people like her."

"Exactly!" Grandma Frida hissed. "She's at the end of her rope. She's beautiful, rich, helpless, and she's desperately looking for someone to save her. And she's Rogan's ex-fiancée. If Nevada takes her case, there is no way the two of them won't have contact."

I stared at her.

"She's a man magnet." Grandma Frida balled her hands into fists. "Men eat that helpless rescue-me crap up. Her husband has been gone for three days. If he hasn't run off, he's probably dead. She'll need consoling. She'll be looking for a shoulder to cry on, a big strong shoulder. Do I need to spell it out? You're about to serve your boyfriend to her on a silver platter!"

Rynda was very beautiful and very helpless. I wanted to help her. I knew Rogan would too.

"It's not like that. He broke off the engagement."

Grandma Frida shook her head. "You told me they knew each other for years, since they were little kids. That kind of thing doesn't just go away. Rogan's people know it too, that's why they didn't give her any information. You're playing with fire, Nevada. Cut her loose. Let somebody else take care of her. She's a Prime. She's rich. She isn't your problem, unless you make her your problem."

I looked at Mom.

"Third rule," she said.

When Dad and Mom started the agency, they had only three rules: first, once we were paid, we stayed bought; second, we did everything we could to not break the law; and third, at the end of the day, we had to be able to look our reflection in the eye. I could live with Olivia's death. I had nightmares about it, but it was justified. Throwing Rynda out now, when she sat at our kitchen table, was beyond me. Where would she go?

"If Rynda's crying will make Rogan break up with me, then it wouldn't last anyway."

Most of me believed the words that came out of my mouth, but a small, petty part didn't. That was okay. I was human and I was entitled to a little bit of insecurity. But I was damned if I let it dictate my actions.

"Thank you, Grandma, but I've got it."

Grandma Frida threw her hands up in disgust. "When your heart breaks, don't come crying to me."

"I will anyway." I hugged her.

"Egh . . ." She made a show of trying to knock me off, then hugged me back.

I opened the door to the office and started down the hallway toward my desk and laptop that waited on it.

"It's James," Grandma Frida said mournfully behind me. "He ruined all of my practical grandchildren with his altruism."

Mom didn't answer. Dad had been dead seven years, but hearing his name still hurt her. It still hurt me.

I grabbed the laptop, a notepad, and the new client folder just in case, then walked back into the kitchen, sat down at the table, and opened my computer. A few keystrokes told me Bern was home and online.

I fired off a quick email. "Please send me the basics on Brian Sherwood ASAP." I set the laptop aside and switched to the writing pad and pen. People minded notes on paper a lot less than a laptop or being recorded, and I needed Rynda to relax. She was already keyed up.

"Let's start at the beginning."

"You don't like me," Rynda said. "I felt it back in the ballroom. You were jealous of me."

"Yes." That's what I get for deciding to take on an empath as a client.

"And when you walked in and saw me, you felt pity and fear."

"Yes."

"But you are going to help me anyway. Why? It's not guilt. Guilt is like plunging into a dark well. I would've felt that."

"You tell me."

Her eyes narrowed. Magic brushed me, feather-light.

"Compassion," she said quietly. "And duty. Why would you feel a sense of duty toward me?"

"Have you ever held a job?"

She frowned. "No. We don't need the extra money."

That must be nice. "Do you have any hobbies? Any passions?"

"I . . . make sculptures."

"Do you sell them?"

"No. They're nothing spectacular. I've never participated in any exhibits."

"Then why do you keep making them?"

She blinked. "It makes me happy."

"Being a private investigator makes me happy. I'm not just doing it for the money. I'm doing it because sometimes I get to help people. Right now, you need help."

The laptop dinged. A new e-mail, from Bern, popped into my inbox. I clicked it.

Brian Sherwood, 32, second son of House Sherwood, Prime, herbamagos. Principal business: Sherwood BioCore. Estimated personal worth: $30 million. Wife: Rynda (Charles), 29. Children: Jessica, 6, and Kyle, 4. Siblings: Edward Sherwood, 38; Angela Sherwood, 23.

Brian Sherwood was a plant mage. Rynda was an empath with a secondary telepathic talent. That didn't add up. Primes usually married within their branch of magic. As Rogan once eloquently explained to me in his falling-on-his-sword speech, preserving and increasing magic within the family drove most of their marriage decisions.

I looked back to her. "I don't know yet if I'm your best option. It may be that you would be better served by a different agency. But before we talk about any of that walk me through your Thursday. You woke up. Then what happened?"

She focused. "I got up. Brian was already awake. He'd taken a shower. I made breakfast and fixed the lunches for him and the kids."

"Do you fix their lunches every day?"

"Yes. I like doing it."

Brian Sherwood, worth thirty million dollars, took a brown bag lunch his wife made to work every day. Did he eat it or throw it in the trash? That was the question.

"Brian kissed me and told me he would be home at the usual time."

"What time is that?"

"Six o'clock. I said we'd be having cubed steak for dinner. He asked if fries were involved."

She choked on a sob.

"Who took Jessica to school?"

She glanced at me, surprised. "How did you know her name?"

"My cousin pulled your public records." I turned the laptop so she could see.

She blinked. "My whole life in one paragraph."

"Keep going," I told her. "How did Jessica get to school?"

"Brian dropped her off. I took Kyle on a walk."
Lie.

"I called Brian around lunch. He answered."
Truth.

"What did you talk about?"

"Nothing serious."
Lie.

"I'm not your enemy. It would help if you were honest with me. Let's try this again. Where did you and Kyle go and what was the phone call about?"

She set her lips into a flat, hard line.

"Everything you tell me now is confidential. It isn't privileged, like conversations with your attorney, which means I will have to disclose it in a court proceeding. But short of that, it won't go anywhere."

She covered her face with her hands, thought about it for a long moment, and exhaled. "Kyle's magic hasn't manifested. I manifested by two, Brian manifested by four months, Jessica manifested at thirteen months. Kyle is almost five. He's late. He's seeing a specialist. I always call Brian after every session because he wants to know how Kyle did."

For a Prime, a child with no magic would be devastating. Rogan's voice popped into my head. *"You think you won't care about it, but you will. Think of your children and having to explain that their talents are subpar, because you have failed to secure a proper genetic match."*

"Your anxiety spiked. Why? Was it something I said? Is the specialist important?"

"I don't know yet." She would be a really difficult client.

She registered every emotional twitch I made. "Did Kyle manifest?"

"No."

"What happened next?"

She sighed and went through her day. She fed the kids, then they read books and watched cartoons together. She made dinner, but Brian didn't show. She called his cell several times over the next two hours and finally called his brother. He was still at work. He walked down to Brian's office and reported that it was empty. He also called down to the front desk and the guard confirmed that Brian had signed out and left the building a quarter before six.

"How far is your house from Sherwood BioCore?"

"It's a ten-minute drive. We live in Hunter Creek Village. BioCore is at Post Oak Circle, near the Houstonian Hotel. It's three and a half miles down Memorial Drive. Even with heavy traffic, he's usually home in fifteen minutes."

"Did Edward mention if Brian was planning to make any stops?"

"He didn't know. He said he wasn't aware of any meetings scheduled that afternoon."

"Did he sound concerned?"

She shook her head. "He said he was sure Brian would show up. But I knew something was wrong. I just *knew*."

All the standard things someone does when their loved one is missing followed: calls to hospitals and the police station, driving the route to look for the stranded car, talking with people at his job, calling other family members asking if they heard anything, and so on.

"He didn't come home," she said, her voice dull. "In the morning I called Edward. He told me not to worry. He said Brian had seemed tense lately and that he would turn up. I told him I would file the police report. He said that he didn't feel there was a need for it, but if it would make me feel better, I should file it."

"How did he seem to you?"

"He seemed concerned for me."

Interesting. "For you? Not for Brian?"

"For me and the kids."

"And Brian has never done anything like this before?"

She didn't answer.

"Rynda?"

"He disappears sometimes when he's stressed," she said quietly. "He used to. But not for the last three years and never this long. You have to understand, Brian isn't a coward, he just needs stability. He likes when things are calm."

That explained why his brother didn't immediately sound the alarm and bring all hands on deck. "Can you tell me more about it? The last time he disappeared?"

"It was after Kyle's one-year birthday party. Edward asked if Kyle manifested, and Brian told him no. Then Joshua, Brian's father—he died a year later—said that Brian and I better get on with making another one, because Jessica is an empath like me and a dud can't lead the family."

He called his grandchild a dud.

"Thank you," Rynda said.

"For what?"

"For your disgust. Brian's anxiety spiked. I felt an intense need to escape coming from him, so I told them that it was late and the children were tired. The family left. Brian didn't come to bed. He got into his car and drove off. He came home the next evening. That was the longest he had ever disappeared."

"Did he say where he went?"

"He said he just drove. He eventually found some small hotel and spent the night there. He came home because he realized that he had no place to go and he missed me and the kids. We are bound, he and I. It's us against the world.

He would never leave me and the last time I saw him he was calm and content."

Truth.

I rubbed my forehead. "Did you share this with the police?"

"Yes."

And they dismissed her as being a hysterical woman whose husband bolted when the pressure became too much.

"Do you have access to Brian's bank records?"

"Yes." She blinked.

"Can you check if there has been any activity? Has he used his cards in the last few days?"

She grabbed her purse, rummaging through it frantically. "Why didn't I think of . . . ?" She pulled the phone out and stabbed at it.

A moment passed. Another.

Her face fell. "No. Nothing."

"Rynda, did you kill your husband?"

She stared at me.

"I need an answer."

"No."

"Do you know what happened to him?"

"No!"

"Do you know where he is?"

"No!"

Truth on all counts.

"There are several possibilities," I said. "First, something bad could have happened to Brian as a result of House politics or his job. Second, something traumatic could've occurred during the workday on Thursday that caused him to go into hiding. I can look for your husband. Alternatively, I can recommend MII. They are a premier agency and very well equipped to handle things like this. You can afford them. You should be aware that we're a small agency with a fraction of MII's resources."

Rynda sat very still.

Someone pounded down the hallway on small feet.

"Mom!" A small boy ran into the kitchen carrying a piece of paper. He had dark hair and Rynda's silver eyes. She opened her arms and he thrust a piece of paper at her. "I drew a tank! They have a tank in their garage!"

Catalina walked into the room, dark-haired, slender, and a small smile on her face. "Kyle wanted to show you."

"That's a scary tank," Rynda said.

"Come on." My sister held out her hand to the boy. "I'll show you more cool stuff."

Kyle put the paper in front of his mother. "It's a present for you. I'll draw one for Dad!" He took off at a run. Catalina sighed and chased him.

Rynda watched him go with an odd look on her face.

"I've talked to MII." She swallowed and I saw a shadow of her mother's ruthless logic in her eyes. "Montgomery turned me down."

Interesting. I was really her last resort.

"Very well," I said. "I will look for Brian."

She shifted in her seat and blurted out. "I want a contract."

"Okay."

"I don't want this to be an act of charity because you killed my mother. I want to pay you."

"That's fine."

"I want things defined and professional."

"As do I."

"And our relationship is that of a client and service provider."

"Agreed," I said.

I heard a door swing open. A thunderstorm appeared behind me and moved through our house, churning with power and magic. Rogan.

I turned. He reached our kitchen and loomed in the doorway, tall, broad-shouldered, his blue eyes dark and his magic wrapped around him like a vicious pet snapping its savage teeth. If I didn't know him, I would've backed away and pulled my gun out.

"Connor!" Rynda jumped up from behind the table, cleared the distance between them, and hugged him.

And jealousy stabbed me right in the heart.

Rogan gently put his arms around her. "Are you okay?"

"No." Rynda choked on a sob. "Brian is missing."

He was still looking at me. I nodded. *Yes. I'm okay.*

Rynda pulled away from him. "I didn't know where to go. I . . ."

"I'm going to take care of it," I told Rogan.

He finally looked at Rynda. "Nevada is the best you can get."

I checked my laptop. 5:47 p.m. "Rynda, I have some paperwork for you to sign. There are some preliminary things I can do today, but tomorrow I'll go and knock on BioCore doors. It would make things easier if you called ahead and advised the family that I'll be coming by."

"I'll come with you," she said.

"It would be best if I went by myself," I told her. "People may say things to me that they might not mention in your presence. If I'll require access to Sherwood family spaces or other restricted areas, I'll definitely ask you to come with me."

"What do I do now?" She was looking at Rogan, not at me.

"Sign the paperwork and go home. Brian might call or show up," Rogan said. "You're not alone, Rynda. Nevada will help you. I will help you."

"I hate you for killing my mother," she told him, her voice strained.

"I know," he said. "It couldn't be helped."

"Everything is falling apart, Connor. How can it all just crumble like that?"

"It's House life," he said.

Rynda's shoulders stooped. She turned to me. "Where do I sign?"

I walked her through the paperwork, fees, and stipulations. She signed and went to collect her children.

Rogan waited until she was out of sight before stepping close to me.

"She'll need an escort home," I said. "And someone to watch the house." There was no telling where this investigation would lead and extra security was never a bad idea.

"I'll take care of it," he said and kissed me. It was a sudden, hard kiss, fierce and hot. It burned like fire.

We broke apart and I saw the dragon in his eyes. Rogan was preparing to go to war.

"Your grandmother is in the city," he said and pressed a USB drive into my hand. "You must decide tonight."

He turned and walked away, the memory of his kiss still scorching me.

I took a deep breath and plugged the USB into my laptop.